BABY LOVE

NOVELS BY RONALD ARGO

Baby Love

The Sum of His Worth

The Courage to Kill

Year of the Monkey

BABY LOVE

Ronald Argo

HotDamn University Press
SAN DIEGO, CA

This book is a work of fiction. All names, characters, places and incidents are the product of the author's imagination.

HotDamn University Press
www.ronargo.com

CATALOGING-IN-PUBLICATION DATA

Argo, Ronald.

Baby Love/Argo, Ronald.—1st ed.

ISBN 978-0-9969802-0-3

1. Human trafficking—Fiction 2. Reporters and reporting—California—San Diego—Fiction 3. U.S. Immigration and Customs Enforcement (ICE)—U.S. Border Patrol—California—History—Fiction. 4. Syndicated crime—International—Fiction 5. Baja Norte California, Mexico—Ensenada—Fiction 6. Pai Pai Indians—Baja California, Mexico—History—Fiction. I. Title.

Cover designed by Michael Kellner

Cover photography: Getty Images

In memory of
Vance Bourjaily and Michael Barry
and my brother Larry

for
Margaret Zehren and Richard Moore

ACKNOWLEDGEMENTS

A note of tribute to the near extinct Pai Pai Indians of Baja California Norte, Mexico—a centuries-old native tribe that's held on to their nation and ways against years of encroachments from the federales, narco raiders and Americans' destructive toys—for graciously putting me up for a short stay.

It was my friend, fellow scriptwriter and IBM ad-madman Michael Barry after whom the character Sidney Rhoades was molded and fleshed out. Michael was a lover of Mexico and I'm privileged to have adventured there with him.

To the Princess of Bombay, Yasmin Mogul, whose years of tolerating a peon like me were equally tolerated and of course savored as exciting and rewarding times. And my friend, *artiste extraordinaire,* Valerie Dawn Smith, for her contributions to my work.

A salute to the dulcet milieu of Key Largo where the bones of one of the key characters in this novel—Bubba—originated. This had little if anything to do with my wife and I sleeping in the same bed previously slept in by Keys author James W. Hall. No osmosis of mind over matter of fictional character similarities, if such were to be interpreted.

Thanks goes to Professor Jason Renzi whose scholarly acumen and exuberant enthusiasm (which is to say hyperbolic zest) never got in the way and in fact cushioned the ego at times.

And to babies all over the world, may they never not be loved.

CHAPTER ONE

~California's Imperial Valley along the Mexican border~

November 2003

Myers didn't see the buzzards. Carol Finley did. Finley would, she had the artist's eye.

"Over there, eleven o'clock," Finley said, one hand pointing, the other blocking the sun. "See them?"

Myers couldn't see anything but heat waves through the sweltering desert haze. He gave it another shot and narrowed his eyelids to slits, now making out a salvo of pinpoints on an otherwise vacant sky. On his own, he would've left it as floaters from a hangover.

"Take a look?" Myers said and edged back toward the car. "C'mon."

"I'm not out here to shoot some stinking animal carcass."

Myers bent a smile. "Sure, you say so."

His crooked grin didn't change while he waited for her to gather her senses.

The two of them were on assignment in this oven near the no-town of Ocotillo Wells, a barren wind-blown landscape beyond the last outpost of modern civilization. The section chief wanted a Sunday feature along the line of "fall hues in the desert." Myers didn't know squat about desert botany. He was a crime reporter. He was good at it. The assignment came directly from the managing editor, who'd been miffed at the veteran reporter's "method of inquiry" into a police shooting. Since the homeless victim had been known to hallucinate but had no violent priors, Myers asked the officer involved why he hadn't used mace or tased the perp, thrown a net over him, something less than lethal since he had no weapon. Maybe Myers' tone had been a bit sarcastic, that was possible. The piece found print in one graph buried in the B section.

Myers waited in the car while Finley finished her roll of thirty-six. Finley, among the last of old-school photographers, still used film for artsy work because film was real, and in some ways easier to manipulate in the darkroom than digital images. He scribbled a line that might become a caption for a giant barrel cactus with a single, stunning pink blossom. Hard to believe such a nasty plant could come up with a bloom that gorgeous. He wrote the description figuring she hadn't missed seeing it.

Finley didn't say a word when she got into the car and Myers revved the Escort onto the blacktop of State 2, dipping east into Devil's Canyon and crossing under Interstate 8. Dust bulbs chased the car at high speed. The buzzards were farther away than they had appeared back at the cactus shoot. Myers then discovered what attracted them. The abandoned boxcar had also drawn three Border Patrol SUVs.

Myers didn't have to guess what was inside the boxcar. A brown plastic body sheet covering a five-and-a-half foot lump confirmed it. He stopped the car a good hundred feet away so his dust wouldn't blow onto the crime scene. He sucked a tooth, said to Finley without any sense of crow, "What I thought."

"Damn, Ray … Damn!"

Finley fitted the camera with a long lens and strapped the instrument around her neck. "We better call the desk, they'll need to hold some space."

"Let's see how bad it is first."

"You *know* it's bad, all these cops around … You know any of them by chance?"

"Agents," Myers said. "Border Patrol."

"Okay, then. You recognize any of these friggin' *agents*?" Finley wasn't pleased having to deal with death when she was supposed to be doing flowers.

They walked toward a switch track overgrown with weeds. Judging by its deterioration, the Lackawanna freight car had been there quite some time, measured in years.

"See what I can get," Finley said in her work voice, then broke away. She moved resolutely, her jaw leading. He admired the hell out of that photographer—that woman.

Myers found a Border Patrol agent who looked like he knew something and flashed a press card. "What's up?"

He swatted at the sweat rolling out of the hairline at both his temples. His throat felt dry as the desert itself.

The agent narrowed his eyes at Myers.

"How'd you get out here so fast? Man, *we* just got here."

Myers nodded toward the four-cylinder Escort with *The San Diego Journal* printed in medieval script on the door. "You ought to see under the hood … "

The agent grinned and tapped back his brown baseball cap. Tufts of red curly hair puffed out, not a lawman's typical military burr cut. His nameplate read, *T. Cousins*.

Myers cocked his chin toward the sky. "We were out searching for cactus blooms and happened to spot those buzzards up there … How many's in the boxcar, Agent Cousins? What about that bagged one, what happened there?"

The agent looked up. "Blooms, huh?"

"Some folks like to look at the hues of fall." Myers was looking at the boxcar now.

"Poor bastards. Suffered like hell," Agent Cousins said. "They might have survived without the bump in heat. Strange thing is there's no evidence they were prepared to walk any distance.

"*That* one," he said and pointed toward the covered corpse a few feet in front of the boxcar's door. "Coulda been three hundred degrees, didn't matter. That one's a homicide. Multiple knife wounds."

"Any evidence you can share might explain what happened?"

"Working on it." He looked at the hills in the distance. "Desert's pretty this time of year, that's true. All the colors."

Myers said, "What about the ones in the boxcar?"

Cousins kicked dirt with his boot. "Can't tell you."

"Can you tell me how many there are?"

"Found two more in the scrub out near Boulevard yesterday. Apparently unrelated to these poor folks. Usually it's just a few days of wandering, when they're out of water, before the delirium sets in. Not like this. Looks like they went pretty fast, being older."

"Older, huh? About how old, would you say?"

Agent Cousins kicked some more dirt and said, "You wanna take a look, go ahead. But don't get too close. I don't want nobody losing their lunch on my crime scene."

Myers said, "Thanks."

A couple of agents climbed speedily in and out of the boxcar holding handkerchiefs or field caps over their noses. Myers watched another one slide the heavy door partway back and forth. It squeaked but rolled.

He waited until the agent finished with the door and then took a breath and stuck his head inside. Right away his throat tightened and his eyes started watering. The stench was unavoidable. There were five bloated bodies, rigored into awkward positions. The two closest to the door were men. The men had unclothed themselves; that would have been the delirium, Myers figured. The condition of the bodies reminded Myers of the carnage he'd seen at Guyana's Jonestown more than twenty years before but always current in his memory, as it always would be for everyone who had been there to see it. He could tell by the facial structure that the victims' lineage was Indian, probably Mixtec, even with the changes death and then exposure bred—distension, fissures in the skin, the black voids from the insects.

He stepped out and away. It was a grisly sight and it made Myers feel tired.

Finley still shot from a distance, using the long lens. Eventually she'd move closer.

A glint in the sunlight down the railroad track caught Myers' eye and he followed its source about 20 feet to some broken glass. It might have been a cheap brand of mescal. He picked up the neck using his ballpoint pen. A bleached-out label that laced the bottleneck floated to the ground. He put the piece of glass back in its place and slipped the skin of paper gently into his pocket, mindful that it could be evidence he was confiscating.

Finley had changed to a wide-angle lens and now took shots of the boxcar's interior.

Agent Cousins approached, shaking his head. Myers figured he was about to be called down for tampering with possible evidence. He wasn't.

"Probably Salvadoran," Cousins offered, glancing to the distant south as if searching for El Salvador. "Getting a lot of 'em lately. But that's what I don't get. Your jumpers are sprouts looking for work. These folk, well …"

"Punishment they didn't deserve," Myers offered. He wiped his face with a sweaty forearm. A drop of sweat slipped into his eye anyway. He usually took a recorder whenever on assignment, but not today, not for fall hues in the desert.

"How'd they get locked inside?"

Cousins removed his cap and scratched his head. His red hair had darkened from sweat. "That don't make much sense, either." He hesitated. He wasn't kicking dirt now. "They could've spotted our colors and hid in there to get out of sight. Or there coulda been a windstorm made them close the door and it caught … Hard to figure. The door's a little rusty. But it *was* locked down."

"Would it lock automatically by shutting the door?"

The agent shrugged. "I suppose it could. I'm not that familiar with train cars—even if I did spend some time around 'em as a kid."

"Yeah?"

The agent nodded, almost shyly. "Yeah. Down there with the hobos."

When he didn't go on, Myers caught his eye and held it. "You think maybe someone closed the door on them? That possible?"

The agent shrugged again, then diverted his gaze. He kicked a rock. "We're waiting on the techs to tell us what's possible." His voice hardened. "In the meantime, this is a crime scene. No tampering."

"Gotcha," Myers said without expression.

Agent Cousins was a peculiar one, but the guy was a talker—even if he didn't say much. Myers loved talkers. They were the thermidor on his lobster.

He flinched at a sound he recognized before seeing. The rotor swirls making wind devils in its approach. "Sky 10's" multi-colored bubble copter whipped near and hovered like some disoriented Jurassic wasp, raising dust and debris over the crime scene. Myers protected his eyes with a hand. He thought about grabbing a rock.

He watched as uniformed agents waved and mouthed frantically. *Get the fuck back. Get outta here.* The pilot got the message and pulled up and banked away, but not too far.

"Ought to pop the tail rotor, teach 'em a lesson," Myers said to Agent Cousins, not entirely in jest.

Cousins tilted his cap back. He grinned at Myers. "Sonsabitches can be a royal pain in the ass, that's for sure."

"Yeah," Myers said, "but I won't quote you."

CHAPTER TWO

The newsroom was in full swing, clamorous as a weekend Lakers crowd. On worthy news days it got that way approaching deadline. In addition to the usual hard news of the ongoing Middle East turmoil, tomorrow's edition had three hot leads—the emergence of a scandalous cell phone shot of the First Lady touching the Democratic House Speaker; a story that heralded untold deaths from an explosion that, until now, had been an unknown nuclear facility in Iran. Good news story for years of continuous follow-ups, like Chernobyl. Myers' story was the only big local item and, after Channel Ten's anemic "Breaking news" aired at six, it would be *the* story, a bona fide exclusive.

The managing editor, L.C., personally sought out Myers, breathing in loud gasps as he waddled up to Myers' inactive area. He leaned all 300 pounds of himself on the edge of the desk, breathing hard and frowning and showing a desperate glaze in his eyes, the glaze of fear all mediocre editors got closing in on deadline when there was something at stake. At stake here was the rare opportunity for his rag to jack television. It would be a first for him.

"Good work out there, my boy, good thing I sent you ... Whaddaya think, maybe some cult ritual going on?" Coaxing Myers. "You sure *nothing* was found, not even drugs? ... I got it, they were missionaries! You think?"

He was working himself into a frenzy. "Any goddamn thing, Raymond? You gotta have *something* the buzzheads missed. Get back on the horn. Do something, man, for chrissake. Don't just sit there!"

His voice was now a scream. His way of expressing the fondness he had only now rediscovered in good ole Magic Myers. After all, he'd called him Raymond.

"You got it, boss." Myers wasn't arguing, he wanted it too. He hadn't had a front-page story in three months, an exclusive in three years.

But nothing was happening for him. He had collected no more information than what he'd gotten at the scene. He'd paced and waited to hear back from sources at the Medical Examiner, the Sheriff's Department, the BP. He knew his calls to Homeland Security and ICE wouldn't be processed, not for a day or two no matter how often he called them. None of his usual contacts were responding and that was troubling.

The story was front-page bound if it went only as a first-person narrative. Which should have satisfied him. It didn't.

There were unanswered questions with big inferences. Mainly, why did the victims' handler put them inside a boxcar, which could've been the case. It sure looked that way to Myers with the unexplained locked door. Why was the one outside stabbed to death? Those immigrants died not just of dehydration and suffocation; at over 200° they boiled to death.

Myers rolled his neck to crunch out the stiffness then took the stairs to the fourth-floor photo lab. The photographer manning the activity desk was a strain of Ape-man named Kreig Kayko, a lumbering bohemian always wearing the same brown baggy slacks and brown buttoned-down flannel shirt. A stoic, strange individual. Myers admired him. His talent with the lens was second only to Finley's.

"Yo, Kreig. Finley in?"

Myers used simple English to phrase the question, but the Ape-man fluttered lazy eyelids as though making a genuine effort to interpret. He seemed to make a connection, as he silently pointed a sloth's arm toward the darkroom. Myers grunted and entered through the double-U tunnel. After adjusting to the dark, he saw Finley facing a row of trays.

He tapped the wall, well aware that photographers did not like reporters inside their darkroom; they tended to ask questions and make requests. The cool walls of the lab were covered with prints of unpublished works that Finley and the other photographers favored and this room was their hallowed gallery.

Claustrophobia grabbed Myers. It was sudden but he expected it when entering a tight place.

"Carol, hey—"

"Hold on, be through in a flash."

He grunted at her pun, which she probably didn't even realize. He studied the back of her thin neck. The fine down glowed under the infrared like tiny embers against her skin. She hung another wet paper on the clothesline above the countertop where paper towels caught the dripping. Myers had taken a look at the contact sheets Finley sent earlier to the city desk. These hanging prints were apparently the ones the editor ordered. None of the wet prints were "fall hues."

"Mind if I take a look?"

"You won't find much there," Finley said. "I'm finishing some blowups now that'll work better."

"What am I looking for?"

"Just a sec."

Computer technology had become so competent that there was little need for the photo lab or a photographer's input; editors had only to crop and adjust computer-generated prints on their screens. But a few devoted old school photogs still preferred to breathe life into their work, like Finley and Ape-man, and grounded it out in trays and under enlargers, burning in contrast and highlighting faces or guns in hands, whatever they decided needed emphasizing—things robotics intelligence in itself could not yet fully accomplish. Not here at the *Journal*, at least.

"Here's one," she said with the excitement of an undertaker.

He watched the print come to life in the solution but could not distinguish details until Finley laid it on the mat and flipped on the incandescent.

"Holy shit!" he said.

"You're quick. I figured you'd forgotten what diapers looked like."

"And what about that thing?" he asked.

"So you have forgotten. Weren't you a father once upon a time?"

Myers felt heat in his face.

"Well, it's a baby bottle," she droned, without looking at Myers. "We don't use 'em much anymore in this country ... See the bag? It's a tote bag for—you guessed it—baby bottles and diapers."

Myers pulled at his collar as if it would help get him some air. The walls were closing in.

The bag in the photograph, emblazoned with Sesame Street's Big Bird, lay mostly hidden under the bloated leg of a corpse. It took the flash of a camera to identify the bag, which investigators had said nothing about. Sticking out of the bag was a folded diaper, what appeared to be a baby's bottle of milk and possibly a hand cloth.

"But no baby," Finley said. She still had not looked at her visitor. "What do you make of it, Ray?" she finally asked. Was she serious, he wondered.

Myers shrugged.

"C'mon, really. What do you think?"

"Can't say … I hope the baby's alive?"

"Jesus … Well, the whole thing's bizarre." A frown reshaped her face. Her face was close to Myers. "A missing baby, illegals too old for beating the bush." She shook her head in consternation. "Very strange indeed. And strange you have not a clue. Baffling."

"They were told to wait in there," guessed Myers, still trying to make sense of it. "A *coyote* locked them in the boxcar to wait and the handlers on this side didn't show up. The person who got stabbed to death fought with the bastard, maybe over the baby. So it was probably a woman. She knew it was a deathtrap in there and didn't want them to put the baby in there."

"So the *coyote* took the baby—or babies—to settle the score with the dude that was supposed to show and didn't," Finley offered. "That is callous, man."

Myers said, "Maybe. But that still leaves you wondering why elderly people were out there with babies."

"Family. Grand kids, nieces. Maybe they were nannies, smuggling them in to reunite with their father or mother."

"Couldn't afford nannies, but family's a good guess. Fathers sending money and never see their children who are growing up without him. It gets old with them, I'd guess."

The reporter and photographer looked at each other glumly, both shaking their heads, maybe thinking the same thing. Finley said it.

"Still leaves the obvious question—"

"Where'd the baby go?" Myers finished.

Myers wanted two things right then, to get out of the small room and to show his gratitude for her discovery, a touch on the arm. He didn't touch her, not in her domain.

He turned to leave, then remembered the reason he'd come. He removed an item from his shirt pocket. Sure enough he wanted a favor.

"Say, Carol. Can you blow this up to where I can read it?"

It was a small ribbon of sun-bleached paper, the label off the broken mescal bottle he'd found on the old tracks.

"What is it?"

"Could be a tax stamp. Probably not important but it could lead to something."

"Take a while."

"No rush … Could I take this print?" He indicated one of the eight-by-tens drying on the clothesline.

"There are better ones."

"Appreciate it." He returned to his desk with the still-wet print. It was grainy from blowup but unmistakable in content: a baby's bottle among the rubble on the boxcar floor, lying there in the background, death all around it. Finley knew what she'd been shooting but hadn't mentioned it to Myers on the silent drive back; she had to have the visual.

He threw out the standard tragic death-in-the-desert lead that had been done so many times the reader was blasé and started over—

Somewhere in the boiling desert heat, as cruel death came to six immigrants, a baby has gone missing ...

An old fire coursed his veins. It stirred in him a gratification he hadn't felt in a good while. The feeling was visceral, like biting into warm prime rib, or a catch in the throat as when some special memory suddenly grabs you.

He didn't hear the newsroom clamor or the voice speaking to him until a wadded paper hit his computer screen. He had finished 25 graphs and was next to done, just the grabbing final line saying, in essence, "stay tuned."

"Huh?" he said and looked around to see Tina Lubrano grinning. Lubrano rarely grinned. She may have been pleased to see Myers absorbed in his work.

"They're tearing hair on the rim," she said, pointing at the huddle of mousy editors waiting only on Myers. They didn't look as eager as a lynch mob.

"Yeah, yeah, gimme a minute." He keyboarded rapidly then threw his hands up with a flair, the conductor at crescendo. Did that for the rim eyes.

Lubrano said, "Good. Now I can tell you about Channel 10's footage—I know you didn't catch it." The entire newsroom knew Myers didn't watched television coverage of stories he was on. He got sniggers for that every now and then from every department on the floor, he'd even gotten the pitiful head shakes from affluents in Advertising on the next floor up. It seemed one could grasp the simple reason for it, the potential mind tainting. But no one seemed to.

"Dubbed it the 'Ocotillo Massacre.' Dressed it up with horrific sound bites," she said with excitement. "But they didn't get squat. No body shots, no revealing comments, just dusty footage."

Myers leaned back in his swivel. "Yep, figures."

Tina Lubrano had shared space and personals with Myers forever it seemed. She and Myers co-wrote on occasion and sometimes held forth at bars. Short, butch-cut and feisty, she'd made her bones covering city hall and now had the clout to pick and chose her stories, which were generally women's issues but only the ones that could invoke controversy. Controversial writing was one of those familiarities they shared and one reason they got along, even when they differed. Go figure.

"They didn't mention anything about babies, I'll bet," Myers deadpanned.

"Babies? No, why, whaddaya got?"

"Then the first round is ours."

"Not ours, Ray, yours. Damn if I don't sniff something big in this one."

"Believe it."

CHAPTER THREE

There was a playhouse in the backyard where Maggie Frazier lived. Her landlord once mentioned that he built it for his little girl. Clearly it had been a labor of love with its single swing-open window with shutters in scrollwork of daisies and crescent-moons and its peaked roof. The original pastels of yellow and green paint still covered its plank walls, only faded now. Maggie had dressed it up inside to look like the dollhouse she never had in her orphaned childhood.

She had hung a white lace valance embroidered with tiny red roses over the window and tacked four American Girl pin-up posters to two walls, while a bookcase took up the back wall, overstuffed with baby dolls of all kinds.

Maggie took a seat in the small girl's chair behind the undersized mahogany desk she'd picked up cheap at St. Vincent's and refinished herself. She took a moment to admire the view outside the window: two old trees, a eucalyptus and California pepper, standing like humongous guard towers protecting the dollhouse. She imagined that little girl swinging from the car tire that still hung from the pepper tree.

"Okay," she said out loud for no reason and pulled open the top of a two-drawer file cabinet. She'd painted the cabinet a girlish bright pink. It contained the paperwork files that made up her child-adoption dossiers—"packets," she called them—papers required to legalize foreign-born children. USCIS material, Immigration and IRS forms, and photographs of children and other related material were all here.

As a facilitator, or baby seller, Maggie was the best in the syndicate, they'd said.

She had slept in this morning, wanting her eyes and head clear for the lunchtime appointment. The rain helped her sleep through till nine o'clock. It was ten before she made the dash to the dollhouse. She'd brushed the rain out of her hair before sitting at the desk.

She gathered paperwork then searched through baby photographs, filed alphabetically by nationality and then by sex and age. She selected two 4X6-inch pictures from the "Latin—Boys" file. Every client she'd had so far was white and they all wanted a white baby. She felt a responsibility to be honest and it was a hard sale convincing some that that wasn't going to happen. Despite Russia's recent openness to U.S. adoptions, there were too many obstacles for too few healthy white babies they housed in "asylums" there. Some clients she even lost for laying it on the line. But others just wanted a baby and those were the good sales, the rewarding ones.

This couple today was on the cusp, but she thought they could be persuaded once they saw the pictures she'd picked out. Didn't matter it wouldn't be the actual baby the couple would be getting—a little deception to go along with her honesty. When you think about it, how could the selling merchant possibly have a picture to show of the actual smuggled baby anyway? But a color picture could sell them in a sec. When it came to adopting a baby, people acted on their emotions and Maggie could play on that with the best of them.

She opened the bottom file drawer and lifted the lid of a gutted silverware box. Ten neat stacks of one-hundred-dollar bills were there, safe.

Though she collected the cash payments in full, only ten percent of it belonged to her. But ten percent was way short of the amount she needed for the down payment on her *Casa Libre*, the house for the orphanage she had dreamed of opening and was now near reality. Which meant keeping all of the money from the next two sales.

Her boss called again last night asking if she'd made the deposit yet—then *when*? Like that, nasty and nervous. Maggie lied, told him Mack was shorthanded at the restaurant and she was pulling overtime and couldn't get to the bank. In fact, Mack had had to lay off a waitress. She was lucky it wasn't her.

She placed the packet in the attaché, then hurried through a sprinkle of rain to the house. The golden retriever stood vigilant, her long tail swishing faster the closer Maggie came.

"C'mon, Sally girl," she called brightly, "let's get you out of this weather."

Maggie pulled off her sweatshirt on the way to the bedroom, the dog following. She removed her jeans and sat before the dressing table mirror and began the transformation that would maker her the older and wiser sales queen Sylvia Fischer—"Sylvia, please," as Maggie insisted of most clients. Maggie relished the challenge of acting more sophisticated than a cafe waitress. By channeling Sylvia Fischer, Maggie was surprisingly more capable of indulging the emotional whims of people mad with baby love.

She inserted tinted contacts into her eyes. Dark eyes were more professional than her natural sky-blues. Blue eyes were good for lunch tips and honky tonks, but they didn't go in this industry. She applied her magical aging makeup then brushed out and donned an auburn wig that hung shoulder-length over her own tastefully clipped sandy-blond mane. The wig added as much age and maturity as the gray pantsuit and beige pumps she now slipped into.

The doe-eyed goldie lay quietly with her snout resting on paws, mildly fascinated, eyebrows shifting as Maggie stood before the closet mirror fully dressed. She studied herself from front, a swing to the side and a twist for a back shot. Not bad looking, she opined, for a woman of Sylvia's age. Maggie Frazier was 29 years old, Sylvia Fischer had passed childbearing years.

"Talk to me, Sally, what do you think?" she said to the goldie, speaking in Sylvia Fischer's tamer voice. "Can I pull this one off? ... How's that? Won't be a cakewalk? You're right about that."

She shut the dog in the kitchen. "We'll do a nice hike this afternoon. Okay, sweetie?"

The dog's tail beat the linoleum knowing the word "hike." Maggie laughed. "Too bad I can't take you with me. You'd melt them."

She'd just shut the front door when the phone rang. She had set it for a single ring. She opened the door and listened to a man's painful-sounding voice. Maggie's stomach clenched. She rushed back inside.

"Dad, what is it?"

The phone voice exhaled, then took in air. "Hey, honey. You must be busy, screening calls."

"I was out the door. What's cookin?"

Maggie tried to sound upbeat, even though she knew it wouldn't make any difference.

He didn't answer.

"I'm closing on a sale today. That's where I was headed," she said. "We're getting there, Dad. Don't you give up on me, Okay?"

"Maggie, honey. I want you to listen," he said. His voice caught and she heard a gasp. "Something's happened … Can you stop by?"

"When? I mean, can't you just tell me now? What is it?" Despite her effort, her voice shifted, quicker, higher.

Maggie waited. She checked her watch.

"Dad, just tell me what's the matter."

"Forget it," he said.

"Ah, don't be like that. Talk to me."

"Really, honey. Let me call you later. I can see you're in a hurry. Okay?"

He sounded better and Maggie sighed. But she knew he was faking it.

"Dad?"

"Yes?"

"I mean it. We are so close. Just a couple more sales and *Casa Libre* will be open for business."

"You were always the dreamer, huh, Maggie girl?"

"I'm not dreaming, I'm doing it. *We're* doing it. You'll see."

"Of course we are. I love you, honey."

The phone went dead. She punched numbers and got a busy signal. She checked her watch again. Shit, this wasn't time to play nursemaid. She returned the phone to its cradle and left.

Maggie picked up the morning paper on her way to the car, threw it in the seat, then started up the old wagon. She lit a cigarette, backed out of the driveway and lowered the passenger-side window all at the same time. Nobody would've noticed her unsteady hand on the wheel. After all her rough years, she'd become an expert at masking her feelings.

But then she said firmly but softly, "You'll see, Dad," the cigarette bobbing on her lips.

Once on the freeway she put everything Maggie behind her and focused solely on Sylvia and the challenging clients she *had* to sell today. She changed the radio from rock to a country station. She felt insular and secure in the self-assured persona of Sylvia Fischer—until the Eagles came on telling her, "You can't hide your lyin' eyes."

CHAPTER FOUR

Myers arrived at the office around 10:30, not much later than usual. His head felt a little clearer than usual and his eyes didn't water. He took his time collecting items from his pigeonhole. There were two letters that appeared to be from John and Jane Q. Public, an interoffice envelope from the photo lab—good, his mescal label blowup—a bill he planned to pass on to the paper, today's early edition, and the a.m. sked. He sorted through the material on the way to his desk. The letters, he decided without opening, would be irate or complimentary readers responding to the last in his two-part series on Logan Heights gangland crimes, specifically its ebb following multiple year-long work programs in the barrio where homicides and armed robberies were the city's highest. The solution had been a no-brainer: Give them some kind of purpose for existing and they'll stop robbing and killing each other.

The midmorning newsroom was the flip side of deadline hour, quiet and hollow as a mausoleum. Rita, the M.E.'s secretary, looked up from her night-school textbook and gave him a friendly nod as he passed by.

"Morning, Rita. Test tonight?"

She confirmed with a worried nod.

He did not glance in the direction of the city editor's desk, six slots from him, figuring Max Cullen would wave him over. Cullen fixated on waving Myers over, as though Myers was the pet whose head he couldn't wait to pat, then rub his nose in some crackerjack assignment only he, "the Magic," could handle.

First thing, Myers checked last night's final edition. He was not dissatisfied; the headline remained the same in content and size as in the first-inked editions, which was also acceptable:

Mystery Shrouds Deaths at Ocotillo Wells
Evidence Points to Role of Missing Baby

His phone sounded. He glanced at the city editor's desk and saw Cullen waving him over. Myers sighed, answered the phone.

" … Yeah, Max, I'm here. See me? Could I at least get my coffee first?"

Cullen waved faster. Myers slowly found his way around desks to Cullen's block and sat in the only wing chair in the newsroom, an overstuffed chintz nearly as old as Cullen. Even the Editorial chief didn't have a chair as comfortable in his lavish cube.

"Afternoon," Cullen said derisively and handed him a note.

Myers curled his lip but otherwise ignored the slur. He half-read the note then tossed it in the trash.

"What's the man's problem?" he said casually. "He oughta make up his feeble mind if he's gonna fire me or not. Or do I just have to fucking re-sign?"

"Maybe you just ought to cool it, take a holiday or something."

"Max, you know how long I've been at this rag? I've seen three M.E.'s come and go. I can make it through this idiot too. Or not."

"I don't know, Ray. L.C.'s got his own agenda, and more importantly, he's her majesty's man."

"He's just another ad exec, so what's new."

"Well, it's best you recognized his position more often. This business … It's dying, you know." His voice trailed away in a vapor.

"Not before your time, boss. No worries."

"Hate to see it, is all."

"*C'est la vie.*"

"Anyway, you got a pass for a couple of days. L.C. left for Denver last night."

"In the middle of my exclusive!"

"I'm in charge of the team. We'll meet in an hour; I'm bringing Lubrano in."

"Good," said Myers.

The note from L.C. that Myers tossed was a reminder for Cullen to make sure he finished his desert floral piece for Sunday's Currents section, in addition to his other assignments. It was absurd; the man was a child.

"You'll have the flower piece, don't worry, Max … You ever heard of an outfit called Casa Amiga?"

Cullen lifted his eyebrows. "You got something?"

"How about Child Quest International?"

Cullen waited.

"Me neither before last night. Last night I spent a few hours finding out about these types of outfits. Casa Amiga returned an e-mail this morning and we had a live conversation—which is the reason I'm in five minutes later than usual."

Myers sat back in the easy chair and thought seriously about the vending machine, its bitter coffee. He gave Cullen another moment to feel guilty for his rebuke then told him, "They're out of Ciudad Juarez in Mexico. They mostly provide shelter for traumatized abuse victims and relatives of all those drug thugs getting murdered down there. They take in girls who've been in the flesh trade who somehow managed to get out alive. They also keep records of missing persons and may have identities for some of our dead migrants. Thing is, Max, it's possible to trace back and see if there were babies with those people, and where they might have come from."

Cullen beamed. "Of course that's what you were up to. I knew you were working. You're always working."

Myers shook his head. He didn't expect a follow-up from Casa Amiga. That's the way it was in this business; you get leads and they go cold. People wanting to help you out but don't have the time it takes to help you run things down. And understandably so, as it would be a massive task tracking victims without any identification who *might* have come from Guatemala, where fingerprinting and other forensics were useless with no databases to work from. The victims in the Ocotillo desert were all Doe's to U.S. authorities, simply more dead illegals. Where would the source begin a search for missing babies from parts south?

The same held true for the other organization he'd contacted, Child Quest International, a nonprofit group that searched for missing children. They would love to help but needed a name or at least a town where the child may have been abducted, *if* the child had been abducted, or at least a region of the suspected country—any bit of factual information to get the ball rolling.

Locating a relative of a missing baby from a country south of the border seemed insurmountable. He had also spoken with an immigration lawyer named Peter Snowdon, twenty years experience helping foreigners attain visas and naturalization, an expert in foreign adoptions. So said his web page. Snowdon himself shined Myers on with a bark meant to imply the infinitesimal odds against Myers or anyone identifying the elusive infant or even the adult victims.

"The child was trafficked, most likely from Guatemala. That's the hot spot right now. But it could've been Honduras," he'd said. "There's no way you'll ever know even if you were to locate the child. Jeeze, good luck doing that. Feel free to quote what I've told you. That's Snow-D-O-N, not Snow*den*."

Myers recalled that the talkative Border Patrol agent out there, T. Cousins, also offered up Guatemala as a probable origin of the migrants. So, Guatemala sounded good as any place to get started.

Myers opened the yellow envelope Carol Finley had sent, found three enlarged and darkened prints of the label off the mescal bottle, clearly readable. It might have been sold in any number of border towns on the U.S. side, but it had come from Mexico, from the state of Sonora, which bordered Arizona. The bottle had been sold in Caborca, a small relatively well-off city in a farming and wine-producing area about three hundred miles from Ocotillo Wells. The local tax was half a *peso*, the state tax slightly higher at 70 *centavos*, which made this one a cheap mescal.

There was no way to draw much of a conclusion with the information he had, but he made an assumption. The broken mescal bottle had belonged to a smuggler and because the ink wasn't completely faded, it probably hadn't been in the blistering desert sun more than a few days, about as long as the migrants had been broiling in the boxcar.

He assumed they traveled through the frontier of Sonora, Mexico. He was pretty sure of that much. If they crossed the border at the most direct route to Ocotillo from Mexico's Highway 2—the northernmost east-west highway down there—it would put them in an open, rough area where they should have been spotted. They weren't, apparently. Which meant the Border Patrol did not routinely monitor that area or the smugglers were lucky. Or both.

Myers went over possible scenarios: Bandits lay in wait for the smugglers, killed one robbing them. The baby or babies were a bonus. Or the *coyotes* themselves did it. Stole the babies and killed the woman who resisted.

He Googled a map of the terrain below Ocotillo Wells, in Baja Norte. Surprisingly that remote stretch of parched land could focus down to two hundred feet. Along Highway 2, he distinguished cars from trucks on the black strip. There was a narrow valley that ran across the Mexican highway and in it he made out what looked like adobe or concrete structures like small square homes spread out some distance apart. Perhaps farm houses on an *ejido*. Mostly, it was barren sandy land.

He then called the Investigations Division of the Border Patrol station in Imperial Beach and got hold of a crime lab officer he had once interviewed—a man Myers remembered as a helpful source. He told him what he'd found on the railroad track and waited for the scolding for removing possible evidence from a crime scene. Myers knew he had taken a chance offering this information and it was his luck the agent didn't threaten to report him. The agent, in fact, thanked him for the information. Myers said he would send him the stamp along with the photographs and hoped that it might help in the investigation.

"One more thing if you could," Myers said. "Who's a good ground tracker out in that area?" He jotted down a man's name and number.

The newsroom had turned busy during the time he'd been on the horn. Lubrano had arrived even later than Myers, by nearly an hour. As he hung up the phone, he heard her speaking gibberish.

"Yuh uhann oohnuh, Ay?"

Her mouth was stuffed with sweet shiny pastry, the kind that had a hole in the middle or toes of goo. She sipped coffee, swallowed and started to repeat herself, but Myers knew what she'd said.

"No time, thanks." He rolled his chair toward her, smelling and craving her rich, dark coffee.

"The boss is skiing in Colorado," he intoned sarcastically of a man way too fat to stay vertical on skis. "Cullen's in charge and he's assigning you to me. There's a lot of legwork to do."

"You got it, baby," she said, "long as I get a byline."

"You want a lot, Tina. I don't know."

Lubrano shrugged.

"I'm off to sniff around in the desert," Myers said. "I want you to contact the Guatemalan Embassy here and ours there. See if either is willing to talk about trafficking of babies or at least missing babies."

"They won't help."

Myers shrugged. "Gotta try. Check back with the sheriff's office and the State Department's law enforcement affairs office, Okay? See what they can tell us. And if there's time get hold of an adoption center or two; they may have some ideas about baby smuggling through Mexico. That ain't so much to ask, is it?"

"Piece of cake. What are you expecting to find in the desert?"

"Babies, what else."

CHAPTER FIVE

Pacifically Fish was packed with Friday suits, the kind of boisterous crowd Maggie hoped for when working nervous clients, as it tended to stifle emotional outbursts.

Inside the doorway she took a moment to smooth her knit skirt and touch the wig to see that it had not slipped in her dash through the drizzle.

She spotted the Bischkes seated at a window table for two with an extra chair in the aisle. The couple sat across from one another, inanimate as mannequins. *Here we go,* she thought. Jack caught Maggie's eye first, then Jane turned. No nods, howdy-do's, nothing. Maggie took a breath, smiled and strode gracefully their way. *Okay, Sylvia, show us your stuff.*

There was a single red rose in the middle of the table that immediately bolstered Maggie and she greeted her clients with a flair, giving Jane a cheek-to-cheek, her husband a warm smile and firm handshake.

She took the aisle chair and propped her material against the chair's front leg.

"I'm sorry you two had to get out in this awful weather." It was 72 degrees outside, a light drizzle with no wind, not quite a squall off Lake Superior.

Both nodded without humor. They weren't holding hands as clients often did; they weren't doing anything. They looked ready to explode, Maggie thought.

"I know you're anxious but, please, try to relax?" She leaned in and spoke above the crowd. "Believe me, it's best to meet in a place like this, where it's open and loud—maybe a little too loud today. I apologize for that. But you would be surprised how some expectant parents will act, especially at this stage. Honestly, the noise helps."

The waiter arrived and Maggie made a suggestion. "I know it's a seafood place, but they make the best Greek salad here."

She looked up at the waiter, a tall affect-less Armenian, whose nod may have been in agreement or in disdain at her suggestion. He wouldn't look her in the eye and she wondered if he recognized her from the diner where *she* waited tables. Impossible, she thought.

Greek salad was fine with the Bischkes and she ordered for all three of them. No wine. Alcohol too could tip the emotional balance.

After the waiter left, Jane finally spoke. "I guess, … " she hesitated, her voice a thin whisper. "I guess for us, it's just, we're a little unsure about this whole thing—"

"I understand completely," Maggie said. She touched both their arms to draw them close to her, then spoke evenly. "As I have tried to make clear, the adoption is processed through the State Department. All the papers are documented legally. There's absolutely nothing for you to worry about. Just remember, you are getting a baby, a healthy infant, not some half-grown kid with issues."

Her effort to reassure them seemed to have no effect. They blinked; they didn't even share a glance. Jesus, what did she have to do?

It tore Maggie up inside to turn a baby over to reluctants, but today money ruled; she couldn't have her father's faith in her slipping further down the bottle.

She sat back, frowning, leading them to make a decision. When they both made eye contact with her, Maggie spoke a little louder, a little rougher. "You tried it the other way. Tender Hearts, I believe? Surely you haven't forgotten the runaround you got from them."

Jane and Jack straightened. They remembered all right. They remembered how Tender Hearts and the Russian government, as if collaborating to break the back of any adoption deal, threw a mountain of offensive and discouraging obstacles their way. It would take years to finalize an adoption. The Russians required at minimum three expensive host-country trips with no guarantee of a particular child or that the child would be both healthy and under three years of age.

"No guarantees, remember?" Maggie reminded them now. She had seen how this kind of treatment cowered clients. Tender Hearts' domestic rules proved even worse.

The thing that did it for the Bischkes, as they had lamented to Maggie, was their asking for supportive medical evidence of Jane's infertility and Jack's erectile dysfunction. Maggie had been hard pressed to keep body-double Sylvia composed hearing this, but she did. And she could do it now, too, even though she knew these two weren't going to make the best of parents—she could see the kid 10, 15 years from now, a crackhead delinquent in and out of juvenile hall. That was a thing that violated her basic tenet, which was a pledge to place all her babies in worthy hands. This couple's interest was superficial, transparent even, more of a novelty than a true selfless desire to raise a child and make a loving family. As an orphan herself, in and out of foster care until the Fraziers finally adopted her, Maggie knew a lot about parental love—and the lack of it.

Maybe Jane really was infertile, and if so that was too bad. But Jack's ED was a poor excuse for not making babies; it just proved him the wimp that he was. Jane and Jack, Jack and Jane. Sounded like characters in a bad nursery rhyme. They were in a fantasy, they didn't even know what they were doing, wanting to adopt a child.

But realizing her dream demanded she push it through.

She sighed. "Jane, you are only experiencing a case of pre-delivery nerves. Most of my clients get them at this stage; it means you're taking the matter seriously. As well you should."

Jane gasped. "Oh! … Does this mean?—"

Maggie nodded modestly. "Your wait is over. The stork is ready to deliver your son … " She gently squeezed Jane's arm while glancing at Jack. She could not work up a smile as she asked, "Are you ready on your part?"

The waiter killed the moment. He took his time peppering their salads. His detached manner was provincial and it didn't take an experienced waitress like Maggie to see the bastard was better suited to a *French* restaurant. She would never treat a customer with such snootiness, as if the customers were mere cellophane. He was begging for a penny tip.

When finally he finished and left, and now anxious to get the business finished, Maggie crossed her arms on the table and squared her jaw facing Jack. "You did bring the money, didn't you?"

She stared at him. She had never liked dapper men. Black hair was Okay, standard, but his beady little snake eyes and that Hitler mustache made Jack into a shyster car salesman, a *used* car salesman.

She watched his dark eyebrows change positions, draw closer together to form a wedge of doubt. When Jack cleared his throat, Maggie frowned in dismay.

"We would like to see the baby first, if that's possible," he said. It didn't help that his mousy voice reminded her of her girlyman boss, Mr. Swabb.

Maggie froze the frown and added a touch of hurt in her eyes. "Of course you would," she said and fished around in her attaché. She placed the picture of a cute little Latin boy between the two of them, then plucked a pepperoncini from her salad. Waited.

Jane and Jack shot each other a look of disappointment. Jack cleared his throat again.

"What I meant, Sylvia, is to see *him*, not a picture … This is him, is it?"

The couple took another look at the print. The child was cute—pudgy, almond-colored, bright brown eyes and a cheerful, expectant face.

Jack lingered over the picture. He wasn't eating; neither was Jane. A positive sign in Maggie's experience. She lost the frown.

"That's him, trust me," Maggie said with conviction. "As you can see he's a beautiful, healthy baby, two-and-a-half months when that picture was taken, just recently. But let me be up front with you, Jack." She lowered her fork. "Our affiliate in Mexico City has notified me there are other Americans interested in adopting this baby. You might have guessed that seeing him. They need confirmation ASAP if you are to take this child. I need to see some money for that to happen … "

Just then Maggie decided to hit them the way middle-class DINKS understood things, in the pocketbook. "I'd suggest that if you really want this baby, you up your bid. Another five thousand is probably sufficient. I'm willing to take a check for the extra amount. I know you don't carry around that kind of cash … And don't forget, you receive that very big tax bonus for an additional dependent."

Jane stopped dabbling with her salad. Her eyes widened. She spoke in a quick tongue. "Of course we want him. Jack, give her the envelope."

Maggie allowed the slightest of smiles.

The husband put his fork down quietly, then glanced with nervous eyes to a table close by with four women, every one of them in suits, working their second or third bottle of wine. He looked at Jane again, then removed a bloated white envelope from the inside pocket of his suit jacket. "It's all here," he whispered, dipping a shoulder as he handed it under the table. The gesture wasn't as obvious as a blackbird landing on the rose.

Maggie took the package and laid it on the table by the blackbird. She took her time shuffling through fifty- and hundred-dollar bills for the benefit of anyone who might be interested in seeing a big money transaction going on, four tight women in suits for starters.

"Twenty, right?" Maggie's face was hot. She thought she might be blushing despite herself, despite Sylvia's incredible self-control.

Jane and Jack nodded glumly.

Maggie said, "And the check, Jack? That would be for five. You can make it out to me personally, Sylvia Fischer. Or to 'cash,' if you prefer to keep it anonymous."

His hands fumbled opening the checkbook but he wrote it out quickly and handed it to her, then hid his trembling hands under the table. Maggie tried charming him with a few eye blinks and a tiny smile. She fluttered a hand at the couple to indicate they could now go ahead and finish eating. She fingered through her briefcase and extracted forms and a ballpoint pen and placed both on the table. She put the envelope of money inside the attaché. Her ankle held it tight.

"When you get a chance," she said. The N-643 and application form for the baby's citizenship had already been filled out and only needed their signatures.

Jane and Jack held their forks but neither ate. They both signed the forms and Maggie slipped the papers in with the dossier and home study report, which she would now forge since she had the money. There were other requirements, fingerprinting, obtaining a Social Security card and ITIN number for the IRS, which had to wait until after delivery of the baby.

She handed Jack a copy of receipts showing a deposit of $5,000, delivered to Sylvia Fischer toward "Finder's Fee" and the down payment for legal services and partial adoption expenses in the amount of $20,000, along with an adoption affidavit signed and sealed by a legal agent that released through a judicial court in Mexico City a male infant named Manuel Cardoñez Sofía. Attached was a copy of Manuel's birth certificate with the baby's footprints, DOB, weight, length and the time, township and clinic where he was born, along with the names of his birth parents and other information. Not all the information was false; the weight at 7lb 9oz fit most Guatemalan newborn boys.

"When will we hear from you?" Jane said, blurting the words with apprehension.

"Very soon. I'll call." Maggie put her napkin on the table and slid back her chair. "You don't mind handling the tab, do you, Jack? I really must be going."

"Sure," Jack said passively, used to paying the bill. "Um, Sylvia, do you mind if we keep little Jackie's picture?"

"If you must," Maggie said.

Little Jackie? Shit. She snapped her attaché closed. She thought: *Sylvia Fischer, you are mothballed.*

CHAPTER SIX

aggie escaped Pacifically Fish and made it to her car without blowing a fuse. She slammed shut the driver's door, making sure the Bischkes were nowhere in sight, and then let it rip: "Aaawww-*fuck!*"

She huffed and puffed and when she was done she angrily tore off the wig, firing up a cig and taking a series of quick puffs. She slunk in a pout.

She did it, she got the money. She might have been in awe with her collected alternate, but the real half remained pissed as hell. Maybe she, Maggie, was too righteous, too unforgiving. But never again would Sylvia live, with all her insufferable self-control and tolerating ways, the fake merchant's disgusting catering to their stupid needs.

"Goddamn shitheads," she muttered, but it had lost power now.

The drizzle let up.

Maggie thought about going shopping at nearby Horton Plaza for some new pedal pushers supposed to be on sale at Ross. Shopping for clothes was good therapy any time but especially in times of stress.

She thought of "little Jackie," the life he would have with those two, and that was most of what had done it; that and the Bischkes' total lack of tact by treating the purveying of human life with no more regard than any other negotiated purchase. Like buying something cute on eBay.

On the other hand she knew they at least were not abusers. She could intuit it in their demeanor, and in their eyes. Maggie had learned early in life the types of persons who abused and who had the potential to abuse; she had been around both and neither of these people fit the profile. For that reason she would not renege; she would deliver their child.

But that didn't make her feel any less disgusted with herself. She still needed to go shopping.

She slipped the newspaper out of the damp plastic wrapper as she smoked. She saw the headline and her head swooned. But it was the smaller headline that made the cigarette drop out of her mouth onto the gray skirt:

Evidence Points to Role of Missing Baby

Not *my* babies! she thought, almost shouting it out.

For a moment she couldn't find her breath and thought she might pass out, and then thought she might be sick. She smelled then felt the cigarette burning into her skirt and slapped at it, sending embers flying under the steering wheel. She lowered the driver's window for breathable air then found and tossed the still-lit cig onto the damp street. She re-read the headline and blurted, "Oh my God! Oh no ... "

She tried to settle down enough to read the story. She knew there were four infants there though the article didn't give a number. She knew there were supposed to be three girls and one boy, the Bischkes' promised son. It said evidence at the scene indicated one or more babies had been traveling with the migrants, though authorities had not confirmed their presence. No babies were among the dead.

Thank God for that. But where were they? Those were *her* babies.

She punched numbers on her cellular and waited through three puffs of a fresh cigarette for a lengthy message to end. Then she spoke quickly, "This is Sylvia. I need to talk as soon as possible. Those people in the desert, I need to know—"

A pinched-nose voice broke in, sounding like that loveable old actor Peter Lorre in *The Maltese Falcon*. "I'm here. What is it?"

Her lip bent at the sound of his whiny voice.

The voice belonged to the man in the smuggling group that she answered to, her boss. She knew that Mr. Swabb was an immigration lawyer and that was about all she knew. He mailed her the material for her adoption packets. He was her only contact so she didn't know how many people were involved; he may have run the whole show himself, though she doubted it, a man with that voice.

"They were our caretakers, weren't they?"

"Just a minute," Swabb said, an edge to his whine.

The shrillness of his voice forced Maggie to keep pulling the phone away. She smashed out the cigarette in the Buick's huge ashtray, an ashtray designed by men of a bygone era, those fat middle-aged guys who smoked fat cigars in a fat Detroit who could not accept lesser being better, much less more efficient.

The rain came in earnest now and she rolled up the window to suffocate on the last few drags off the cig. She could hear Swabb cup the phone and speak to someone in Spanish, something about the secretary having lunch or going to lunch.

"Sylvia, you know you're allowed to call only in an emergency. You know that," Swabb said.

As much as possible they kept conversation formal and vague when talking by phone.

"What happened to my babies?" Maggie said, not so vague. Her tone was more intense than she intended because of his flippant attitude, his indifference. He must have known about this.

At the moment she wasn't thinking about the money; all she wanted was to hear that the babies had made it to Chula Vista and were all right, hoping he would assure her of that.

"Those people, they *weren't* our caretakers, were they?" Her voice cracked.

"I really can't say," he said matter-of-factly. "Maybe, maybe not."

Maggie gasped. "No. I don't buy that."

"Then don't. I would have contacted you if there was a problem—"

"A problem!" she shouted. "All those people are dead and our babies are missing. *That's not a problem?*"

"Calm down!" Swabb said. "Everything is fine. Didn't I just say?—"

"What does *fine* mean?"

"It means what it means. I'm telling you. There is nothing for you to worry about … I'll have to talk to you later, Sylvia, I have a client. Just do your thing."

"I *am* doing it," she shouted. Tears gathered in her eyes. She took two quick breaths, then said, "I have a couple that's expecting to hear from me; they'll be devastated if they don't get their child. Don't you know how anxious they are?"

"Of course I know."

Maggie hesitated. She raked a hand through her hair; her elbow rested against the cold driver's window. Her eyes darted around; she measured her lie carefully. "I'm going to see these clients tomorrow. What am I supposed to tell them?"

"Nothing, just make the deal. Illegals are dying out there all the time."

Maggie moaned. "How can you be so callous!"

Swabb sighed into the phone. "In my line, I see it all the time … Look, Sylvia, tell them they may have to wait a bit longer, that's all. That unexpected complications have come up; it happens in this business. You should've told them that already.

"At any rate just get the money. And don't call me again unless it's an emergency. By the way, did you get to Great Western yet? I don't want to hear you don't have the money you owe."

Maggie was not one to tolerate threats. Nor could she tolerate people who didn't care about children—like foster parents who were in it only for the money or this money-hungry bastard boss of hers. Her voice hardened. "I'll tell them the truth."

"What? What did you say?"

"You find those babies or I swear I will tell these people and the others that their adoptions are off, and I'll tell them why. Translated, that means you get no money," she said. "I mean it, bud."

Swabb was used to having the last word, but not this time. Maggie left him holding a buzzing phone.

CHAPTER SEVEN

Rain chattered against the big wall of glass in Earl Warren Swabb's twenty-third floor office. He sat on the edge of his leather swivel behind a slick mahogany desk, sweating in the cool air. The law firm recently moved its suite to the coveted west side of the half-block NBC building, Broadway and Third; the firm was doing well these days specializing vigorously in immigration law. Every client stepping into his rich wood-and-books office wowed the view, and no wonder. It was a Chamber of Commerce panorama of San Diego's harbor with the picturesque Coronado blue bridge spanning sparkling deep turquoise water and the lush hunchbacked peninsula of Pt. Loma that kept watch over incoming vessels. Soiled clouds hid all that today.

Swabb of course didn't have a client with him as he'd told Sylvia, and his secretary was halfway into her lunch break. He tapped the glass-topped desk with a fountain pen and considered what to do about the frustrating woman he himself picked; she had crossed the line. He moaned and wiped fingers along his sweaty forehead, then phoned *his* boss.

Swabb's given name—Earl Warren—was not the only burden he had to bear. Nor was it the lack of authority in his voice. The thing that burdened him most was his uncanny resemblance to Richard M. Nixon—short, hefty, dark complected with beady, furtive eyes hidden under heavy eyebrows. And of course a telling propensity to sweat heavily, as if he was always guilty of something. It didn't help him or his client in court. Tiny beads formed on his upper lip from no more exertion than punching in a phone number, as he'd just done. He patted his entire face with a handkerchief.

After five rings of the phone he began tapping the fountain pen harder. Cutting her out of the business would be the best thing all around, he thought. But how would she react? She was emotional and vindictive;

this episode with the missing cargo showed him that. Would she really nullify sales?

Five more rings and a female's recorded voice asked him kindly to hold. That took another minute and fifteen seconds. Finally the man he called picked up.

"This is Richard Mendez. How can I help you?" The deep, resonant voice was a study in contrast to Swabb's bird tones.

"Ricky! Earl. Sorry to call. Just got off the horn with Sylvia," he said. "We have to meet. And I mean pronto—now!"

"Calm down, Earl. Take a breath; take it in steps."

"Okay. Step one—she's hysterical. Step two—she threatened to stop deliveries. Step three—I think she's holding out on us, lying to us. Ricky, we—"

"Don't get hysterical yourself ... "

There was a pause.

"I don't know what in hell she will do," Swabb whimpered. "But I know this; she could ruin us, she could ruin us bad."

"Badly," said Mendez. "Earl, listen to me. She is not our only problem ... I'll see you in an hour, at the place. Don't be late."

"All right. But, Ricky, where *are* the—"

Swabb looked at the phone incredulously; he'd been hung up on twice in a matter of minutes.

CHAPTER EIGHT

The ground tracker who met Myers at the site of the boxcar tragedy had worked the Imperial desert for a decade. Never a duty day went by, he said, that he didn't sweat a bucket. Myers could see that. He'd sweated off all the fat on his body and was down to about one-twenty sopping wet with sweat, so skinny he'd vanish behind an ocotillo stem.

Glen Paulson introduced himself with a strong handshake and a grin that put the wrinkles in his face to work. He held firmly a liter-sized water bottle that dwarfed his bony hand.

He showed Myers some tire impressions in the sand. "These are them," he said and pointed to a vague set of dual tread stamps running parallel along the south side of the railroad tracks about twenty-five feet from the boxcar. The tracks headed south.

"You're lucky that weather system in the city didn't make it out here," he said. "Would have compromised all this."

Myers watched him tilt the water bottle till it was empty, breathe "ahh," and wipe his sweaty brow.

"Vehicle that laid down these marks? Six-wheeler, probably an old Chevy ton-and-a-half, definitely heavy, with twenty-five, thirty-year-old tires."

Myers lifted his eyebrows. "That old, they should've blown already, don't you think?"

He nodded. "You'd think."

Myers wasn't sweating much, a trickle on his temple. He had brought water but it was boiling in his car.

"It's the weight of the vehicle that's interesting," said Paulson, "not the tires per se. If they cross the border at all, they usually use vans, but this vehicle was a very heavy truck, and that's a curious thing. It was a crazy snake that crossed this prairie to make his drop."

"And not get caught," added Myers. He eyed the pencil-thin ground tracker start on another water bottle, a smaller one. He didn't go ahh.

"Yeah. Didn't get caught. Anyway, all this is on file. We obviously didn't save the migrants, but you gotta make out the report, keep the stats. And you always want to know when and where new corridors might be opening."

"This going to become a new corridor, officially?"

"Now it's official, far as I'm concerned."

Myers kicked up some dirt. "They didn't have survival kits."

"Nope. Fact is I'm not sure if they are actually issuing those Happy Boxes anymore; if they ever did issue them, cause I haven't ever seen one in my area, and my area is big." Paulson grinned. "Want some water?"

Myers grinned back. "You bet."

The agent took ten measured steps to a white and red cooler sitting under the sun, dug a bottle out of crunchy ice and water and handed it to Myers. It was cold and wet.

"Happy Boxes," Myers knew, was a satirical reference to a one-time idea of issuing survival kits to illegals that crossed the border in the desert—like a complimentary sample handed out at a 5K race for cancer. The idea came from a joint U.S.-Mexican committee on migrant health, seeking ways to lower the desert's soaring death rate.

"Let me show you," Paulson said and pointed to the tracks. "Here, they had the migrants in the truck. Now come on over here."

He led Myers, in no hurry, to a spot a hundred feet south and showed him tracks behind a clump of scrub that had been protected from the prevailing easterly wind.

"Here's your tracks after the smugglers unloaded them off the truck. Not as dense and the vehicle was leisurely driven away. I guarantee you these tracks don't vary from due south to the highway across the border, about 24, 25 klicks from the spot we're standing at.

"Where the truck went from there? Your guess is good as mine."

CHAPTER NINE

~Four Days Earlier, Hwy 2 Sonora, Mexico ~

Sanchez had popped peyote in Caborca and now he was seeing objects in the headlights—a salsa-drenched carne asada tortas chasing a bowl of red menudo. The bowl of menudo danced across the asphalt, spilling itself. Weird. The *coyote* was too fascinated by the Carl's Jr burger somersaulting behind the other stuff to bother analyzing his altered vision.

He glanced at his partner. "We're stopping at the focking safehouse. Don't give me any shit."

Chacon frowned. He turned to the blackness through his window. There was a desert racing by out there but he couldn't see it. "Boss will be pissed we don't get there tonight."

At the wheel, Sanchez sneered but kept his eyes on the steady line of Carl's Jr burgers in the road, scooting along like a whiplash of ducklings. He mooned his eyeballs and shook his head but the crazy images wouldn't get off the road. The thing was they moved with the traveling truck. He *couldn't* run over them. His glazed eyes shimmered in the dashboard light as if coated in oil.

Another hour passed before he sharply broke the ton-and-a-half and wheeled off the highway onto a weedy dirt road, careless that it would shake up the *campesinos* in the back. "We're focking stopping."

Chacon sighed and held on against the bumps.

After seventeen hundred miles, the smugglers had less than a hundred to go before reaching Ensenada, their destination.

A few scattered lights illuminated ranch houses across the *ejido*. The first ranch they saw was supposed to be the safehouse. Sanchez cut the engine behind a grove of yucca near the only lighted adobe in sight. "Keep them quiet," he said and got out.

The usual commotion of baby cries, shushes and bumping noises commenced in the rear of the truck though subdued under the thick cocoon of canvas. Chacon tossed open the cover against the harsh odor of diesel fumes and flicked a light on the huddled migrants. Tiny knotted fists quaked as caretakers tried to quell the infants' cries.

Chacon doused the light, whispered, "Shh, climb on out." The migrants eased over the tailgate, nervous-looking but relieved to be standing on their feet.

"Gather some firewood," he said, "I will see about some food." He handed one of the men a book of matches and walked off toward the house.

The flickering light from inside the adobe danced among the shadows across the dark desert floor. Chacon ignored the sleepy dog at the doorway and acknowledged with a tooth-sucking sound the stooped farmer standing in the curtained doorway. He pointed toward the yuccas and said seven people needed food. The old man nodded.

Out back, Sanchez sat on a rock eating a meatless plate of beans and corn tortillas, staring up at the black night. "It's focking perfect." He could have been talking about the food satiating his craving or the vast heavens.

Chacon squatted. He drank from his bottle of mescal, sputtering as if he might throw up. He spooned some of the steaming beans onto a cold tortilla. "We can get there by midnight," he said. "Boss said any later and we would be out of favor. He talks polite but he means we won't get paid. Even worse."

Sanchez flashed a wolfish grin, the metal caps on his teeth catching light and slashing at Chacon like razors. "Fock him. We'll get paid all right."

"You gotta stop doing that shit, cousin, it's fucking up your thinking." Chacon watched a scorpion as he spoke.

Sanchez pushed the last bite of burrito into his mouth and spoke with food protruding from his lips. "Chacon, you want to be poor all your miserable life?"

Chacon screwed his face up with disgust without looking at his cousin, knowing there would be particles of food spewing his way. He sipped mescal and bit into his burrito.

"Well I don't. I want to be rich. I want to be king of my focking destiny—*Un rey*. My destiny is to be as Al Pacino."

Chacon chewed and listened to the peyote talking. He pushed a dried ocotillo stick under the scorpion and waited till it climbed aboard. He brought it eye level. "You want to pick its legs?"

Sanchez knocked the scorpion off the stick and stepped on it, twisting his boot into the sand.

"You don't know who I'm talking about, do you? Old Scarface, you imbecile … You will be rich too, because we are going to take these focking babies and sell them ourselves."

He punched Chacon on the shoulder.

Chacon narrowed his eyes. "What gringo will buy babies?" he said, sneering. "What kind of story will you tell boss? What about them?" he said, nodding toward the *campesinos* out there in the dark.

"Ha! You think I haven't thought of that stuff already? I have a plan. We will be wolves—as Al Pacino!"

Chacon lured the worm with his tongue from the half-full bottle of mescal, chewed it up, then raked an arm across his mouth. "I think you are full of shit."

The migrants had taken orders from the ill-tempered Sanchez for eight days. They had traveled across mountains and avoided the cities and conquered a huge desert, tolerating the cruel *coyote* all the while. They stood helplessly by as Sanchez violated the group's only girl at will and cowered pitifully when he put a stick to the backs of the oldest ones. The other smuggler, Chacon, did nothing to stop him.

When Sanchez now said, "In the truck, we're going," they scrambled back into the truck bed, leaving their chow unfinished.

Sanchez used fog lights along the arroyos of the dry *Rio Coyote*. The vehicle bounced and rocked on the pitted desert floor. Luck came to Sanchez in the form of a rare cloudy sky that cloaked the desert like a great eyelid.

In time the truck came to a railroad track and Sanchez cut the engine. He backhanded his pouty partner and pointed through the dusty windshield to the vague outline of a train car.

"There it is, just as I remember … You know what to do."

The empty mescal bottle tumbled off the floorboard and shattered as Chacon got out. He stood aside as Sanchez untied and threw back the canvas, then shined a torch into the bed.

"Get out." He waved his stick. "Leave those squawking babies in the truck."

The migrants at first appeared confused, then reluctant. "Tell us what is going on," an Indian woman said.

Sanchez took hold of the woman's thick forearm and pulled to get her out. No one at first saw the knife in his hand. "You stinking *pollo*, I told you, get out of the truck!"

The woman was bigger and stronger than Sanchez and she pushed him to the ground.

Again she asked, "What is happening?" The woman's name was Jovita, a woman known across her mountain home for the good food off her stand.

Sanchez this time held a beam of light on the woman so the others could see as he pushed the knife into her lower stomach. He twisted it to make her cry. His breath came in gasps, like hers.

Jovita swung her elbow around and caught Sanchez on the nose, again knocking him down. Quietly, she fell to her knees and moaned. She rested on hands and knees, panting like a dog, unable now to get back to her feet.

From his knees Sanchez plunged the serrated knife again into the thick of her body. Then again and again until his arm lost power and he could no longer lift the blade.

The *campesinos* huddled in pathetic silence as they heard their companion's last breath slip away.

Sanchez held his shirttail to his bleeding nose. Panting, he hastened the group into the boxcar at knifepoint. "Not you," he told the teenage girl. "You stay with the babies."

He said to the others, "Don't worry, you will be picked up in the morning and given jobs. You are in *el norte* now!"

Chacon could have stopped his cousin with a quick punch to the throat. Sanchez was an addict and a runt, but he was blood. So the stockier Chacon let him be.

It took Chacon's help to slide the big Lackawanna door shut.

The girl had crawled into the back corner of the truck bed, weeping and shaking in fear then crying out when the torch hit her eyes.

"Shut up," Sanchez said. "Get up front and bring them."

Emboldened by his own savagery and full of grandeur, Sanchez became reckless on the return, driving fast across the black landscape, the girl beside him and the babies in hers and Chacon's arms.

A searing flood of light broke on them. A bullhorn blared, commands to halt.

Chacon screamed, "See what you've done, cousin. We are dead meat now!"

"You idiot, we are in Mexico. *La migra* can do nothing."

Sanchez baited the enemy with a blast of horn. He didn't slow. Chacon watched in amazement as the enemy agents did nothing, just as his cousin, King Al Pacino, had said.

CHAPTER TEN

Earl Swabb waited on his boss in front of the Star of India, the designated meeting place. Gulls miked shrilly gliding around the historic schooner. An overland bus pulled up and a hoard of Japanese tourists quickly disembarked and swarmed Swabb. Most of the Japanese men were taller than him, which forced him to step onto a piling to continue his vigil. He made a picaresque if not applaud able presence poised on a pedestal in a three-piece suit, mocked it appeared by the gaggle of both seagulls and Japanese.

Swabb bided his time studying the tourists. He tried to pick out the ones who might have lied when applying for their visas. It was hard to tell with Japanese. He was generally suspicious of all traveling foreigners and in particular of rich Latin nationals, the core of Zehren Bagdonavich & Magoo's clientele. They tended to forget some aspects of their financial wealth when applying to work or live in the U.S. over differences with the IRS.

He spotted the black luxury sedan as it turned off Harbor Drive into the bayside parking area. Swabb yanked his hands out of his pockets and jumped off the piling. He nervously straightened his vest and tie as if preparing to face a known xenophobic judge.

Richard Mendez stepped out of a Lincoln Continental and slipped the maximum number of quarters into a meter and walked briskly toward the tall ship. Well-heeled and heavyset, his cropped black hair had the impeccable, gray-tipped wavy mane of the manicured executive, a man in his mid fifties with little obvious body fat under buttoned-down pinstripes. He might have been a Wall Street broker or an Italian movie producer. He might've been the paranoid mastermind of a baby smuggling ring.

Swabb greeted him with a dead-fish handshake and got a bad-smell look in return. He didn't say anything about his being late. Maybe he, Swabb, had misunderstood and Mendez had actually said an hour instead of thirty minutes. Perhaps Swabb was making excuses to conceal the intimidation he felt, even after years in a business relationship with the man. A partnership as Swabb imagined.

"I'm not feeling comfortable about her, Ricky."

"You worry too much," Mendez said. "Every lawyer I've ever known worries too much. You taught that in school?"

They walked a few steps from the noisy crowd.

"I'm serious … If I was in the loop, I would know how to deal with my people. What was I supposed to tell Sylvia?"

"You know the saying, 'What you don't know—'"

"'Won't hurt you?'"

Mendez said, "Earl, if I'd told you I don't know where the merchandise is, what would you have told her?"

Swabb said nothing.

"Exactly. It serves no purpose to worry our operatives with information unnecessary to them. Of course *you* need to know, and that's why you're here now."

Swabb thought, *Excuse me but who the hell called this meeting.*

Instead, he said, "I told her everything was fine, but Ricky—"

"You want to know."

"Sure I want to know."

Mendez walked back toward the tourists and Swabb followed.

"The cargo's still missing."

"Damn … They're not dead are they?"

"Use your legal noggin, Earl … The *coyotes* you hired for the transport, what do you think—you following me?"

Swabb nodded. "Yes, of course. But, uh, what do you mean?"

"To clarify. It appears your thugs decided to take our merchandise for themselves."

"No! … They did?"

Swabb said nothing more because Mendez showed him a hand meaning silence. "How much do you think they would get if the cargo wasn't breathing?"

The bastard couldn't even say the word, wouldn't call them what they were. It disgustedly Swabb—even if he himself didn't say the words. *Ba-*

bies, humans. Little humans, but still *human beings.* Ricky Mendez was a sick man.

"I see your point," he said, not quite groveling. "Ricky, don't think for a minute that I personally selected those men. I had nothing to do with hiring them. Okay?"

Mendez gazed at him. "No? I was sure they were friends of yours."

"The Inspector assured me—"

"Yes, well, I will be speaking to *Señor* Guerrero about his employment pool. As for the renegade *coyotes,* and the whereabouts of the cargo, I'm putting a specialist on it. A man who knows how to get answers and take care of business."

"Great, but listen, Ricky, it's not my fault. I—"

Mendez raised the hand again only this time he wagged a finger. "It will be in your best interest that our operative finds the merchandise. That he finds it alive and gets it back. Because if he doesn't—"

He spoke in a level voice but suddenly grabbed Swabb by the throat and lifted the smaller man to his tiptoes. He used just one hand. Mendez did not appear concerned that he stood on the open sidewalk in front of fifty Japanese tourists and directly across the street from the County Administration Building where plenty of bigwigs knew him by sight.

Mendez released him and smoothed the lapels on Swabb's suit, all seemingly in one move.

"Because if he doesn't," he went on, same steady voice, "you will be covering the loss in more ways than financially. You see? Are you understanding me, Earl?"

The lawyer nodded furiously, gasping for air.

The Japanese tourists finally grew silent as they gathered in an orderly line and began moving, one by one, onto the ship's gangplank. Evidently, they had not noticed the red in both men's faces nor the sweat covering Swabb's brow on a cool, mid-November afternoon.

Swabb shook in his polished shoes but he didn't lose bladder control, and when he again spoke it was as if nothing had happened. "Ah, what about Sylvia? I know she lied about her latest deal, I called the clients who said she already collected the down, even got a bonus. She got it *before* she called me threatening to cancel the sale. We cannot trust her anymore than your Mexican guy, Guerrero."

Mendez listened intensely, frowning. "What is it, five transactions she's done over the last three months?"

"Six now. But she hasn't deposited the money for the last three. This one makes the fourth."

"This is information I needed to know earlier, Earl. Explain."

Swabb took a swift pace backwards, keeping out of Mendez's long reach. He had not stopped sweating. He pulled a handkerchief from inside his suit jacket. He patted his forehead and then worked down the rest of his face and then to the back of his neck and then back to the forehead for another swipe.

"Uhh—what I mean, Ricky. She could have deposited it today. I, uh, I didn't think to check before I came. She's always put the money into the account on time until lately—"

"Not kosher, Earl."

"But … but, I've never had a reason to think she wouldn't. Well, I mean, until now, that is."

Mendez shook his head and let his eyes burn into Swabb.

"Check on it before this day is over. *Comprendes?*"

"*Sí, yo comprende,*" Swabb said instinctively. He was unnerved.

"I hope we can continue this working relationship, Earl." His words were as chilling as a slasher's, in that kind of movie.

Swabb nodded like a schoolboy. He started to say something but Mendez, once again, raised a finger.

But Swabb wouldn't be cut short again, not if it cost him his life, not for a third straight time in one day. He mustered up all his courage and said, "Maybe you could have your specialist pay Sylvia a visit, too. Collect the money; do whatever's necessary—you think?"

"First things first, Earl. But, yes, I will take that matter under advisement."

CHAPTER ELEVEN

Travis and Roxanne Cousins had lived in the same trailer community since their arrival in San Diego four years earlier. "Bubba," as everyone outside the BP called him, had been ecstatic to leave the hellhole of Sasabe, Arizona, come serve the greatest and biggest border crossing in the country, in the world.

Their rented trailer was second in from the entrance gate and only steps from the community pool. They'd lucked out getting an envied silver-bullet Airstream, which had an attached screened-in patio twice the trailer's square footage, a nice bonus, especially for Roxanne who spent a lot of time reading her romance mysteries.

The park could have more seductively and simply been called "Paradise Lagoon," but for reasons only known to management it went with the hard-hitting, no-nonsense name "Paradise Lagoon Trailer Park." Other than the constant roar off Interstate 5, it did offer a semblance of paradise, for the lagoons across the 5 and below the commercial shipyards offered an ornithologist's dreamland. The sensitive wetlands served as a protected sanctuary for the endangered least tern, the elegant sandpiper and the tiny, prim California gnatcatcher, soon to go off the endangered list again, as well as the larger birds not on the list, the pelicans and red-tailed hawks and osprey, the great white and blue herons. Even with his powerful, heat-seeking, night-vision-capable Border Patrol-issued binoculars, Bubba had only once or twice spotted one of those endangered bird in the lagoons—and Bubba considered himself somewhat of a bird watcher. Rox did, too.

Roxanne was stretched out on the patio chaise reading her Harlequin, a captivating Apple Valley romance by thrilling new author, S.A. Skains. Her twin schnauzers were being lazy with her, Trixie and Dixie both snoring piggishly in the same doggie bed just below her, looking like one dog with two heads. She had one page to go in the chapter when the phone rang. Her eyes were misty, ready to spill. She frowned at the interruption. The phone continued to ring. Trixie woke and barked.

"Darn it! … Bubba?"

Bubba was under the Chrysler changing the oil and filter, just spitting distance from the screened porch. Today was the first of his off shift days. He ignored his wife's call. Let her answer it herself.

The phone started ringing again and Roxanne compliantly put her book aside and stepped up into the trailer. "Cousins residence. Mrs. Cousins speaking."

"Travis, please."

Roxanne recognized the weighty voice that had called a couple times before, but she turned her head and shouted out the door, "For you, Bubba. Man won't give his name."

Bubba could hear her big voice loud and clear, as did everyone else in the vicinity. "Shit," he mumbled, crawling out from under the vehicle.

He wiped his greasy hands on a rag before taking the phone.

"Travis. Who'm I talking to?"

"Your services are needed."

Bubba straightened. "One sec." He took the phone into the tiny bathroom and shut the door.

He didn't know the man's name; that was a condition for both their protection since the "services" the man spoke of were nasty affairs.

Richard Mendez spoke in his low-res, clear executive tone so that he would be heard over the background noise on the phone. First he suggested Bubba use a cell phone in the future. "Let's don't get others involved."

"Rox? She don't matter."

"Everyone matters. Do it. Can you meet this afternoon?"

"No problem, what time?"

"One."

"Okay, thirteen hundred. Should I bring anything?"

"You'll know what you need after we talk." The phone went dead in Bubba's hand in the tiny chamber. The bathroom was big enough only for an average-size woman, not Bubba. He didn't much care since he took most of his showers at the station.

Bubba didn't take the time to install a new oil filter. He tightened down the drain bolt then added four-and-a-half quarts of Quaker State 30 weight. He changed clothes and told Rox he had to go, overtime call, could be an all-nighter. He grabbed his personal piece but didn't take time to charge his cell phone.

CHAPTER TWELVE

~Outskirts of Tecate~

For their last set, the mariachi bandleader took a chance and suggested the boys try their hand at some tejano. The farmhands and street roughs making up their small audience were pretty juiced by now, so he, Juan Pepe, figured this was good a time as any to practice the worn Mex-Tex style, which had just now become the rave here in Tecate. None of Juan Pepe's boys liked tejano, too much gringa/German influence bastardizing their musical tradition. They didn't work an audience very well as it was. They weren't out there strutting like matadors, though they did depend on flashy tights and sequined sombreros to make them stand a little taller and pull them through their off-key weaknesses. Juan Pepe expected the band to fuck up tonight since they hadn't rehearsed a single tejano piece.

Outside the tavern, standing in the shadows, a gringo listened and watched. Peering through the saloon's doorway, light caught his pale eyes. The gringo had time and patience on his side, which he needed waiting on the crowd to get loaded and drop its guard. He waited until the flashy but tired-looking band finished its set, then he stepped casually through the doors into the smoky interior.

Several faces turned anyhow when he entered; he had that kind of presence. The eyes that caught his belonged to the thieves, men with something to fear, not the farm boys who had only came out for a little fun. The rogues narrowed their eyes, as though they could tell by his carriage the man was *la migra*, as if they smelled the law on him even in street clothes—the black leather across his chest to the snakeskin boots.

They were right, he was Border Patrol. But not tonight. Tonight he was servicing an outfit he knew little about except that they wanted him to find a murdering *coyote* named Miguel Sanchez, then kill him—with cruel prejudice.

Bubba had worked the Ocotillo boxcar tragedy and he knew his man was fearless and beyond redemption. He knew his man was a drug user based on the mere bravado of the act. He knew also that the man was smart and dangerous.

A snitch had tipped Bubba that his man might be here and Bubba brought with him an official capture-and-release mug shot of his man. It pictured a narrow-faced, sneering individual with three tin-capped teeth and a heavy brow hiding small eyes. In the photo, his hair was big, bushy, but Bubba wasn't depending on hair to ID the punk; he could have cut it off or shaved his head. Still, mugs sometimes deceived and he would require confirmation that Sanchez was the Sanchez he was after when he found him, so he strolled to the bar and took a spot near two women who looked as if they had known a lot of local men. The women wore similar black-vinyl micro body wraps that enhanced their bulges and left a lot more skin exposed than the fabric covered.

The musical group hit the stage again and the cantina soon throbbed under the base strings and trumpet and Bubba had to shout his choice of drink to the barkeeper. "Bud, *por favor.*"

He studied the layout. Men occupying all the tables who wore either feathered Stetson knockoffs or corn straw hats. There were a couple other women sitting at tables in the back. Working-class Mexican bars typically didn't welcome women. The establishment had only one bathroom, which he figured would have one urinal and one doorless stall with a toilet that no woman in her right mind would sit on. All the windows were high and had iron bars on them. Bubba noted that the back door was the only other way in or out.

The women in vinyl gave him the come-on with their eyes and sidled closer. Both were past their prime. He acknowledged them, as any decent Texan would, by tipping his hat in a kindly way. He wore a real Stetson, short-rimmed and short barreled.

"Good evening, ladies," he said in border Spanish. "You look lovely tonight…"

They eyed him skeptically, so he got right to it. "I am looking for a skinny little dope addict with silver teeth. *Su nombre es Sanchez.*"

He showed them the arrest mug shot. "Either of you lovely ladies see this man tonight?"

Both women backed away as if something smelled bad. Bubba figured it was him.

One said, "You are *la migra*, huh? I know, I can see it in your face … But you are handsome, anyway. So what you want to know?"

He was right. Bubba again tipped his Stetson and the red curly locks puffed out as if spring-loaded. He shrugged. "I'm not here to bother you. You help me and I will do you a favor."

"What favor?"

"Do you know this man?"

"There are many men named Sanchez, eh?"

Bubba sniffed. "Not looking like a corpse from all the dope he shoots into his body. This Sanchez is a thieving *cholo*; he rapes young virgins and robs *campesinos* just to get high. Where is he? I know he comes in here … The favor I will do for you is in the future."

The other woman was shorter, slightly pudgier. She turned her head sideways and appeared to spit at the floor. "I know this man. I would see him dead. He comes here for the drugs. Never for us. I would never let him touch me."

"Look in the dark out there," the first woman said, pointing to the back door. "You may find him with his dope friends. Take him away. That is a favor you can do for us."

A fistfight broke out at a table close by and one of the scrappers stumbled backwards into Bubba. The women moved quickly out of the way. Bubba forgot for the moment that he was off duty and took the man by the wrist and locked his arm behind him, about to grab for the cuffs. He let go in the same movement, said, "*Lo siento, amigo*," and grinned, then shoved the man back into the fray.

The first woman grabbed his arm. "Look! There is the coward. Get him!"

She jabbed a finger at a shadowy figure by the bathroom. Bubba saw a thin man wearing drab and baggy knee-length pants slung low, his bushy hair in the mug shot now a buzz cut, as Bubba figured.

"You sure that's Miguel Sanchez?"

"Get him, *kill* him!" She was pulling on the sleeve of Bubba's tight leather coat. He figured the man somewhere along the line had done her wrong. Her passion was enough assurance this was his man.

He moved slowly toward Sanchez. "Miguel, just a moment, man. I need to see you."

Sanchez's eyes grew wide, quick to sense the man was not a buyer. He made a dash for the back door.

Bubba picked up the pace, pushing aside a table and two men to get by, barking apologies in his haste. The lighting did not carry out into the parking lot and he was momentarily blinded. He held back, listening and ready for an ambush. Then he heard a car engine start up. It revved and spit gravel. He could make out a heavy-bodied car speeding off without headlights.

He had anticipated the perp making a break and accordingly had parked his Chrysler where it wouldn't be blocked. In a short few seconds he pursued a late-70's model Monte Carlo. Sanchez had chopped the car and that was a big mistake, Bubba thought; the car could not stand a chase without bottoming out.

The outskirts of Tecate proper had few paved streets and even fewer lights. Darkened shanties on dirt streets cutting through a scrub brush landscape. Bubba had only to follow the trail of billowing dust and listen for the loud glass packs that proved now to be Sanchez's second big mistake. He eased off to give him a good block or two lead and clear the raised dust.

The last street light fell away and soon the unlit shanties dissolved; the terrain became rough desert. The Monte Carlo's lights came on. Bubba knew his perp was thinking he had lost him, with no tailing lights.

~

In the Monte Carlo, Sanchez kept his eyes moving suspiciously between the inside and outside mirrors. He didn't notice the *vado* until it was too late. The low rider suddenly dropped and smashed into the opposite bank of the sandy gully, throwing Sanchez first against the roof and then into the steering wheel. He cried out from the hammer blow to his chest. The car's back wheels spun; the glass packs screamed. He could feel a knot forming on top of his head. He backed up, got a little speed and hit the bank again.

The Monte Carlo dug deeper into the porous earth until finally it would go neither forwards nor backwards. He was in a panic or he would have known to turn into the *vado* instead of trying to barrel through it. The oil pan had hit something hard and soon the sweet, rancid scent of hot oil drifted through the open window. His prized car—home of so many lustful and high times—wheezed like an asthmatic old smoker until finally it sputtered and died in a languid hiss.

Sanchez felt sick. He turned over the ignition, begging *El Dios Todopoderoso* and *Santa Maria*. He pressed the key until the battery was drained.

He felt even sicker spotting in his door mirror the flickering beam of a flashlight that wavered side to side, a light heading closer. The beam closed in, now hitting his eyes.

~

Bubba held the torch on the *coyote's* face. He saw a scared, sweaty, contrite face. A guilty look seeking mercy. He took a moment to study the face of a woman killer.

"You got a gun?" Bubba said in English. Sanchez raised his hands. You could see that the *cabáon* knew *la migra's* drill. There wasn't much doubt this was his man, but Bubba double-checked the mug shot anyway, looking for that look in his eye. It wasn't there but satisfied anyway, he put away the picture.

Bubba scanned the interior. No exposed weapon. He put the light back on Sanchez' pleading face.

"How old are you?" Bubba said contemptuously.

Sanchez suddenly banged open the door, knocking the flashlight out of Bubba's hand. He took off like a cartoon Wile E. Coyote, stumbling to get out of the gully. Bubba sighed and let him go. It was just a game now that the sick-looking addict had no chance of winning against a trained lawman in decent shape.

Bubba took his time checking inside the big car. He found some crushed cocaine in a glass vial in the open ashtray of the console along with a small metal cup. He'd been expecting to find meth but the coke was better for his purposes. Still no weapon. He grabbed the vial and cup and took off after the smuggler, only slightly concerned that Sanchez might be holding. If anything it would be a knife.

Bubba loped along the ravine behind the beam of his flashlight. He caught up to the addict in no time. Sanchez had tripped over a rock and was on his knees wheezing. Bubba sat on him. He laid the flashlight on the ground facing them and performed a hand search, turning up a hunting knife in a sheath attached to the killer's ankle.

"This the one you used on that old lady at that train car?"

Sanchez breathed in gasps. He didn't answer.

Bubba tossed the knife into the night desert and held the vial of coke in the shaft of light for Sanchez to see.

Sanchez looked at it as though puzzled. "What is this?" he said, going for innocence. Like they all did.

"This is the shit that's ruined you."

"I didn't do nothing, why you chase me, man?"

Bubba squeezed Sanchez's wrists together in front of him and cuffed him. Sanchez didn't resist. He moaned.

"I'm going to tell you straight, Miguel. Tonight you're going to die. In a few minutes … The only way you're not is if you tell me what you did with the babies."

"Huh?"

"Okay, then, let's start with this one. Where is Chacon?"

"I don't know no Chacon, man. Who's that?"

"At least you got enough character not to rat on your own blood. But he's a dead man, too, pardoner."

"Man, don't talk that. I tell you right, I don't do nothing."

"Looking at you, I shouldn't even bother," Bubba said. "You're gonna kill yourself soon enough, anyway … Get up."

He pulled Sanchez to his feet.

"One last chance. Tell me where the babies are. You do, I'll give you a break."

"Okay! Okay, man. I take you to them."

Sanchez's profusion of sweat released a putrid odor, like rotting flesh. Bubba held him at arm's length. "You are one worthless piece of shit, you know that, *cabáon*? … Come on, we're going for a ride."

Bubba took a handful of Sanchez's shirt at the back of his neck and guided him to the Chrysler.

Before putting him in, he said, "If you've gotta puke, do it now. Do it in my car and I'll cut your tongue out, understand?"

Sanchez nodded and went in without having to be shoved.

Bubba leaned over and fixed the miserable doper with a glare. "Once again, and last time, where are the babies?"

"Ensenada."

"Who has 'em? I want a name and place. Chacon? They with him?" Bubba asked his questions in an even voice. He propped himself on the window of the passenger door as if there was no hurry. The night could pass into day and it wouldn't matter to him.

"Chacon, he don't know nothing." Sanchez wiped his dripping nose on the sleeve of one of his cuffed wrists. He looked up toward Bubba but not at him. "True. I tell Chacon, go on to TJ. He live there with his mamma."

"So it was all you. You killed the old woman and it was your brilliant idea to steal the babies ... What did you do with those babies, Miguel?"

"Okay! They are with this woman. You know, women know about babies. She keep them for me while I look for some people who maybe buy them. Babies are not easy to sell. You know?"

Bubba narrowed his eyes and Sanchez gave in. "Okay, man. She is my mamma. I swear. She live on Rio Avenida, all the way south at one-hundred-ten."

"That a real address? The babies are there now?"

Sanchez nodded.

"One-ten Rio Avenida, in Ensenada. What part?

Sanchez gave him the look then that told Bubba there was no doubt. "You know. Shit."

"Yeah, okay. How many babies are there?"

"Four. There are four of them."

"Are they sick?"

Sanchez looked offended. "My *mamma* take care of them, man. The girl, too."

Holding the torch on him, Bubba walked around to the driver's side and slid in under the wheel.

Sanchez started to cry. "Man, I didn't do nothing. Me and Chacon, we only hauled those *pollos—*"

"Save it."

"Man, the Patrol catch us. On my mamma's—"

Bubba popped him on the nose with the butt of his flashlight. Hard. "Don't talk to me about your mother, you fuck. Your mamma didn't bring you up to kill women."

Bubba cranked up the Chrysler and drove slowly along the gulch, listening to the *coyote* suck blood back into his nose.

"I have friends who can pay, you let me go," Sanchez said clearly, despite his nose swelling.

He leaned toward Bubba. Bubba caught the shift in his demeanor, sounding confidential and friendly now. "Hey, buddy. I give you a young, beautiful girl, you want."

Sanchez brushed at his nose. "You don't like girls, I give you money, huh. How much you want? I get it for you. You just give me a price, huh? Miguel can make you the deal. I am the king, old Scarface."

Bubba sneered. "Al Capone, huh? King that died of syphilis while incarcerated? You picked a real winner to admire."

"*Capone?* Who is this? Is Al *Pacino*, man, old Scarface. I am him."

"Yeah, I can see the resemblance."

Bubba stopped the car after a couple miles. He turned off the headlights and got out and took a few steps under a black sky full of pinpoint stars. No wind and quiet. Desert critters were there but they weren't chattering. He shined the light around and spotted a barrel cactus about the size of a trashcan. That would do, he thought.

Bubba removed things from the car trunk, a bundle of rope, some bungee cords, rags and duct tape he'd purchased at a clean *mercado* in Tecate that was more expensive than Home Depot, then got Sanchez out of the car.

"Hey, tell me what you want, huh. The beautiful girl?" Sanchez clearly had run low on confidence, seeing the stuff Bubba was carrying. Trickles of blood sprayed on the wind with his words.

"What all this stuff for, eh?"

Bubba paid no attention to him. He held him by his trousers where he should have worn a belt and dragged him to the barrel cactus. He shoved him to a sitting position. He gave Sanchez the vial and a lighter. "Go ahead, it's yours."

"Aw, man, *you* take it. I give it to you."

Bubba removed a pill bottle from his pants and shook out four round tablets. "Here, take these too. They'll help."

Sanchez began to tremble. "What? Wha—"

"Open up. Take them. This is the break I'm giving you."

Bubba had to pop him with the flashlight once more before Sanchez would open his mouth and take the oxy.

"I gotta pee while you get yourself high, don't move," Bubba said. He walked out into the open desert, giving the *coyote* a precious last moment. Though he did need to urinate. This was his body reacting to excitement, he knew, because he was too young for prostate problems. Usually it happened only around women he found attractive and he'd have to run to the bathroom. Got to be a drag.

The sky was so beautiful and full of awe that Bubba nearly got a crick in his neck looking up at it. It gave him pause to reflect. He didn't like what he was doing; he was nothing but a common thug, he thought, doing a job like this. Not a whole lot different than the *cabáon* he was about to kill.

The twinkling stars made him think of his wife, the way things were when they were first married. It was funny, but lately with Roxanne it was hard to feel the love for her he felt when he was not with her. How come that was? Was it that way for other husbands after eight years of marriage, he wondered, or did they love their wives the same all the time, when they were with them or not with them? He was the quiet type and didn't get that close to the other guys to know how it was with them. He didn't feel all that sexy around her, not like when they tied the knot, back when she didn't wear curlers in the afternoon and smoke cigarettes and read romance books. Rox read more books in a month than Bubba had read in all his adult life, other than manuals and a couple of Tom Clancy paperbacks sometime back in the '90s. He hated to think it, but he saw his wife as just another south Texas trailer tramp. He pined for affection at this very moment, under this clear black sky with all its brilliant stars. He saw a satellite, he thought, or a real slow shooting star.

Now sobbing, Sanchez looked up at his kidnapper as if full of penance.

"Those people you put in that boxcar, you know what it's like to die like they did?"

"*Muertos? No!* Man, I don't know nothing about that. Man, you gotta believe me."

"Your blood starts to boil. Your organs heat up and start to swell. You feel that happen. The organs blister and then blow up inside you. Maybe you get lucky and go unconscious first. Maybe not. Either way, it's an awful way for a person to die."

Sanchez started blubbering. He tried to get to his feet and Bubba had to kick him in the chest to settle him back down. The murderer began to babble like a Pentecostal fanatic gone to tongues.

"None of that stuff," Bubba said and gagged his mouth with a rag and taped it. He shoved Sanchez hard against the quills of the cactus. Sanchez froze in surprise as the needles penetrated his backside. His legs began to quiver. Bubba pressed a knee into his chest to hold him in place and swung the rope lasso-like around the barrel cactus. He tossed the rope around the giant plant again, then pushed his knee hard against Sanchez's chest and throat, driving the needles deeper into his back, at the same time tying off the rope.

He removed the cuffs from Sanchez's hands and bound them at the wrists with another length of rope. The gag muted Sanchez's screams, making it mere moaning. Bubba wished he would puke so he would drown and bring his suffering to a quicker end, since it was just going to get worse.

He moved behind the cactus with the rope attached to Sanchez's wrists and pulled his arms as far back as they would go. He flashed the torch to watch as he carefully interlaced the rope with low-sided quills and then tied it off. To finish his job he needed to have the man's belly exposed.

He stepped around the cactus to face Sanchez again, screwing up his own face at a rising fecal odor. He watched Sanchez's bulging, horrified eyes. It pained Bubba to see the killer wasn't unconscious, that he hadn't suffocated.

He stepped on Sanchez's ankles and lingered over him for only a moment, then knelt and put his knees with his weight on the man's quivering thighs. He spoke softly.

"This is the last thing you're ever gonna hear, Miguel, so listen up. You are scum on the sewer floor. But if it was up to me I'd still just shoot you and get it over with. But I got my orders, amigo."

He ripped away Sanchez's shirt. The silver blade of the Buck knife caught a flicker of reflected light off Andromeda before it dropped and sank in Sanchez's abdomen just below the rib cage. The *coyote's* swollen eyes registered the sharp dissecting pain as the knife raked across to spill his belly. His ashen face turned vapid then faded under the starlight to neon white.

Bubba rejoined the stars till he thought the *coyote* was good and gone, then he took an ear to show his employer the job got done.

CHAPTER THIRTEEN

He pushed the Chrysler harder than he should have on dangerously dark Mexican roads. It took him less than two hours to get across the central Baja mountains to the coast. To shake visions of the man he left dead, Bubba played old tapes that came with the car, Boz Scaggs, a hot Santana, Linda Ronstadt, the one recorded in Oakland with the Eagles. But he kept seeing Sanchez's bulging eyes and hearing him say, *"Muertos? No!"*, thinking that maybe the poor bastard really didn't realize he sent those old people to their maker. It was troubling, but he would get over it. All he had to do was remember the woman the punk stabbed sixteen times.

He decided not to go after the other one, Chacon. If Sanchez had been straight with him, and he thought so, the other guy didn't deserve to leave his earthly life; so Bubba let him be despite his boss' orders to finish them both.

The seaport city of Ensenada was a wealthy town, relatively speaking. But it had its slums just like every city and Rio Avenida, on the south, fell into that class. Once in the *colonia*, Bubba noticed no parked cars and only a few pickup trucks. There were plenty of chicken coops, bicycles, buckets and bad odors. No electricity and probably no running water.

Taking a chance, he left the Chrysler under a low-slung willow tree a short block from the place Sanchez had said was his mother's home. It was after two in the morning when he tapped on the corrugated tin siding at 110 Rio Avenida. A wool blanket covered the door space. He heard the unmistakable cry of a baby from within. A promising sign.

"Hola. Señora Sanchez?" he called out and pulled aside the blanket to flood the room with the beam of the BP-issued flashlight. Two platform skids pushed together and softened with colorful blankets served as the bed. A woman under the blanket sat up. Next to her a young female showing only part of her face lay deathly still. There was a tiny person squeezed in between the two of them. The girl would have had a pretty

face if it hadn't been twisted in terror. She would be the one Sanchez wanted to "give" him, Bubba figured. He didn't see a man in the room. He held the beam on the woman. She shielded her eyes, but she didn't flinch.

"Your son, Miguel, sent me for the babies," Bubba said in Spanish. "My name is Travis."

She struck a match to a lantern and the room came to dull life. Bubba noticed first the bucket of washing water in a corner that every drunk gringo mistook for a piss pot, if the gringo happened to be in a Mexican whore's bedroom. Then the colorful shrine centered with a photograph of a man, a farm hand by all appearances, at the foot of the bed on the floor. He knew the flower-adorned shrine praised her departed husband. Women such as Mamma Sanchez all had departed husbands, it seemed to Bubba. Departed in death or to *el norte*.

Bubba detected two more people under the covers, both infants. There was another in a cradle-basket beside the bed. To a man with a trained eye for identifying nationalities, that one, the one in the basket, seemed to be Filipino, Indonesian at any rate. Here he stood with all four babies present and accounted for.

Bubba at that moment felt an odd pleasure.

The pretty girl, Carmela, alarmed but not screaming, scooped up the baby next to her and jumped out of bed as if to make a run for it.

"Don't be afraid," Bubba said. He had entered the room now.

The baby in the girl's arm was the one crying. It now wailed.

"Is the baby sick?" he asked.

Mamma Sanchez answered. "His ear. It hurts and I have no medicine … Are you going to take these babies? This late in the night?"

Bubba nodded. "That is why I have come; they have homes to go to."

Carmela shrieked and then coughed. She was sick, too. Carmela was probably fifteen years old, a girl who should be thinking of nothing more than her *quinceñera*, but she looked far from that age, her face yellow-tinted and gaunt from the diet of heroin Sanchez must have forced into her veins.

Mamma Sanchez said, "The girl, it is her child … Do you understand?"

Bubba made a couple of quick decisions that weren't going to jibe with the boss. He took out his billfold.

"Here, take this," he said, handing the older woman some money, all he had except a twenty, which he needed for gas, maybe a Pepsi and a fish taco.

"Use it," he said. "More will come later."

The second decision would be the unwelcome one. "The girl and her baby can stay. You can help her get well."

The heavyset woman counted the money; it came to a hundred and ten dollars. She nodded with the slightest gratitude.

"Why is Miguel not here with you?" she asked.

"How many children do you have of your own?" Bubba asked back.

"I have seven. Two have died. Where is Miguel?"

"Are your living children well? Do they work?"

She was not a tall person, her eyes reaching only as high as Bubba's neck; Bubba himself was not that tall. But she seemed to inch higher with pride from the question. Her eyes were steadfast. "Is he dead?"

"Look to your other children for comfort, *Señora.*"

Bubba stepped back against a wall and folded his arms to show them he wasn't rushing anyone. He felt a sudden warmth sweep over the room, as though the sun and the songs of birds and the good side of life had suddenly seized them all, opening like a flower.

Carmela's eyes were aflame, probing Mamma Sanchez. The baby's wailing had turned its wrinkled face so red Bubba thought it might burst into flames.

Mamma Sanchez seemed to read Bubba's alarm. "The girl is afraid her baby will die," she said. "It has fever and we must get medicine for the infection."

"I'll take you to a pharmacy, and maybe you can help me make the other babies comfortable in the car," Bubba said, contemplating the three hours he had to spend in the Chrysler by himself with three crying babies.

The woman grinned. "Yes, good," she said. "Where will they go?"

"Chula Vista."

"How can you cross the border with these babies?"

Now Bubba grinned. He knew half a dozen places to cross in a car. "Don't worry about that."

~

Driving north along the winding and bumpy free road, Bubba played a Celine Dion cassette he found in the floorboard box. The babies seemed content with "Beautiful Boy," so he rewound the lullaby repeatedly. It wasn't as bad a trip as he thought. Getting close he veered off the main roadway near the Otay Mesa crossing, closed at this late hour, and drove three mile east, then crossed over the border along a dark stretch of flat land where a section of the corrugated fence without razor wire could be swung aside. Less than three weeks ago he had busted a bunch of *coyotes* using the passageway to smuggle in their load of well-paying human flesh.

Before six o'clock in the morning, before dawn broke, the babies were safely in the United States, snug as bugs in a rug, and Bubba was feeling more like a decent human being again. All he'd done was help the law get rid of a scumbag and deliver three children to a brighter future.

CHAPTER FOURTEEN

Pulling up to the front of the Royal Arms Hotel, Maggie Frazier squeezed the monster Buick station wagon into a space meant for a "compact" the size of a Metro Geo. Impossible as it seemed she did it. She inserted the only coins she had into the meter; a quarter and three dimes would not be enough but maybe she'd get lucky and beat the meter maid back. She glanced at the big bay window on the third floor facing west; her father often stood there staring out at oblivion, as lonely persons will do. He wasn't there now.

In its heyday the century-old luxury hotel accommodated all walks of royalty, including European kings and princesses as well as U.S. presidents going back to Calvin Coolidge. But after WWII, the Georgian-style brownstone lapsed into disrepair and by now it was used to house fixed-income singles. It was one of the few buildings near the downtown Gaslamp remaining in its original state, now a refuge for those who otherwise might be on the street. Just the place for a downtrodden soul like her adopted father, John Frazier, whose life was in shambles—some would say unnecessarily.

She climbed the stairs rather than taking the snail-speed elevator with its bad karma. Earlier she'd called the desk and left a message to alert her father she would be there around noon, that she wanted to buy him lunch. But her real concern was finding out what was troubling him so much he wouldn't tell her on the phone.

Her dad answered the door in his pajamas, his face pasty, his hair matted. He looked terrible, Maggie thought, smiling at him as if he was still her savior. His eyes were red and puffy, the way eyes become after tears are abruptly rubbed dry.

"Sugar!" he said, clearly surprised. He hadn't gotten the message. "Come on in. I was just about to get cleaned up. I'm, uh, I'm glad you came by."

She stepped past him, brushing her hand against his unshaven cheek in greeting. They had never been much on touching, though Maggie wished they had. She liked to touch, to show affection. But from the time the Fraziers adopted her around her ninth birthday, Maggie had been savvy enough to know it wasn't good for the "father" to display physical affection for a young foster "daughter," and she had not encouraged it. As if understanding her reasons perfectly, he obliged. It held after the adoption was finalized, all the way till now.

The big suite had been a blessing, getting him out of the dark backside efficiency onto the street side with sunshine flowing through the afternoon window and he could hear and see life going on in the streets below. It had helped bring him out of the lapse he was having then. He'd been third in line to move in when the two old guys in front of him dropped like flies, just after the previous tenant succumbed from a bleeding ulcer while waiting for that ancient elevator to get three floors down. The thing still seemed to smell of death.

The apartment had a separate bedroom and bath and the great corner bay window that was a small room in itself. At night the streetside blue martini-with-olive neon flashed high on the ceiling through one of the windows, like a flag of Frazier's allegiance.

He had managed to hold on to the apartment going on a year now.

Maggie saw the opened photo album on the couch, which explained his red eyes. Feeling sorry for himself again, she thought. He'd no doubt stopped taking the medications that kept him from the depressions that twice had him hospitalized as suicidal. It took two decades before the VA finally acknowledged the "possibility" that Frazier suffered from PTSD resulting from his traumatic memories of combat for which they had finally started prescribing antidepressants, Fluoxetine and Prozac. They also diagnosed bipolar II disorder and put him on lithium, which Maggie thought absurd.

He was no more bipolar than she was. They both knew his problems stemmed only from fighting Immigration all those years to get his Amerasian son a visa. The "bipolar disorder" didn't start until long after he began that battle.

"Get dressed, Dad. I'll take you to the Cafe … You could use a square meal."

Maggie could have fed him for free at Jimbo's but El Cajon was too far away to make it worthwhile. Besides, he liked the food and the people at the Golden Hill Cafe and so did she.

"Oh, Maggie, I'm not really hungry."

She wouldn't listen. She steered him toward the door. "Trudy wants to see you. Now get yourself dressed."

"All right, all right."

Maggie sat on the floor by the couch and turned the photo album to face her. It was opened to the section allotted to his son Minh, his *bùi đôi* or "child of the dust," as he often said. "Amerasian" as we Americans called the boy, a half-breed. Minh was born after Frazier left the war in the early '70s. The boy's mother, his mamasan, had located Frazier years after the war was over and sent a letter and photographs of a good-looking kid with limbs of twigs. She claimed he was their son. She sought him out, asking for his help getting the boy to America.

Frazier first reacted like most GIs trying to regain their lives after war. He wanted nothing to do with the country or the boy. He was married then and he and Cloris were trying to get along at the same time they were trying to raise a sweet, pretty, smart-alecky foster girl named Margaret. They were learning how to function like a family; bringing in old garbage from the war was an intrusion on that life, particularly on his unforgiving wife. He feared the ridicule of raising a half-Viet boy, even if the boy turned out to be smart and as handsome as he appeared in the photos.

It was in raising the misplaced preteen Maggie and the fulfillment he got caring for her that changed Frazier's mind about the Viet boy. He saw that bringing Minh to California was not only a duty and the right thing to do for the mother but it could help him make amends to the country he had helped destroy; he had a conscience about the war that haunted him long after leaving it behind, and he hadn't appreciated that for many years. Looking at it that way he felt there was no other choice. The boy was Frazier's blood, his son.

But Cloris resisted adopting "that" boy, arguing it would be way too hard handling two children with such diverse histories, and they couldn't afford it anyway. "We don't know what kind of horrible things happened to him in that re-education camp, do we?" she complained. "Isn't he supposed to hate Americans? He doesn't even speak English, for chrissake."

They could not agree so it didn't work out. And neither did Cloris.

If he had known about Minh sooner, it would have been easy to acquire the visa to bring him to the U.S. for adoption. But at that time, years later, the political climate of forgiveness and charity for Amerasians had passed and neither the American consulate in Ho Chi Minh City nor the INS would sanction a visa or any kind of adoption.

Before the divorce, Frazier took their savings and went to Vietnam to work out a way to bring Minh back. The boy's mother—Spec4 Frazier jokingly had nicknamed her *My Sin*—had left out a critical bit of information in her heartfelt letters. Turned out Cloris was right. The boy had a dire attitude about American servicemen and when Frazier arrived, the boy immediately ran away, from his home and his mother. Frazier only got a moment to look at his son, a soft-faced teenage lad with an angry, hateful glare. It was a dagger he hadn't expected. He had not even gotten to touch the boy, not even a handshake.

Looking at the old pictures, Maggie noticed what a beautiful bronze-colored round face belonged to that boy, as did most Amerasian children regardless if their fathers were black or white or brown. Skin the color of sienna and smooth as water. But in Minh's most recent picture, five or six years old, he sported a sparse goatee that Maggie associated with a gangster trying for a spot with the Asian mafia; the expression on his handsome boyish face was streetwise and bitter.

She closed the album when her father reappeared in the living room. He wore a wrinkled cotton shirt and blue jeans, sandals and white socks. He wore his hair tightly drawn into a tail, which gave him the forlorn look of a rough-faced Bogart. His watery eyes enhanced the likeness.

Frazier's listlessness didn't sit well with Maggie. But she offered him a reassuring smile. "Ready?" She took his arm. "Let's boogie."

No ticket on the Buick's windshield. Maggie took that as an omen of good fortune to come her way. She still had her youthful sense of expectation.

She drove east up Broadway away from town and the harbor.

San Diego's first inland mesa had been named Golden Hill a hundred and fifty years ago. It was the original neighborhood of San Diego. In the later 1800s, sea captains built their homes on the hill to better keep watch over their harbored vessels, which back then were docked at the foot of Broadway. With sweeping panoramas from their bedroom windows, the sharp-eyed captains had only to look westward down the street, as if from a crow's nest, to see their ships sailing away under piracy or going up in flames or calmly docked.

"Have you read the paper?" she asked, working into a subject she had rather not discuss. "About those people who died in the desert?"

"Awful. Just terrible," Frazier answered. She took it he had heard but didn't made the connection.

"Those people were our caretakers, Dad. Somebody stole our kids, four of them."

"Oh, Jesus. That's not right," Frazier said, slow to assimilate. A frown gradually grew on his brow. "Those people you're working for?"

She nodded, glancing at him. "It's gotta be their fault, yeah. But I don't know if they stole them. Nobody seems to know anything right now. Or they're not telling me."

"They're a bad bunch, Maggie. I'm telling you, you gotta quit this racket."

"That's the plan, Dad."

She patted him on the knee and changed the subject. "You get to the reservation lately?"

He shook his head without speaking.

Frazier laid claim to being part Indian. He didn't know what tribe, "maybe Australian Aborigine or some southwestern Mexican tribe." Something obscure like that. Or he could have just been nostalgic for association with the mountain tribes of Montagnards he serviced in Vietnam. For some years now he paid occasional visits to a reclusive band of Baja Indians—sometimes taking Maggie to their village in the hills. He would bring back basketworks and jewelry that he consigned to an Old Town novelty shop. The Royal Arms took a lot of phone messages from the shop's proprietor, who having quickly sold out of the Indian-made merchandise would be asking for more. But Frazier stubbornly wouldn't exploit the Indians' craft, said he didn't want to turn their art form into a production line, like stocking Gucci in Wal-Mart.

He could have made good money off their products, but Maggie's dad wouldn't budge. Stubborn as all get out, she thought.

Maggie changed course from the restaurant at 19th Street and made a right turn.

Frazier didn't notice. He seemed preoccupied.

She finally brought it up. "Why'd you call yesterday, Dad? Why're you being so secretive—and so gloomy?"

Frazier silently turned his head, looked out his window. She watched him pull a half-pint bottle out of his coat pocket, take a noisy swig. He passed it over. She pushed it back, glaring at him. He was looking at her now with his sad, watery eyes. "Jesus, can't you wait at least till after you eat something?"

"Where we going?"

She shot back with cheerfulness. "Oh, you'll see in just about half a minute—take that back. Here we are."

She pulled the wagon into the overgrown driveway of a low-slung '20s Craftsman that hadn't received much pride-of-ownership in the last 50 years. The house sat back in a dirt plot. An ancient live oak shaded the front yard.

"What do you think? Look at that tree; there's a *porch*." Maggie looked at her dad excitedly. But seeing his expression, her face fell flat.

"C'mon, Dad, what is it? I thought you'd like it. It's not perfect, but it's going to be ours … Come on, let me show you inside. I know the lockbox combination."

Frazier took another slug of bourbon and got out of the car in no hurry.

"It's big enough for eight, if they're all toddlers," she said on the move, working back into her excitement. "I've got one more client tomorrow. That'll be it. That'll be enough for the down payment and some extra for fixing up. Dad, don't give up, not now. Come on now. Please, tell me you *care*."

"Goddamnit, Maggie," he gushed fiercely. Booze exaggerated his emotions. "I care. You know that. But—you know, it's just a dream …

sooner or later they'll find out their money's missing. Don't think for a second they'll let you slide on this."

Maggie stopped and faced him. "Oh yes they will—I'll turn on them if they mess with me."

His eyes burned with intensity. He slowly shook his head. "They will hurt you, honey. It was a bad idea. You've got to give them back their money."

"I'm their best seller, Dad, their top dog. They need me."

Frazier shook his head sadly. "They don't deal that way, baby. They'll come after you."

Maggie flashed her famous smile. "I've got *you* to persuade them otherwise," she said. "You're a tough guy, they'll listen to you."

Frazier grunted. "I used to be."

Before they entered, Frazier spoke, sounding disconcerted and desperate. "Can't you just drop all this nonsense, sugar? Go out and get yourself a decent boyfriend. Make babies of your own, for chrissake!"

Maggie laughed. She didn't mean to, as the comment hurt her to the quick, but it was so unlike him to give up after all this time.

"Imagine that," she said, her voice a sheet of ice. "Me having a *decent* boyfriend, having a *baby*. Dad, I can barely handle my goldie!"

"I'm sorry," he said and slumped against the cedar-shingled siding as if spent.

"I know, I know," she said, opening the door.

The orphanage may have been Maggie's hard work, but it was her dad's idea and his enthusiasm that kept her going with it.

Frazier made it two steps inside the vacant house then suddenly collapsed.

She thought he'd stumbled, too much whiskey on an empty stomach. Maybe that was so, but then she saw the raw pain in his face.

"*Dad!* Dad, what *is* it!"

He pulled himself next to her and wrapped his arms around her legs, holding on to her. The shivering in his thinning arms gave Maggie a sick feeling, as though his wasting away made her see he was one step closer to doom. He took a deep raspy breath. His torment tore through her.

Frazier said, "He's dead, Maggie. My son is dead."

CHAPTER FIFTEEN

Myers trailed a Metro bus down Texas Street into a valley of fog. An old Kristofferson flipside called "Sunday Mornin' Comin' Down" played on the AM. It was Sunday morning. It was wet and gray. The song throbbed; it conjured the memory of a long ago lover, a long-legged woman who hypnotized Myers with gypsy love, a blaze that burned so very hot before going poof. Only for him, the embers still glowed. She was something, Dark Eyes, deceptive eyes. The tune wept like the droning melody of rain against the flat windshield. He descended on into the depths of the gray valley seeing nothing now but the Metro's brake lights.

The indulgence lasted as long as the song, yet something lingered. He wheeled into the newspaper's employee lot.

The third-floor newsroom was a house of ghosts, a mere handful of reporters, editors and clerks sprinkled about, everyone appearing lulled by the saturating mist that enveloped the mostly glass building. Sunday morning coming down, thought Myers, still stuck in his reverie.

He went on to his desk. He sat and glanced around the hushed office, then woke the computer and propped his feet on the drawer he'd opened for that purpose. Inactivity was Sunday duty's consolation. Not much was happening out there that required a reporter, though something would. It always did.

Once here and at it, Myers actually enjoyed working Sunday mornings. Without much connection to the present, this morning reminded him of a time when a young Myers climbed out of bed on dark Sunday mornings against a whistling cold wind to deliver newspapers, a kid of ten, straining uphill on his one-speed Western Flyer with a hundred thick papers, his route two miles from the workroom where boys stuffed their newspapers with sections and supplements. But once he finished the route, or almost finished it, there came the light of day to usher in springtime Sunday mornings; those were the times to remember, when nature woke and he was part of it.

Who would've known that he would still be associated with newspapers.

By now he had earned the right to self-indulge. Take time to read the book review section, listen to Click and Clack, just enough time to call his mom in Georgia before she went to morning services at her church or his brother in Chicago who didn't go to church but would probably be at his drafting board. If nothing else Sunday mornings eluded the usual.

Myers forewent those things to check his e-mail. Only fifty-three new entries of junk mail. He wasn't so popular. There was a note from Casa Amiga asking if he had discovered where the immigrants had originated and he responded saying he was "working on it" and thanked them for keeping in touch. Another from the immigration lawyer, Snowdon with an "o," who had before put him off with "good luck." He wanted to know if Myers had had any luck.

When his phone lit up, he automatically glanced at Max Cullen's desk. Cullen was the only editor on the floor, so naturally he waved Myers over to his desk. The city editor's gesture was overdone, dramatic, so Myers picked up the receiver.

Cullen spoke sharply. "Get your raincoat on."

"I don't have a raincoat."

"Well, goddamnit, wear mine. Some nut's holed up out at Cabrillo point, raving about dead people. Could be connected to your desert folks. Let's go."

"They are not mine."

"SWAT's there. Get going, Ray!"

Myers' Sunday morning indulgence had been effectively terminated before it began; he didn't get his java again.

~

The single road along the crest of Point Loma's peninsula was cordoned off with bright yellow police cones and tape. Myers produced his press card to a soaked and sullen motorcycle cop who waved him on. He steered the Journal's Escort along the single road that ribboned the four-mile spine of the peninsula. The U.S. Navy's ocean systems headquarters and its tiers of WWII-vintage barracks occupied both sides along the first stretch of road. Further down lay the Fort Rosecrans military cemetery with thousands of grave markers overlooking the vast blue Pacific to the west and the emerald bay to the east, views that never failed to bring tears of envy to the eyes of developers and realtors the world over. Burials no longer took place here as the acreage was filled to capacity; you needed to have died years ago to make it in.

Today's fog drew a curtain on any decent view of the hypnotic headstones or the vast space beyond.

The Cabrillo monument stood at the peninsula's southernmost tip. Local brochures will tell you foreign guests visit Cabrillo National Park more than any other historical site in America. It beats out Graceland, Niagara Falls, and the Alamo, even 1600 Pennsylvania Avenue. Myers knew the stat was a fountain of pride to the overseers of America's Finest City—a city otherwise in dire straits from corruption and flirting with bankruptcy.

The old lighthouse at land's end—what did the Chamber of Commerce call it, the National Park Services' "Crown Jewel?"—was a simple white cinderblock house standing like a proud requiem to a more glorious time in the nation's illustrious history, a time when foreigners were not only welcomed to America but encouraged to come and prosper, to help build a nation. Once upon a time Cabrillo Lighthouse kept its welcome beacon burning bright. That was then; today it was dark and as useless as the U.S. Congress when it came to a sound immigration policy, or any policy.

Myers appreciated the editor's urgency and was glad he had not stopped along the way for coffee. SWAT wasn't the only law there; he counted four black-and-whites, park security, a Navy SP vehicle and a city fire engine, all parked haphazardly in the lot and on service roads leading to the old structure.

Incredibly, not one TV van was there. Myers held back any notion that he would singularly cover the story; no doubt other media had their scanners running. TV was bound to show up at any moment. Still, he was there first. Sweet.

Climbing the hill in search of the OIC, he phoned Cullen and asked for a photographer, Finley if he could get her.

A San Diego PD patrol car under a wind-twisted Torrey pine stood as a command post. It was positioned in full view of the lighthouse. The lighthouse cupola was a misty turret in the low clouds. Loony Tunes, the guy, was reportedly up there, with a gun of some kind. Myers spotted his old buddy Millard standing by the black-and-white. Detective Sergeant Johnny Millard (pronounced "Mah-lard") was a burly, black cop overdue for retirement who was sure to eat his gun when he finally did give up police work, when they kicked him out. He and Myers had a history that went back to the paddyfields where Millard was pronounced "LT."

He waited for the detective to get off the two-way. "Johnny," Myers said, cordially. He seldom called him LT anymore. "The hell you doing out here in the rain on Sunday?"

"How'd you? … Give me a second." Millard opened the car trunk and pulled out a megaphone.

"How long you been set up? Why aren't the buzzheads here?"

"Having trouble with your ears, Scoop?" Millard's sidekick, Pedroza, said. "The man said wait."

"Maybe you'd like to talk, Detective. Get your full name in the papers? Not shy are we?"

"Fuck you, Gonzo."

Myers let that pass. "You shouldn't mind telling me what's going on here."

Pedroza turned his back. The rancor between the two could be traced back to the Janice Parrish murder case years before; there was no reason for the junior cop's attitude, he just hated Myers. Myers knew Pedroza would shoot him given the opportunity. He just didn't know why.

Millard blew into the megaphone, playing with the dials, then said to Myers, "Glad you're here. We need you."

"Need me? That's a twist." Myers threw a thumb toward Pedroza. "How come you still got him with you?"

Pedroza unfolded his arms.

"Hot dog," said Myers, "Junior wants to play."

Millard said, "Cut the crap. Both you."

Myers asked, "What's up with all the firepower?"

"Not my call. I'm just trying to keep them calm—don't go quoting me, Ray."

Myers nodded.

"The guy's armed," said Millard. "I don't know what we've got here. He's mentioned something about Immigration and missing kids. None of it makes much sense, not to me. Just ramblings."

"Could it be the Ocotillo murders?"

"Maybe, yeah," Millard said, helpful as a corkscrew to an empty bottle of wine.

Pedroza stepped in. "He'll only speak with a member of the press corps. That's how he put it—'the press corps.'" His fake lisp dripped of sarcasm.

"The guy's up there in the cupola," said Millard.

Myers took a look, frowned and said, "And me being the only hack here, you want I should go talk to him."

Millard's grin brought out the pale scar on his ebony cheek. He stood under an umbrella that had been jury rigged to the door of the black-and-white and the Torrey pine. He was mostly dry. Myers wore Cullen's too-tight plastic raincoat, which kept his back dry, but his hair and his pants and the socks in his Rockports were soaked.

"So what's keeping you from sending a couple of boys up there and bringing him down?"

"What'd I just tell you? That maybe he's armed?"

"He fire it yet?"

"Not yet," Millard said. "Butted out one of those big windows is all … Hasn't threatened any of our people, but he's a troubled person. We can't get to him without exposing ourselves and I'm not ready to gas him … So I was thinking that maybe you, as a member of the press corps, might wanna pay him a visit, talk. Maybe we can clear this whole thing up, get a nice cup of coffee."

"Close quarters with some armed nut? Think I'm crazy as him?"

"Know you are, Spec," the detective said with a grin. Called Myers that back in the day. "I'll announce you're on your way up."

"Hold on. Who is the guy? Tell me something about him."

"Name's John William Frazier. Caucasian. Fifty-six, brown hair and eyes, weighs one seventy-five according to the driver's license we found in the wallet on the steps just over there. Maybe he dropped it on purpose. A taxi brought him out here earlier. Suspicious cabbie called us."

"Okay. Anything else?"

"Guy's wearing military camouflage, same kind we wore. That right there's enough."

"Nam, huh?"

Millard shrugged. "You ready now?"

Millard was pampering the man. The shrapnel scar on his face told you why. His perp was a patriot, a scarred man himself, and Millard wanted to help him through this. If he could.

Myers put the wet notebook away and glanced down the hill to see if the TV vans had gotten there yet. In a city with a press corps larger than China's, he was still the only reporter on the scene. Amazing.

Millard stepped out onto the open concrete. The lighthouse sat on the crest of the hill at a steep angle above them. He adjusted out the bullhorn's squeaking feedback and said, "Got your reporter, John. He's coming up … Okay?"

A small voice from the tower said, "Send him in."

Millard turned to Myers. "Don't incite the guy. And don't be a damn hero."

Myers walked uphill with his eyes fastened on the high point of the tower. It looked twenty stories tall but wasn't of course. It eluded him how some individuals had no fear of heights. He admired skyscraper laborers probably more than any other working human being, like the admiration famous writers were know to hold for famous artists.

Myers walked inside and climbed the narrow spirals, looking not at the museum of the old living quarters but above at the wooden trap door to the cupola. He pushed and the trap door swung partially open. He got a glimpse of the man, and his gun. Average looking guy holding a small gun that looked Myers in the eye. Frazier motioned him up.

"I write for the Journal," he said. "Myers."

The man's blank expression didn't shift. Neither did he ask Myers to prove it; Myers could've been a cop. But it took the edge off the apprehension Myers felt and he lifted himself the rest of the way into the cupola. Once in, as the trap door shut, a different thought crossed his mind.

The guy had a death wish, he wanted Myers to be a cop so he could blow him away, no further action required.

But that was rational thought in an irrational situation. Myers told himself to just do his job. Stop thinking.

Frazier locked the trap door.

Myers studied him. His hair was long and stringy. It concealed some of his face. He avoided eye-to-eye. He wasn't jittery. Drugs weren't his problem, but those eyes were wide and fixed, such as the look of a man set on something important to him. His face was gaunt and sunken, as if he couldn't sleep and hadn't for some time. The shoulder patch on his frayed fatigue shirt bore the patch of the 1st Cavalry Division. Myers knew it well.

Rain blew in through the void left by the plate glass window the man had destroyed. There was a cut above his right eye with some dried blood that most likely came from flying glass. Despite the breeze there was a familiar odor of something old. He squatted next to the obsolete fuel-burning lantern. He waited.

Frazier finally looked at him. Sizing up the reporter. A good sign. Myers didn't see a wacko. He saw a man at the end of his limits.

He didn't say anything so Myers did. "I used to could sit like this for a length of time." Keeping it casual, bobbing on his haunches. "But not so much these days."

Myers nodded at the arm patch. "First Cav. Means you did your time in the field. I humped it too, in the Delta. River rat."

"Don't matter," the man said.

"No, I don't talk about it, either, man. What I just told you? Most I've said to anyone in a long time. But I gotta think something matters, or you wouldn't be here."

Frazier shifted, looked at him for the first time. "What I did there's not the business. What I left there is. I want people to know about it. I want to see those hypocrites at Immigration on their knees."

Myers nodded. "Okay. Can you tell me why? I'm here to listen."

"The whole goddamn bureaucracy. Justice—if you can call it that—is dished out on who you are, where you've been. Fuck me. You can forget it."

"You're right as rain," Myers said, meaning it. "What'd they do, or what didn't they do?"

Frazier gauged him again. "I'm talking about how they decide who gets to come into this country. I'm talking about the attitude, the prejudice. It's not policy I'm talking about. This right here?" He jerked savagely at the sleeve of his aged fatigues with the horse-headed patch still holding its brilliant gold-and-black color.

"This is the reason they've fucked me over for so long. They won't recognize anything moral and right could come out of that war. Nobody will. Nobody will recognize it, period. They have no sense of conscience about those children we orphaned—" His voice caught. "Motherfuckers!"

Myers in his own right understood him and felt his anger. "I know you're right," he said. "But, man, it's been a long time to carry it. Tell me what happened that made you come up here today."

Frazier cast grievous eyes on Myers. "Yeah, it's been forever. And I've lived with it all this time. All this time, just holding it in. But no longer ... Listen to me. When our boys came home from that little scrimmage in the first Gulf War, I was peeved with all the hero worship and mythmaking that came back with 'em. But, you know, I was okay with that. Bottom line, I was proud of the troops, they're Americans and good fighters, damn good fighters. Never mind the shit we got coming home. I'm over that; I can handle it. And I'm fucking proud of every troop serving in Iraq right now, I hope God speeds them home, every last one. But ... "

His lips stuck to his teeth. Myers offered him the water bottle he'd brought along. He shook his head.

Frazier got off his knees, made a sudden move toward the broken window as if to jump through it.

Myers started, his heart leapt; he felt helpless. Had the man jumped he could not have stopped him. Instead, Frazier kicked away some of the window's glass fragments.

He looked again at Myers.

"My boy is dead," he said, his voice a monotone.

"Your boy? ... I'm sorry."

"I should have seen it coming. All the signs were there." His raw eyes stayed fixed on the floor. "They wouldn't let me bring him home, not in twenty goddamn years. Oh, they were real fucking sorry, but there was nothing they could do. Nothing they could fucking do! And now, that boy … my boy is dead. I never even got to hold him."

The sudden tinny blare from the megaphone, shrill and inhuman, ripped through the cupola like a bullet. Both men winced. It was probably Millard's voice, but Myers couldn't tell. "John, let us see the reporter. Myers, show yourself."

Myers turned to Frazier. "All right if I stand, let him see me?"

Frazier shook his head but he didn't seem to hear.

A gust of wet wind slapped Myers' face as he inched to the broken window. He peered into black open sky, imagining being sucked out, falling at great speed. He may have gotten vertigo at a time not so pressing as now. Still, he didn't show himself, he waved an arm.

He pressed his back against the iron-plate wall. "They don't know what to make of you coming up here in combat fatigues, John. Bringing that pop gun with you, breaking the window."

"It got you up here … " Frazier's grin was bitter, not a grin at all.

That wasn't all that got him up here. It was the story, the opportunity. And the familiarity. "They said you mentioned immigrants, illegals. You meant your son?"

Frazier raked a hand through his stringy hair, showing fatigue.

Myers pushed. "Not those old migrants found dead last week?"

Frazier glanced at him, his mouth turning upside down. Myers couldn't tell if it was restrained rage or something less.

"They weren't Americans either so nobody gave a fuck," Frazier said. "Didn't care that there were four infants, four little lives gone. Vanished. Nobody cared but the goddamn smugglers, the slimeballs that stole them. Won't hear anymore about it. You can count on that."

"Not if I have a say," Myers said. His mind worked fast trying to figure out how the man would know babies were missing from the massacre, and four of them. The authorities didn't even know how many there were.

He feared asking his next question but asked anyway, trying to sound only mildly interested. "Smuggled, huh? Got any idea what might have happened?"

He waited while the world rotated, feeling the adrenaline rush his veins. On the verge of discovery.

Frazier could not be read; he only shook his head.

"You got a tape recorder?" he asked, surprising Myers.

Myers nodded and tapped the inside breast pocket of the rain jacket.

"Turn it on."

"Already have, hope you don't mind."

"Let them know that I respected the law," he stated in a flat, for-the-record tone. "I've always lived by the rules. Followed them even when I knew they were wrong. It's—"

He choked, struggling it seemed for the right words. "All I wanted was to get my son home—and for my girl Maggie to find her happiness. That wasn't too much to ask. I was a good American; I did what they wanted me to do—I destroyed people's lives for my country. I took a bullet for them; I learned in a heartbeat what fear was, what life meant … I played by their rules. But all it ever got me was fucked! … Now it's too late."

Frazier dropped his head. He covered his face in his hands.

Myers looked at the rifle propped next to him. Grab it! Throw it out that window, it was a cinch—no, you won't violate the man's trust. But he was hard to figure and Myers wasn't sure.

He watched Frazier shake in his private pain. It was pain Myers recognized, the kind of raw grief you experience in the lull of a firefight when you see your buddy's life flow from him. When you lose someone dear.

Myers didn't stir. The recorder ran. He waited.

Frazier stopped weeping and looked up. The color of his worn face was gray now, the light gone from his eyes. He spoke in a slight voice and Myers wasn't sure he heard right.

"What?"

"Why are the children always the ones to pay." A child's soft voice.

Frazier raked his sleeve across both his cheeks to collect the tears, wiped hands on his fatigues. Then he reached into his shirt pocket and removed a folded paper, a snapshot. He opened and smoothed it on his leg and stared at it a moment without speaking. His hands trembled. "Will you tell it right?"

Myers nodded. "It may not all go, but I'll get it right, I promise you that."

"The tall one," he said, referring to the picture, and started to hand it to Myers.

Myers didn't get the chance to take the snapshot, a big noise roared in, stealing their attention. It arrived with a blizzard wind descended on the cupola. Myers knew the helicopter was not a television lightweight; it was a full-bodied chopper, Sikorsky, one of those monster rescue machines, its whomp a common denominator of anticipation and fear for every foot soldier who took to the field. The pounding put both men on notice.

Alert now, Frazier grabbed the rifle.

Myers said loudly, "Easy. Take it easy."

The unwieldy Coast Guard chopper dropped lower and hovered. A blazing spotlight shot through the pencils of rain illuminating the cupola's interior.

Before the light washed out Frazier's face, Myers saw a thin-lipped grin appear. A grin did not fit the situation.

Myers said, "Don't do anything crazy, man. I know the cop in charge. He wouldn't call in the chopper. It's a mistake ... John! Put the rifle down!"

Frazier glared into the light. "It's too late. It's over. I can't—"

Now Myers lurched for the rifle. "Don't, don't do it!"

Frazier's eyes pleaded, but Myers knew now it wasn't help he wanted. The man swung to his feet and crouched in a stance used in the bush against treetop snipers, leveling the rifle through the broken window.

Frazier screamed, "I'm sorry, Maggie. Forgive me!"

He seemed to take aim at the hovering copter, but with all the noise and gale-force wind it was not clear if he fired the little gun. It wouldn't have mattered.

Myers lunged in earnest for him. He didn't need to. Frazier recoiled, falling hard against Myers as though someone a lot bigger had shoved him. Myers fell back with his weight. Frazier's legs collapsed and the rest of him surrendered; the body convulsed.

Myers eased the limp body off him and rested it in a sitting position against the rusty wall. The spasms ceased. Blood covered Myers' hands, the front of his clothes, his face.

Frazier had found his way out of the overwhelming battle within.

Myers turned away from the damage. He'd grown soft over the years despite all the ugliness and desperation he'd encountered.

He stayed low, avoiding the spotlight and made ready to climb down from the cupola. He first located and then folded Frazier's snapshot as it had been folded and slipped it into a dry pocket. He didn't look at it. He suspected the image portrayed at least one Vietnamese-American child from a long time ago somewhere in the Republic of Vietnam. He was sure of it.

CHAPTER SIXTEEN

Myers descended the spiral in no hurry. He stepped out onto the landing and shoved his face toward the driving rain, letting it wash away the blood.

He did nothing for a moment but stand there. His hands trembled; his hands seemed useless. The scene had ended as badly as it could and he struggled to check his fury before facing Millard.

A state of confusion surrounded him. It seemed to generate a kind of electric desperation. Highly motivated cops appeared dangerously close to panic. A quick movement, a cry in the still-soaring wind, anything at all could shout hostility. The scene, he thought, was that close to exploding.

The incongruous whirring of an SLR camera got his attention. Carol Finley stood not more than five feet away, shooting *him*, the bloody reporter. Of course, the sole eyewitness. He was the last person to see the victim alive. Myers hadn't yet thought of it that way but she had, and she was there at the precise moment he emerged from the lighthouse to recorded it. Finley seemed to possess another sense, as though she had an inner aperture that could view things before they happened.

Myers was now part of the story he would write. It was a new experience. He sensed the power of it, along with its unsettling weight.

SWAT officers stormed past him on their way inside. "There's no rush," he said, knowing it wouldn't diminish their intensity.

Detective Millard found Myers before Myers found him. Pedroza followed, hands in his pockets as though nothing important had happened.

Millard, though, was enraged. "What the hell happened up there? I called you out, goddamnit—"

"Who brought in the chopper?" Myers asked just as furious but holding back. "Was it your pathetic sidekick here?"

Pedroza didn't like that. He stopped sucking his teeth. "You're goin' down for this, fuckwad." He turned to Millard, "I'll cuff him right now, give me the word."

Millard snarled, "Get lost, Rosy. Just get the hell away."

Stunned, Pedroza stalked off.

"Talk to me, Ray, goddamnit!"

"Whoever called in the chopper's the one that caused this casualty. Don't tell me it was you."

"You think that, I'm disappointed. Just answer my questions. Did he fire the weapon? Why in hell didn't you show yourself when I called you out?"

Myers ignored the last question. "He had a .22, single-shot. You must have known that. I don't even know if it was loaded … Who brought in the Coast Guard, Johnny? I thought you were in charge here."

"Any rifle is a lethal weapon," said Millard with little enthusiasm. "He's wearing military fatigues, for chrissake. He took aim."

"At a chinook!" Myers shouted. "You'd need a fucking RPG to scratch that thing."

He stepped close to the big cop; he smelled his aftershave and didn't like it. He needed to take a walk and knew he needed to take a walk.

Millard looked upward at the gusting wind that threw rain darts down at them. He shut his eyes and wiped his forehead with the back of his hand.

Both men knew an impulsive cop would be called down for the shooting and that a SWAT commander had already started sweating. Myers knew Millard wanted to hear that the victim was the initiator, that the shooting, in the end, was clean. He wanted it badly.

"I'll give you this," Myers said. "Wearing the uniform was his way of protesting what he went up there to protest. He had some serious issues with Immigration about a son born in Vietnam when he was there that he claims is now dead. I know, it was so long ago, how is it that he's done this now? …

"I'll depose that he pointed the rifle—he could've fired off a shot, you'll know that soon enough. It seemed to me the action from the ground was justifiable."

Millard nodded, said, "Let's go over to the car, get out of this rain."

Myers still didn't see any sign of TV, but that no longer mattered to him. He did see a 30-year-old Buick station wagon arriving and a young woman about the same age as the car get out of it and storm up the hill. There was an air about her that said if the day could be saved she was the one to do it.

CHAPTER SEVENTEEN

Myers didn't go to the office. He called in, said he would be work-ing at home. Max Cullen didn't like it but didn't quarrel.

The old house groaned and bumped under the wailing wind, but its fixed solitude provided the sense of familiarity he needed at the moment.

His legs felt weak and ached as if he had a cold. His hands wouldn't stop shaking. The smell of blood in his hair nauseated him. He had a two-ounce shot of scotch then stepped into a hot shower and scrubbed himself from head to toe.

He slept for four hours, oddly without a single disturbing dream.

In the late afternoon he washed three-day's worth of dishes and cleaned the countertop and threw out old food from the refrigerator. The cat showed no appreciation when he fed her.

Myers went into another room and picked up the gut-string guitar he once played routinely. He strummed "Malagueña," a practiced tune that took some effort but sounded sweet in the lofty room. But his fingers made mistakes on the frets and he put the instrument back on its stand.

Dark now, the house turned quiet but for the Sunday evening jetlin-ers arriving at nearby Lindbergh Field. When planes ascended inland, as occasionally they did in foul weather and Santa Ana's, the old mansion's windows and doors rattled in their frames.

The Victorian had twenty-seven rooms and Myers lived in it alone. He had inherited the house from the aunt he'd looked after for years, until she took off with a younger man in what would be her last trip. Selling the place would make him a millionaire, more in this up market. He didn't need that much space and he didn't spend a lot of time at home. But he liked the house, its tranquility, its location uptown. He grew up in old homes and the Juniper House, as it was listed with SOHO, felt like home. It had for seven years now, since his last divorce.

The stormy weather brought a chill and he pulled on a sweater and took a walk up Fifth Avenue to trendy Hillcrest, a bustling community of coffee shops, boutiques, bars, restaurants, theaters, tattoo shops, bookstores, porno and curio shops. Sunday evenings were alive with its flux of costumed LGBTs and straights and gawkers crowding the sidewalks as one. Tonight Myers played zombie, though envious of the merriment, the casualness, the carelessness, the cluelessness brought on by nature and by fantasies.

He passed the Safari Lounge without a thought of having a drink. The old joint was a wart on the uptown de rigueur culture. It was Myers' bar. He had been patronizing the place since he started working at the paper nearly two decades ago. In a coffee shop he had a hammerhead and for a while watched the street scene from inside.

Back home he spread half an avocado on rye bread and made a pot of French roast decaf and went to his office. He could breathe now and his eyes were clear and his hands weren't shaking except from the punch of the hammerhead. He would put the bigger effort into the sidebar, writing from the observer/witness perspective, as he had treated the Ocotillo story. The voyeuristic nature in all people favored emotional connection and gritty detail over mere fact telling. The reporter-as-witness could easily backfire into exploitation, gore for gore's sake, become yellow. So Myers minimized the drama by minimizing his language, even when he knew it would irk his editors.

Myers had scribed myriad tragic stories in his time, and most of them he treated by the book as hard news. Child killings and suicides were the hardest to report. Rarely had he stretched the facts or truth in a piece and then only by nuance and the subtle choices in describing a thing. He had done that in a story years ago—a young mother who dressed her three-year-old in a new Sunday school suit then threw him off a 300-foot bridge. Buckled the toddler into the car seat with a carton of apple juice and drove the fourteen miles from Kearny Mesa to the apex of the Coronado Bridge and stopped. Timothy Betts was the boy's name, Little Timmy. Myers interviewed the killer three times at County and walked away knowing nothing more than the facts, but he made the merciless killer the object of hatred for the reader, even as he delved sympathetically into the woman's appalling childhood. A week later he wrote the hard news story of the mother killing herself in lockup with one severe head bash on the toilet.

Though he'd been shaken plenty from years of writing such stories, he still fancied himself void of aloofness or cynicism. Neither did he think a solitary lifestyle, a life at his age without the companionship of a family or even a single close friend, equated misanthropy or even aloofness. It was merely the way things had worked out. He wasn't a happy man.

Myers phoned Millard, who was still at PD Central. The detective informed him the police officer that fired the fatal shot had been put on paid administrative leave, which was standard with shootings. He also told Myers the dead man's daughter, Margaret Frazier, would be going to the morgue to positively identify the man. He emphasized there had been no new developments.

Millard left him with some advice. "And listen to me, Ray, don't go turning this thing into something bigger than it is just because you happened to be a witness and also a reporter. This shit happens frequently. You've got your future to think about." He spoke without sounding malicious or threatening, though that's exactly what he meant.

Myers thanked him for his interest in his future and hung up. He called the morgue to see if the next of kin had arrived. The daughter had been there and gone; yes, she made a positive ID. Lastly he looked first in the phone book for Margaret Frazier and found a listing for that person with an El Cajon address.

He had met the woman briefly at the scene of the shooting—it was she who approached Myers afterwards. She'd come in a rush, asking frantic question about her father, what had happened to him. Myers had seen desperation and grief in people just informed of someone's death, and he could tell in her face that she had loved him. She was in no shape to answer a reporter's questions at the time; she still wouldn't be now. He phoned her because it was his job. He learned nothing more from their brief conversation than to confirm she was the same woman he saw charging up the hill and that it was her father who'd been "murdered."

He finished the hard news piece in an hour and sent it electronically to the paper. He got a fresh cup of the dark coffee and right away began the sidebar, slanting it with what he thought had really been going on with Frazier in his frustrated pursuit with Immigration. Myers didn't use the word "suicide" in the copy, but he might have implied it when he observed that the man "seemed out of options."

He finished 30 inches by ten o'clock, leaving plenty of time for Cullen and the rim to chop it up, send it back for a shot at a rewrite if they felt that generous, and still get it set before first-run deadline at midnight.

He scratched the cat's ear, turned off lights, and walked back to the Safari Lounge and drank scotch straight up until one a.m. He brought his cell phone but no one at the paper called. He might have stayed until closing except he couldn't bear yet another yarn from the bartender about the animal heads mounted on the walls.

At home he took a bottle of Chivas Regal to the living room and listened to a moody Tom Waits album from his island days until he was ready to call it quits.

He could have had a dozen more drinks, but it wasn't going to help him sleep through the night.

The thing he couldn't shake was not stopping Frazier from picking up the gun when he had the chance. A blind man could have grabbed it and thrown it through the gaping broken-out window; it probably would have saved the man's life. He could have muscled Frazier down without breaking a sweat. But Myers did nothing, and that was the reason he was going to be paid a visit from an unwelcome companion in his boozed-up struggle to sleep. It wasn't the first time he'd failed to save someone's life.

CHAPTER EIGHTEEN

The body lay on a steel plate that was ice cold to Maggie's touch. She had to hold the table to steady herself when time came to uncover the hump. A man slipped the sheet back just enough to expose the head and neck. She wanted to touch the undamaged side of her dad's face but feared she would break at the feel of his cold skin.

His sadness was gone now. For that she felt deep and lonely relief.

"It's John. It's my dad," she said and turned before they could draw back the cover over the corpse.

Another man wearing a loosened paisley tie, apparently in charge, said more as a question, "We should be able to release him day after tomorrow most likely. The VA can make the necessary arrangements, if you like."

"I'll do it," Maggie snapped.

The Buick's right wiper blade had worn down to metal months ago. It made one shrill swipe before she remembered and shut it off, too late to avoid another arched scratch on the windshield. On the freeway she lowered her speed and listened to outlaw music, Willie and Waylon. It was heartfelt and sentimental and she cried.

The phone was ringing when she opened the house door; she decided to take it. It was the reporter calling, the one at the lighthouse. Now he wanted to ask questions. She was too nervous to talk; what if she slipped up and said the wrong thing? She tried to be polite but it wasn't easy; she wanted to say, "Fuck off!" and slam down the phone. She hadn't thought the media would be interested in her father, even when he had pulled such a crazy prank. He was just a mixed-up old drunk.

"I'm sorry," she said to the reporter, "I'm too upset to talk now."

"I understand. Tomorrow may I call you?" Ray Myers persisted and she said, "I suppose."

Right now, though, she had to keep her mouth shut.

Maggie killed the ringers on both her phones and unplugged the message machine.

She popped a Valium along with half a Vicodin she'd taken from her dad's meds and got into bed. She dreamed but she didn't know what it meant, only that it was unpleasant—a fierce tidal wave uprooting everything in its wake, houses, little children, dogs, her collection of glass fishes, trees, a car tire swing, her and her dad in the house that was to be called *Casa Libre*.

She awoke before eight the next morning, early for a swing-shift waitress, and crawled out of bed with a sedative hangover. She lingered in the shower until the water turned cold.

Making coffee double strength might help unglue the cobweb in her brain. It did the job after one cup. She played with the goldie at the kitchen table and sipped her second cup with a cig.

Reluctantly, she turned on the phone ringers in the kitchen and bedroom. The phone rang right away. Maggie was ready for the reporter but it wasn't him calling. She greeted the realtor pleasantly, glad the woman called. Her dad's name was going to be co-owner on the title for the 19th Street property and she needed to make that change.

The agent didn't much care about names on a title. She had something else to say: "Margaret, I'm so sorry for your loss. But ... " It was that "but," the emphatic finality in its tone, that immediately infuriated Maggie.

The cigarette dropped near the snoozing goldie and she ground it out on the linoleum. She was on her feet and heard herself say, "'*But?*' what's that supposed to mean?"

"I am sorry, Ms. Frazier. There are certain rules we must follow—"

"I thought your only rule was to sell houses, period ... Look, I have the money. I'm over twenty-one, for chrissake. You know my credit rating is good, over seven hundred, I believe."

"Let me repeat, McGillis Realty has integrital standards we must meet, Ms. Frazier ... "

Integrital? Maggie thought. Was that a real word? Or realtor-speak?

She said, "I can deliver fifty thousand dollars to you today, in cash. You can't stop our deal. We have an agreement." Her voice was rising and she took a breath and counted numbers to help control herself; she only got to three. "Ms Richards. Let me ask you. Do you know how many orphaned children there are out there? How many that you're turning away because of your goddamn integrital standards?"

Maggie slammed down the phone, maybe even breaking it. "Damn *bitch*," she screamed. The pitch of her voice, if not the mauled cigarette butt, had already run Sally out of the kitchen.

She hated realty people. They were so fucking phony. Acted like they knew exactly what you wanted then wasted your time showing you properties that were nothing like you'd asked to see. They were frauds. Realtors pretended to sympathize with your situation, until your situation meant you did not qualify. That was probably it, she thought now; the price tag on that wreck of a house was four-hundred-and-fifty thousand dollars when Maggie signed the acceptance offer. They must've thought it would go for more now. This whole thing probably had nothing to do with her dad's shameful death. Ms. Richards turned hardcore so she could kill the deal and get more money from some other interested party. That's what Maggie did not like about realtors—they were two-faced, deceitful, disingenuous. All those things.

The rain gave over to blue today, another ho-hum beautiful day in San Diego. The newspaper had been dropped at the sidewalk, twenty-five feet from her stoop. Next week the carrier would probably drop it *on* the sidewalk, lazy jerk.

She had hoped the story would be hidden somewhere inside the paper, but it wasn't. There it was on the front page, up top, with a headline so pronounced you'd think the Big One had finally hit:

MAN KILLED IN STANDOFF
AT CABRILLO LIGHTHOUSE

Wasn't something more important happening? Maggie wondered. Still, she felt a fleck of pride that the newspaper thought her dad bore *some* importance, or at least his death did.

But that was probably not true, either. The real reason her father's death was flagrantly splashed all over the front page was because the paper's reporter had gotten an exclusive story. Instead of a picture of her dad, the victim, they put his picture there, along with another article:

Journal Reporter Chronicles
Victim's Final Moments

She read the second story. She couldn't imagine what her dad thought he would prove dressing like an old soldier and breaking into that light-house. It was sad. Her dad was crazy lost. Had Minh's death alone sent him over the edge? How upset could he have really been, the boy hated him, after all. The boy had been "re-educated" against the American imperialists and her dad understood that. It seemed incredible that John did something so drastic.

"'Why are the children always the ones to pay?'" her father was quoted as saying. It could be his epitaph; his concern for children had always been the essence of his being, the sum of his worth, and his words struck Maggie with pride. He was a man with a heart, even if he was pitiful.

The reporter saw those qualities in him, too, and this eased her ill feelings as she read on. He wrote of her father's despondency and grievances just as Maggie knew them to be, especially the way she perceived the hatred he'd had of his runaround through the immigration system. The article didn't say much about Minh. She supposed her father hadn't said much about him.

Then the article took a turn. An icy chill raced through her when it mentioned the babies that went missing in the desert. She read the quote, "'Four little lives have vanished and nobody cares.'"

"Oh, christ," she said aloud, flushing on her chest and cheeks.

It got worse. The article kept going on about illicit babies smuggled into this country. "'You can blame their disappearance on a smuggling operation that went bad,'" the article again quoted her father. Just like that, in quote marks on Page One of the _San Diego Journal_.

How could he do this to her? she thought, and immediately felt guilty for thinking only of herself. Still, she couldn't believe what she was reading. Something was wrong here. Her dad wouldn't say this stuff. He knew she was involved and the matter of all that money she had yet to turn over to Mr. Swabb; her dad would know the trouble it would put her in.

She lit a fresh cigarette and circled the kitchen table with her arms folded across her breasts, holding the cigarette between long fingers close to her mouth. Don't panic, she thought. Think!

Maggie took her coffee and a new pack of cigs and ashtray into the living room and sat on the davenport. She tucked her feet under herself and put a throw pillow on her lap, then tossed the pillow away and got up, too edgy to sit. She stood by the double bookshelf that held her glass fishes. On an entire double bookcase there was nothing but colorful blown-glass figurines of fish. Her pretend rescued orphans, she thought of them that way even if they weren't always dust free.

She lifted the statuette of a hefty blowfish with fins and quills, colors of a sergeant major. It weighed six pounds. She touched it to her cheek then put it back on the shelf. She wanted suddenly to disappear.

This was going to hit the fan with Mr. Swabb. If he had any brains at all, which he did because he was a lawyer, he would figure out that her father knew about her involvement in the ring. She thought of calling Mr. Swabb right then, before he called her. But what would she say, her father made all that up? He would threaten her, he would demand his money. God knows what else.

The phone rang. The ash jumped off the end of her burning cigarette. Collect the money before you do anything else, she told herself rationally. Money talks; the more she had the better to negotiate with. It could buy her a way out of this mess. Maybe.

The phone rang more than four times before she remembered she had not plugged the answering machine back in; it wasn't going to stop. She bit her tongue and answered after the seventh ring. "Yes?"

"You broke the code." Swabb's shrill voice blared out. "Just how much did he know? Quickly, tell me everything."

"Go to hell," she said. The response surprised her.

"Hey, don't you hang up." Swabb said.

"My father's *dead*." Maggie spit the words. "He's lying in the morgue. Don't you respect *anything*."

A moment passed. Swabb said, "What in hell did he think he was doing in that lighthouse, anyway? For chrissake."

"Well, it had nothing to do with you. I didn't tell him squat about the company. I don't know where he got that stuff about the babies, maybe he just made it up. Maybe the reporter did. Okay?"

"Too lame. I don't buy that."

"I'll call you later."

"Don't you dare hang—"

She decided in that instant to pack up and go, maybe to the reservation, help Margarita with the kids—but not before she delivered that Filipino baby to the big-money La Jollan.

CHAPTER NINETEEN

Madelene felt the pain as she stretched to hang the baby's mobile. Quick and sharp, low stomach. She thought she'd had similar pain yesterday morning, a touch of nausea afterwards. She thought she might get nauseous again now but scoffed at herself and went on about the job. The idea of having morning sickness was preposterous, for Madelene Schaefer could not bear children. How strange the power of the mind, she thought.

She had already drilled the 3/8th-inch hole in the ceiling after rolling the baby's bed aside to avoid falling dust, and now she inserted a toggle bolt with a florid gold hook, twisted and twisted until it was tightened down. Then she hung the mobile. Once hung she separated the strings then blew the strings of pyrite seagulls to assess—and approve—its delicate motions and soft sounds.

Madelene heard the vacuum cleaner as it swept from a distant bedroom into the hallway. She called out, "Villi, come here, please."

Mrs. Ruvalcaba heard the summons all right; it was loud and clear. But the housekeeper was in no mood this morning for the mistress' little whims. She grinned wickedly and continued with her vacuuming. She would work her way down there soon enough. It had taken forever to get through the border this morning, which meant she would be two or three hours late getting home tonight and would miss the episode of *Al Diablo con Los Guapos*.

She sashayed down the long hallway with the apparatus churning a path in a carpet thick enough to sleep on, refusing to answer a second summon. When finally she got to the master bedroom, she switched off the growling motor and grinned at the lily-white woman she deemed too thin to be healthy. Her boss stood there in a fluff-ball nightgown when it was noon, looking like a vampire. Villi's unwilling grin, upon seeing her, suddenly turned upside down.

"You call, Mis-iz?" she said, trying in her faulty frontier English to emulate the haughty tone of an ancient American soap opera heroine now the passion of Tijuana television.

Madelene smiled pleasantly. "I want you to be absolutely certain the baby's room is spotless … Do you know what I found?"

Villarmini Ruvalcaba leaned against the doorjamb, tapping her fingers on the handle of the vacuum cleaner, noticing with disapproval the useless string-thing hanging from the ceiling. And the mess on the carpet underneath it. She held the frown, not amused with these games the mistress played. "No, Mis-iz. What you find?"

"Dust," said Madelene.

"Dust? Where you see dust?" The housekeeper acted offended. "Don't you worry. I will have that baby's room *muy limpio* … Today maybe is the day, huh? That baby gonna have one good life here. You go down and Villi make you up some lunch."

"Yes. I could eat a horse … Isn't it a lovely day?"

The housekeeper watched her skinny mistress roll the crib bed back in place. She didn't offer to help nor vacuum up the drywall dust. She leaned off the doorjamb shaking her head at her boss' unseemly comments. She said, "A horse? I don't know. How about you have some *chorizo y huevos*? You know how good it is I make."

The vacuum cleaner took off on its own back down the hallway, Villi just hanging on to it.

Madelene changed into a silky pink blouse-and-pants outfit, mauve slippers, and a pinkish afghan; it would be chilly in the enclosed patio where she regularly took her lunch. She pampered her shoulder-length coriander hair, slowly stroking it with a bubble brush as though the world had stopped to wait on her. The stomach unpleasantness turned out to be only gas. Surely from that awful dressing she put on her salad last night.

After hearing from Sylvia, she had thought of nothing but the baby, given to electric moments of fantasizing her strange new role as "mother." She pictured the child on her arm, its adorable fingers clenched to hers like tiny C clamps. Madelene let her heart run as it would.

But she had been on pins and needles these past few days. Sylvia had said "very soon now." Very soon, she knew, meant *any* time. The phone rang and she would start. She had lost sleep the past three nights. She knew she was being too hard on the help. She adored the housekeeper even if she was acting up lately. Mrs. Ruvalcaba had been with her off and on for ten years, more, and though she was as candid and utilitarian as they came, having little humor or patience, she had bore five babies; Villi knew a thing or two about babies.

She was trying to keep her emotions in check, because, as her agent had warned, in this fragile and shady business there are no absolutes. Buying a baby on the black market was risky business for anyone. Double that for a convicted felon.

It was a burdensome irony that Madelene's criminal past was part of the reason she had to conspire in another crime now if she expected to adopt a child. Madelene could actually do hard time if she were caught. The thought of prison set off in her a chilling mix of fear and turmoil. Was it worth the chance? She'd weighed the question and knew decisively that, yes, it was worth it. So worth it to have a child she could raise and call her own. "Mom," how sweet the sound.

On a whim, one day not so long ago she blurted, "Villi, why don't I adopt a baby?" Villi smiled, and there had been no turning back.

She had tried several adoption agencies at first. The people were cordial and supportive until the first mention of "a prior." Then, in subtle ways, things turned. E-mails and calls were not returned, sympathy turned to doubtfulness. In the end all but one agency rejected Madelene's application.

The Adoption Center of California offered her a twelve-year-old male with muscular dystrophy. The agency suggested it would help if Madelene converted to Catholicism, the boy's religion. They also required thirty-five thousand dollars for "reserve funds" toward the child's outpatient therapy for the coming year. It forced a decision no one with a conscience would ever want to make, a damned if you do, damned if you don't double bind that could only lead to guilt because she had to decline. The agency assumed correctly that she wouldn't take the offer, and that was fine with the for-profit company, which stood to lose its handsome federal welfare revenues if the orphan were adopted.

Call it another irony, one serendipitously positive, that at the same agency Madelene met a nice person who took her aside with some advice: "When you get fed up fighting these self-righteous godheads, put an ad in the personals and on Craigslist. You'll get your baby, promise."

Sylvia Fischer was among those who contacted her through the personal ad she placed in the newspaper. Madelene liked the woman from the get-go. Her mild voice, her girl-like laugh. She was a straight-talker, questioning Madelene about the prior conviction without prejudging her … That sit-in thing she and some of her Stanford friends did at Berkeley back in young Maddy Wayne's impetuous college days had escalated into a firebombing in the Political Science building, for which she had been wrongly arrested but still convicted and sentenced by a decidedly unsympathetic judge.

Sylvia grilled her with questions from the MMPI psychological test to see if she was, as the baby merchant put it, "the abuser type," making it clear she would not work for anyone who had even a latent potential to abuse a child. That's the only reason Sylvia wanted to know about her felony. Madelene appreciated the kind of person who scrutinized so carefully someone to whom she might sell a baby. Sylvia was also motherless and appeared to be around the same age as Madelene, maybe a year or two older. She could empathize.

By their third meeting, Madelene had no qualms at all about forking over twenty thousand in cash to get the process rolling, opting for a Caucasian baby from Russia or another Eastern bloc country. The sex wouldn't make that much difference, although she preferred a girl. Good news to Sylvia. That had been less than a month ago, hardly enough time to get ready. Then Sylvia called and the baby was coming, ready or not. Madelene gleaned it would not be from Russia, however, not that quickly. It didn't matter to her.

The pungent scent of chorizo filtered into Madelene's bathroom as she stood bent toward the mirror finishing her minimal morning makeup. Villi could cook faster than any short-order wizard and of course much better, the only caveat being Madelene's inflexible prohibition of lard in the Windnmar house. That was a problem Mrs. Ruvalcaba could easily solve simply by using more sausage.

Preened and ready for the day, Madelene journeyed along the hallway to the glassed-in patio. The patio overlooked a kidney-shaped pool one graded level down. Beyond that, well down the mountainside, lazed the Pacific Ocean, which today was invisible under a lingering marine cloud, a common occurrence in the hills of La Jolla.

The phone rang and Madelene shrieked. Still in the hallway, she picked up her pace, shouting, "I'll get it, Villi!"

But Mrs. Ruvalcaba had it before the second ring. By the time Madelene got to the kitchen, the maid had finished with the caller.

Madelene glared in disbelief. "You hung up! ... Who was it, Villi?"

"Baby sales," she sniffed. "We no want."

"*What!*" Madelene cuffed her small white hands against her hips. She was now irate. "How dare you decide what we—what *I* want without asking me first. Maybe it was her."

"No, Mis-iz, it was not *her*." Mrs. Ruvalcaba knew about Sylvia, but she did not have to trust the person who was supposed to bring her mistress a baby. Just like that, bring her a baby. The mother of five was suspicious of anyone who would promise such a thing.

"From now on, Villi," Madelene said sternly, jabbing a finger, "I will take the phone calls when I'm here."

The maid hissed.

"I mean it—What's that smell?"

"*Santa Maria!*" Villi leaped to the stove. "You make me burn the tortillas. You see what happens when you come too soon, I still cooking. Huh?"

Madelene left, throwing the kitchen's swinging door behind her. She went into her study and busied herself at the computer, chewing a cuticle as she waited for the computer to check her mail. She was hoping for word from Sylvia. Nothing, but that was not necessarily bad. She had said she would call her by phone when the time came.

A few minutes later she heard Mrs. Ruvalcaba's call. "You food is ready."

Madelene came back to the marble and glass room. Before she took her seat the phone rang.

"Don't you dare touch that phone," she called into the kitchen, seeing the housekeeper scowl from the doorway.

Madelene took the call in the study. She answered nervously, her voice warbling like a bird's song, "Hello? This is Madelene Schaefer."

"Hi, there. It's me, Sylvia," Maggie Frazier said.

Madelene's heart leaped to her throat.

"Good news. Your daughter is waiting for you to come get her."

Madelene managed to hold herself together listening to the particulars. She carefully cradled the phone and then she collapsed and vomited on the beige carpet.

CHAPTER TWENTY

Hating herself for reneging on her sworn oath to mothball Sylvia Fischer, Maggie donned the guise. But this was it, never again. As she did it, old Sally lay at her side, the dog's paws on its snout as if covering her eyes in shame of her master. Maggie noticed. "I know, I know," she said pleadingly of the dog, "I gotta do it. For the baby's sake."

Once at the mall, she lit a cig and watched for the client's luxury car to arrive, a silver Mercedes. All your La Jolla women drove a silver Mercedes. She also kept an eye peeled for Madelene Schaefer's other car, the cream-colored Jaguar. She had a hunch it would be the Merc, though. Mercedes were safer and she was one of the caring clients.

Maggie had parked her unsightly old Buick out in left field of Bonita Mall's gigantic north lot, in "F". The client's baby was not in Maggie's car breathing secondhand cigarette smoke. The baby was inside the shopping center, presumably, in front of Payless Shoes nestled in a warm stroller and under the care of Mrs. Rodriguez from the Chula Vista safehouse.

She'd rushed to get here, fighting 25 miles of noontime traffic after cashing the Bischkes' bonus check at her bank in El Cajon.

Maggie spotted a silver Mercedes coming in near the Robinson/May entrance, over in Section "E". She spiced her breath with a spray of Bianca and jumped out, assuming the car was the client's. She sped on foot through another entrance to beat the client to the perfume counter where they had agreed to meet.

This part of the job, the baby exchanging hands, was the most rewarding of the process. Seeing the excitement in the client's face had its own reward for Maggie. Also, there was little doubt at this point the client would renege with only a final payment to hand over. Maggie could tell the ones inclined to skip out, even after the non-refundable down payment, and Madelene Schaefer wasn't one of them. This woman wanted a child so much it actually frightened Maggie a little, but she had no misgivings about her. She was good at heart and sound, and wealthy. She would make a fine mother. Maggie could read it all over her, anyone could.

For the client, the first sight of their baby brought with it the highest anxiety and it was the reason Maggie of course selected a wide-open venue like a busy mall. She'd had a near-disaster once, and only once, when conveying the baby to a gay couple at their residence. Without any forewarning, the pair launched into a duel tantrum over the child's not having a say about his own circumcision. The circumcision had been performed before reaching his new parents. But they were inconsolable. Their argument was untouchable: The boy had not been given the choice and he must now live the rest of his life knowing someone else had made the discretionary decision that he exclusively had the right to make. People were strange, the things they chose to lose control over. There was nothing she could do about it. Maggie almost lost the couple until she coolly reminded them that there was no "choice" in the matter because state policy required performing circumcisions on orphans in Eastern bloc countries before conveying. "You'll just have to live with the disfigurement," she'd said without sympathy and so close to laughing out loud she was afraid it might kill the deal. She doubted they would have thrown that kind of fit in front of Baskin-Robbins.

She spotted her client coming and waved. As a proper La Jollan, Madelene responded synthetically. "Sylvia! So good to see you again." Acting as if she'd by happenstance bumped into an acquaintance from the Hill, when in actuality both would be scandalized for being caught slumming in the dumps of what San Diegans called "Nasty City."

Maggie watched her scan the area with darting eyes, obviously searching for the baby. She wasn't panicking, not yet. Maggie adjusted the handbag strap on her shoulder, biding a little time for the client to settle down. The young woman behind the counter stood by, bored but patient.

"Where is she?" Madelene blurted, surrendering manners and all else. "Can I see her now? Please?"

"Yes, of course you can," Maggie said. "Relax, be patient."

She led Madelene out of the department store into the enclosed concourse. They walked by clothiers, Chico's, Gap, passed B. Dalton Bookstore where Elmore Leonard's forty-ninth release, *Urban Turban*, took space on an outside rack alongside Danielle Steele's hundred-forty-fifth, *Mediterranean Diary,* and Michael Connelly's new one, *Stink Street.* Gay Talese's third autobiography, *Myself, My Love,* was not outside.

~

Madelene's excitement had surged so high it was all she could do to control her bodily functions; she kept repeating to herself, *Stay calm, don't panic.*

She then spotted a stroller near an arrangement of waterfalls between escalators. It made her squeal and look expectantly at Sylvia Fischer. "Is that—?"

"That's your daughter," the agent said calmly and smiled.

Madelene again focused on the stroller. Several Hispanic women about Mrs. Ruvalcaba's age had gathered there, looking a lot like Villi. In unison the women leaned over the stroller to take a peek. Then, suddenly, they all at once jumped back as though they'd seen Rosemary's baby.

It paralyzed Madelene. She watched the women pat their chests breathing hard and then leave, mumbling among themselves.

~

Maggie hadn't noticed the ladies' reaction. But she did notice her client speeding up, almost running to the stroller.

"I must tell you," Maggie said, hustling to keep pace, "there's one little snatch. Well, two, actually."

Mrs. Rodriguez from the Chula Vista safehouse sat calmly on the bench, slowly moving the stroller back and forth, tilting it gently at arm's length. She greeted Maggie with a warm smile. *"Buenos días, Señora."*

"Y también, buenos días, Señora." To Madelene, she said, "Let's have a look, shall we?" The client hesitated. "Don't be shy, Madelene."

Maggie gently lifted the bundle from its bed and handed it to the new mother. Madelene wiped her tears and took the bundle. "Oh, my ... Thank you so much."

Maggie dismissed Mrs. Rodriguez. The stroller stayed; it would go with the client, gratis.

"Let's sit over here," Maggie said.

They sat side by side. Madelene tried bouncing the infant on her lap, being very careful. She smiled innocent as a teenage girl. "Gosh, she's so beautiful."

Not a word about the infant's non-Caucasian complexion. Maggie smiled. "The other matter? Don't worry, it's nothing at all. Just a minor problem with Customs. But we can wait on that for the time being."

It didn't seem to make any difference to the rich La Jollan that the child was Filipino. Maybe she thought the child was jaundice. Maybe love had blinded her. Who cared?

Maggie said, "I'm just going to forget about this little problem with Customs, okay? Is that all right? … Madelene?"

Madelene hadn't heard a word she said. Just sat there ogling her new daughter. Maggie took a peek at the baby. It was cute as a button, she thought, the black-as-night hair, the delicate nostrils. There didn't seem to be a nose at all, just the subtle rise and fall of two little nostrils. The baby opened her eyes and cooed at them. The baby's new mom cooed back.

"Okay," Maggie said. "Then here are your final papers."

Maggie removed a large envelope from her shoulder bag containing documents that would naturalize the child under ICE and State Department laws for international adoption.

"You have the cash with you, I assume? Here, let me hold her while you look these over … If that's okay?"

Madelene made goo-goo sounds.

"Madelene? … Ms. Schaefer? I'm sorry, but if you didn't bring the balance of the payment, I will have to take the child back."

That did it. While Maggie held the weightless bundle, Madelene squared up, giving her a purse from inside the bigger purse. Maggie stuffed it into her bag. She trusted the woman; she would count out the twenty-five thousand back in her car. No embarrassment that way. No sheepish under-the-table hand-off like Jack Bischke.

"The last thing you need to know?" Maggie said. "Okay? … You haven't received this baby yet—in case anyone in the company asks. This is important for the baby's welfare. If they do call you, say you're expecting me to bring the baby to you later this week. Got it? … It's just, I know

how anxious you've been and I wanted you not to have to wait any longer."

"I understand. Do I owe you any more money—or anything?" Madelene asked.

"You are paid in full," said Maggie, who continued to bounce the baby
on her knee, also falling in love with it.

~

Villi Ruvalcaba did not realize how thrilled she'd been until now, after the mistress actually left to pick up the child. Her absence—the silence brought the reality home. She could feel the nesting instinct take
hold. It was an instinct that took her back to her last and final child, the
son she had finally given her late husband, Enrique, after having those
four girls.

Now the mistress was getting a child and Villi would be the baby's
nanny, her *Abuelita*. Like having her own little *niña* again, after so many
years with no help from those daughters, all of whom remained unmar-
ried to this day and still at home hiding under their mother's skirt.

She dusted the baby's room for the second time today, vacuumed the
carpet again, scrubbed the changing table again. The currents of air
caused by her swift movements set the mobile of seagulls aflutter. Mrs.
Ruvalcaba changed her mind, deciding she now approved of the blue
sky-and-clouds wallpaper the mistress had chosen instead of that pink
flower wallpaper. Even the light blue carpet, which would show the
slightest stain, seemed right.

She walked through the house, checking things, straightening hallway
pictures of her employer. The photographs went back through the
years—her youthful days with the big hair, the one with her ex-husband
and their twin dalmatian dogs on a rock in La Jolla Cove, several photographs with her and her parents before they were killed in that freak
flying accident at Vail, Colorado. Villi knew about her mistress' life, even
if the memories had meant little to her. But now the housekeeper grew
nostalgic looking at the wall of pictures, the story of her mistress' life.
She recognized that love was the same for gringos as for her own family;
not all gringos were as hard hearted as they wanted you to think.

She sterilized a dozen bottles and rubber nipples, even though the
mistress had weeks before purchased pre-sterilized disposable plastic

bottles by the cases, stacked on top of boxes of canned formula in a corner of the huge pantry and in another pantry in the garage. There was enough baby food to feed quintuplets till they were teenagers.

Mrs. Ruvalcaba then did something she had never done on the job; she had a shot of brandy with her coffee. She sat at the mistress' place on the marbled patio, nervous feet going a mile a minute. She wondered if the baby would mind if her *Abuelita* sang traditional Mexican to her.

At lunchtime she stood over the stove pan-frying a fillet of yellowtail, the mistress' favorite. She heard the garage door motor clank on and waited with bated breath as the car door shut. Madelene soon walked into the kitchen, a big smile riveted on her face. Madelene put a finger to her lips to hush Villi and continued on into the living room with the bundled-up baby in her arms.

Mrs. Ruvalcaba followed excitedly, hoping to get a peek under the blanket.

"Please, Mis-iz. Let me see her. I can hold her, huh?"

"Yes, of course you can, Villi. But don't burn her with that utensil. Be careful, she's sleeping."

Mrs. Ruvalcaba placed the oily spatula on the coffee table, on a copy of "Parenting," then smoothed out her skirt, pressed back her graying hair under the palms of her hands, and gently took the bundle in her hands.

"What do you think?" Madelene said, "Do you like 'Consuela?' 'Connie Schaefer?'"

Madelene sniffed the air. "What's that burning?"

She dashed into the kitchen to find sparks and smoke rising from a pan on the stove. Unrushed, she threw the pan with smoldering fish into the sink, not aggravated in the least.

Hearing a shriek from the living room, Madelene grabbed for her heart, just knowing the housekeeper had dropped Connie.

Mrs. Ruvalcaba entered the kitchen with the child in her arm. "*Santa Maria!*" she cried. "It's a jellow baby!"

CHAPTER TWENTY-ONE

Myers usually got no more notice entering the newsroom than a taciturn rim rat—those mousy copy editors who sat around a horseshoe rim waiting on reporters to get the hell done with their articles so they could get their paws on them. Today was different, heads popped up, some cheery, others glaring, some jealous. It wasn't his fifteen minutes, but it was front-page notoriety. He acknowledged the sulkies as well as his fans, then marched straight to the city editor's desk. He had something to talk to Max Cullen about.

Settling into the cushioned side chair, he got to it. "Before they shot him, Frazier gave me a snapshot of some kids. I didn't mention it to the police. I'm going to track it down. What I want to know is, what happens when we later want to publish the shot. How's that going to stand with Legal?"

Cullen turned ninety years old as Myers made the confession. "Jesus H. fucking Christ!" he raved in a rare display of lewd language.

"He can't help—look, Max, I can run it down today, then turn it over to the PD and still get a follow-up, if there's anything to follow up. I believe there is."

"Not the goddamn point, Ray. You gave your statement to the police, you should've told them about it then. They can get nasty if they choose. You've put the paper in a bad place … I am disappointed in you, Raymond."

"Fair enough. But a snapshot of some kids wasn't going to change anything that transpired at that lighthouse."

Cullen shook his head looking at his belly. In a tired voice he said, "Let's see it."

Myers produced the tattered snapshot. "They're Amerasian. It was taken somewhere in the Nam, I Corps probably. That's up north where most of the fighting went on. I'm going to find out what kept a Purple

Heart veteran from bringing his son to the U.S. when they were letting them in right and left."

Myers pointed to the tallest kid in the picture. "That one."

"Looks like he's put together with Twiddle Sticks." Cullen handed the snapshot back to him. "Forget this. So much time's passed. It won't make any difference with anything anyway."

"That's the kind of reaction that had Frazier so screwed up. It turns out this kid really was his son, the people at Immigration have some explaining to do. That's a story. Whaddaya say, Max? Carry me on this one, will you?"

Cullen threw out his hands. "It'll be the last straw with L.C. You know that. I see trouble with the law, too—but, what the hell. You *are* Raymond A. Myers, Mr. Magic. Just don't take long. And this conversation never happened."

"Good boy, Maxie. Buy you a drink whenever."

Myers caught a couple more knuckled fists going to his desk. He took the glazed donut Tina Lubrano offered him. A copy clerk had a mocha from upstairs waiting on him. It was still warm. How bout that, he thought. His phone light blinked. A picture of him was on the front page of a metropolitan newspaper. Maybe it *was* his fifteen minutes.

"You'd think this rag's never produced anything original," he said to Lubrano.

"You sure pulled some heart strings, though, maybe even mine," she said, dangerously close to sentiment. "Appears you might be back, doing what you do—"

"Max's sentiment exactly." Myers grinned proudly.

"Don't let it go to your head, big shot." Lubrano pointed to the flashing light on his phone. "Want me to secretary for you?"

Myers shook his head, kicked back in his chair and again soaked in the front page, leaving the ME's gal to take his calls. Seeing his own picture there played both to the hauteur in him and conflicted him—he got his scoop, but at what cost, to him and the paper? Using the reporter's mug was a cheap shot owing to an editorial assumption that the reader was fascinated by what witnesses to violent death looked like, probably more than their interest in the victim—the voyeur watching a man get his head blown apart, so close that the splatter of hot blood stuck to his skin. Made excellent latte-on-the-run reading. Using the reporter's mug shot only stooped to the kind of self-promotional image boasting you'd expect from FOX News. And CBS. Okay, all of them. And then there was the writer's skillful persuasion. But to what affect? The real truth or manipulated truth?

It should have been the victim's picture, not Myers'. As it was they used Frazier's driver's license shot on the jump page, and that was better than nothing.

He swallowed some donut before asking Lubrano, "You get anything from Guatemala or State?"

"Matter of fact they got 4,000 cases of missing persons on record down there since summer. That could be for the fiscal year, they weren't really sure at the consulate."

"Missing babies not specifically mentioned, I take it. How about adoption agencies?"

Lubrano shrugged. "Cold shoulder. Agencies won't talk about it. Policy, they say. You think that's how *they* do it—agencies get their stock from black marketeers?"

She was being factious—maybe. Myers said, "Well, you tried."

Lubrano wasn't done. "Called the VA. Got something there might interest you."

"Yeah?"

Lubrano held back. She took pleasure in stringing Myers along whenever she could. At length, she said, "It ain't all that easy getting info out of the VA. You ever tried it?" She gave him a big Italian grin.

"Okay, okay, go on, talk."

"Frazier couldn't have children. Type of wound he got in Vietnam."

Myers mumbled, "Fuck me."

"Some credit, please. God, do I have to beg?"

"You done good … But could be his mamasan and he got together before he was wounded."

"Could be. Info came from the outpatient psych clinic in Mission Valley, not La Jolla, for future reference … Anyway, my squeal there said it was pretty hard on Frazier since he and his wife had both wanted children of their own. Probably why they divorced, the squeal said. Even after they adopted a girl."

Frazier's extreme intensity now made a little more sense to Myers. "Who's the squeal?"

"Personal acquaintance."

The morning was slipping away. He said to Lubrano, "I'm going to pay a visit to the good people at ICE."

She swallowed the chewy bear claw, it took a moment. "Be nice, Ray, you know how you can get."

"Sure, sure."

Myers right away called the office of Immigration and Customs Enforcement, seeking an interview with any ranking official. Surprisingly, he got an 11:45 appointment for this morning.

Then he phoned Margaret Frazier, hoping she felt up to talking and might give him something that would be helpful at Immigration.

He was just about to hang up when she answered.

"Hello?" She sounded reluctant and winded.

He said his name. "I hope I didn't catch you at a bad time."

"I was just out the door."

"Please give me one minute, Ms. Frazier … Again, I am truly sorry for your loss. Your father seemed like a decent, caring person. That was my impression talking to him."

"Thanks, he was. Look, I need to—"

"Please. Your father gave me a snapshot of some Vietnamese boys. Can you tell me anything about it, who the picture is of?"

"I really don't know much, Minh—" She stopped.

"Minh?" Myers said. "That's Vietnamese. Is that his name?"

"All right. I don't know about a snapshot. All I know is Minh's mother located my father way back when. She wrote Dad a letter through one of those agencies."

Myers noticed the change in her voice after the faux pas letting slip the boy's name, now somewhere between frosty and nervous. She was a step ahead of him and he had to fill in what was missing on his own.

"When did all this take place, Ms. Frazier? Had they assigned a particular case worker?"

There was a pause at her end. Myers figured she was trying to decide how much to tell him. But why hold back? he wondered.

"It was so long ago … I can't tell you the year Dad found out he had a son. And, yeah, he had caseworkers. One guy later on seemed to care. His name was Rhoades. But he didn't get anything done either. Way too much red tape, hands were tied, all that crap."

"Did your dad have a case?" Myers scribbled as he spoke, *Minh, Fr's son in VN. Rhoades—still at ICE??*

"He had a birth certificate. Didn't help him get Minh home, though … You were with him, Mr. Myers. Why did they have to kill him? Dad wouldn't hurt anyone."

"I don't think he would've. But dressed up in combat clothes gave them another impression. They spook easily these days."

"They didn't have to kill him."

"It was bad judgment on their part. You can sue for wrongful death," said Myers. "Look, I don't want to offend you, Ms. Frazier, but most GIs who fathered children in Vietnam didn't want anything to do with them. What was it about your father made him different—if I may ask?"

No hesitation. "Dad believed family was more important than everything else—even if Minh didn't want anything to do with us."

Myers glanced around the newsroom to see whose ears were tuned to him—nobody's. The fame had gone. Lubrano was buried in her computer. He took a breath and got to the subject he most wanted to talk to her about. "Ms Frazier. You saw my article, I'm sure."

"Yes, I did. And I wanted to say you treated Dad like a real human being, not some crazy lunatic."

"Thanks … Let me say that in the lighthouse your dad told me straight out that those migrants who died in the desert last week had babies with them. Do you have any idea how he might have known about them—the babies?"

Myers waited, deciding she wasn't going to respond. He said, "I should tell you also, before things got out of hand, your father apologized to you. His words were, 'Forgive me, Maggie.' Those were his last words. He wasn't rambling, he was preparing himself, trying to make amends. I believe that. He spoke of you at least twice."

He listened to the sound of her softly weeping and wondered cynically if she was crying just to avoid his questions. "I'm sorry, Ms. Frazier. Your father was a good man who had some bad breaks. I was in Vietnam, too, and I think I understand a little bit what made him hole up like he did in that lighthouse. I'm going to try and set the record straight for him. He deserves that."

"I—I hope you can, Mr. Myers. But what—I mean, how are you going to do that?"

"Ask some questions. I was hoping, too, that I could come out and talk with you again—before television starts crowding you."

Another hesitation. She said, "Uh, why would they do that?"

"I find out what I think I'll find out at Immigration, they'll be all over you. Believe me."

CHAPTER TWENTY-TWO

The abundance of ceramic tile in the Amtrak men's restroom magnified even the slightest sound. Rubber soles squeaked like train brakes, a cough became a cannon. There was little traffic here to interfere with business. Which must have been the reason Bubba's boss chose it.

The patent-leather soles of Bubba's reptile boots woke the tile when he entered. He peered under the door of the first stall and saw his man's shiny brown Florsheims, then examined the other three stalls, all unoccupied. He slipped into stall number two.

He tapped the partition twice and watched at the top of the stall as a hand appeared waving a folded piece of paper. He took the note and read to himself: *Margaret Frazier. A.k.a. Sylvia Fischer. Caucasian, tall, sandy hair, late-twenties. Lives alone. 1304 Paseo Place, El Cajon.*

"A woman? ... Shit," he said, facing the divider.

"It's on a cul-de-sac," Mendez said in soft baritone. "Watch for inquisitive neighbors."

Bubba silently mouthed the address and both names on the paper before wadding the note and dropping it into the toilet. He flushed and watched it float on top of the swirling water until, at the last moment, the vortex sucked it down. Bubba exited the stall so he could keep an eye on the bathroom proper and stood outside his employer's stall. He was frustrated.

"No way," he said. "Who is she?"

"Tell her you have come for the money. She should have eighty thousand in cash. She may claim to have less. Don't buy it. See the cash, then take her somewhere. South is good. It wouldn't be unusual for her to be in Baja. I understand she goes there sometimes ... Make it look like an accident, or it could be from morbidity—despair over a recent loss. We want to avert any suspicion of foul play. Understand?"

"Fuck, man, I don't know, I don't think so. You can give me all the *cholos* you want, but I ain't doin' a woman. Fuck no … Who is she?"

A sudden drop of water in a porcelain sink echoed across the room.

"Think carefully, friend," Mendez said, his tone hardening. "There are witnesses who can tie you to a murder in Tecate. You know we have extradition with Mexico."

Bubba stepped in tight circles, scratching the itch on the top of his head. "*Damn!* … Is she a citizen?"

"And need I remind you of Sasabe, the favors I did you there?" Easy as flipping a coin, Mendez lost the hostile tone. "Don't be a bonehead … Keep twenty thousand for yourself. Just get the job done and bring me sixty."

Bubba's eyes lit up at the figure. He could get Rox the used Miata she had been hounded him for, seventeen thousand dollars. *Oh, please, Bubba … I'll be so good to you, sweetie!*

"Who the hell is she?" Bubba didn't shout his words for fear someone in the grand hall outside would hear, but he came close.

"Did you read the paper today?"

"Naw, not yet."

"Don't delay. Could be she's thinking of leaving town."

"You say twenty?"

"That's the figure, provided I get the desired results."

"An accident, huh?"

"Or suicide."

CHAPTER TWENTY-THREE

Bubba gobbled the sandwich-size bag of Cheerios he'd brought from home. That was it; that would be all he had to eat this morning. Lately he'd gotten concerned about his weight, in particularly the developing waist ribbon; he could still fit into a 33-inch waist, but his 501s, after washing, weren't as easy to button anymore.

He was in no rush to get there and didn't push the Chrysler to keep pace with the traffic flow, which broke the law by at least ten miles per hour. He hadn't Googled her—by either name—he hadn't looked up her phone number, so he couldn't call. If she'd been in a hurry, maybe she had already skipped town. Maybe he hoped she had. He felt a little sick thinking about the job, something like having rocks stuck in his gut. Knocking off a woman. She must be a bad one considering the amount of dough he was getting paid. Must be worse than that stinking *coyote*. Nah, no way. He could only hope she was a real dog, which would make the job a lot easier to swallow.

The man asked if he'd read today's newspaper, which presumably would tell him something about her. He purposely did not pick one up on his way to her house; he didn't want to know anything about her. Even though he was curious.

The boss suggested taking her south; Bubba was comfortable with that. Once there, and in possession of the money, he would contact Fitzsimmon who in turn would put him in contact with someone in Ensenada who would see that his needs for the body disposal were met. The organization had a shitload of contacts down there. Bubba would need an official ruling on her demise, so he would be dealing with someone crooked in Baja law enforcement, which of course was no problem. The only problem he could foresee would be getting her down there without knocking her in the head first, and having to drag her outside her house unconscious or dead in front of all the cul-de-sac busybodies.

From state Highway 94, he merged into the eastbound Interstate 8 traffic heading around the big curve out of the pleasant city of La Mesa to enter the wide El Cajon valley. The quintessential Southern California community of El Cajon was an urban sprawl of wild-colored cookie cutters, driveways with motorboats and covered-up dune buggies, queen palm and poisonous oleander and ficus roots raising sidewalks. There were thousands of dogs kept unsecured behind three-foot chain-link fences, half of them pit bulls. The city had a gargantuan mall and many smaller strip malls and no Asians, not yet. All of it lay under a canopy of carcinoma-colored smog that regularly drifted in through the foothills from L.A.

Bubba and Rox stayed in a motel out here a few weeks before they moved to the Paradise Lagoon Trailer Park. Rox couldn't stand it, said if her schnauzers weren't eaten by pit bulls they would die from breathing the air. So they got the hell out of El Cajon.

He felt the burning in his sinuses soon as he climbed out of the car, which he parked around the corner from the cul-de-sac and walked the short distance to the house.

The houses on Paseo Place were ground-level stuccos and cinder block set close together but not too close to the sidewalk. They all had similar low-maintenance landscaping—boxwood, mock orange, lemon trees, oleanders—the kind you saw in working-class neighborhoods all over Southern California.

The old station wagon parked in 1304's driveway was bigger than his Chrysler. Bubba studied the car for a second, admiring it—rusted, faded to a dull brown, it sagged on blown-out shocks and had a black rug underneath that caught the oil drips. The consummate Mexican jalopy, a perfect car for the plan he already had been formulating. He wondered, would it get them seventy miles down the road to Ensenada.

~

Maggie jumped at the sound of the doorbell. She was on the phone with a reporter and inadvertently squealed. Her goldie Sally barked from the backyard. The old dog's bark was more of a smoky croak, sounding like it hurt her, and she rarely barked at the doorbell. Like her owner, Sally sensed danger.

Maggie abruptly got off the phone.

After finishing with the La Jollan, she'd been packing clothes and other chores—making calls to get the dog and yard taken care of, writing out checks for late and upcoming payments, stopping the newspaper and mail—getting ready to run from the mobsters she knew would be coming.

Tears came easily. She couldn't keep from thinking about her dad. She was in shreds over her own future, *if* she even had a future. Her baby-selling days were over and uncertainty loomed. Much as it had in a childhood filled with the fearful uncertainty when you bounced from one residence to another, hoping for a home. She felt that emptiness of the unknown again now, on top of the fear. She blamed herself for always getting into these situations.

Her neighbor Sarah, who lived in the house behind her, would be happy to look after Sally for a week or two, put her in at night, feed her, walk her to the park, all for free. A good neighbor and she loved Sally.

The front door did not have a peephole and Maggie was afraid to open it. She had no choice, her car was out there in the driveway. She patted her eyes with a wet tissue to take out the puffiness. Maybe it was Ginger from across the street bringing a neighborly mourner's dish. Maybe another neighbor.

Maggie wasn't at all concerned with the way she dressed, in pedal pushers and an Abercrombie form-fitting halter—a teenager's clothes that worked well on her long frame.

She took a breath and opened the front door just as the bell went off again.

A man she didn't know stood there, thumbs in his blue jeans. She knew it wasn't Mr. Swabb; Mr. Swabb was sure to be squirrelly and wimpy-looking. Probably really short. Weren't all lawyers really short?

This man wasn't all that tall but he was thick and had curly locks of red showing under a cowboy hat and he wore a black shirt with pearl buttons that were buttoned all the way up to the neck. He'd been to a honky tonk or two, and rodeos. An involuntary smile sprang onto her face when it shouldn't have. And she knew it.

He grinned sheepishly, saying nothing for a couple seconds. Then, "Howdy."

Maggie responded, "Howdy?"

"Well, yeah. Howdy, *ma'am*. That better?"

Bubba took off his Stetson, his red curls springing.

"You're an honest-to-God cowboy, aren't you?" Maggie said.

"Used to be. Mustanger. Long time ago … Can I come in?"

"Who are you?" Maggie said, not moving aside.

"They sent me for the money."

Maggie's smile dropped. "Oh." She inched the door toward him. "I usually deposit it. He knows that."

Bubba shrugged. "Can I come in all the way? The neighbors might start to wondering."

"Most of them work," she said, but stood aside. "All right, come in."

Bubba smelled her natural scent as he stepped by her into the living room. He pressured himself to keep his eyes off the perky breasts in that skimpy shirt—the opposite of Rox's oversize knockers.

She was no dog.

His forced his eyes away, had to get his thoughts back on track. He glanced at the shelves where a bunch of glass figures collected dust. They looked sort of like fishes. A bowhead whale, spotted goldfish, tiger sharks.

"Go ahead, you can touch them," Maggie said, seeing his interest. "Everybody wants to touch my fishes. They're not that valuable, go ahead."

Maggie spoke evenly, but she was screaming under her breath, *Make up something, quick!* Tell him the clients stiffed her, or stalled her. *They're fickle, they got buyer's remorse and wouldn't ante up.* Anything, just figure out how to hang on to the money. She still hadn't decided what to say, but here she stood, at the moment of reckoning, facing the collector.

"I was going to transfer the money over today," she said. And there it was, her decision made and sealed. "Didn't they tell you that?"

Bubba carefully removed a spiny object from a shelf; it might have been a blowfish. "I don't know. I'm just the courier. These aren't amulets of some kind, are they?"

"No, of course not. They're just for looking at. I try to get one whenever I go to Tijuana," she said. "There's this glass factory that's—"

"Off *Revolución* on one of them shadier side streets, right? Where you don't want to go alone." Bubba saw opportunity knocking.

"*On Revolución*, sort of," said Maggie. "Near the fronton—you know, the *jai alai* building?"

"Yeah. Sounds like you like it down there. Folks are strange about Baja," Bubba said in a lawman's preachy voice. "Did you know there's more than half the people live in San Diego won't go south of the border, not even to TJ? Think they're going to get their throats cut in the alley by some sorry-ass drug dealer or *cholo*. Shoot, it's as safe in Baja as—well, as it is right out here in El Cajon."

For a second Bubba thought he might get giddy at the cleverness of his own sick joke; he came up with a joke about as often as an ocean liner sinks.

"You sure it's all right to handle the fish?"

"Sure, I thought I said that about ten times already."

Maggie's dad started the glass collection for her nearly twenty years ago, on the first "birthday" of their adoption of her. He'd walked into the house with three hand-blown fishes. He contributed several more over the next few years but Maggie had built the menagerie when she would make the trip down with him and kept it up, much as she had kept the orphanage effort going once he climbed back inside that bottle. Because each of the statuettes had a flaw and sat unsold on the store's back shelves, she thought of them as her little adopted orphans. She thought of them like Minh, her dad's only real child who had been an orphan all his misled life.

"I've heard that word used before, *cholo*. What's it mean?"

Bubba stood tall so he wouldn't have to look up to meet her eyes. She had the long legs and wore the tight pants. The little innie button of her flat belly shined like a diamond between the halter and the pants, begging to be tickled. There wasn't even a tattoo or piece of metal piercing the belly button. She liked her body, and he liked that about any woman. He was getting nervous and knew he would have to excuse himself soon to pee.

"Ah, *cholo*'s another kind of bandit. Kind that lives off *pollos*. Lowest form of scumbag known to man. I know. I chase 'em day and night. Border Patrol."

Maggie shook her head. She didn't quite know how to take the man. He sounded like a lawman with that quick, droning drawl—"I know. I chase 'em."—but he seemed so open at the same time. She didn't think cops were like that, especially crooked cops, which he had to be.

"You sure got a load of 'em," Bubba said, turning back to the shelves of fishes. He lightly caressed another figurine, an octopus with seven delicate tentacles and an ink sac filled with multiple bright colors.

"How the hell they do this?" he said, studying the object.

"Something, huh? They're artists … How much do they want?"

Bubba continued examining the octopus as if admiring a thousand-carat diamond.

"All of it," he said. "The full eighty K."

"Shit," Maggie said out loud. "What makes them think I have that much?"

"They said you'd say it was less, but that you owe 'em eighty."

"But that doesn't even give me my commission." Maggie didn't want to whine, or cry. But she felt it coming.

Bubba remained cool. "You're right about these things. Blowing glass *is* an art. Man, this is off the heezy what you got here."

"So, you got a name?"

"Travis. What's yours?"

"You don't know? They didn't tell you my name?"

"Yeah, sure they did. I just meant what do you go by, what do you want me to call you?"

"We going to get to know each other or something?" Maggie said, working a flirt. She could tell he was interested in her. "I go by Maggie." She smiled crookedly and crossed her arms under her small breasts, forcing them to swell above the halter, show him little. She thought he would notice and he did. The cowboy quickly averted his eyes.

Bubba said, "Could I, ah—where's your head?"

"Bathroom?"

"I gotta go. Sorry."

"In there," Maggie said, grinning.

He stood over the toilet and looked around the modest bathroom. It didn't smell of high perfume like Roxanne's. She had photos hanging in the bathroom. Didn't photos wilt in the steam? The pictures were of kids and men, one of herself with an ore-colored Irish Setter with her holding its ears. Kind of like pictures hanging in the academy of LBJ pulling on the ears of his beagles. Bubba wondered who took the picture of her and the dog and who the men were in the other photos. He saw a pill bottle on the sink and picked it up. Vicodin. Prescribed by a Dr. K. Abbas seven months ago through the Veterans Administration Medical Center for John William Frazier. There weren't many tablets used out of a quantity of ninety.

~

In the living room, Maggie nibbled a cuticle and drew on a cig at the same time. She wanted to make a quick call to her dad for advice, and with that thought she almost burst into tears. There was really no one she could call. She would just have to think like her dad would. *You're going to have to give it back*, she could hear him tell her, as he had done the day before he died.

"Sorry," Bubba said, returning. He wrinkled his nose. "You a smoker, huh. Not good."

"I just hold 'em between my fingers," she said, stupidly. "So, what are *pollos*? Doesn't that mean 'chickens'?"

"In literal translation from the *español*, sure. But it's also slang. The *cholos* call them *pollos*. It's derogatory, they are their chickenshit prey. Peasants from the boondocks, meek and innocent people that don't know shit about sneaking into *el norte*; they don't know shit about any-thing. They give all the money they have in trust to these sorryass hus-tlers. They're only trying to get across the border to the good life and they get robbed and raped and murdered. Sometimes they get left in the desert to roast to death in the heat. Did you know there's been over 300 this season alone that died out there? Poor bastards."

"Were you there where those people died last week?" she asked, alert-ly.

"The ones locked up in that boxcar? Yep. They were locked in there on purpose, I guarantee you. And the scumbag that did it—well, let's just say he wished he hadn't."

Bubba was talking too much. He was doing it to avoid looking at her. It was hard not to. She was knockdown gorgeous. He grabbed and ogled a foot-long glass shark, holding it tight. He put it to the window light. The shark had gold zebra stripes that refracted into other colors as he rotated it, turning his eyes from blue to green and back again. A hump on its back was supposed to be a dorsal fin.

"A tiger shark, right?"

She didn't respond.

Bubba couldn't help himself; he looked at her. "Is something wrong?" he asked. "You look a little outta sorts, kinda worn out, if you don't mind me saying. The Vicodin ain't gonna help, you know."

"You snooped."

"The bottle was out."

"I've had a couple of rough days," she said. "That's how come I haven't sent them the money yet."

"I understand," Bubba said.

"I'll have to go get it, I don't have it here."

"Not a problem. You wanna do it now, get it over with?"

"That's fine. I need to feed Sally first. Do you mind waiting a minute?"

"Sally?" Bubba's face sank. "Don't tell me you have a kid?"

Maggie half-laughed at the notion. "I don't have a kid. It's just my dog. It won't take long."

"All right. I'll hang around with the fish."

Bubba watched from the back door. He still didn't want to know about her, maybe more than ever now that he'd met her. She went into a shack under a pepper tree, followed by the big bronze-colored dog, the one in the bathroom photograph. Bubba went back into the house.

He performed a cursory search of the small place, breezing through the dining room and into one of two bedrooms. He found a dirt-colored wig hanging on the closet door and considered that for a second. Maybe that other name, Sylvia something. There were more pictures on the dresser of the same man in the bathroom, maybe her boyfriend if she went for older men—in this picture the guy was in green fatigues that he knew weren't from either of the gulf wars, earlier than that.

He wondered about her. He swore to himself he wasn't going to get curious, but here he was, checking her out. He went into the kitchen and saw the newspaper. On the front page he saw what he didn't want to know. A man had been shot and killed at Cabrillo Lighthouse and the man, if her name was correct, was her father, the same name on the prescription bottle of pain killers. No wonder she'd taken them, he thought, and she had the right to light up, too. He wondered if she might have been suicidal, a thought that made him cringe despite that being the reason he was here. He just felt sorry for her at the moment, but he would get over that.

~

Maggie glanced back and saw the man standing in the back door. He filled up the frame, the way he stood. Thick limbs, head cocked, a thumb hooked in the belt loop, the other hand high on the door frame. Entering the dollhouse, she saw him turn back inside, as though to allow her a moment of privacy. Hard to figure him.

Maggie took a moment to pretend she was just a girl in her dollhouse, sitting in the small rocking chair with the only teddy she'd had. But now it embarrassed her. Maggie the girl had moved in and out of foster homes until she was eight, until John and Cloris took her in, then later adopted her. Some of those homes had five or six other children. No privacy. She would have liked to have children of her own, but everybody knew that orphans made the worst parents and that was why she resisted even the thought of it.

She didn't know what to do now. Pretend, she supposed. Just like she did in her job as Sylvia Fischer. She didn't pretend at the diner, in her regular life, she *was* real. She was getting like her dad, feeling sorry for herself. And look what happened to him.

She hastily put the ragged doll on a shelf. It took her just a moment getting the moneybox out of the cabinet. She fanned the bundles of $100 notes, fantasizing just for a sec. Silly stuff. But it was all she had now, those dying dreams. Maggie knew things were coming to some kind of head, maybe to an end. She did know this—nothing from here on out would be routine.

Bubba was in the living room when she came in carrying a silverware box.

"You keep your silver outside?"

"I don't own sliver," she said without humor. "Just some old stuff I've been meaning to bring in from the dollhouse—just thought of it now for some reason."

"Dollhouse? Huh … Cool."

"Let me clean the dog slobber off my shoes and I'll be ready."

"Go ahead."

In the kitchen she used a paper towel to wipe off one of her sneakers where Sally really had drooled. Then she dashed into her bedroom and transferred the clumpy units of bills from the box into a large purse and grabbed a jacket. She let Sally out back where she could curl up on the porch couch, even sleep through the night if need be. She returned to the living room.

"I haven't eaten and I'm starved," she said, working on a vague idea how she might keep some of the cash. "Could we go over to Jimbo's for something before we get the money?"

Bubba shrugged. "Don't see why not." At the front door, he stopped her. "Say, I got a better idea. How 'bout we go ahead and get the money, then hit TJ. Get yourself another fish trophy. I'll get one for myself. A couple hours is all it'll take … I'll spring for lunch, maybe we'll get fresh Baja *langosta*. How's that grab you?"

Maggie blushed for affect. She thought she might have the cowboy in the palms of her hands, and hence hang on to the money. It's what she had planned to do anyhow, hightail it to Baja, hide out with the hill Indians. Now, she would just have to deal with this cowboy "courier." Her eyes glinted with devilish and real excitement. "Only if I get to drive. I love to drive in TJ."

CHAPTER TWENTY-FOUR

Myers recalled a story he co-wrote with Tina Lubrano on an amnesty program the INS grudgingly proffered illegals in the late '80s, way back before they became ICE the cold nasty. Illegal immigrants working here as seasonal farm hands and those who could prove they'd been in the U.S. for the previous five years would be granted amnesty, all they had to do was step forward and register. "Amnesty." The word touches all kinds of nerves today resulting from September 11th, but wasn't such a negative back then. It was a major national reform policy. Myers' minor assignment, a fluff piece, had been to interview as many illegals as he could find who would talk. As he recalled from those interviews, the immigrants—mostly Mexican—and some native Central Americans, thought the program was a trick arranged by the snakes at Immigration to arrest and deport them. It took a lot of cajoling to convince many of them to accept that they could be naturalized after many years of running and hiding from *la migra*.

Myers listened to their grievances and doubts; he heard the question repeat itself: "Why they doin' this for?" Immigration officials didn't exactly roll out the red carpet either in their effort to welcome those hundreds of thousands of aliens who had snuck into the country fraudulently and would now get away with it. It humiliated the Service. Agents had to process these people *in,* the same ones they'd worked like hell trying to keep *out.* Every INS official Myers encountered was contemptuous of the amnesty program.

He'd written his piece with a playful bent, taking the migrant's superstitious point of view. He didn't have a personal beef back then. Today he did. Today he wanted to make amends for a man who died *because* of the snakes in the INS and the cold nasties at ICE.

His outrage included the needless death of that man's son, a half Viet-half American kid who spent his life trapped in an unyielding cultural divide. Minh's death, ironically like the boy's very life, resulted from the same poor judgment that put the country at war when war was a political and business choice and not a necessity—and not winnable. Even now, Vietnam had not stopped hurting people's lives; the same thing was being repeated now in the unacceptably high number of Iraq veterans' suicides. Vietnam was a place Myers himself had had the most personally affecting experiences of his own life, accounted for now, more than thirty years later, in a problem familiar to many returning soldiers, PTSD.

The Bureau of Immigration and Customs Enforcement took up most of the federal building's second story, the same downtown location as the old INS, on Front Street a stone's throw from Horton Plaza and the cool waters of today's sunny harbor. Myers checked in electronically and was escorted by an armed guard into a room with a plethora of gray desks, looking every bit to Myers like work stations in a sweatshop. Mother of all ironies. There were some semi-private booths and a couple of closed-off executive offices. Myers headed to the one marked "Assistant Director" and entered. A secretary had her own little office and he stopped in front of her desk.

"I called earlier, Myers? I am in the right place, aren't I?"

"From the *Journal*?" said the woman, a middle-aged, middleweight lady who appeared pleasant enough. "It just so happens Mr. Mendez has had back to back cancellations. I can let you see him. I'll let him know you're here."

Myers nodded courteously. He stayed on his feet, took a few step one way and then the other, then stopped. Masking an attitude, he sat down and waited like a prim little unbiased reporter.

The secretary took her time to show Myers to the only other door. He stepped through it. The glare from double windows made it hard to distinguish the features of the man sitting behind the desk. That man enjoyed a commanding view of the twin-tower Federal Detention Center across a concrete and mature green plaza. The quietness of the office stood in marked contrast to the labor force in the big room just the other side of the movable wall.

The man's desk begged a new term for cleanliness. Spit-shined would have to do. A long, thin, gold-plated nameplate facing Myers read, "Mr. Ignacio Ricardo Mendez Salazar."

Without looking up the man motioned Myers to take a seat. Myers stood where he was. The assistant director was coming into focus now and Myers could see he wasn't making eye contact and that put Myers off; the guy would be a challenging interview. Which of course is what he expected. These types always were, he'd found. Always passing the buck, never responsible.

He studied the man, Mr. Mendez or Mr. Salazar, he wasn't sure which he would go by. He had the gray-winged black hair of Ricardo Montalban, a groomed, beefy physique and, when Myers got a glimpse of them, dead black eyes.

Myers didn't like anything about him, even though he liked Ricardo Montalban. He said, "It's going to take up a lot of precious space using all those names when I quote you. Which one do you prefer?"

"Mendez … You're with the *Journal*, Freida says." Myers was pleased to see that Mendez tossed an attitude right back at him, which would make the interview cozier. "What can I do for you? Myers, was it?"

"You'll not want to talk to me, but you had better," Myers said , his tone flat, rude even. He gave the man a glimpse of his press card.

"Is that a fact. And why might that be?"

"You don't read the paper? … You remember John Frazier, the man who was shot and killed yesterday at Cabrillo?"

Mendez came out of his chair. He made a more imposing figure standing, about six-two, two hundred plus. "Of course! *Myers*. You were the reporter out there. The one who didn't get his facts straight."

He seemed to study the reporter as if deciding whether he could throw a hundred ninety pounds through the window. He didn't come around the desk to try.

"I haven't finished that story," Myers said and inched closer. "You might say I've just got started. I'm trying to clear up some things about Frazier that I think indirectly caused that shooting. I think you—your department—can help me do that."

The assistant director lifted a suspicious eyebrow that seemed to lack curiosity. "Maybe, what things?"

"About the Amerasian son he tried for years to get immigrated."

The look turned amused. "That's ancient history. We don't make those decisions here, anyway. You're in the wrong department, you need to go over to State, talk to the people in Consular."

"Been there," Myers said tersely and not exactly truthfully. But he figured records didn't move just because the acronym changed. "I'm not in the wrong department, Mr. Mendez, you and I both know it. Frazier's case got bounced around for a whole lot of years, decades, so it shouldn't be hard to run down. You aren't going to tell me you wished you could be of help, are you?"

Mendez appeared bored now. "You people in the press. You take every little exception to the norm and blow it out of proportion. You distort things you don't know anything about. Well, I'll tell you, friend, obtaining an immigrant visa is a long, complicated process and any number of things can cause delays, even preclusion."

"You'd have to admit yourself that two decades is a little excessive," Myers said. "The boy could have easily immigrated from the time the Amerasian Homecoming Act took effect. You recall that, of course. They immigrated those youngsters by the thousands. All that was needed was for the child to *look* part American. It was a rubber-stamped process. What happened to Frazier's son? That's all I want to know, Mr. Mendez. You clear that up and I'll be on my way."

Mendez took it in stride, the practiced bureaucrat. He seemed to hold back a yawn. "I can't answer that, Mr. Myers. The consulate over there would have processed him. Certainly they would no longer have records. But I can assure you that back then the agency granted citizenship to legitimate immigrants. Along with refugees, distant relatives, even re-education camp detainees. Understand I said *legitimate*. That's the operative word."

Myers wasn't giving up. "Frazier had a case worker, maybe he still works here. A person named Rhoades? You know that person, Mr. Mendez?"

Mendez checked his wristwatch. "That's all the time I have for you, Mr. Myers. But you are welcome to schedule another appointment."

Myers took one step closer, his face now over the edge of the glass-covered spit-shined desk. "I could do that. I can leave now and call your boss in Washington, find out why a decorated veteran of an American war was refused family immigration for his birth child. The public doesn't like its soldiers getting shafted, not anymore, Mr. Mendez. My editors live for stories like this. 'Purple Heart survivor loses son and commits suicide after decades of continued denials for custody by Immigration.' Does that paint a picture you'd like to see?"

The color darkened on Mendez's face. Myers had gotten to him. But Mendez said nothing. He was used to confrontation. Then, the assistant director shook his head and turned perfunctory. Easing back into his chair, he pushed a button on his phone and said tiredly, "Freida, would you please run a search on—just a minute."

He cupped the phone and said to Myers, "What's his full name?"

"John William. The boy's name is Minh something."

Mendez spoke into the phone, "John William Frazier, child's name is Minh, Viet. Check post-Vietnam records. Pronto, Freida. Thank you."

Myers didn't move. He was an unwanted fixture in the man's private sanctum.

It took no time for Freida to tap and enter through the door. She carried a single-page print out that she handed to her boss and started to leave.

Mendez looked at the paper, then quickly said, "Send in Rhoades, please."

"Yes, sir."

Myers' eyes flared.

Mendez continued in his mechanical manner. "According to this," he said, "Frazier completed the I-130 in May of 1985 and in September of that year a Le Nue Nyugen applied for the visa petition with the consulate general in Ho Chi Minh City. She was the mother. That was before the Amerasian Homecoming Act." He shot Myers a smug glance. "So they would have been petitioning under the Amerasian Immigration Act that preceded it. It seemed to be moving along—I don't see ... "

There was another soft knock on the door and a rotund man with long hair entered, tie askew. Tall and straight for a hefty man, he exuded a sense of humility, not your typical Immigration field agent, who looked nasty, intimidating, Myers thought. A pair of black bushy eyebrows hadn't so much sprouted above his eyes as they had landed there, twin caterpillars that now crawled up the forehead with uncertainty as to why he'd been called into the chief's office. He tried a little smile on Myers and Myers decided he liked the man.

"Agent Sidney Rhoades," Mendez said, less as an introduction than routing information. "Mr. Myers is from the *Journal*. He's here about a man named John Frazier, the one killed by the police at Cabrillo. He wants to know—"

"Mind if I ask myself?" Myers interrupted. "It's what I do."

Myers turned to the big man. "You played football or basketball. Basketball, right?" he asked.

The question seemed to take Rhoades by surprise. He blushed. "Well, ah, yes, I did. Pitt."

"Panthers. Forward?"

"Yeah—"

"If there are *pertinent* questions ... " Mendez broke in, and let it trail. He appeared to direct the comment toward Rhoades.

The big man seemed to shrink when his boss spoke. "Uh, I'll have to check my files."

Myers frowned. "Tell you what, that's okay." He sensed the man's reluctance, more likely fear, and didn't want him lying to Myers. "I'll call you later today," Myers said, "give you a chance to check your files."

Mendez spoke, "Now, if that's all ... "

Rhoades seemed grateful, glad to get out of there.

Myers wasn't satisfied. He let the big guy pass him and exit, then he faced Mendez again.

"Perhaps we could get together down the road to discuss another subject your agency might know something about," he said. "Smuggling. I'd like to do a piece sometime on trafficking operations across the border. I'm thinking in particularly of some infants disappearing in Ocotillo Wells recently, the same ones Frazier mentioned to me up in that lighthouse before they shot him. Ties not in any small part to his story. What do you think? Could you offer any insight into that subject?"

Without expecting it Myers saw that he got to him and good. He had baited and hooked him when Myers was mostly being the curious snoop. The Assistant Director stiffened, turned brittle.

Then he did something Myers found very peculiar. He took two Chinese silver balls from his desk drawer and began to rub and rotate them in his hand. Reminded Myers of Bogart as Queeg in *The Caine Mutiny*. It wouldn't have surprised Myers to see the man start sweating and pull on an earlobe, twitch a watery eye. Something about him was unsavory. More than annoyance, it seemed to Myers, Mendez was worried.

"Not likely, friend … I'm going to let this go as a bad day," he replied. Evidently, palming the silver balls calmed him. "But if you persist with the same kind of irresponsible conduct and inaccurate writing, I'll personally talk to your publisher, Mrs. Compton. You don't want that."

Myers pointing a cocked finger at him and made a soft "pow" sound, as if to fire off a round, right between his eyes. "Give the old broad my regards."

He left partially gratified though with nothing he could write about. Not yet.

He looked around but didn't spot Agent Rhoades anywhere in the sweatshop. He rode the escalator down. Standing at the bottom, the rotund man stared up at Myers from under eyebrows plucked off the face of Sam Donaldson.

"You wanna get some lunch and talk?" he said.

CHAPTER TWENTY-FIVE

Sidney Rhoades went for the carnitas platter, the largest meal served at the Old Town Mexican Cafe. A waitress of Mexican descent in a brilliant, sweeping costume took their order. He started off with a margarita, salt and tall. Myers ordered two fish tacos a la carte and water. No booze on the job.

Rhoades hadn't eaten since breakfast, he said, only coffee, lots of coffee. It was now pushing two o'clock.

A waiter wearing the standard white tight-collared shirt, also Mexican, served up a bowl of warm chips and *salsa fresca*. Rhoades dug in. His caterpillars expressed exalted pleasure, crawling upward by degrees of sensual abandon with every salsa-laden chip.

Myers placed John Frazier's old snapshot on the table facing Rhoades. "What can you tell me about these kids, if anything?"

Rhoades wiped his hands on a paper napkin and picked up the photograph. Then he looked at Myers.

"I am going to talk to you but I am going to ask that you don't identify me," Rhoades said. "Too close to retirement. Too much to lose."

"They can't fire you in government work, next to impossible."

Rhoades chirped out a small laugh. "Maybe not, but things could get real bad for me."

Myers said, "'Anonymous source close to the investigation'—which I'd already intended to make it. Now, can you identify these boys?"

"Buster's in the middle, the tall one. The others are orphans as well—his pals. They're all *bùi dôi*, children of the dust," he said. "John showed me several shots of these boys. The kids stuck together for their own protection."

"How can you recall this boy that easily? Was his case special in some way?"

"A little."

"Buster, huh?"

"That's what John nicknamed Minh, after Buster Brown—you know, the chubby blond kid in the Dutch cap with the bulldog? In the shoe?"

He spoke affectionately and grinned looking at the picture. Then he handed it back to Myers.

Myers looked again at the wispy figures in the snapshot and said, shaking his head, "I don't see the resemblance."

"Of course not, that was the point," the portly man said. "Crazy, huh? It was a thing to put off the Vietnamese authorities."

"Authorities of the orphanage, or re-education camps?"

"I'll tell you the story … "

A large chip dripping with salsa pulled a disappearing act behind Rhoades' large hand, followed by another chip without salsa. He chewed fast and chased it with a long sip from the salt-rimmed, blue-tinted icy margarita. Myers watched him with wet lips.

"First, let me tell you that your article was moving. Even when it cuts the agency pretty good. Which it rightly should have—we aren't exactly exempt from John's loss. And then you come down in person to give Ahab grief. Good for you, he needs it."

Myers shrugged, as he did when complimented. He eyed the chips and salsa; but that was all, just eyed it. Working lately on improving his overall health, less booze, minimum sodium, less carbs, less carbonation, less everything worth tasting. More tennis, more running, more pain. Generally speaking, newspaper people were slovenly even though they were on the run, and then had to work harder than most to hold a fit look. Of course, avoiding the bars a little more would help. Newspaper writers, at least of the old school, died around the life expectancy age. That was 75 latest count—and counting down.

He watched Rhoades finish off the tequila drink and lick salt halfway around the rim of the glass. After that Rhoades said, "John first petitioned about fifteen years ago, or longer, after World Vision notified him of the boy's existence. The new Hanoi government sent Buster and his mother to a re-education camp in the 70s. Later they moved Minh to an orphanage in Quang Tri, up around Hue, probably where your picture was taken. Tell by the thick luster of the foliage. She wouldn't see her son again until 1983 or '84. That's when she started the search for his father. She wanted a better life for her socially ostracized son."

Lunch was served. They brought Rhoades' on three plates and he went at it, spreading chunky strings of roasted pulled pork on a six-inch corn tortilla, sprinkling it with cilantro, chopped onion and dried oregano. Then he smothered the contents with green salsa and half-rolled the tortilla. He prepared and rolled three before starting on the first one. Myers took absolute delight watching a man who so enjoyed eating.

"John wasn't sick then, alcoholic sick," Rhoades said between bites. "He didn't yet have a mental history. In my opinion, it wasn't PTSD alone that started him spiraling down. It was the series of disappointments after discovering he had a son he couldn't reach. I watched him grow more and more depressed. It showed on him. He went in the ER a couple of times that I know about, dehydrated, ulcers, overdosed. None of that helped his cause."

"Can they deny a family visa because of a mental or medical condition?"

"Not unless there's some criminal element involved … I guess you could say the paperwork could not keep up with the movement of all the people involved."

Rhoades spoke apologetically, as if the problem had been his fault. "Once the mother put in a visa request, the government relocated Minh to another camp. I don't know the full story of the mother, but I know she was John's girlfriend and that she worked for the U.S. military when the two met. Many Viets worked for the American military during the war, but the communists considered her a dissident even after her so-called rehabilitation. It was because she had a half-breed child. They made her life miserable."

Myers frowned. "There's your reason, but I'm still confused. Since Minh was Amerasian and a social outcast, he was a walking reminder of the aggression we perpetrated on them. Why wouldn't the new government want him gone?"

"Oh, they did. But they also wanted to punish the mother, whom they saw as a nonconformist. So they interned Minh in one camp after another as they saw fit."

"Couldn't the consulate have done something for Minh under the McCain Amendment?"

Rhoades shook his head. "He wasn't over twenty-one." The black caterpillars leaped up as the second tortilla approached his mouth, his eyes growing in anticipation. He held Myers off with a hand while he chewed.

"Those kids," he said after swallowing, "are detainees of re-education camps who originally weren't qualified on the first go round. There are some five hundred such cases that we still have on the books. Also, it was relatively recent that the consulate general in Ho Chi Minh City started processing visas. But of course by then it was too late for Minh and pretty much all the remaining Amerasian orphans."

Myers started on his second taco, now using a fork, leaving the tortilla, even though it was corn.

Rhoades waved to the waitress for another cactus drink, the big one, he indicated. Myers thought about joining him. Not good.

"What finally broke John's spirit," said Rhoades, "was all the money he wasted on traffickers who kept ripping him off—thousand of dollars over time. And when he finally met Buster, the boy wanted nothing to do with him. His father was the enemy, the camps had trained him well. John gave up after that."

"He had to have trusted you."

"We could have expedited the case," Rhoades said, shaking his head. "Buster got lost and turned up later in Bangkok. I heard he was killed in some kind of gang war … Just a sad story."

"Then you kept track of the boy?" Myers said. "Even after Frazier gave up?"

Rhoades shrugged his shoulders.

The margarita arrived in a glass the waitress had to carry with both hands; it was the largest one they served as an individual drink, twenty-two ounces in a heavy birdbath glass. Rhoades gulped about a third of it. He might have been getting a little tight by now, though for a man his size, it didn't show.

"Listen, Mr. Myers, there's something might help make this story even better," Rhoades said.

Myers didn't respond; he routinely showed disinterest in tips because they often turned out to be something personal, like a vendetta.

"John did business in Baja that wasn't just turning imported baskets," Rhoades said, as if he might be offering something for sale.

"If he was smuggling dope, not interested," Myers said.

"No, no, nothing like that." Rhoades looked surprised. "It's this: He and his daughter had an arrangement with an Indian tribe that ran some kind of refugee center for abandoned children. He bought his crafts from them."

"Interesting. Sounds peculiar, though."

"Yeah. I never went down there. He just said it was a village where—I guess it was mainly Maggie, his daughter—where she would arranged placement for the kids they get. She used to be a facilitator for an adoption agency, I believe. John told me; he was real proud of his daughter for that."

Myers straightened. This was the most compelling thing Rhoades had told him. "You know where these people are, where their village is?"

"Not sure," the big man said, finishing up the last pork-laden tortilla.

Myers tidied up with the napkin—fidgeting, actually—while waiting for Rhoades to finish, which didn't take long. Myers was glad to see he didn't lick his plate. His last wife did that.

Rhoades said, "I suspect the reservation's in the mountains outside Ensenada. John once mentioned Hussong's—"

"A saloon. I know the joint," Myers said. "I don't see a notorious bar having anything to do with deserted babies—unless it's something illegal."

"Who knows, but it's where one of the Indians draws quick-sketch charcoals of tourists. John mentioned him, sounded like a colorful character."

"This Indian got a name?"

"Probably. But that's all I can tell you. Talk to John's daughter. She would be your source on that."

Myers nodded. "Thanks, I'll check it out … I'm still interested in your *Ahab*, how Mendez came about getting that moniker. He aware of it?"

Rhoades shook his head slowly. "Richard Mendez doesn't give a hoot about refugees from any Third World country—unless the applicant has a stand-out resumé. He'll push through only the elite from advanced Rim countries like South Korea and Taiwan. Looks good on his sheet; the bastard's motivation is purely selfish. He wants the directorship of Western. Wants to conquer that white whale, be the great rat dictator of the west. He won't, though, the guy's xenophobic."

The cactus juice had loosened his tongue. Cocktails do their job assisting reporters.

"I can see you're fond of your boss."

He made a face. "We administer decisions about people's lives, often life-and-death ones; Ahab administers himself. He's obsessed with himself, just like the mythical Ahab. He's cold-blooded, got no conscience, no soul."

Myers smiled easily shifting subjects, "You work in any way with other kinds of adoptions?"

"I have. Good work, means something. But now? Now they got me stuck doin' real important stuff," he said. "You know, going after nannies and maids, real tough work."

"I thought ICE had stopped busting nannies, with all the emphasis now on the borders," Myers commented. "That really what they got you doing?"

"Hell, yeah. I've been an agent twenty-three years. After lunch I'm headed out to run in another little old lady," Rhoades said and sniggered. "Never mind the cases that *really* need working—your immigrants stuck in La Mesa prison awaiting trial, for instance. Families separated for months, sometimes years, because we can't move on their cases. No-oo, we're too busy out busting old granny maids."

"Mendez' orders?"

"That's right."

"You ever thought of getting out of the racket? Sounds like you could be doing something better with yourself," said Myers.

"Yeah, but there's this little thing called retirement benefits."

A sudden gleam came into the senior agent's eyes. He edged over the table closer to Myers. "Say, you like, you can come along. Make a dynamite story—another courageous, humanitarian act by ICE."

Myers thought about it. "Be fun."

"A cartoon."

CHAPTER TWENTY-SIX

Madelene Schaefer cracked opened a south window in baby Connie's bedroom and the delicate sea gull mobile tingled on the drift of a not too cool afternoon breeze. The baby slept like a baby.

She leaned over the crib to sneak a peek. Then she decided to pick Connie up. The baby opened its eyes wide, bunched its tiny face into a wad of wrinkled skin and broke into a piercing wail. She certainly has good lungs, thought Madelene.

"There, there, little one. You want your bottle now? Okay, we'll just take a walk and find you some delicious warm milk."

Madelene felt awkward and self-conscious, even frustrated cooing over the baby. But you had to talk to them, let them know you're here, reassure them. Consuela would need reassuring. God knows what she had gone through in her short three or four or five months of life. Madelene didn't even know the day of her daughter's birth. She hadn't looked at the paperwork. But she would get around to picking a date that she liked anyway, one with a good star. Poor baby couldn't have had much tenderness or affection how ever old she was, which explained why she started crying soon as Madelene touched her. Yes, having a baby was going to take some getting used to.

Soon as she heard the baby cry, Mrs. Ruvalcaba warmed the bottle and brought it to Madelene in the living room. Madelene sat in the new rocker. She stuck the bottle's nipple between Connie's puckered lips and watched the child suck as if totally starved.

The sound of the door chimes startled Madelene who inadvertently jerked the nipple from Connie's mouth—which she quickly reinserted. She was still jumpy over the fear of losing her child, particularly so after a man with a squeaky voice she thought was imitating that cuddly little author, Truman Capote, phoned and threatened to take Connie back if she didn't answer his questions truthfully. The man said he was a lawyer with the firm contracted by her adoption agency, and that she would not get into any trouble telling the truth. He just wanted to know if she had paid the money; he didn't really seem to care all that much about Connie. Madelene didn't want to get her agent Sylvia into trouble, but neither was she about to lose this baby. She told him the honest-to-God truth. Yes, she had paid in full.

Now, seeing Villi dwarfed by two big men at the front door, the housekeeper's elbows akimbo spelling defiance, Madelene was frightened into a state of physical weakness. She froze in place and concentrated solely on not dropping baby Connie.

"What you want?" Mrs. Ruvalcaba had just asked the men. "You not here about that baby, I know."

Oh, God! Madelene thought, and rushed to the door before the woman gave the whole thing away.

"Villarmini Ruvalcaba?" Sidney Rhoades asked in a voice like a song. "Are you she?"

"She who? So what I am. Who are *you?*"

"Just a minute, please," Madelene said, bumping Villi to move her over. She intended to sound authoritative but was anything but. She held Connie tightly in the fold of her arm and rocked sideways, which only exaggerated her apprehension. "Can I help you gentlemen with something?"

"I'm sorry, are you Madelene Schaefer?"

"Why? Ah, yes, I am. But—"

"I'm sorry, ma'am … My name is Sidney Rhoades. I'm with Immigration and Customs and I've come—"

Villi stumble backwards, as if blasted by a shotgun. Myers moved in a flash to catch her if she decided to faint. She didn't, but she had given away the truth of her illegality, sure as rain.

"Oh my *God,*" Madelene snapped, herself just short of collapsing into a cold faint. *The ICE.* She, of course, thought they were here to take Connie—and throw her in jail.

"Christ," mumbled Rhoades, who hadn't completely sobered up from his margarita lunch. He backed away from the door, wearily, as if to regroup for another approach—or just to forget it and leave. Myers wasn't sure which.

It was a noteworthy scene for a sober newshound like Myers, who glanced among them all, taking mental notes of reactions and trying to piece together connections and relationships and thoughts. He could easily assume the gloomy thoughts of Mrs. Ruvalcaba, with "illegal" written all over her. She was an innocent. But the homeowner's overreaction led him to notice the baby clutched in her arm, dramatically clutched as if to protect the child from the world's evils. Not to mention the maid's initial outburst about their assumed interest in the baby. He thought Rhoades might be leaning toward leaving the housekeeper in peace. It was an exhibition, a situation Myers was thinking might just make a lively little story. At least in concept if not in fact—the names have been changed to protect the innocent and the guilty because everyone is both.

Myers broke in to say, "I'm with the *Journal*. Ray Myers. But don't let that make you assume anything one way or the other."

He looked at the housekeeper and grinned. "I don't think Agent Rhoades is going to take you away. Isn't that right, Mr. Rhoades?"

Rhoades nodded and then smiled. "That's right, ma'am," he said, addressing Madelene. "I'm just going to say in my report that Mrs. Ruvalcaba is unlocatable—I do love that word—that there is no one at this address who's working illegally. Furthermore, I did not see the baby you're holding—Thai descent, I believe?—and would consequently have no reason to ask to inspect either a visa or adoption papers. Or anything else related to any breech of U.S. policy."

"My baby is perfectly legitimate, sir," Madelene said defensively, missing or passing over Rhoades' magnanimous intent to leave all in peace. "And Connie is Filipino, not Thai."

"This a *beautiful* baby," said Villi, also the defensive tone.

Myers said, "What do you think, Mr. Rhoades? Should we take our leave now?"

Rhoades never opened his brief.

Myers handed Madelene his card. "Can I contact you later?"

He was glad he'd come along for the ride; the woman was hiding and the snoop in him wanted the skinny.

CHAPTER TWENTY-SEVEN

"South of the Border ... Ooh-yeah, down Mexico way. Du du du du du du."

Bubba's crooning wasn't half bad, he decided. He felt spirited; going south did that to him despite the barbs of his occupation. For the moment he'd put aside the other thing—the ungodly reason for coming south of the border.

He reclined in the front seat of the woman's old Buick, feeling safe with her behind the wheel, even admiring her driving skills and fearlessness. Tijuana's bustle didn't intimidate this lady in the least.

"They are trying real hard to die," Maggie said to him, speaking of the pedestrians dashing every which way across a big intersection. She grinned at him—like a she-wolf, he thought. A come on. He grinned back with more admiration.

Maggie wheeled onto *Avenida Revolución* from *Calle 6*, which she'd taken after bypassing the loop-de-loop freeway. Bubba figured she'd taken the locals' route to impress him of her expert's knowledge of the streets of TJ. It did, but she hit *Revolución* two blocks short of her destination, into stalled traffic.

"Darn, it's been so long," she said. He gave her credit for admitting it; *he* wouldn't have.

"Don't worry, I'm enjoying the ride. It ain't often I get down here that I don't have to drive myself. And not usually for pleasure—uh ... "

Bubba shut up and gazed at the people and the shops, noting how much the town kept changing. Working the U.S. side of the border, the fences and arroyos, he hadn't actually been in the city proper in some time. There were cobblestone streets and ceramic-tiled inlaid sidewalks. Like a Chula Vista shopping mall, he thought disapprovingly. Here was an upstairs glitzy Hollywood disco joint over a row of colorful curios and there another Kentucky Fried Chicken, two of them just a block apart. He spotted a five-member mariachi band waddling along the spiffy new sidewalk and thought to himself, "There's the old TJ." But even though the men were all potbellied except the kid of the group, their sequined black-and-silver suits were clean and creased.

"Jesus, would you look at those guys," he said to Maggie. "Their pants are *pressed*, for chrissake. Looks like the Lawrence Walk Band."

Maggie glanced at him and chuckled. "Welk, Lawrence *Welk* Band."

"Yeah, I know, they just sway like 'em."

There weren't many tourists due to the saturation and exaggeration by the media up north of the rampant gangland slayings, hanging up headless corpses across the city these days. Which made the drive even more leisurely.

"Shoot. Even with all the changes," he said, waving a hand to include everything on both sides of the street and the street itself, "this town *still* has it. You can feel it, can't you? And smell it. I love that smell. It's like magic on the air."

"It ain't Disneyland," Maggie responded, "but, yeah, it's still got it. Something—freedom, adventure, wickedness. Makes you wanna just let go, huh?"

Bubba said, "Hell yeah, that's what I'm talkin about."

Then Maggie nodded toward some street urchins. Her mouth flipped suddenly downward, as if seized by some unpleasant news. "Look at them. It breaks my heart, all these lost children. Where do they go at night? Who's there to take care of them?"

"They're scrappers, they survive just fine."

"They're not so tough. They're only kids."

"You serious?"

"Sure I'm serious. I feel so sorry for them."

"Jeeze, Maggie—is that all right, I mean that I call you Maggie?"

"Sure."

"All that's wrong with these so-called poor orphaned kids, Maggie, is what us gringos make of it. We're the ones think the world's in shambles, everybody dying from terrorist acts, uprisings, world economic instability, floods and mosquito bites and famine. We're afraid of birds, for chrissake. I'm not saying all that ain't true. But people—human beings— are tough as nails. That's how come we ain't gone the way of the coo coo.

It's us gringos who aren't so tough, what with all our fears. So we think nobody else is either."

"Well. Mr. Philosophy … But not the children, the orphans. They need love and caring for, they're still innocent. Hey, there it is."

Bubba looked where she looked, at the large painted window of the Inco Glass Factory storefront. "Let's go get you a fish, then," he said.

He had been serious about letting her get herself a glass fish for her collection. Where's the harm in that? It was just extending the inevitable, even as he felt terrible at the thought. She had been a good sport so far, caused no problems; she hadn't pulled any punches about the money. She even seemed relieved to tell him they could skip going to the bank, that the cash was in the purse that lay right there on the seat between them. Eighty thousand smackers, minus a few bucks for personals, you know, she'd said. He thought about not even counting it; that was how much he wanted to believe her.

On the way down they had talked some. Bubba tried to avoid anything personal. As she sped south he took as long as he could to count the cash, just to keep his mind from the unpleasant job ahead. It didn't work. She shed some tears telling him about her father, that he had been such a loser, that she dreaded seeing her so-called mother at the funeral. Maybe she'd just skip the funeral. The woman wasn't her real mother, she'd said, and they had a long-standing mutual hatred for one another. That left her with nobody, Bubba learned, and he felt pity begin to form down there in his otherwise merciless heart. That was not good.

She told him about the mom-and-pop import business her dad worked for in Old Town and that she would travel with him into the mountains to purchase pottery and jewelry from some Indians, and then Bubba felt sorry for *him*, her dead dad.

By then they'd crossed the border and were heading into town.

On the corner stood the picturesque jai alai fronton arena. Bubba had been to a game or two. It was the world's fastest ball game, played with a rubber ball hurled by a wicker scoop against a wall at 150 miles per hour by players who were trying to kill their opponents; some had been killed by the *cesta*, others only blinded and crippled. But it still wasn't as violent as American football and ultimate fighting where you also try to kill your opposition.

Maggie wheeled the wagon into a pay lot behind Tijuana Tilly's. She wasn't afraid to carry that much money on her shoulder down the streets where drive-by killings took place. No fear. Bubba was fascinated. He paid the attendant and they crossed the street, passing at least five eateries with strong and delicious aromas, including the outdoor area of Tilly's right there. With only the Cheerios under his belt, Bubba was starved.

"You wanna eat first?" he asked Maggie, who shook her head.

"How about after?"

"Sure."

The glass factory's showroom featured shelf after dusty shelf of human-blown glass objects, all shapes and sizes. There were glass crucifixes, glass nativity scenes, glass Virgin Marys, glass flowers, glass animals, even glass cathedrals and glass hacienda-style houses. There was a wall of wine and tumbler glasses and tables of colorful clay plates and bowls. Thousands of items. But no glass fishes.

"Where's the fish?" Bubba said after a while, disappointed for Maggie.

No one seemed to be around. Bubba shot a furtive eye about and thought not unlike one from the other side of the law would think—hell, just take what you want and leave. Except there were no glass fish to take. He sure didn't want a figurine of Mary Magdalene.

"Maybe I was the only person who ever bought them," Maggie said. "They might've stopped making them when I stopped coming back. But they'll blow one if we ask. C'mon, the kilns are in back. That's the fun part anyway, watching them create their art."

Bubba noticed the supple movement of her buttocks in the tight pedal pushers as she walked on ahead, the titillating display of bronze skin between halter and pants. Bubba wasn't at the moment thinking of Roxanne in her curlers reading a dime store novel, Trixie and Dixie on her lap, gurgling like little piglets.

He followed her through a double door and down a darkened hallway with more dusty merchandise and then along another hall that was narrow with nothing on the wall. The passage led to an alley covered by a tin canopy and into a drab concrete building. Inside was a huge open area that was hot and clamorous.

Maggie kept the big purse squeezed in tight under her arm.

She stopped in front of an empty viewing gallery. Bubba stood close behind her. On the floor men busily orchestrated ten-foot rods weighted at the far end with molten, glowing glass. Using scissors they snipped off whole segments of the softened substance, pinched and twisted remnants with metal tongs into the shape of some figure that took form before their eyes. At this point Bubba wasn't paying too much attention to the glass blowers.

Maggie tilted back until her head touched the rim of Bubba's cowboy hat. Did she want him to make a move on her? Bubba wondered, hands ready by her sides. The moment was saucy. Time slowed as the two of them stood close while dark muscular men naked to the waist slip their long metal rods in and out of the burning-hot kilns, their chests swelling then blowing life through the rods into fluid glass.

Maggie nestled her hips closer against him and turned her head sideways and spoke, casting her eyes slightly down, coquettishly, and almost touched his lips with hers.

"There something, aren't they, Travis?"

Bubba forced himself to look at the sweaty young men at the smoldering kilns. The blasts and roar from the furnaces were so loud and mesmerizing he could barely hear her voice. He gave in, deserting the pressures of restraint that so far had kept him going. He put his fingers on the soft part of her arms, then glimpsed from her lips down over her shoulder to the rise and fall of her perfect breasts, the curves of flesh, the hint of nipples straining under stretched linen.

"Call me Bubba, Maggie," he said, sucking back saliva before it dripped onto her shoulder.

Maggie kept her eyes on his lips, milking the moment for all she could. She let the double syllables of the name roll off her tongue, bubble over her lips. "Bubba. Bub-ba ... I like it, Cowboy."

The purse didn't shift an inch under her arm.

CHAPTER TWENTY-EIGHT

Myers sensed it soon as he stepped out of the elevator, and he knew it for certain entering the newsroom. The grim hush that fell over the room told him. Those cheery, gung-ho faces that received him just yesterday had made a U-turn to pity.

Undaunted, he strode on to his station, anxious to get on the story that would hack away at the Achilles of the giant called Immigration. The story would of course get watered down if not trashed altogether, but that wasn't going to deter him. What was it the poet said, "The bigger they are, the harder they fall"?

Rita, the managing editor's secretary, had left the confirming note on his desk. It read: "L.C. wants you **IMMEDIATELY!**" the last word underlined twice just in case bold caps didn't rouse him into action.

Myers sighed, got up, walked past Rita, who mouthed, "He's mad as hell!" and entered the managing editor's smoky cubicle. He started to close the door before the shouting began but didn't since he wanted to breath at least some unpolluted air. He hadn't fooled himself; he knew what was coming.

L.C. took a couple of puffs off a fresh Merit and came forward in his chair.

"You're finished, Myers," he shouted. He was mad as hell.

"Welcome back," Myers said. His eyes were lidded. "You do any downhill in the Rockies? Bumps?"

The heavyset M.E. might have competed in the big-splash belly-flop contest, but there was no way he could maneuver his three-hundred pounds of soft flab around on skis, much less over moguls.

He ignored Myers' mockery. "You know who called me this afternoon? Got any idea? ... " Oddly, he stopped, appearing to study Myers.

Myers brought his hands from around his back where his fingers were intertwined prayer-like, although he had not been praying. His hands got in the way in moments of nervousness.

"Lady Gargoyle?" said Myers. He thought about sitting. Maybe L.C. would flip his cigarette at him and Myers could sue. Maybe he would sue anyway for cross breathing in a tight chamber full of carcinogens. Cigarette and cigar smoking was supposedly prohibited in private office buildings as well as everywhere else. America's Finest was shooting for a smoke-free city.

The managing editor eased back in his chair, tapping a finger on the desk, as was his habit when aggravated. "What happened down there?"

"Down where?"

"Don't mess with me, goddamnit. At ICE."

Myers shrugged in an effort to plead innocent of wrongdoing. "You're talking about *Señor* Mendez, the man was a hostile interview. I hardly pushed him."

"What made him hostile?"

"You kidding? By association; he works for *ICE*. Immigration's been our fodder for—forever. I have to explain that to the editor-in-chief?"

L.C. shook his head. "God and Magic Myers—one and the same."

Myers stepped forward. "If ever there was a bureaucrat needing bad press, it's that guy, Mendez. His own people hate him. Hell, the field agents call him 'Ahab.' I kid you not. He's paranoid; but that ain't all, he's xenophobic—high official in the business of processing foreigners and the man *hates* foreigners. He's fucked up, L.C. Not unlike the well known sea captain of yore."

"Shut up, Myers. The publisher wants your resignation—"

"And I thought it was only you all this time. I am hurt."

"But I told her that wasn't good enough; I suggested she fire you instead … She finally agreed."

The M.E. grinned bitterly and blew more smoke at Myers. His office would have made a wonderful set piece for a heart or lung disease commercial. Camera pans in on stubby fingers mashing out a cigarette in a hubcap ashtray containing thirty-seven Merit butts. Some wheezing sounds, some phlegmy coughing perhaps. A digital clock next to the hubcap indicates it's just past noon, suggesting a heavy smoker, an excellent high-risk candidate for early heart congestion or stroke. Is this you?

It gave comfort to Myers who gave up the habit long ago.

L.C. wasn't through with him. He ground out his cigarette in the hubcap and decreased a triple chin to a double shoving his meaty face at Myers in a gesture of finality. "The publisher want you out of here by the end of the day. Time enough to clear out your stuff and turn in your ID."

Myers hissed. "A disgruntled call to her highness after an experienced newsman asks a couple of tough questions—that wouldn't get me fired. That's bullshit. What's the *real* reason, L.C.?"

"The killer reason? You want the fucking truth? Your arrogance—you went too far with the Cabrillo shooting, lying to the cops about the picture the victim gave you. You lied to us, your own people. The paper *will* be sued, bank on it."

"I never lied. The most harm you'll see is a slap on the hand from someone lower than a regional assistant director of ICE; he's not that high up. The paper won't be touched at all."

L.C. sighed, as might a man feigning grave remorse. "First thing, running a correction explaining that one of our ex-reporters is in jail for withholding evidence in a police shooting ... Now get out of my face!"

"Imagine the fun TV's gonna have with *that*. In particularly my response." Myers couldn't help losing his magic. He had to get in his dime's worth before departing.

At his desk he pulled up an in-depth story he'd been working on before Frazier's suicide. A story revealing dozens of child abuse cases occurring in San Diego that related to the LA Catholic clergy. It was a subject he knew a lot about after the Janice Parrish story and all his follow-ups with other women coming out, at least to Myers, and now he was thinking why not take what he knows to the *Los Angeles Times?* Maybe they would hire him here at the San Diego bureau. He copied his files on a clean CD, plus a few other ideas he'd scribbled down to look into.

Myers wasn't going to lay down and die just because he'd been fired from the job he had held for the last eighteen years, all benefits denied with justifiable dismissal. That's the way it was with a free press that had struggled two centuries to enable workers' rights; they turn on their own. He would only be able to collect unemployment for a few weeks.

Maybe the guild could save at least his puny pension. He might even have to put in for compensation from the VA; he was certainly entitled.

"Sounded heated in there," Lubrano said from her desk.

"Sonofabitch finally did it. You couldn't hear?"

She grinned crookedly. "Don't kid around, Ray. You did it just to keep from covering the funeral. You'll do *anything* to avoid a goddamn funeral."

The word put another furrow in the frown on Myers' brow. "Forgot all about that."

It was a fact known by every writer, editor, secretary, rim rat and copy clerk in the *Journal's* newsroom that Myers hated funerals. What they didn't know was why—that he'd seen too many during and after Vietnam. He never saw a reason to mention it.

"Uh-huh. I'm not taking it, no way, buster," Lubrano said with as much finality as the M.E.

CHAPTER TWENTY-NINE

This was not how Bubba figured it would go. He had thought, sure, she was a fox and she was fun and, all right, he could mess around a little. But sooner or later he had to take care of business. Here it was getting on nightfall and he had her where he wanted her, very close to Ensenada, with all the money on the seat between them. With his cut of twenty thousand, that little red Miata was going to tickle Roxanne pink. Maybe she would let him wheel it out to the estuary to search for wounded birds. Or maybe, instead of the Miata, he'd talk her into getting a giant HD flat screen instead with Bose surround, the works. Update the stove and fridge since the ones management provided weren't worth donating to the Goodwill. Rox did the cooking, she'd like that.

But right now he couldn't think about Roxanne's happiness or a stove you had to light with a match. He didn't want to think about doing Maggie, either. The assignment went against every grain of his being, killing a woman, who it turned out was hotter than his dreams and even nice—a citizen that had done what? Steal some money, something that sure didn't warrant getting murdered over. Took a little dirty money from an outfit of criminals. Didn't hurt nobody, big fucking deal.

But he was getting antsy. He had to do something, and soon.

Earlier, in the steamy glass factory when Bubba touched her skin and then kissed her lips, something came over him that wasn't purely lust. A kind of mystical repose, something he couldn't describe. It seemed to take away his control of the situation and made him want to hold onto the moment. He wanted just to please Maggie. It was a sensation entirely new to him, a man used to dishing out aggression. That was his job. Instead of rushing off to a hotel in the heat of passion with this sexy beast, he talked the glassblower guy into making Maggie a fish. It was the pretense upon which he had gotten her down here, after all. She wanted a barracuda, a fish she said she'd pictured since childhood as fat and all teeth, a scaly Pac Man or maybe piranha-like. Knowing barracuda to be pencil thin, like mackerel, Bubba humored her and translated her description to the glass blower, who laughed it up then produced a toothy turtle-like creature with frog legs that seemed to be caught in mid-leap. It had yellow and mauve coloring. Maggie adored it, said it would go just right with her other "orphans," which was what she said she called the glass figures in her fish collection. The girl had a thing about orphans.

Bubba held off even longer by ordering something for himself, an iguana, which another young man started as Maggie's "barracuda" was being fired, then fine-tuned and cooled, shaved of sharp bumps and chips. He thought maybe a translucent yellow-eyed lizard might scare hell out of Roxanne's schnauzers, letting him get some peace in front of the new TV he'd decided definitely to get.

"Don't know which one's the ugliest," Bubba had joked outside the factory.

"Yours—that iguana-thing, of course?" Maggie remarked. "Your guy must have been in a seriously foul mood today, cause I know you didn't tell him to make something that hideous. Did you?"

Bubba grinned. He didn't say a word about her purple turtle-froggy, leaping barracuda with teeth outside its mouth.

They had a cold shrimp-and-whitefish-cocktail lunch from a vendor on the street corner and shopped *Revolución* into the late afternoon, and all that time he carried the bulky paper-wrapped objects, one under each arm, guardedly like they were a pair of Maltese falcons.

He thought Maggie had gotten out of the mood. Then she suggested going to Puerto Nuevo for lobster. She'd said, with the abandon of an uncaged bird, "Let's blow it out, have a feast. It's not like we can't afford it, right?"

Bubba needed no persuading; not only was Puerto Nuevo-style lobster—split and deep-fried—just about his favorite dish, it would get them closer down the road to Ensenada, where he needed her to be for the plan he could now clearly see.

Middle of the week in the off season, there were no more than a handful of European travelers at Miguel's Langosta Restaurante, even thought it was the most popular eatery in the celebrated seaside fishing village. Apart from the other restaurants, Miguel's was perched on a cliff a hundred feet directly above the ocean, commanding the best view in town. No one else seemed to care for the breezy rooftop seating, so they were alone. Maggie and Bubba pulled up chairs to enjoy the red sunset at sea. Three cheerful waiters spread a white cloth on the small round table and placed a cut-glass vase with clippings of red and white bougainvillea among three red candles inside glass bulbs. A sweating bottle of Santo Tomas chablis stuck out of a bucket of ice next to the table. Bright hand-painted tile lay at their feet and around the wall of the parapet. Bubba sprang for the two-person mariachi, allowing them to select the tunes; the duo cranked out two warbling, sentimental love songs—*Amor Eterno,* and *Sabor a Mi* —ringing pitch perfect for the wine-and-candlelight setting by a sibilant ocean. The moment was storybook romance for Bubba, silent, deep eye-to-eye stares, a moment too intense to survive and shortly sank with the dying sun into the remnants of a fiery-orange horizon, like the seeming chemistry between them.

After the corpulent lobster dinner, Bubba excused himself and stepped out of the restaurant. Earlier he'd noticed a pay phone near the front door of Miguel's. He used it, wanting no trace on his cell phone.

He made a collect call to his contact, Rory Fitzsimmon, a Border Patrol agent. He had never met Fitzsimmon but knew he'd been a brother agent who somehow got busted and was now a dispatcher at the Imperial Beach station, a job no one in their right mind wanted. He worked swing. He spoke informally, buddy-like, the few times they had conversed.

"Rory, it's me. Got only a minute to talk." Bubba kept his hand curled around the phone to keep his voice from traveling. "I'm down here with the one. Is everything still good?"

"Nobody's indicated otherwise," Fitzsimmon answered.

Rory Fitzsimmon had the perfect temperament for the high-wired job of law enforcement dispatching—always contained, observant, sure. It was the right job for his kind of personality. Nothing shook him, nobody could throw him while he was broadcasting. Never needed the boost of antidepressants, tranquilizers or any drug to maintain a collective calm. That kind of clarity of mind helped him decipher quickly what was being told him on any given call. As such, it might have struck him now as odd that the contractor would question if the job was still on. But he didn't reveal it if he thought so.

Bubba asked, "You got the guy's number in Ensenada? I need to call him before I get there."

"Yeah, I got it, hold on … " He gave him a number, adding, "That's a mobile."

"Who is he?"

"Name's Guerrero."

"Don't know him," Bubba said, "he got any authority? Cause I gotta know what I gotta know before I go any further with this thing."

Fitzsimmon took a moment, maybe to phrase a response or clarify in his head what the contractor meant about going "any further with this thing."

"Sergeant on the force there. Veteran. Want him to be your pal, call him 'Inspector' … You can handle things okay down there, say it don't go right?" the dispatcher asked, as if to solicit some clarification.

"No problem," Bubba said, giving him nothing to work with. "Nothing won't not go right."

Fitzsimmon wasn't stumped; he figured out instantly what Bubba had just said. "Call if there's a problem."

Bubba hung up. He would wait to call this Guerrero guy with the obvious inferiority complex—call him *Inspector*—until he and Maggie got to Ensenada. If he could talk her into going.

~

The headwaiter wore a bullfighter's getup. Maggie looked him over, smiled and sent him downstairs for a strawberry margarita after she finished off the chablis. Alone on the rooftop, she stood in the corner of the tiled parapet high above the ocean's surf. She could hear it hissing and see it pounding rock; there was nothing pacifying about the way the Pacific smashed against the land at the end of its run. She removed a handful of hundreds from her big purse and then loosened her pants and pressed the bills inside her undies on both of her hips. The thousand-dollar traveler's checks already lay horizontally under her pants just above her ace of spades; those would be the five notes compliments of the Bischkes. Neither Mr. Swabb nor Bubba knew about that money— unless the couple cracked when asked, *if* asked.

She figured a couple grand was padding her hips. Still, tucking some of the money away didn't do much to reassure her; if the cowboy was a typical guy he'd want to rip off her clothes. And maybe in the heat of the moment she'd forget it was there and money would start flying everywhere. What's this? he'd say, hopefully with a playful grin. But what the hell, she thought, it really didn't matter. She was cooked anyway even if things *didn't* go bad between them.

She felt torn. She could make a break right now, or she could play it out. She was attracted to the guy, she even liked him in a kind of flighty way, corny as he seemed to be—which was part of his appeal, she had to admit. She also had to admit her tastes in men leaned toward the easy-to-read-and-manipulate, like this cowboy. Still, he had a job to do, but he didn't seem in any hurry to get it done. Thank goodness. She had already decided she wasn't going to let things get negative if she could help it. But what was she going to do when he got tired of playing around, demanded the money and dumped her? She needed a plan. She thought she could keep him feeding for a while, at least until they went to bed together, if she decided to do it. She figured him to be the wham-bam-thank-you-ma'am kind of guy. He was a cowboy, wasn't he?

And after that? What then?

She sipped her frozen drink and puffed rapidly on a harsh-tasting Mexican Marlboro Light.

What did it matter now. She had to stop kidding herself. Her life was shot. Her father was dead, her hopes of opening the orphanage as good as gone, the company had turned on her. She never really thought she could get away with cheating them, even for a worthy cause. Mr. Swabb didn't have to threaten her. She would have paid them back somehow. Maybe. He had no feelings at all, completely insensitive about the babies, about her dad, and about her. The whole thing had escalated because of him. Everything was that man's fault, she now thought, licking the salt off the glass rim before killing off the drink.

"I'll have another one of these," she said waving to the waiter, who now stood silently in his ridiculous matador clothes. At least he was far enough away to let her think undisturbed.

She was going to get crocked and forget it—maybe, she could bring the cowboy over to her side, make him see things her way, that it wasn't fair what they were doing. Be upfront with him about the problem. If she could make Bubba understand that Mr. Swabb was the bad guy in all this, that she had a righteous thing going, then maybe she could convince him to let her keep some of the money, cut him in if necessary.

It seemed like a good idea, so she could go ahead and get crocked and throw wise to the wind.

CHAPTER THIRTY

Myers palmed his chin with both hands to hold his head off the bar. He gazed across the bartender's causeway into the cracked mirror behind the rows of booze bottles, glaring morosely at the pathetic image of himself. The crack in the mirror split his face square through his offset Roy Scheider nose, the broken image of a man. He dropped his eyes, unable to accept that he *was* broken.

The Safari was dead tonight. It was dead every Monday that the NFL played, the drinkers and revelers hanging across the street at Miss O'Leary's glass-and-wood palace with those big plasma screens, screaming and hooting like teenagers. Here, Sam had an old 21" tube high in a corner turned on, broadcasting the Giants-Patriots game. The sound was off.

Myers liked football and he loved seeing the Giants behind at halftime on Monday Night Football, since they played every Monday night. But tonight he would not be caught dead with those young, bright, cheerful people, just as they were not about to venture over to the musky Safari Lounge and tolerate cheesy patrons like him, an aging, dour, nostalgic newspaper reporter. *Ex*-newspaper reporter.

"Fuck it," Myers said out loud, "fuck *me!*"

His thoughts hung low. Where would he be a year from now, next week even? He hoped like hell he wouldn't end up a wretched barfly like the one snoring a few stools from him. Wispy thing swallowed up inside a pea coat that looked like some girlfriend of Mickey Rourke's.

His harsh utterance had disturbed the person and she rotated her head, wiped her nose on a sleeve, tried to focus his way.

"Huh?" she muttered. "You talkin to me?"

Myers was the only other patron in the Safari Lounge. He was about to throw another insult at the drunk when the bartender stepped in.

"Ray!" Sam exclaimed, as though Myers had just arrived when the bartender had already handcrafted him four Dewar's-on-the-rocks. "I ever tell you about the time I took this baby down?"

Sam leaned back from his side of the bar and pointed to the mounted head of a warthog above the mirror. Myers figured he was trying to divert him from his only other customer.

"Noticed it already," Myers said sullenly, still eyeing the slumping woman.

"You only think it's a pig," the bartender pushed on, as if reading Myers' irritable mind. "It's a javelina. Vicious as hell. Smart, too. She's a prize trophy … Just look at that mug. *Beautiful*, ain't she?"

Myers knew the bartender wasn't joking. He glanced at the creature—a gnarled-lipped, saber-toothed beast with sparse wiry hair growing out of a pink and wet-looking snout. The lips were stretched back in a mad grin revealing more grimy teeth. Myers shook his head; it was about as ugly an animal he'd ever seen.

"You ought to get that thing out of sight, Sam," he said. "Christ, no wonder you don't have any customers."

That was not exactly true, or fair. The Safari Lounge had languished over the years, turning into a mere relic of its heyday back in the 50s. But it had its regulars, always a few customers dancing in the shadows or shooting pool, or hunkered down at the bar. It might have been the mounted animal heads hanging on every wall that turned off the trendy, largely vegan Hillcrest crowd. On those colorless stucco walls hung the heads of cats, deer, moose, a buffalo, gazelle, and strung birds of prey, most of which appeared so alive they might have crashed through the plaster only to be hoodwinked and trapped that way in perpetuity.

"It starts chargin' me right after I fire off an arrow and miss," Sam said, mulishly. "Comin' straight for me, shaking the ground like a damn rhino. Then it does this flip and stops in its tracks, just that quick. Turns out my guide saw it had me in the straights and struck the deathblow. I was scared shitless. That guide shot true, saved my life. Those little fellers have been known to chase a man down and thrash him within an inch of his life. On the other hand, they can be real sweet."

"Uh huh."

"Find 'em in southern Arizona, out around the Chiricahuas, even in the neighborhoods far over as Tucson," the barkeeper went on. "But this one, we bagged her in Baja."

"Hit me again."

Sam pointed a finger at Myers. "You got it." He raked a fresh glass through ice from the open-top machine, poured a hearty slug of house scotch, and wiped the bar before placing the drink in front of Myers, the whole process taking no more than six seconds, or the blink of a drunk person's eye.

"Here's lookin' at ya," Myers said as thanks, not looking at the bartender. Few patrons did.

Most everyone resisted eye contact with Sam because of the fake eye, which remained motionless while the good eye darted here and there. That glass eye remained front and center at all times, like the eye in an Aztec statue. Disconcerting for anyone, drunk or sober.

The woman nestled her head back against her forearm on the bar. At the same moment her foot slipped off the stool ring. Myers lurched to catch her. She didn't fall.

"You think she'll feel anything when she falls?" he said to the bartender, a bite in his tone.

"Relax, Ray," the bartender laughed. "She ain't going nowheres. Velma has never fell off a stool, long as I've know her ... Something, ain't she? Ole Vel."

Sam grinned. His good eye split off toward the woman; his glass eye stayed put as if to burn a hole through Myers. He shook his head sadly, looking at the slight woman, all dressed up for Alaska.

"Don't know if I'll end up calling her a cab or an ambulance tonight," Sam said.

"Call a taxidermist."

The bartender chuckled despite himself. He leaned closer to Myers. "If it weren't for that crazy bird of hers, parakeet she called Tweetie—"

"Tweetie?" Myers glanced again at the woman, settled comfortably now, drooling onto the bar.

"Actually a Rainbow Lorikeet. Ole Velma'd come in for a draft around three in the afternoon, flitting around the jukebox. You'd think she was a ballerina or something, quite agile and feathery on her feet—maybe she *was* a ballerina once. Four, five years back. Look at her now."

"How come I haven't seen her before?"

"How should I know … Oh, she loved that bird. You know how people get with their pets."

"Uh huh."

The bartender had a big heart. He was generous beyond his means, a virtual saint to the uptown drunks. The young entrepreneurial owners of Miss O'Leary's never worried the Safari would lure away their clientele, so long as Sam remained proprietor and the staring beasts hung up there to haunt.

The sound of Velma's light snore drifted toward them. A half pack of No Bull cigarettes with a matchbook tucked into the cellophane wrapper lay next to her half-empty beer. Sam would say the beer was half-full.

The bartender continued and there was nothing for Myers to do but listen, "Story goes one day she's got Tweetie out of its cage, letting it fly around the apartment. Meanwhile, ole Velma's getting her bath water going. Tweetie hears it and thinks it's a birdbath. It swings into the bathroom, into the cascade of running water and gets knocked down and drowns. Next thing, Velma's sitting and singing in her bubbles and feels around for her washrag. Almost uses it on her face but sees it's the dead bird. A wet bird's just like a limp washrag, you know. The rest is history, her downfall … She had that parakeet memorialized."

Sam's eyes separated again as he pointed to an area in the rear near the pool table. "Tweetie's over there on a wire, close to that antelope. See it?"

"Which one's the antelope?"

"One with the four-foot horns, African gemsbok. Right back there. Damn, Ray, you don't know what a antelope is … where the deer and antelope roam?"

"Sure, I do. I see it. Front of the bighorn moose."

"Caribou," Sam corrected. "Tell by the antlers. Much bigger than the moose's. You didn't know that, Ray?"

"Sure, I knew that. I knew it was a caribou … And antelopes play, Sam, they don't roam."

"Anyhoo," said Sam, smiling now from his playfulness with his only paying customer, "I figured it might help her a little, you know, to have it stuffed, but I was wrong."

Myers felt no inclination to walk to the rear of the bar in search of "Tweetie." He stared at the bartender for a rare moment, marveling at him. Sam wore a tan hunting jacket tonight that had twenty pockets and several rows of shell pleats. He kept an unwrapped cigar in one of the pleats. Hanging on the wall directly behind him and near the warthog was a well-known faded picture of Ernest Hemingway, the Great White Hunter himself, holding up the horns of three gemsbok, Africa in the background. The author often had an elephant gun in his African portraits, foot propped on the neck of a king of the jungle, and wore a hunter's jacket, one like Sam's.

"Bring down that bottle of Cuervo Gold up there, Sam," Myers said. "You talking about Baja makes me want some. Velma can drink with me. Hey, Velma!"

"Shh, Ray. Let her be."

Sam stretched for the tequila. He poured shots for Myers and himself, threw his back and poured another one.

"Pour one for Velma," said Myers. "On me."

The bartender leaned on elbows to match Myers, looked at his patron, smiling. "Reckon you can afford it?"

Myers shook his head when Sam's eye split off left. He said, before thinking, "Sam? I don't mean to get personal, but you ever thought of wearing a patch over that eye? Hey. Not that it bothers me, I could care less. It's the place I'm thinking about, your well-heeled customers. You know, the ones that don't come back."

The bartender had a big laugh, one that matched his sense of humor. "You know what they say, 'You only got two.' Let me tell you about it."

Myers squirmed, thinking maybe it was time to mosey on down the road. But where to? Miss O'Leary's? He stayed put. "I always wondered."

"There's this place in Ensenada, a wildass bar—"

"Hussong's."

If it had been quiet before, it was tomb-dead silent now.

"Don't ever mention the name in my presence."

Myers wasn't sure if he was serious and maybe that was what got his attention.

"How come? The pretty boys there come on to your woman?"

Sam recoiled, as if Myers had poked him in his only working eye. "The Don Juans, how'd you know? I tell you the story before?"

He *was* serious.

"I don't tell the story to just anybody, Ray ... But you look in the mood for a heartbreaker."

"Maybe you ought a forget it, save it for a rainy day."

Sam smiled crookedly. "Maybe I oughta but this looks like your rainy day."

Myers wiggled his jigger glass and his little finger at the same time and Sam obliged. He downed the rust-colored tequila and went, ah, and wiggled the jigger again but not the finger.

"Maybe you should hold off a bit, there, Ray. I got to look after my customers, you know ... You driving tonight?"

Myers shook his head. "You going to smoke that cigar in your hunter's vest? Cause if you aren't let me."

"She was the woman of your dreams," Sam said, fingering his cellophane-wrapped cigar. "I loved her true."

"Yeah, I know what you mean."

"I lost the eye over her. Them little fucks, they are bad. B-A-D, bad."

Myers offered, "They're a bunch of worthless maggots. I nearly lost a girlfriend there, too. Had to kick some ass before I could get her out of the place. I haven't been back since. Haven't seen *her* since, either ... Dark Eyes."

"Thing is I didn't know whose ass to kick."

"Don't talk about it, you don't want to."

Sam went on. "It's true the Don Juans instigated the whole thing, strutting their stuff and all. But I mean I *lost* her to them boys."

Myers' interest piqued. "What do you mean?"

"Just what the hell I said."

"They kidnapped your girlfriend?"

"You know out back, where they have the fights?"

Myers nodded. "Sure. Dog or cock?"

"Cock that night. She went out there with one of 'em while I had hit the head. Took me a long time to locate her and when I did—shit, man ..."

"Forget it, Sam," Myers said pitifully, like some guy in some old noir film. Sam looked on the verge of tears and Myers suddenly wondered if he *could* make tears in that blank socket. Does the tear duct dry up when there's no eyeball?

Velma had come alive sometime during Sam's yarn, for she piped in, "You poor man ... Say, Sammy, mind if I have another little shot of that stuff you're pouring for the gentleman?"

"Give her a double," Myers said.

Velma didn't move closer to the men, having the good sense to keep her distance when men were speaking of lost love. You never knew when they might go off the deep end. Sam poured everyone a round; the Cuervo was half empty now, but there was still half a bottle left.

"What happened, Sammy?" asked Velma, chipper after her shot.

"Maybe it'd be better we lay off it," Myers said in a gentle voice. He no longer cared to hurt the woman's feelings anymore than Sam's.

But the bartender took the onus off both of them. "I saw how happy she was, licking up that hot Latin stuff, and it just pissed me off. So I made a bet."

"You did *what?*" said Myers.

"I bet the little shits—'scuse my French, Vel—I bet her against fifty bucks on this cock."

"Christ almighty!" Velma roared. She wiggled her jigger and this time Myers slid down and poured her to the brim.

"It was then I lost the eye ... Sodomon and Gomore of the western world, that place ... You wanna see personal?"

Sam turned his back on the two customers and in a flash wheeled back around with the glass eye in his hand, a dark hole in his skull. He laughed heartily.

"Ho-ly shit!" exclaimed Myers.

Velma decided to slide closer, perhaps to better see the glass orb in Sam's hand, or maybe Mr. Cuervo.

She said, "I think the man's right, Sammy. You need to patch that hole up."

Sam laughed again, and in his sport with the customers the eye slip out of his hand. It rolled into the sink. Myers saw it bounce against the stainless steel casing, and he quickly stretched to grab it. But he was clumsy and slow due to his blood alcohol level, and the eye rolled like a marble down the tub's inch-wide drain.

"Damn!" he said.

"Don't worry. I got a spare." Sam hadn't made any attempt to retrieve it until now, as he tried to dig it out of the drain hole with a spoon.

"Well hell, *that* eye's gone, I guess."

"You can loosen up the trap, don't run any water," Myers said, curling his mouth at the thought of an eye rolling down a drain.

For no particular reason other than a proclivity to pedantry when drunk, he added, "And, Sam, it's Sodom and Gomorrah, the biblical cities consumed by fire and brimstone for their rampant sin ... Ah, so, yeah, you're right about Hu—that place."

Suddenly, there came a loud fist-slam on the bar. Velma jumped and grabbed her throat. They all looked at once.

Detective Pedroza stood about where Velma had been most of the night. His demeanor could not be described as happy. Dressed in a suit would have been enough to draw attention inside the Safari, but he was looking for respect when he slid back his suit coat to reveal the sheathed Beretta and badge on his belt.

Velma eyed him sourly, apparently not seeing the gun. "Where's your goddamn manners, young man? You nearly frightened me to death with that banging."

Pedroza smirked. "Over here, Myers. *You*, fuckwad, are under arrest."

Myers didn't move. "Since when did Millard let you out all by yourself. And fuck you, detective."

Sam leaned over the bar, thrusting the eye socket side of his face toward Pedroza to no effect.

The junior detective said to the bartender, "Don't speak. I'll run you in too. C'mon Myers, you just added obstruction and obscenity charges. Wanna try for resisting? I ain't taking all night with you—"

Velma stumbled into Pedroza; she had moved as if she meant to attack him but tripped over her own shoelace. Pedroza helped her down with a backhand on her way to the floor. Infuriated, Sam jumped over the bar and rushed him. Pedroza knocked him down, too.

Myers tried to catch Velma but failed, then knelt to help her to her feet when a jarring and whirling pressure burst into a bright flash as he folded in a sea of red squalor.

CHAPTER THIRTY-ONE

Maggie herself suggested driving on down to Ensenada, saying she felt like dancing discotheque, the night had barely started.

Bubba shrugged behind his bumpkin grin and said, "Shoot, why not."

Both were energized from frosty margaritas and hearty, two-pound lobster tails at Miguel's Langosta Restaurante.

Now, wide-eyed but tired after an hour of disco dancing, Maggie wheeled the Buick slowly through a dark area of potholed streets and pool halls. Bubba said, "Just yonder," and she pulled forward and stopped when he said to. She hunched over and looked through Bubba's window and viewed a steep and dim staircase entry leading up to total darkness.

Of all the fine hotels to choose from in the Emerald City, Bubba picked what appeared to her the seediest. "I don't know. Isn't this the kind of place you stay at when you got nowhere else to go?"

Bubba said, "Ain't it the truth."

It was a special hotel, he explained. Said the Hotel Mexico had a certain ambiance you couldn't find anywhere else in Ensenada. "Something out of the past, you know? It's kinda feels like the soul of this city back when … Wait till you get upstairs in the room, you'll see what I mean," he said.

"I mean, it's not like we can't afford a *good* place," Maggie argued.

"Just one night, okay? You'll see."

Maggie said, "Well, of course … What do you mean, just one night?"

Bubba got out of the car, slipped on the tight-fitting brown leather jacket he'd picked out on *Revolución* with money Maggie gave him. Maggie thought he looked good in slick leather, stout and hard, like an off-duty cop ought to look. He fitted the Stetson just so and double-stepped up the stairs into the darkness.

Maggie locked up the Buick and followed at a slower pace. Halfway up the dark stairs she became frightened and pressed herself against the wall. The fear hit quick, like a thief in the dark. She clutched the bulky handbag to her chest with both arms and called out for Bubba. She wasn't even sure what it was that spooked her. Just the darkness, she supposed.

"Right here, Maggie. Here I am. C'mon up."

He appeared then and took her hand, scooting her up the remaining stairs straight into a room. He quickly turned on lights and the overhead fan; then he dashed to the French doors and pitched them open with fanfare. He turned with a big, proud grin plastered on his cowboy face.

"*Voila!*" he sang.

Framed through the doors beyond a Romanesque carved-stone balcony stood a huge orange harvest moon, as if from van Gogh's brush, poised over a shimmering cityscape.

Maggie said, "Wow!" and dropped her handbag with all the money onto a chair. She sashayed toward the cowboy, forgetting all those bills pasted against her hips and ace of spades, just as she figured she'd do. She cast aside her trivial fretting and abandoned everything, her "plan," her coyness, her very self.

She pulled money out of her pants like a magic act, with a broad smile and a lot of graceful hand and hip movement. "Extra," she said, "just in case."

The moon rose and the bed springs squeaked. Maggie let go and for a while the shrieks and moans carried out the French doors into the glow of moonlight and down into the streets and alleyways.

Afterwards, they lay side by side for a while, and then Bubba got up. He smacked the pert, round buttock mooning him out of the sheets.

Maggie stared at a bullfight poster glued fast to the wall beside her. It was dated "1938, May 29, Tijuana," still with its bright colors. The bed was probably that old too, she thought. The hotel's sputtering neon sign, a three-story tall obelisk next to the balcony, threw flickers of orange and red across the bed and wall and bullfight poster.

From the bathroom Bubba said, "Dan Duryea was on the lam in this room, wounded, sweating profusely … You remember that movie?"

She didn't know Dan Duryea from Nelson Rockefeller but went with him and pictured an actor's giant face in black-and-white, grimacing, furtive eyes, a tormented man struggling just to pull his tie from the shirt collar—a man over the edge.

But wouldn't he be in Morocco or The kasbah, thought Maggie?

"Maybe that was Sidney Greenstreet," she said, an actor from old whom she recalled because of the dignified way he carried himself for a fat man always sweating under pressure from swindling some other bad guys.

She heard Bubba turn on the water in the shower and pull the plastic curtain. He shouted, "*Ah-ah!*" then started singing.

Maggie listened. She knew the tune to "La Cucaracha" but she had never heard any of the lyrics the way he sang them:

> *When a man doth love a woman*
> *and that woman doth not love him,*
> *it's the same as when a bald man*
> *finds a comb upon the highway.*
> *La kook-a-rooches, la kook-a-rooches …*

Craziest love song she'd ever heard—bald man finds a comb.

She was reeling now, in a strange room under a lover's moon, lying naked on a creaky bed, her outlandish new cowboy lover singing crazy in the shower—her life in shambles, ruined. *She* was on the edge.

As darkness settled in, the flashing neon grew brighter against the wall. Maggie rubbed her thighs together and squirmed under the sheet, still charged from lovemaking. Rudimentary sex for the cowboy, just as she expected.

But she didn't mind. Caution and pride and giving a damn were not qualities she recognized or went by, not anymore. Just as caring and giving and loving weren't relevant either. It was a new time for her, another chapter. Survival, freedom, security, those were now her objectives. Living was the only thing that counted, living it up. Behavioral modification of the base element—Sin. Maggie felt she had discovered her new self, or rediscovering the person within, the one she may have always been, the character that lie latent until now. She wondered if that was it. Could she be the bad girl she felt like being?

Bubba came out of the bath wearing a towel too small to fit completely around him, and Maggie's eyes climbed his exposed flesh from toes to neck, coming back and locking on the suggestive bulge in the towel that seemed to be leading him towards her. She took it as a sign of his eager-ness to rejoin her—hop back in the saddle, as he would put it. She flicked her eyebrows at him and ran her tongue around her lips, made a trilling sound.

"Come over here, cowboy," she whispered, and dramatically tossed the sheet to her ankles. She turned on her side, pulled up a knee, showed him her curves and bulbs. She ran a finger along the dark hollow behind her thigh and moaned.

Bubba grinned at the curvaceous creature, a purring, lustful vamp in the sheets. He sat on the bed's edge. He didn't touch her. Instead he picked up the phone. Old black phone without a dial that James M. Cain might once have used, or one of his desperate characters. Bubba spoke in Spanish, gave a number and, waiting, turned and winked at Maggie.

She walked her fingers along his waist. "Who're you calling?"

"Rox."

"Rox, huh." Maggie had not heard that name. "I give, who's Rox?"

"The mother of Trixie and Dixie—twin schnauzers."

Maggie said, "Oh."

Bubba patted her on the leg, said Rox was his wife of eight long years. "I was supposed to have the car back for her tonight. I don't let her know I'm still tied up at work, she'll go into a panic, think I'm face down in some canyon slit ear to ear."

"Isn't that what cop's wives are supposed to do, worry?"

Bubba puckered his lips, thinking that over. "Yeah, you're right."

He fingered the phone button, told the desk clerk in English to forget the call and racked the receiver.

Bubba put on his black shirt with the pearl buttons, pulled up his 501s and slipped into his snakeskin boots. The clothes were a little per-fumed from sweating under hot disco lights, though Maggie didn't wrin-kle her nose. He stood at the small mirror opposite the single bed and slipped on the new leather jacket.

"I'm gonna go out and get us some tequila, okay?"

Maggie pulled the pillow over her breasts. "I don't really need it, Bubba. But sure, go get us some tequila. I want to take a shower. The water hot?"

"Yeah, you bet. I'll lock the door. Don't answer it for anybody."

"You expecting somebody?"

"Course not. Just being—"

"A cop, I know."

~

Bubba checked to see if she would follow him. She didn't. He went to a wall phone by the front desk and called the number Fitzsimmon gave him for this local guy Guerrero, the "Inspector." The man answered, sounding as though he'd been asleep. It was getting late, though Bubba hardly noticed. He spoke in Spanish, "What I need may sound crazy. Can you meet me in an hour?"

The sleepy voice spoke in English, "It is late, amigo. But okay, where?"

"Hussong's. One hour."

"You say one hour, I meet you one hour. No need to say again. What is this business you want?"

"Tell you then."

Bubba knocked on Room 203, said his name out loud so Maggie would know it was him and entered using the key.

"I got a better idea," he said to her.

Maggie was still in the shower and he went to the bathroom door and repeated himself.

"Your better ideas are always interesting. What is it?"

"Hurry up, I'll show you."

CHAPTER THIRTY-TWO

Bubba suggested dividing the money. Leave some in the room, carry some on their bodies—at which Maggie was already adept—hide the rest in the Buick. "So we're covered in case of theft."

Maggie went along, seeing an opportunity to get away with a lot of the loot if she had to abscond, if she *could*.

She tossed the cash on the bed and separated it, putting aside six or seven thousand dollars, and bagging the two stacks in plastic trash bags she got from the bathroom. She rearranged a handful of hundreds into her hip-side banks while Bubba did something similar inside his pants. Maggie had already folded and stuffed the thousand-dollar traveler's checks in her shoes when Bubba took his shower. *That* money she hadn't revealed in her moment of surrender. It hadn't been total abandon.

Bubba jammed one of the moneybags behind the old chifforobe serving as a closet and left the other one for Maggie to take with them.

"We'll walk," he said.

"Where?"

"Get some drinks, hear some loud music. Have a good time."

"We just had a good time. I did."

"Yeah, me too. But, we gotta talk some."

"Yeah, I know … But we could do that here, couldn't we?"

"Better where we're going."

He sounded like Sylvia, Maggie thought.

She brushed out her hair and slipped on the soft cashmere pullover sweater she'd purchased on *Revolución*, which seemed to her like days ago.

Maggie slipped the second bundle of cash under the Buick's front driver's seat and locked the car. They walked in cadence along the nighttime street, moving as though, like lovers, they'd walked sidewalks together forever. Bubba gave her a hand up the steeper corners, some three feet off the street that shorter legs would have to climb up. She had been in Ensenada before but always stuck to the main drags—the vegetable and fish markets, the novelty stores, the pottery and tile factories, places she went with her dad. But never to the nighttime sleazy sections. Never walked the wild side of this town. She was excited and cautious, but not afraid with Bubba at her side.

Bubba was hungry again. He had an old gentleman at a street cart shuck two oyster cocktails. Maggie watched the man's scarred, rheumatic hands work and thought about salmonella and high mercury content and God knows what other sea and land borne diseases they had picked up. But if Bubba wasn't worried, then neither was she. The cocktail was savory, the oysters rich and sweet in a piquant salsa, the best oysters she thought she'd ever had.

Pounding the sidewalks again, she peered into some of the smoky bars and cafes where hard black eyes threw stones at her.

"Where're we going?" she asked again.

"There," he said, pointing out Hussong's Cantina across and up the street.

Maggie had heard the stories, though she had never been to Hussong's. Reckless, violent, depraved. Even surreal. Watch out for the Don Juans, those cocksure young locals whose only aspiration was to make it with American chicks, in front of their amigos. Rumors she'd heard in Jimbo's and the honky tonks around El Cajon.

She held on to Bubba as they entered the saloon. Two federales with assault rifles locked and loaded didn't feed on her with their eyes. The young federales' eyes were the blackest yet. Bubba's step quickened with the roar inside and Maggie had to put an arm lock on him for fear of getting separated amid the jammed bodies. Bubba shoved people aside making his way to the bar. She was real glad to be with a man like him right now, a man without fear.

It was close to midnight and the place had just woken up. A string-and-wind mariachi quartet worked the crowd. There was a fireplace without fire. Caricature sketches, some in black diploma frames, hung from all the walls and overhangs, covering the place like wallpaper. The bar was full of men and they moved across the sawdust floor as if they had somewhere to go. About every tenth person was gringo, she noticed. The rest were cardboard images in decorative polyester shirts opened to the navel, gold chains draped from necks, tall feathered Stetsons bobbing in the smoky haze like a meadow of black quail.

Maggie didn't expect to see any Mexican women; they didn't dare patronize Hussong's. But American women did. American girls loved to flaunt their stuff in rowdy Baja bars. Maggie counted three gringas, all sun-bleached college-age girls, probably all southern Californians but not college girls; too cheap looking for higher education. The open room held two hundred drunk men and four young women including Maggie Frazier, who wasn't sun-bleached or in college or even college age.

Soon as she squeezed up to the bar between Bubba and a high-smelling Mexican, the bartender handed her an icy margarita. Bubba clicked her glass with his.

"To us and the horse we rode in on," he said and grinned a boyish grin. He seemed less jubilant than preoccupied, Maggie thought. It put a little knot of apprehension in her stomach. He finished off the drink in one toss and called for two more.

Maggie nestled against him and said, teasingly, "You lookin' for a date, handsome?"

"I gotta ask you something, Maggie," Bubba said close to her ear, over the roar.

She saw his studied look turn into a hungry look. Her hair after showering was ratted out into a bouncy fine fizz against her face. He touched her and quickly withdrew his hand, a frown stealing over his hungry expression.

"I was wondering. You, uh, you own that house you live in or just rent it?" His eyes were lowered.

"Rent, why?"

"Good. That's good."

"That's a funny question, Bubba. You thinking of maybe moving in with me?" She felt giddy but desperate at the same time. It was a duality that had always been a trait of her personality, though she seemed only now to recognize.

"I'd just hate to see you lose the equity if you owned it."

Two margaritas appeared before them, fat and tall this time.

Maggie narrowed her eyes, silently demanding explanation.

"See, it would go to probate, unless you got a will. You got a will, Maggie?"

"Bubba, what are you talking about?" She held her margarita with a shaky hand.

"See, Maggie, it's supposed to look like an accident, and if I can arrange everything I got planned out in my head, it will—I mean *look* that way, not a real accident."

Maggie's legs turned to mush, her arms were too heavy to lift; she began to tremble. She didn't think she could speak, but she did. "Accident? … What is supposed to look like an accident?"

"You know, with you. I thought you'd a figured it out by now."

"Oh, God—you mean? … " She let the unthinkable trail.

Bubba nodded, then shook his head. He put an arm around her shoulder.

"I figure you got a right to know what's going on, Maggie. Especially after a while ago … you know?" His voice syrupy, sincere.

"But why?" Her fear began to snowball into panic. "You—you're supposed to *kill* me?"

Bubba's eyebrows lifted with comprehension. "Oh. No, Maggie. I'm not really gonna do it. I … I think I love you."

Maggie could not have guessed that Bubba had never told a woman he loved her, not even his wife on their wedding night. She was too upset to even imagine anything about her *killer*.

A commotion arose at one of the tables near them. A blond girl in cutoffs and tank top jumped onto the table as if tossed onto it and started flailing in some crazed trance, her limbs at first going berserk. The audience of Don Juans egged her on, dousing her with beer from shaken up longneck Coronas; someone then threw a pitcher of beer on her. The effect worked and she began rubbing her wet torso through the wet fabric as a lover might, then lifted the soaked shirt over her head and wiggled her cutoffs down to mid-cheek with lust and desire in her movements. She splayed arms and legs and writhed in spins like a drunk and very limber flamingo dancer until she reeled and fell off the table into a dozen pairs of groping hands. There followed a clamor of hisses—Hussong's cultural response for more, Maggie figured—then a wild flailing of arms and fists amid a roar of laughter.

"Shit, look at that," said Bubba. "They coulda broke her neck."

The things Maggie thought she had been running from suddenly flashed across her mind, as if she were falling from a skyscraper to her death—her father's dead face, the baby she still owed the Bischkes and wasn't going to deliver, her father's funeral, the loss of *Casa Libre*, Sylvia Fischer, her job at Jimbo's, her old goldie. Oh, goodness! Did Sarah remember to feed Sally? Her mind whirled in desperate thought. She felt numb. He had brought her here to *murder* her; there was no reason for him to lie about it.

His voice in her ear, somehow reaching her, broke into Maggie's nightmare.

"Listen, Maggie, listen. I mean it. I'm not gonna do you," he said. He was looking sharply into her face. "I got a plan. You wanna hear it?"

"But why?" Her tears were about to spill. She thought of her father's warning that they wouldn't let her get away with stealing their money, that they played dirty. Oh, how right he was. She should have listened to him; her father knew better.

Bubba said, "I don't know why. I don't get told—" He stopped cold.

She caught it. "You mean you've done this before? You *murder* people?"

She tried to move away from him but bumped into a baby-faced Mexican whose broad smile produced a flicker of diamond light in his front tooth. His rough eyes stayed glued on the bare skin in the V-neck of Maggie's cashmere sweater.

"Buzz off," she shouted.

Bubba squirmed closer to her; he sighed, looked around, squeezed his chin, paying no attention to the advances from the diamond-toothed Mexican.

"I'm a BP agent, Maggie. Sometimes I have to do this stuff. It's part of the job. I don't like it, believe me."

She wiped the tears out of her eyes, tried to calm down. "You're lying," she whined. "Why me? They want me *dead*? Over the money? Oh, God. I cannot believe this!"

"Okay. I'm gonna tell you, Maggie. Just try and get hold of yourself, for chrissake. I told you, I ain't gonna do it. Okay?"

He waited until she nodded.

"Listen up. This is the truth. This guy I know has me contact these greaseballs—twice I've done it is all. Worthless fucks, *coyotes*. I don't ask why. I don't *know* why. He's got his reasons. The guy's fucking nuts, I guess. I got in some trouble once that he's holding over me … Look, I do know that the world's a better place without those lowlife rapists, and I get paid. That helps. I got a nice little nest egg saved up. Was planning on someday buying me and Rox a place on the Pacific—guess I can dream on with that. But maybe have us some kids. Total commitment."

"But *me*? I'm not a fucking *coyote*, Bubba—or a greaseball. They know that, don't they?"

Bubba shrugged, stared at her with beady mice eyes. "You must a done something, huh? Something to do with that other broad, Sylvia Fischer? After all, you got all that money; it had to come from some-where I guess ain't completely kosher."

"You know about Sylvia?"

"Uh-huh."

"That was supposed to be kept confidential between me and my boss. How could you know?"

"Never mind that now. It just shows you I don't care. See?"

"She's somethin', ain't she?" Maggie somehow said.

"He said you were—"

She cut him off. "Who said?"

"The Man."

"The Man? *The Man*?" Maggie echoed, her tone all mockery. "Now that's fucking original."

"I don't know what his name is. That's the way he works."

Maggie wiped more tears on the backs of both hands. She wanted to believe him, and she was curious. "Does the name Swabb ring a bell?" she asked.

"What the fuck kind of name is that?"

"He's my boss, a big-time lawyer," said Maggie. She had nothing to lose. "He runs the smuggling ring. Sylvia sells the babies. Mr. Swabb gives her the documents for the adoptions and Sylvia gives him the mon-ey, or rather puts it in the bank. Only, I've got the money, not him or the friggin bank."

Bubba grinned at her approvingly. He liked the way she separated Sylvia from herself, as if she were another person completely. "He told me you'd lie, not to pay any attention to what you jabbered about … How many babies have you sold?"

"You really didn't know where the money came from, did you?" said Maggie. "Aren't you with the company?"

Bubba said, "Shit."

He licked salt from the rim of his empty margarita. "This Swabb fella, he got a smooth voice? You know, like Sam Rayburn from Texas used to have? Speaker Sam, now there was a suave voice. I used to hear him in newsreels when I was little."

She recalled her last conversation with Swabb. She knew now he had taken her seriously when she threatened to return the clients' money. He should've realized she was just mad at the moment, being fickle; a woman under duress can be like that. But Swabb decided to have her *assassinated*. All over a little bit of money.

Her eyes again got moist, mostly in anger now. She forced a demure grin for Bubba, her new lover and no longer assassinator. She hoped.

"Yeah," she said, "the little fuck can sound pretty nice I guess when he's not whining like a baby."

"Then we know who the Man is," Bubba said with a possum's grin, gloating in false discovery.

CHAPTER THIRTY-THREE

Bubba knew nothing about Sergeant Javier Maria Guerrero. He didn't know that the Ensenada cop worked bunco because he needed the grift to cover his wife's gambling addiction on weekend junkets to Tijuana's race track and up to Barona Casino in the hills east of San Diego. The police sergeant probably wasn't scoring big on bunco shakedowns. But he was still walking in his boots, as they say.

Bubba accepted his fleshy handshake but didn't like it, nor did the man's cave man's face do much for him; it was unreadable. Bubba indicated a direction and they walked in silence toward the Hotel Mexico.

The Ensenada cop wore typical off-duty attire—black leather jacket over a white embroidered *guayabera* shirt, plain beige polyester slacks, authentic alligator boots with elevator heels and pointed silver-steel toes. The gaucho hat covered a mane of thick black hair.

Boosted to five-eight in the elevated boots, the Mexican reached Bubba's height in regular boots. They had a similar gait as well—quick, long strides accentuated by bowleggedness and a roundhouse swing of the arms. Observed from behind, at night, the two were Rorschach copies.

The Mexican hauled around a bean-and-pork-fed paunch Bubba didn't have. His belly was the size of a desktop globe and he kept a dense mustache twisted into arching points with pomade, but short of a full-size handlebar. He kept his thick black hair greased, too, winged back almost into a ducktail, a popular style in the states fifty years ago. A Mexican of Indian blood, Guerrero's skin color at night appeared black. He had a huge head and deep set pinched eyes, a smashed-looking nose and a protruding block jaw that was armed with horse teeth. Smiling gave him a toothy, oafish appearance. He didn't smile around gringos.

The two men hastened on foot along uneven sidewalks, Guerrero listening with a tortured frown to Bubba's plan, issuing little grunts of disgust to show he repulsion.

Bubba asked him, "You ever seen the movie *The Postman Always Rings Twice*?" He was pretty sure the man wouldn't have and Bubba wanted to insult him. He didn't like his attitude and he didn't trust him worth a spit. He figured the Mexican would cut his own grandmother's guts and use her for chum if it'd benefit him financially. The man acted superior, too. Bubba wasn't about to call him "Inspector."

"No problem," Guerrero said without answering the question. "We will look in the morgue of the poor first. And if you do not find the one you want, we will have to go to the hospital or the funeral home. Maybe then we will have to look for someone who still walks. I know places where that will be no problem, too."

Bubba scowled at him; Guerrero scowled back.

"Nobody dies, *comprendes*?" said Bubba. "And I don't have all night, so let's just get it done."

He was nervous about leaving Maggie alone at Hussong's; he knew it wasn't a place a man left his girl alone. It hadn't been just the romp in bed that now made him feel the way he did about her; to him that had been more than just sex. It was when she froze in the stairway of the Hotel Mexico that he knew a hundred-percent he was not going to hurt her. He had felt her fear at that moment and he knew then his feelings were true. Strange but true. He was afraid to think it to himself, much less to say it out loud, but he was falling in love with Maggie. But he couldn't worry about her now.

Bubba stopped him near the hotel and said, "We'll take this car. Get in."

Guerrero looked at the roomy old wagon and made a joke: "You have come in a hearse." He turned officious. "The money, I will take it now."

"You get half now, half when the job's done."

"This is not the way I do business," the Mexican protested.

"Is tonight."

Guerrero sat low against the passenger door while Bubba thumbed off hundred-dollar bills from a sheaf he covertly took from under his seat. He pulled off 25 of them, counting as he went. "Fucking highway robbery," he complained.

"What can you do, is the price of business." Guerrero counted the money by adding on his fingers, then folded the bills into a lump and slid it into his front pocket.

"Go two blocks and turn left and go straight," the sergeant said.

"You get me a car?"

"Sí."

"Good. We'll pick it up after we get through here. There a problem with that?"

Guerrero produced a slight grin. "No problem."

Bubba drove according to his directions and came to a grand old brick building less than a mile away. The Mexican instructed him to drive through an open mesh wire gate all the way to the rear of the structure, then back the car up to a loading dock.

An empty asphalt lot filled a darkened space inside the Cyclone fence. A roll of razor wire topped the fence. Bubba saw some cars parked on the other side of the structure and lights were on there, but no cars here. "What is this building?" asked Bubba.

"Tuna. The old cannery," Guerrero said. "We go in there." He pointed out a heavy aluminum sliding door atop the loading dock. The door was illuminated by a dim light and under the light, stenciled on the brick wall, was a sign with the faded yellow words, *Recepción de Cadaveres*.

Guerrero explained the city leased a small portion of the refrigerated building as a storage facility for the unclaimed and indigent deceased.

Bubba took the tire iron from the rear of the wagon and smashed the station wagon's tailgate window. He picked up a long, knife-like shard of the broken glass, tucked it in his coat pocket.

The Mexican watched him in silent curiosity then jumped up on the dock and slid back the morgue's aluminum door and Bubba followed him into darkness.

Guerrero turned on a light that shone down a narrow corridor. Bubba was right behind him.

"Nobody here?" asked Bubba.

"Plenty people here, but they are not talking." Another joke.

An old man appeared like a phantom, wearing a brown security uniform. He wore a fancy gun belt. His hand rested on the butt of a big gun inside a silver-studded holster. He went into an asthmatic coughing fit.

Guerrero patted the security guard on the arm and told him they had come to identify a murder victim, which they would find on their own.

The bottom floor smelled of pine-scented Lysol. There were alcoves on both sides of the corridor leading to swinging metal doors at the hallway's end. It fascinated Bubba how local governments handled the dead in Baja cities. They'd place them on wooden slats that sat on concrete blocks in the basements of police stations and funeral homes until the family anted up to have them cleaned and embalmed, ready for burial. Autopsies were rare. Unidentified Americans who died in Baja were left in the condition their bodies were found—from the car accident or overdose or the hunting or boating mishap—only moved from the scene to a slab.

The two men took a freight elevator below ground level and stepped off into a dank anteroom. Guerrero opened another sliding door to a blast of refrigeration; he turned on lights, three hanging rows of fluorescence flickered to life. The green-colored walls were bare except for some slatted air vents. Before them was a vast cellar floor filled with bodies under white sheets that hovered, it appeared, a foot off the floor. Souls descending to Purgatory—or all the way to Hell.

Guerrero tucked his flashlight into a back pocket. He said, "We can look for a tag with the name of Julieta—"

"No names, friend. I don't want to know no names. Just find the body."

They split up. Bubba uncovered corpses that looked like they might be women. Most of them were too large, hefty corpses that probably keeled over from heart attacks. He saw no bullet holes or machete or knife wounds, no bruises or evidence of strangulation. Mexican men didn't kill their wives; if anything, wives did in their husbands, who tended to be smaller and usually too drunk to give them a fight.

Then he uncovered a body the right height and size but that was a young Caucasian male, probably an American teenager. The body appeared beaten pretty badly.

Death had left these unassuming corpses more unassuming, to the point of grossness. God bless their loser souls, Bubba thought.

He found a smaller one, maybe about a hundred-fifty pounds. Suitable structure, all limbs accounted for. Kind of short, maybe five-four. Way too short.

"You find one?" he said, seeing Guerrero wheeling a gurney toward the door. "Hey, wait a minute, hang on there."

He rushed over and uncovered the corpse to the waist, took a good look at a blue female, then smiled at the Mexican.

Rigor mortis had passed and the body was flexible; Bubba figured it had not been refrigerated more than a day or two. It looked just about right, right height, right weight.

He took hold at the ankles, pulling the body a couple feet off the bottom, then ordered Guerrero to jump on the gurney and grab hold of the hair.

Guerrero looked at him as though he were insane. "*Porque?*" the Mexican said loudly. "What the shit!" he added in English.

"Just fucking do it, General," said Bubba, not particularly enjoying what he had to do and losing patience.

Guerrero frowned but did as he was told.

"Now pull like you're trying to take that head right off there." He locked eyes with the Mexican.

Guerrero looked not so much like Quasimodo squatting on a corbelled arch as he did a smaller version of Mighty Joe Young not liking himself about now.

Bubba used the shard of glass from the tailgate window and quickly cut across the throat, a strong fast pressure slice that popped the head right off under the Mexican's tug.

Guerrero fell backwards. He let go the head of the corpse and threw his hands out behind him before he struck the concrete floor. The head hit the concrete on its nose, popping an eyeball from its socket.

Bubba grimaced and gingerly picked up the head, holding it away from himself. It was heavier than a bowling ball, all that black hair hanging off it. A front tooth had chipped and lodged in the lip. Something leaking from the neck splattered on both Bubba's and Guerrero's pants and boots.

Guerrero got to his feet with his revolver in hand. Bubba couldn't tell if the Mexican's face was red or not, a face that dark.

"You maybe go too far, *señor*," Guerrero said, speaking in clear English. "Maybe I want to shoot you now."

Bubba avoided his glare and placed the corpse's head on the gurney, making his moves calculated and slow. "Sorry, man ... You see how quick that thing popped off? You all right, not hurt are you?"

Maybe it was thinking he wouldn't get the rest of his money, or shooting Bubba wouldn't fly with his U.S. boss, Fitzsimmon—but the Mexican slid the Colt back inside his shiny jacket.

Bubba said, "It's done, let's get out of here."

"Dead people, they make me nervous," said Guerrero.

It was done all right but Bubba couldn't forget that gun eyeballing him; he felt a fire boil in his gut. "Yeah, me too. Now we need to get some clothes and shoes and some fuel. Then we pick up the other car."

They wrapped the body and head in the sheet that had covered it and carried it to the elevator and then outside and down the steps and heaved it into the back of the wagon. No prowl cars in the parking lot, no civilians wondering around. No noise other than machinery droning at the other end of the factory and some distant street traffic.

Bubba followed Guerrero back through the sliding door and waited in the corridor while the Mexican stepped inside a room and brought out a set of women's clothes—skirt, blouse, undergarments and sneakers.

Bubba said, "Didn't I say jeans? You know what blue jeans are?"

Guerrero spit to the side and headed back into the room. He returned moments later with a pair of men's soiled jeans that Bubba said would do. In the car they lowered the front windows to allow air to pass through. Bubba stopped at a combination mercado-gas station where he bought two gallons of Coleman fuel while Guerrero filled the Buick's tank with premium gas.

Guerrero guided him through the rough dirt streets of a *colonia* where they picked up the other car, a '62 Falcon he said belonged to his nephew. The Mexican drove the Falcon behind Bubba, out of the city onto the coastal byway.

The flicker in the Falcon's right headlight kept drawing Bubba's eye in the rearview. *Fuckin idiot, just put the lights on bright.*

The highway in places ran dangerously close to the edges of jagged cliffs that dropped hundreds of feet to the sea. Tonight, under a cloudless sky, Bubba watched the late moon paint a shimmering silver rug on the ocean. This was Gringo Pass, where drunk American kids occasionally took the dive.

Bubba missed his chosen spot and made a quick bumpy U-turn across the trenched median. He pulled on to a scenic overlook, positioning the Buick in the direction lemmings would take leaping to their demise, and got out of the car. Behind him, the Falcon sputtered and squeaked to a stop. A southbound car breezed by.

"Your headlight has a short," Bubba said.

"No problem. Who is going to stop *me*, the Inspector of Police." The Mexican sat behind the wheel, an arm hung out of the driver's door. Bubba hadn't noticed the gold incisor inside his mouth until now, twinkling in the moonlight.

"It's gotta get fixed, General."

The Mexican climbed out of the Falcon and walked up to Bubba, getting close. "*Esta carro es bueno, es no problemo, ese.*"

"Fuck it ain't," Bubba said. He moved to the rear of the Buick. "C'mon, let's get this thing dressed."

Guerrero paused long enough to lose the hard face then reluctantly pitched in. Both men tried to look at other things—the serene and lovely view—as they dressed the corpse. Once the jeans were up to the knees, Bubba said, "That's good." The Mexican flipped the body on to its face in the cargo bed while Bubba worked the blouse up the arms. He had to get real close to the thing for that. He didn't button it. The sneakers and a bra got tossed on the front floorboard.

They moved the corpse the rest of the way out of the cargo space and hauled it by the forearms into the driver's seat, Bubba crawling in first and posited it flush with the contour. To hold the body in position, Bubba fit the arms through the steering wheel and under the blinker arm and gearshift lever. He got a little queasy through the whole ordeal and stayed queasy looking at it sitting there now, imagining how it would look to see a car driving down the highway, no head on the driver.

He told Guerrero, "Drive the Falcon down to that dirt road." He pointed. "I'll be along in a few minutes." When the Falcon was gone, he doused some of the Coleman fuel over the body, the front and back seats, and then he stood outside and doused a rope's tail strung into the backseat. He left the other can of Coleman fuel in the cargo area, lid off, and tossed the one in his hand into the backseat floorboard. Done.

He stood back. He looked at the road and then the ocean.

Before lighting it up, he sighed. It was a good thing his horse-wrangling daddy had taught him to consider things before jumping in because he had forgotten something.

"Jesus! Thank you daddy," he exclaimed. He dug the bag of money out from under the legs of the corpse and laid it aside on the ground then did the same thing as before, stood back and thought.

"Jesus, the damn head!" He folded the sheet into the form of a hobo's sack, head in it. That done he laid it aside.

Bubba stood in front of the Buick pretending to relieve himself as a string of three cars passed. The plates told him they were citizens, *Bajacalifornianos*. The taillights faded and the scene again grew quiet.

The car stood just feet from the cliff's edge, ready to sail toward that moon. Bubba moved quickly. He wedged the crowbar between the accelerator and seat and restarted the engine, adjusting the crowbar to rev up it. He again shut the door and now put the flame from a cigarette lighter to the fuel-soaked rope tail. He watched the flame move up the rope and inside the car. He moved the gearshift lever, dropping it into drive, then quickly backed away.

The Buick lurched forward then stopped with a clunk. Rear wheels spun and the engine roared but the car didn't move any further. He hustled to the rear of the wagon and pushed. It wouldn't give.

He ran to the side, knelt and saw the problem—the front right wheel had caught behind a boulder. Bubba opened the door amid yellow flames and reached under the body and knocked the crowbar aside, then threw the transmission into reverse. He turned the steering wheel counterclockwise as the car inched back, waited one-mississippi, two ... Then he rotated the wheel the other direction.

Flames licked outside the windows now.

Bubba pushed on the crowbar and slammed the shift again into "D," ran to the rear of the car and pushed with all he had. The car moved forward, the back wheels began to lift off the ground. He pushed till the veins in his face and neck were ready to blow.

Then she gave.

The rear end went heavenward, rising above his head. He gave one last heave against the car's underbelly and the car slowly tilted over, disappearing top first.

Bubba stepped to the edge and watched as it crashed against a boulder fifteen feet down, sending the beefy vehicle into its first flip, wheels upside down, the underside exposed in the moonlight like the belly of a big flaming turtle. It took a crushing rooftop bounce that coincided with the initial explosion, an eruption lighting up the mountainside and roaring with violent energy.

The only thing that could stop it from reaching the sea was a narrow dirt road through a hillside olive grove halfway down, about a hundred more feet. But the way it was picking up velocity, Bubba's money was on it missing the road altogether or just taking a bounce off it and still making a splash—if the tumbling fireball didn't disintegrate first. He had picked the spot on the drive down with Maggie, giving it only a cursory look while she talked about her poor dead dad. He knew then it would make the perfect site. And it did.

Bubba stood over the moonlit sea and watched the ball of fire plummet. He used body motion at every bounce and tumble and boom.

The fireball exploded again and then came apart altogether. The larger pieces made it to the bottom where the pounding deep-water surf extinguished the flames as if they were candles, leaving but puffs of dissipating steam, not even a fizz.

Bubba picked up the sack of money and hobo pouch. He sighed and looked beyond the ocean's edge where the moon glow scooted along the pale surface to its source at the edge of the earth. He quaked from a sudden chill, never having experienced anything quite like the show he'd just put on.

CHAPTER THIRTY-FOUR

Myers sat alone on the concrete bench. His elbows rested on his knees, his hands dangled freely above his shoes. His eyes were closed. He dozed again.

He had managed to ignore the loudmouths and derelicts that strutted around the holding cell throughout the wee hours, looking for something Myers and a few others didn't have to offer, the need to fight, a fix or something personal. Myers was approached but held his ground, dead set on having no contact or engagement. It occurred to him that his demeanor pretty much showed him how he had become—indifferent, aloof, angry even. He wandered through life with little direction, without contact, without emotional commitment. Existing, nothing more. What was that telling him?

No, that wasn't him. He could be emotional, he could be committed. Like now, with this story, the one he'd been so damn committed to it had cost him a job. And now his freedom. He felt obligated to do something about these missing children; he needed to find them, to *save* them. He knew why, but the notion came from the past. And the past was not now.

Myers squeezed his temples to force away the stubborn frown embedded there, like a curse. He needed to relieve the pain from his swollen head. Pedroza. The rat had clubbed him into unconsciousness.

He couldn't manufacture even a grin spotting Detective Millard enter the cell, like a huge dark shadow in his charcoal suit. His eyes located Myers and gave him a nod.

"You've looked better," he said.

There was pity or disgust tinting his stoic face. Myers said nothing.

Myers kept his open hand on the clobbered side of his head as if to protect it from the cop.

"They're arraigning you early," Millard said. "Thank me for that … Planning to sue?"

Myers stood up too fast and his head swooned. He grabbed hold of Millard's arm to keep from falling. "Assault and battery in ambush, intent to kill. Thinking seriously of it."

His mouth felt of cotton and grit when he talked and reeked with the pungent aftertaste of Cuervo Gold. Sleep came to mind as an antidote. They had not followed up with pain medicine after sewing his head. Which was just as well since he would be stuck with the bill, no longer employed and insured.

Millard said, "Rosy's real sorry about last night—I had a long talk with him."

"When?"

"Last night—afterwards."

"So why the hell didn't you get me out then?"

Millard grinned. "He had a bench warrant, don't forget. Something about perjury, don't forget. You *did* withhold evidence in a police shooting, don't forget—"

"Sonofabitch! You're all in it together."

"Could be. I can recommend the best shyster around, Sonny Roy McClellan, Jr. I believe you're acquainted already."

"You don't do cute well, Johnny."

Millard pitched a hand toward the holding cell door. "Any time you're ready to leave ... "

"Someone picked up bail?"

"Your benefactor's Maxwell Cullen. Said he was good for five grand, no more. He wasn't thrilled to get called at four a.m."

Myers nodded in appreciation.

Millard walked with him out of the tank.

"You think I'm not gonna get out of this, don't you?"

Millard grunted, shook his head. "Judge'll decide. You want some coffee?"

It took an hour to get processed and turned over to County for the arraignment, and then another hour waiting on the judge, who apparently hadn't yet learned how bad the south bay commute was, apparently recently becoming a resident of Chula Vista from east county. The arraignment itself lasted two minutes—bail set at twenty thousand on a felony complaint for withholding evidence and also resisting arrest, which the court was inclined to dismiss, court date set two months from now on a Tuesday at ten a.m. A strong admonition from the judge not to leave the State of California or the country. Myers said, "Yes, Your Honor."

Pedroza's gum-chewing smirk menaced him even now as Myers left the courthouse, his head throbbing from the junior detective's cheap shot. Forget it. The courtroom visit brought the reality home, felony charges, the possibility of jail, sweating it out. Fired from his job. He couldn't forget it.

He stood for a moment at the corner of Broadway and Front where the eastern sun peeked through skyscrapers. He walked ten blocks to Salazar's Mexican Restaurant, a family-run diner, and had huevos rancheros with lots of water and coffee. He chatted with the owner whom he had spoken to over the years and whose name he figured was Mr. Salazar though didn't know.

He felt better after eating. A short cab ride and he was home where he showered off the stench of jail and dressed in a solid blue, buttoned-up shirt and tan trousers. The big empty house groaned invitingly, and it was all he could do to keep from climbing into that tall, comfortable bed. But he didn't have the time. He grabbed his car keys and left.

The drive into the valley this time of morning took fifteen minutes. Myers made it in ten. He pulled the Land Cruiser into the high-security section of the *Journal's* parking lot and flashed the press card to the kiosk guard, the same ID that L.C. had ordered him to relinquish. The guard waved him in.

The guard at the desk inside, an old-timer named Henry Boggs, knew better. Employees entered the building from the west side of the building, walking up a ramp through electronic glass doors and past the checkpoint where they underwent an electronic scan. It wasn't always like that. Used to be mutual nods and hand waves of recognition, howdy do's.

"You okay, Mr. Myers?" the octogenarian said. He was concerned. "Your head."

"Oh, that. Nothing to worry about, Henry."

"Well, uh, didn't you get word?"

Myers feigned surprise. "Word?"

"You know, that you wouldn't be returning. You know. Damn, I hated to hear that, we been through so many tall and true tales together."

Myers laid a hand on Henry Boggs' bony shoulder. "Yeah, I know … But I got personal stuff up there, Henry. What do you think I should we do about it, just leave it for the vultures?"

"Aw, hell no … You go on up, Mr. Myers. What are you gonna do, steal a typewriter?"

Myers nodded and smiled at the old man, who probably thought they really did still use typewriters up there. The old man made a delightful grandpa for a flock of grand- and great grandchildren.

The newsroom was dead. Lights on but dead quiet, not a soul in sight. Cullen often showed up before nine, and that was okay with Myers since he wanted to thank him to his face for going his bail and for all his refreshing homespun advice and wisdom over the years.

He rummaged through his desk for the undeveloped film roll he'd shot that went with that Catholic diocese sex exposé that was going to get him a job in L.A. Myers knew that child abuse stories, even while saturated by the news media, would never be dated.

He took a few ballpoint pens stamped with the newspaper logo, a couple of rulers, a ream of paper. He considered the American Heritage; but who needed it anymore. On his way out he was lured by the vitality going on in the wire room. He checked the AP and Reuters releases. He noticed a piece datelined Ensenada, B.C., slugged "Baja Fatality." It got his attention of course. The report had just come across.

"Holy shit!" he exclaimed.

He left the wire room and hurried back to his desk to pull up the AP story on the computer; his password still worked. Maybe he'd just dreamed L.C. fired him.

The story had been filed originally by a former stringer for the *Journal* who covered Baja Norte, one Wilford Reynolds, an old codger who couldn't quit the business even though he'd retired years ago to Baja Mar to play golf by the sea. AP had picked it up from the early edition of the Ensenada daily, *El Mundo Hoy.*

Margaret Frazier's name appeared in the second graph; it would be a bad Alzheimer's day before he forgot the name Frazier.

ENSENADA—A fiery car crash took the life of a U.S. citizen on the toll-road bluffs just north of this city late Monday, Baja officials reported.

The vehicle, registered to Margaret Frazier, 29, of El Cajon, California, apparently left the highway ten kilometers north of Ensenada on a winding section of road known locally as "Gringo Pass," so called for the number of American fatalities that have occurred there over the years.

The vehicle, identified as a mid-1970s' model Buick, was almost completely demolished in the nearly three-hundred-foot plunge. A single recovered body was mangled and burned beyond recognition. Except for the victim's head, the body was mostly intact, according to city morgue personnel. The head, apparently, could not be found.

Officials are awaiting confirmation from forensic tests before making a positive identification of the remains. But it is believed to be Margaret Ann Frazier, whose father, John William Frazier, was shot and killed by police at Cabrillo National Monument only the day before under circumstances still being investigated, according to the San Diego Police Department.

Ensenada Police Inspector Javier Maria Guerrero said the victim apparently lost control on the mountain road early Tuesday morning.

"There [are] no skid marks. It appear[s to be] another accident caused by alcohol," Inspector Guerrero said …

Myers took the stairs to the fourth floor photo morgue, which was open and also uninhabited. Lying on the counter was a folder labeled "Cabrillo pixs, newsroom." Myers filed through the prints and found one of Margaret Frazier facing the camera from the side of him, Myers, and a side view profiling both in a face-to-face from which Myers distinctly recalled the angry, distraught words she uttered: "He's dead? He's *dead.* How, why! *Goddamn them.*"

Myers took of the prints showing her face and went back down to the third-floor newsroom.

He sat at his desk, suddenly exhausted, struggling to keep his burning eyes open. Her death seemed too much of a coincidence. He recalled their phone conversation from early yesterday. She had sounded nervous but not out of control. The Immigration agent, Sidney Rhoades, had mentioned her having some kind of connection with an Indian tribe in Baja; maybe she had been on her way there, overwrought and not watching her driving.

Myers got on the horn to ICE. Rhoades' day began at eight and he was there.

Myers told him about the wire story. He said, "Didn't you mention an orphanage in Baja, run by some locals?"

"I just can't believe it," Rhoades said.

"It's a terrible thing," Myers said. "But I need some answers. The Indian reservation. I need to know where it is. Maybe she was headed there. Maybe these babies are there."

"She wouldn't get drunk and make that drive," Rhoades said. "Something's up, Mr. Myers. I just don't buy it. I knew enough about her that I can tell you it wasn't like her at all."

"What are you suggesting? Maybe it wasn't an accident?" Myers wanted to hear it from someone else. He already thought it.

"*Someone's* responsible for this." Rhoades didn't sound too sure of himself. "Her father just died, and now his daughter crashes and dies, this quickly? That's rather remarkable, don't you think? She might've been a little unstable after John's death, but what in hell was she doing driving down there in the middle of the night?"

There it was, corroboration of Myers' own suspicion of foul play. Myers nodded, as though the big man sat across from him in Tina Lubrano's seat.

Rhoades added, "About the Indians, look for the quick-sketch artist at Hussong's Cantina. Officially, I can run it by Captain Ahab, see where that gets us."

"You sure you want to do that? Your boss doesn't seem to have much humor where the name Frazier is concerned—or my name, either."

"Maybe so, Mr. Myers. But both the Fraziers are now dead and I think I should try to do something."

"It's not your fault," Myers offered.

"You're wrong about that."

Myers needed to get out of the building. People would be showing up any time now. It would take only one of L.C.'s chums seeing Myers and right back to jail he would go.

Just one thing more. He found Madelene Schaefer's number in the phone book. He dialed before deciding what he'd say. But she'd just adopted a foreign child and babies were missing and something needed sniffing out at that residence. Myers' curiosity compelled him to find out.

"Hello, this is Madelene." It was the voice he remembered.

Myers hung up without speaking; he grabbed the photo of Margaret Frazier and left the newsroom, halting for the briefest moment to look over the massive floor. He figured this was it, he would never return. See you in my dreams hopefully not.

Max Cullen ran into him at the guard's station. Myers thanked Cullen for bailing him. He knew Cullen wanted to know why he was here, but the city editor let it slide. Cullen just gave him a mentor's sad, sympathetic gaze. "You need a reference, don't hesitate. But knowing you, something's bound to happen—maybe even better. I've got money on you, remember. Be good, Ray."

"Relax, Max. I'm not going to skip town on you," he said, knowing that's exactly what he was going to do.

CHAPTER THIRTY-FIVE

Madelene Schaefer answered the door. "Yes?" She spoke shyly. "You remember me?"

"Why yes, of course. You're the reporter. Ah—"

"Myers. Call me Ray, Mrs. Schaefer. I'm sorry, *is* it 'Mrs.?'"

"Not in a while," she said with a slight lift of the lip. "Please come in." She stood aside.

"Thanks."

Myers stepped in far enough for her to shut the door behind him but close enough that he smelled lilac. She walked and he followed her through the house. He eyeballed everything within view, committing to memory the details that interested him. Starched and shined living room, no baby items. Whole other story in the natural-lighted den, push toys galore, a yellow-and-green motorized swing and a swinging floor crib standing side by side between a couch and cushioned chair. Blanket on the floor with smiling pink elephant faces and a dozen stuffed animals strewn about.

She led him through the house to the outside. The patio contained more baby items, a wind-up rocker close to a heavy redwood chaise lounge where she had Myers sit. The swimming pool did not have child proof fencing surrounding it, but Myers didn't think he had to ask about that; he suspected that was in the works.

"The little one asleep?" he asked.

"Why, yes. Why?" She sat in a cushioned chair next to Myers.

"You don't have to be suspicious of me, Ms. Schaefer. Like I said before, I'm not out to cause you any trouble. Okay?"

"I didn't think I looked suspicious. Did I, Mr. Myers?"

"Not in the least. Please, make it Ray."

"Madelene, then?"

"Fair enough."

"Would you like something to drink, a beer? Something stronger? ... Are you all right?"

"No thanks. Too early." Myers tried to keep himself from getting too comfortable on the soft cushions, with the warmth of the sun bathing his face. He was seeing floaters again, whether his eyes were shut or open, a true tequila hangover. He gazed out at the unobstructed vista of a blue Pacific Ocean, the floaters taking dive after dive into the sea. He could have fallen asleep in a blink.

The hillside fell off beyond the pool, eliminating even rooftops in the grand view of sky and ocean. Even in La Jolla, it was a spectacular view. The saltillo-tiled patio extended around the side of the house, where Myers saw three walls of nothing but glass and the tops of mature cypress and eucalyptus beyond that.

"Very nice place you have."

"Thank you. Gift my husband left. The only one."

"I'm sorry, Ms. Schaefer, I didn't realize—"

"Oh, no. I'm not widowed; the bum's still around. I should've said that."

"I'm divorced, too. But only twice."

"Madelene, remember? ... Do you have children, Ray?"

Myers nodded. "Sure. Only two. I don't see them."

"I'm so sorry."

"Me too. It's my loss."

She was staring at him. She grinned politely and quickly looked away. "Villi is a wonderful cook," she said. "She—it would be no trouble at all if you would join me for a brunch, or early lunch if you prefer."

She hadn't asked him why he was here. He heard the baby cry, then the muted sound of rapid-fire pats and shushes. He turned to the sound coming through an opened door and saw the short, plump housekeeper holding the baby. Myers thought, *It's an awfully tiny baby for all these toddler toys.* But he didn't say it.

He didn't answer the brunch-or-lunch question. He handed Madelene the black-and-white picture of Margaret Frazier standing in the rain.

"Do you know her?"

She hesitated. "Know her?" Her voice was breathy.

"I guess maybe you do."

"All right. Yes, I do know her. She—she's my broker."

"Stock broker?"

Madelene shook her head. "No, not that. I fired that crook last year—not soon enough. I do my own investing now."

Myers said, "On second thought, I will have something to drink. If it's not too much to—"

"No, no trouble at all."

Madelene returned the photo to Myers. She stood and called for the housekeeper. "Villi, can you put Connie in her crib for a moment and bring us a pitcher of Bloody Marys? Please. Use the crystal, please."

Madelene stayed on her feet, pacing in quick tiny steps. Myers sighed. She was obviously nervous. He was beginning to put two and two together, the baby and the "broker." Getting the picture. But the gauze inside his head muddied things. He supposed he needed the hair of the dog.

"Madelene. If I may, let me explain myself, why I'm here. I'm working on a story—which is the result of that shooting at Cabrillo on Sunday. The man they shot and killed was named Frazier, your broker's father. My story has to do with Immigration and maybe some smuggled babies and an orphanage down in Baja. I think this woman could have been involved. But I haven't figured it all out."

He again showed her the picture of Margaret Frazier.

"She's different, younger looking. I—"

Mrs. Ruvalcaba appeared in a flurry with a silver platter containing a cut-glass pitcher of red, red drink with a silver saucer of celery pieces and lime wedges and two frosty highball glasses engraved with the initials, "MS," presumably for Madelene Schaefer. She was strong as she was stout, carrying the heavy tray in one hand, the baby in her other, cloaked and quiet as a mouse. The new nanny had ignored Madelene's order to first put the baby down, demonstrating the stubbornness he knew of strong-minded Mexican women. Either way, Myers got the bright idea that he could use a housekeeper like Mrs. Ruvalcaba for the umpteen rooms in his unkempt home. Maybe she had a relative available, a niece or daughter.

"May I?" he asked the woman, seeking a closer look at the baby.

The housekeeper recoiled as if from the groping hands of a child molester. Myers gave her a big friendly smile, but she didn't budge. Her stern face had eyes that told him to keep his filthy hands away from this baby. Myers let it go as his beat-up looks.

"*Mrs. Ruvalcaba!*" snapped Madelene. "Give me Connie this instant."

The housekeeper did as she was told, however reluctant. "Humph," she snorted and left.

"I'm sorry," Madelene said, "Villi can be a real bugger at times. Very possessive. I don't know, maybe it's a cultural thing. Sometimes I can't figure her out at all. Oh, here."

She handed the baby over to Myers, who quickly sat back down to take the bundle. He'd only wanted to peek; he hadn't meant to actually hold it. But he let the baby lie in the crook of his arm and found himself swaying comfortably, a spark away from humming a tune he could still recall. He pulled back the gossamer veil protecting the baby's face, seeing a healthy-looking, red-faced Islander. He touched the red forehead with his finger. The baby seemed hot.

"She doesn't have a fever, does she?" he said, a bit anxious. He looked up now.

"You'd think so, but no. I've been to her pediatrician for that twice. She's just warm-blooded."

"Well, she's, ah, she's darling," he said and used his free hand to gulp the Bloody Mary.

"It doesn't matter a hoot to me that Connie turned out to be Filipino," Madelene suddenly said. "She said the baby would be Caucasian and that's what I expected. But I don't care. Really. Actually, I'm glad! But, it's just—she could have told me beforehand and not surprised me with it. You know?"

Myers nodded, following her eyes, paying close and sympathetic attention. Keep her talking. "Maybe there was a mix-up; maybe she didn't know."

"Well, yes of course, that could be."

Madelene frowned as she shifted closer to Myers.

"What happened, Ray?" she asked, lifting a hand toward his head, as if wanting to comfort him. "That nasty looking bandage on your forehead.

Were you after an interview with somebody that turned on you? That happens, doesn't it?"

Myers laughed, then winced from the resultant bolt of pain. "Nothing exotic like that. Bumped it on a bar counter. You'd of had to be there."

"Here, let me take her," she said and lifted Connie out of his arm and put the baby into the musical bassinet close to her chair and got it started moving.

She covered the infant again and sat back down, facing Myers. "It must be difficult sometimes," she said, "the things you have to do in your work. And dangerous. I really admired your story—that you could find the courage to put your own feelings aside to write about such a terrible incident. When it happened right there in front of you."

"Well, thanks, Madelene," said Myers. He was thinking, with that blanket always covering it up, no wonder the baby felt hot.

"No, I really mean it. We take for granted what you newspaper reporters have to go through sometimes. I know I do. Frankly, nobody really cares, you know? It's not like television news. We don't ever see you, we only read you."

Myers's eyebrows raised. "Yeah. It's rare when we get responses from readers, at least nice ones. I'm pleased to hear you say it. You know, with print giving way to this new age with so much more to offer—and immediate—us old writers are soon to fade away."

"That's not true. I look forward to reading my paper every morning."

"I do, too."

Myers finished off his drink and stalk of celery and got himself centered again. He handed her another picture, the snapshot of three Vietnamese boys he had held back from the authorities and over which he had been fired, hit on the head and thrown in jail.

"Do these kids mean anything to you?"

She looked and shook her head. "Who are they?"

"The tall one John Frazier's son. He spent everything he had to adopt get this kid. I haven't told the police all I know, which means I'm concealing information in the Frazier shooting. I'm breaking the law."

Myers glanced at the side table where he observed half a pitcher of spicy red drink. Madelene noticed and poured him a full glass, stuck in another celery stalk and slice of lime and handed the drink back to him.

"Thanks. Whatever you want to tell me, Madelene, even if it's something questionable about your baby, don't let it stop you. If you're worried you might lose the child because of me, you can forget that."

Myers drank thirstily as he waited for a response. It appeared Madelene was fighting back tears. She didn't say anything for a moment, then straightened. "She was really good. She took care of everything, the baby's papers, everything. This time I got my baby, thanks to her."

"What do you mean 'this time'?"

"The first baby I was supposed to adopt—oh, it was terrible. I gave them extra money to make sure the child would be well cared for in transport."

"This was before you got Connie?"

He saw the welling come to her eyes again, but her voice didn't crack. "My first baby didn't make it. She got tuberculosis, and just died. She was from Russia. I just wonder about all the others who don't make it."

"Was that baby from a legitimate agency?"

Madelene froze. Then, timorously, "The first one?"

Myers drew closer to her. "Madelene, just tell me you *thought* it was legitimate, that the person told you they were."

"Oh," she said, brightly, as if that had never occurred to her. "Yes. It's true; I didn't have any reason to think otherwise."

She then said, "Selling babies like this might be criminal but it's victimless. I'll tell you this. I waited two years on those other agencies … You won't go to the authorities if I tell you something, will you, Ray?"

Myers shook his head. "I see no reason why I would or should. All I can see is that your Connie is a damn lucky baby."

She almost whispered her words. "It took her *three months*. That's it, just three months to get my baby—and look what I got!"

"Margaret Frazier was your facilitator, wasn't she?"

"Well," she said, a glitter in her grassy-green eyes, "when I paid her fifty thousand dollars for my baby, her name was Sylvia Fischer."

CHAPTER THIRTY-SIX

Maggie woke to Willie singing softly in the distance, *Mamas, don't let your babies grow up to be cowboys ...*

The French doors stood open and the light of morning bathed the walls. She scanned through Sandman eyes, seeing pale yellow, awakening to the room's consoling antiquity. She clutched the arm of the man lying next to her and held on tight. She trembled slightly from a nightmare, one she had had before: Tall adults screaming at her in a well-lighted room, changing to a dark hallway, their shadows elongated along the floor and walls. Moving closer, turning fully dark. She squeezes her ragged teddy against her chest, standing before the two faceless figures that are blocking her way.

Maggie drew a small sense of security from Bubba's untroubled snoring. She needed him now. He had become her only connection to the previous life. Was there anyone she could turn to, without word getting back to the people who wanted her dead? Maybe Mack and the girls at Jimbo's? No, gossipers. Cloris? Why would she want to tell that woman anything? Certainly not her neighbors. She hardly knew her dad's parents, they lived so far away, too poor to travel. Mr. Swabb and his people would find out no matter whom she told. They would search for her until they were all dead or imprisoned for eternity. Her life had undeniably and inescapably changed. Maggie Ann Frazier no longer existed.

She lay immobilized by that oppressive thought, hanging on until Bubba woke.

When he did, he smacked his lips and exhaled warm morning breath, fluttered his eyelashes in a girlish way, then smiled seeing her next to him.

"Mornin', honey," he said sweetly.

Maggie smiled back. "Howdy."

She let go his arm so he could scratch; he scratched his head, then his ribs, then a knee. She thought for sure he would scratch his privates, but he didn't.

Sitting, he said abruptly, "What about life insurance? You got any?"

Maggie frowned. "Like I would take it out on myself?"

Bubba lay back. "Yeah, guess you're right."

"I'm not worth anything, anyway," she said gloomily.

"Aw, I don't think so … I mean, I *do*."

The comment drew a grin from her. "You say some funny things sometimes, you know that?"

"Well, I don't mean to. Sorry."

Maggie had been in shock last night after he told her what was going on. The thought that people wanted her dead, that they were paying money to have it done. Premeditated murder. That was a capital offense. It probably even had—what did they call it—extra circumstances? Enough to draw the death penalty maybe. Killing her was serious stuff. She might still be in shock.

But Bubba had come clean about it. Then he told her he loved her. Then he went out and said he made things right. Then he told her she was free to keep the money and disappear under a new name, free to start life over. He could talk smooth and straight as Dr. Phil. Sometimes.

Bubba rolled over in the bed and kissed Maggie on the cheek. "We need to talk about your future, you know," he said. "I have to get back sometime."

"I'm going to the village." She pulled the sheet to her chin.

"What village?"

"Indian. My father did business with them. They run an orphanage for strays and other troubled children and sometimes our babies. A sort of safehouse, you might say."

"Hey, you can't do that, Maggie. You crazy? Those are part of the people want you gone."

"I thought of that already. They won't tell. Margarita and I are friends—she's the chief's daughter. What Margarita says goes."

"I don't know. Seems to me you're just walking into more trouble." Bubba's little eyes narrowed. "You're not egging them on on purpose, are you? For revenge? That wouldn't do me any good."

"They have lots of land, Bubba. They couldn't find me there even if they looked—and the only way they would look is if somebody from outside told them I was there." She nudged him.

"Oh, man. Don't even kid like that."

"Besides, I *want* to go. It's so nice in the mountains, Bubba. The children are there. I can help with them."

Bubba sighed. "You know this squaw that well that you can trust her to keep your secret? What about the men there? They all lust after white women, you know."

Maggie laughed. "You're an idiot—and she's not a squaw, Bubba. Shit."

"Okay, sorry. It's just I don't know anything about these people, these Indians."

"Nobody else does, either. That's what makes it safe. See?"

"I guess. But just till your remains are cremated and the death certificate issued. Then we'll get you squared away somewhere else, maybe even back in the states. Sort of a protective-custody deal."

Maggie didn't say anything, but it hit her like a punch in the heart. *Death certificate. Remains.* It took her right back to that awful feeling of despair. This cowboy was no Dr. Phil.

"I'm going to take a shower," she said.

She climbed over Bubba getting out of the squeaky bed. "And then I want to do some shopping."

Bubba grinned and patted her on the fanny. "Anything you want, Maggie honey." She could see he didn't know shopping for her was therapy, not fun.

Willie was off that distant radio now and some cheerful Mexican song was playing, cranked up a little louder. Bubba listened for a moment to the lyrics, chuckling. He lay propped in bed with hands intertwined behind his head, wondering about the Indian land and the kind of people who lived on it. What was her involvement with them that she could trust them with her life? And she hadn't brought up the money thing yet, either. Hadn't even asked about the money stashed in her burned-up station wagon. It sure didn't seem like she was planning on fighting him over who gets to hold on to it. He figured it should go in his interest-bearing account at Great Western, where it would be safe and he could easily get to it. Get it to her as needed.

A bloodcurdling yell erupted in the bathroom. He thought the hot water might have died on her.

Then she screamed, "What *is* this thing?"

"Oh," Bubba mumbled, getting up. He stepped into the tiny room and removed the hobo sack from the shower stall floor. "It ain't nothing, just something from last night. I didn't want to leave it in the car—in case we slept in."

He grinned like a horse.

Maggie made a sour face. "What the hell is it, Bubba? It doesn't look like something that ought to be in here."

He sighed and tried explaining. "See, if something had gone wrong at the scene and the body only got the epidermis burnt off it, and these dingdongs decided to run an investigation, and say they ran a dental check, guess what they'd find?"

Maggie's face changed color first then began to twist and convolute.

He went on, "The forensics sure wouldn't match with the person that owned that old Buick with California plates. You catchin' on? ... So I decided to eliminate that problem by removing the head."

"Oh, God! Jesus!" screamed Maggie, who pushed herself against the farthest corner of the stall. "Get it out of here!"

~

The overhanging sign outside the dental office depicted a huge, bone-white molar with "Dr. Julio Lopez, *Dentista*" written in a fancy cursive stroke across the tooth's fading enamel roots.

Bubba ushered Maggie inside the small waiting room where a dozen people waited, almost all of them young children, hardly old enough to have teeth at all. They were moaning and sobbing on the laps of pampering women. The office was cleaner than one would expect of a dentist on the take; Doctor Lopez had been the forensics examiner for certain law enforcement authorities since one of Guerrero's fraternal investigators discovered "errors" in the dentist's government-subsidized practice. Since then Doctor Lopez had worn false teeth.

Right away a heavyset nurse in a brilliant white uniform brought Maggie in while the moaning kids continued to wait. Bubba waved at the children and trailed behind. He had a magic trick with a quarter he could have shown them but didn't have time. Maggie sat in a worn leather chair with a porcelain spit bowl at her elbow, a spotlight out of a police interrogation room, a belt-operated drill. Equipment Wichita dentists used forty years ago.

Maggie looked frightened and Bubba held her hand.

"Don't worry, honey. He just wants to take an impression," said Bubba, adding playfully, "Won't be any drilling today."

The impression was insurance to cover Sergeant Guerrero if he needed definitive identification, say he somehow came up with what was left of the victim's missing head, a jawbone maybe. No concern over Forensic DNA phenotyping; it wasn't even a dream around here. U.S. officials or next-of-kin occasionally were dubious of Mexican findings, or the lack of them, but that only offended local pride and wouldn't get them anywhere.

"Beautiful teeth, beautiful!" exclaimed a boisterous Dr. Lopez, who flew like wind into the room. His dentures were whiter than the handsome nurse's uniform. "Oh, that mine were so nice."

Maggie noticed his teeth behind the broad smile. "They are," she said, furrowing her brow. "They're perfect!"

Dr. Lopez suddenly poked the upper plate slightly out of his mouth. "*Perfecto, sí.* Ha!"

Maggie closed her eyes.

A baby's cry came from somewhere and Maggie's eyes jerked open. "That sounds like a baby. Babies don't have teeth."

"You are so right, Lady. *Es* why I love them so, so much. They are so innocent, no sharp little fangs to cause infection, to cause pain. They are perfect little people before they get those things."

"I guess," Maggie said.

Bubba spoke to the dentist in Spanish. "Get the impression to Sergeant Guerrero quickly, understand?"

The dentist sucked air between his grand choppers and changed his tone. "He says you will pay."

Bubba said, in English, "I'll kick his ass. You tell him that."

Waiting for the mold to set, Bubba took Lopez by the arm and guided him outside. The dentist smiled foolishly walking through the outer room, nodding as if to impart reassurance to desperate-faced mothers still waiting that he wasn't leaving. They walked around the corner and into the alley to the parked Falcon. Bubba fetched the now-soggy bundle from the trunk and handed it to him.

"Dispose of this," he said and grudgingly gave the dentist three hundred dollars.

~

Locals in droves swarmed the sales bins at Élan's. Maggie didn't have to pick and fight her way through those bins, now that she had money. She found exactly what she wanted on the neatly arranged racks and stacks of new items. She bought heavy clothes, Levi jeans and long-sleeved flannel shirts, a down jacket, a fanny pack, serapes and round-toed boots not unlike Bubba's snakeskins. She purchased a baseball cap with the logo "LA Angels," dark lipstick, feminine products, and then, at a novelty shop, a large fish piñata.

"You'll need some booze, and I guess some smokes," Bubba said. He entered a nearby liquor store and bought five bottles of tequila and took a handful of limes from a wicker basket by the cash register. Maggie stood on the sidewalk.

They walked down the street, Maggie in the serape and Angels cap, hugging the tail part of the fish piñata under her arm. Bubba carried the sacks and packages. They kept their shopping to Lopez Mateos, Ensenada's main tourist drag. The couple stopped at El Charro's for an early lunch of mesquite-fired chicken off the rotisserie with *papas*, authentic *salsa fresca* and freshly-made tortillas, then returned to the alley where they'd left the car.

"That should do it, huh?" he said as Maggie opened the passenger's door. "You ready?"

It hadn't gone over Bubba's head that shopping seemed to sadden her, though she'd earlier used the word "cathartic" to describe the cheering effect shopping was supposed to have on her. He didn't know what that word meant exactly, could be something like a hospital stay to recuperate. But she had only grown morose the more boots she tried on and the more stuff she bought—when everything looked great on her girl-slim figure. The lunch buoyed her spirits a little but it didn't last.

Bubba even went so far as to say, "Aw, come on, honey. It can't be that bad."

But it was.

CHAPTER THIRTY-SEVEN

Earl Swabb failed to reach the green in regulation. Again. From eighty yards out he had to clear a formidable bunker and make his third shot sit if not spin back. Virtually impossible with the pin placement so close to that bunker; hardly ever had he gotten backspin anyway. He talked to himself, settling in on the ball—*Loosen up on the grip, swing through the ball, keep your head down. Keep your damn head down.*

He was the single with three Japanese salarymen visiting the west coast on a tight four-day golfing holiday; they were booked on Torrey Pines North after this round, the coveted south course, and were rushing Swabb in their sly, foreign way—arms crossed, fingers to chins, murmuring quietly, grinning, that grin of spite.

The Osaka boys themselves were terrific golfers, hitting long balls with precision and placing them in neat little triangular salvos on the fairways so that they never had to split up nor postpone a perpetual conversation that allowed no room for Swabb. Swabb's cursed slice had shown itself a few times today, keeping him off the fairways.

On this hole, the twelfth, the tourists' balls lay about thirty yards out, sitting up in the middle like eggs, leaving them simple up-and-downs for three more pars. At least, Swabb thought spitefully, they had not made the green in regulation either. They moseyed closer, before Swabb hit.

Swabb refused to be intimidated. By going ahead of him, he figured they were not so subtly telling him to speed up his game. He swung, popped it good, kept his chin tucked. He lost the ball in the sun but followed the direction of three pointing arms, oohs and ahhs, seeing he'd made an excellent shot, just clearing the backside lip of the volcanic bunker, the ball rolling onto the green. He jumped in place like a youthful Sergio to see his ball stop only fifteen feet past the pin. Swabb was something of an amateur expert on Japanese etiquette and thought that in their culture you didn't point unless intending derision or mockery. Apparently the Osaka boys broke with tradition.

"Thanks, guys," he said of their slight bows. Maybe that shot would rid him of his chip jinx.

He also broke the putting curse, sinking the 15-foot, slight left-to-right, for his par. The par failed to give him honors on the next tee, but second up he powered his drive two-forty just off fairway right into the first cut, safe. Oohs and ahhs.

It had finally turned into the kind of afternoon golf had been invented for, the stuff duffers' dreams were made of. Then, on the fifteenth fairway, just at the pivot of his down swing, his cellular vibrated in his pocket. He didn't pull a Tiger and hold up; he went on through the swing, topping the ball and advancing it about fifty yards at best off the box. It went straight, though.

"God*damnit*," he muttered, glancing at the threesome. They were grinning. If he'd heard right, one of them had even giggled.

He knew the caller was Mendez but answered nevertheless in a sour, formal tone. "Hello, this is E. Warren Swabb."

Mendez breathed into the phone but didn't speak.

"Can't it wait? I'm on the golf course."

Then Mendez spoke, telling him to pack his clubs, now, and meet him to discuss "an urgent matter."

"All right. *Fuck!* I'll be there."

He talked that way to a man he feared more than any superior court judge, all because his golf game had been interfered with. The golf course was sacrosanct; you don't disturb a man on the course, particularly when his game's just beginning to firm up.

Swabb's group was too close to finishing the course to just walk off. Might as well hit the ball walking in.

But the call had effectively ruined his stroke. He bogied the present hole. Double bogied the seventeenth. Didn't even count strokes after hooking it into the drink on the eighteenth's final approach. Swabb never hooked. The Japanese were obviously fed up; they did not bow or speak after the round, just scuttled over to the north course's starter booth to wait their turn off the tee, which peeved Swabb even more.

He angrily threw his clubs in the trunk of the Lexus and left rubber on the asphalt getting out of there. He sped south on the 5 at a safe seventy-three mph. Given his current bad luck, he thought, it wouldn't surprise him to get ticketed even though everyone sped around him.

Twenty-five minutes later he found a parking slot between the Star of India and Anthony's Fish Grotto. Ricky Mendez long ago had chosen the tourist spot to meet when smuggling business was on the docket, the idea that meeting in full view brought less attention. It wasn't all that inconvenient for Swabb on working days since his office was mere blocks up Broadway or even his condo in Mission Hills.

The lawyer arrived first, again, and had to wait. Again, it irked him. He went inside the restaurant this time, instead of standing by the old ship to have the gulls mock him. He wanted a drink.

At two p.m. there were no more than a handful of customers in the lounge. Swabb took a bayside table and stared at the seagulls. The Ensenada-bound ocean liner sat idle at the next-door terminal blocking his sunlight. Hundreds of passengers milled around the dock waiting to board. The gulls frolicked everywhere around the seafood restaurant. With an unwanted sense of déjà vu he turned from the window. He sipped his chilled glass of refreshing Zaca Mesa Reserved Chardonnay while he waited on Mendez to show. He wanted lunch but didn't dare order until Ricky arrived. At two-thirty Mendez sat down across from him. It was too late then to order lunch.

"What's up? What is it?" Swabb asked rather keenly, still bristling from the last part of his golf game. He blamed Mendez for ruining it.

"I have come to a decision I hope you can live with," Mendez said. He was being his enigmatic, stoic, now formal self.

"I'm in no mood for suspense," Swabb said in a foolish display of courage. As a child he didn't know when enough was enough. Even as a grown-up lawyer, he often got admonished by a number of bench judges because of his unchecked emotional retorts.

Mendez eyed him sharply but otherwise ignored the brisk tone. "But first, there's a thing to clear up. I've learned that our shipment from the Rim is arriving early. In two days, it appears."

"But I thought—you said we were looking at a couple of weeks. I'll have to notify people."

Mendez raised one finger to stifle Swabb. "Don't notify anyone, Earl. It won't be necessary ... Let me explain in terms you may understand. You know who came to my office?"

"No, duh!"

Mendez sat back, watchful of Swabb while the waiter took his order—mineral water—and Swabb's—a second glass of the Zaca Mesa.

Then he said, "Put a lid on the sarcasm and listen for a minute ... A reporter named Myers. He had some interesting questions and observations. He wanted to know if I knew anything about human smuggling. Imagine that."

"Smuggling falls under ICE's jurisdiction, doesn't it? Nothing strange about it."

"The other thing," Mendez went on, "is the problem concerning Sylvia—or her father, who caused all this media attention. It's bad news for us. This reporter has tied an old case concerning some war brat to our agent Sylvia—never mind the details, that's not important. My point is, as you can see we have a situation."

Swabb swelled. "Didn't I tell you she's trouble?"

Mendez sighed, a signal to Swabb of his growing impatient, which of course the impervious lawyer missed.

"Do you understand what I'm saying to you, Earl?"

"Sure I do. We have to recruit someone else. Right?"

Mendez shifted in his seat. His face didn't change, nor his eyes. "Try to receive, it's to your advantage. We are in crisis prevention, we can no longer conduct business as usual. We can no longer conduct business at all."

He gave Swabb a chance to tune in, but the lawyer couldn't or wouldn't and Mendez went with a lesser point. "You yourself suggested it, if you'll remember. I wasn't sure if it was the right call then. Now I am."

"Sylvia?" Swabb said and Mendez closed his eyes nodding, apparently pleased he at last had connected that much.

Their beverages appeared and both men sat quietly for the moment, Mendez staring out the window at the blue bay and the water birds flitting about the sky, giving away nothing of his thoughts.

Swabb began to feel a little unsteady with the way the meeting was going. His hands became jittery and it caused him to dribble wine on his tight polo shirt, just above the Nike emblem. He swiped at it.

Mendez turned back to him. He spoke softly. "Obviously, because of my position, I cannot afford to do anything out of the ordinary right now. The Ocotillo problem, just in itself, has forced me to reconsider the future of this business. And now, with our own people turning on us and the press meddling, I'm left with no choice which direction to take. We have to disband … It was inevitable."

Swabb spoke up. "You think it's that serious we can't just make some adjustments, get some fresh blood? There's a lot at stake here, Ricky— money wise. I mean, what about the deals already in the works? Which reminds me, you want me to contact the Inspector for the delivery? Remember, you told me to run it by you when we needed another transporter. You remember?"

Mendez listened with his eyes shut. He sat perfectly still and silent, as though he might be counting to ten. He could have counted to thirty in the amount of time he took before again speaking. "Only you and I know what is happening," he intoned calmly. "As such, you will need to take on additional tasks. Closure requires tying up loose ends … No, do not contact *Señor* Guerrero. We will not need another transporter. Earl, *you* will be doing that job. It will be your final job."

Swabb's mouth dropped, but stopped short of fully hinging. "Uh, what job?"

"I want there to be no misunderstanding," Mendez said in a firm tone. "Tomorrow morning, presumably at eight a.m., a ship will unload our merchandise at Pier Six in the port of Ensenada. You will be there. You are personally going to take possession of the cargo."

"Hells bells!" stammered Swabb. He stood, turned, turned the other way, and sat back down. "For chrissake, Ricky, what am I supposed to do with them? I don't know anything about babies. I have clients to see in the morning."

Mendez spoke to the point, "It's a Panamanian-registered freighter, *La Mariah*. There will be five total, three are Australian; two, I believe, are Thai—yellow, in any case. See Colonel Abreano at the docks. He will instruct you. Pier Six. That's Abreano."

Swabb was incredulous. "You're serious. You're fucking serious."

The lawyer had already begun his sweating, now his color darkened, the Richard M. Nixon transformation working toward full form.

"We cannot let ourselves be traced to this load."

"My God! Listen to yourself. They're babies! Ricky! … "

His words seemed to have no affect. Mendez said, "It's merchandise; it's a business … One word of warning, Earl. Don't let them get in the hands of the Indians—"

"Indians? *What fucking Indians!*" Swabb was frantic. He rose from his seat, but this time didn't make the turns; he kept his eyes on Mendez.

Mendez looked around the low-keyed lounge, then came back to the lawyer. "Shut up, Earl. Sit down and listen … These Indians have often been instrumental to us providing an initial safehouse. They may have found out when the shipment arrives. I don't know. But we can't allow the cargo to get diverted to their tribal compound in the mountains. It would complicate things."

Swabb was sitting now but not breathing any slower, his sweating nearing profuse.

"Tell Abreano we are effectively terminating the business with this shipment and won't need his services hereafter," Mendez continued. "Remind him he can live a fruitful life, it's up to him. As for the cargo, don't you have some rich clients in Ensenada? Tijuana? Maybe someone owes you. One of them might want to extend his family. Split them up if need be. Let the stuff go at bargain prices."

Swabb tried to reason with the man. "That's crazy! I don't know anybody who'll go for that. It's absurd … I won't do it, Ricky. There's no way you can make me." Swabb fell into a middle-schooler pout.

Mendez sipped his Perrier. "I had hoped you would take more interest, be more pro-active—for your own sake … You recall my telling you what happened to the *coyote*?"

He gazed at Swabb, a suave, almost fatherly look, and waited for a connection before going on. "Our thieving smuggler, remember the ear I showed you?"

Swabb scooted back, out of Mendez's long reach. He avoided looking at him, though he was paying attention now, all too well. He reeled inside with fear, knowing exactly what Mendez meant; he had been told the grisly details of the *coyote's* demise, his "sanction."

Mendez said, "Well?" in a whisper that made the question all the more emphatic.

Swabb nodded, then squeaked, "I remember."

"It would probably be better than the thirty years you will otherwise spend in Lompoc, even though you wouldn't last that long in that environment."

Mendez produced a sad face that quickly shifted to serious, then ominous. "If you can find no other solution, rent a boat. Go sportfishing for the day. Just get rid of the merchandise."

CHAPTER THIRTY-EIGHT

Castro Herlinda reached the docks well before daybreak. He honked at the Port's cargo vessels' gate and waited for the armed guard to open up. Castro had learned from one cousin that the early duty guard was Robert, another cousin he hadn't seen since Robert left the Pai Nation three years ago to join the federal militia. That was a bit of luck as it would save Castro's bribe money.

"Good morning, cuz," the guard said, unlocking the fortified Cyclone to let the truck through. "Nice ride, man."

Castro gave him a cold Hawaiian Punch Juicy Red out of the cooler he always carried and asked how life was going in the military, was he getting any from the *señoritas*? Yeah, he was, but it wasn't so hot in the army, low pay, long hours, tough boss, lots of bosses. So Castro gave his cousin the bribe money anyway—a U.S. $20 bill.

In a few minutes he wheeled his souped-up Chevy pickup inside the port. The entire Port of Ensenada engulfed eighty thousand square miles, an enormous affair that accommodated freight, container and cruise terminals at its six piers as well at a large marina. He crept along this section's concrete yard in a thick November fog. The ship was supposed to be there already, but he couldn't see much beyond the ornament on the hood of his truck and decided to park and wait till it cleared. He cut the engine and settled in.

An hour later his freighter sounded a first-call horn. It blasted apart Castro's dream of a sparkling chrome manifold topped with gleaming twin four-barrel carbs for sale behind a gated store window. The horn shattered the window. He could see the vessel now through the dispersing fog, appearing as some fantastic one-dimensional ghost ship.

La Mariah last night had arrived and docked but remained inactive till daybreak; Castro knew the horn blast was to get the crew ready to unload. The huge cargo containers brought thousands of assorted items from three or more Pacific Rim countries. It was a good thing there weren't many security procedures in place or else Castro wouldn't be here. Government regulations were largely on paper and not vigorously overseen, so getting the contents of containers into transit to points beyond went smoothly and quickly—virtually no customs, agriculture, narcotics, and weapons inspections to hold things up. Which also made it easy to smuggle in biological agents bound for America, sarin, any number of other toxic chemicals—and little people from points east. One just had to know how to do the paperwork, which of course was beyond Castro but not an immigration lawyer such as E. Warren Swabb.

Now that he had daylight, Castro raised the Chevy's hood and went to work. He adjusted the two-barrel carburetor air intake so the big 306 would run leaner; it pinged too much from the batch of lousy gas he'd filled her with last night at the Pemex. He finished and wiped his hands first with a sanitized wipe from the Colonel's value pack, then at length used a clean rag and then closed the hood. From the cab he took a large bassinet that fit when the bench seat was let back and walked to the gangplank where he waited to board while several crewmembers disembarked; they noticed with amusement the pink baby carrier under the Indian's arm.

Bear-like through the chest and six-feet-two, Castro was not likely to be laughed at to his face or questioned, either about carrying around a pink bassinet or why an unauthorized civilian was boarding the transporter. His face was chewed-up but friendly looking because a curious, perpetual grin embraced it. He waved with familiarity at a man standing at mid-deck.

Castro spoke in English to the man when he reached him. "B'chi, you old dogface. How in the fuck you are?"

"A year it's been, my friend? I have new teeth, look." B'chi was *La Mariah's* first mate.

B'chi poked out a lower partial for Castro to marvel at. "My wife, she have them, too," B'chi added.

"Colorado! Business is fuckin very good, huh?"

As a boy, Castro learned his American tongue from white, black and brown sailors with a dab of Aussie lingo thrown in. He'd later picked up quirky expressions from the rowdy foreigners at Hussong's Cantina, where his quick-sketched charcoal portraits hung on the walls and pillars. The sketches hung there because many gringos were insulted by his caricatures and wouldn't buy them.

Two sailors with swaddled bundles in their arms stepped onto the deck through a nearby starboard door. They awaited B'chi's instructions.

B'chi looked at Castro. "I see you still have the '53. Beautiful wheels. Maybe you want to sell her to me, huh? I pay you handsome—we load her up right now. I take her home and show off!"

"Oh, dog meat, in your fuckin dream," Castro chided.

B'chi smiled big for a nice view of his new upper choppers, then told his two men to help with the bundled babies. "Put them in the car. Be careful!"

"No, no, I bring my own carrier. Let me see a peek at these little ones," Castro said. He took one of the babies and tossed it in the air. He hummed a native tune, did a dance turn, made a face at the baby. The infant seemed happy in the hands of the moon-faced Indian.

"They are cute buggers, eh?" he said, laying the bundled baby inside his pink baby carrier.

He checked the other babies, taking an Asian infant into the fold of his arm. "This one, he don't like me so much, huh."

"I want to tell you, my friend," B'chi said. "This one is sick. It is the cholera, maybe. The eye is bad, she may have the malaria, too. Your wife must treat her very soon."

The fixed grin fell from Castro's face. "Okay," he said, still looking at the child. "What happened to her? Why you no take care of her?"

B'chi shook his head vehemently. "No, no, no! She was sick before."

"You could maybe steal some medicine, though, huh?"

"Impossible to do. You don't know—they got guards because of the dope fiends in the crew. Big regulations with the infirmary. Even the captain hisself, he won't help."

Castro frowned but said nothing more.

The sailors standing by tried imitating Castro by making faces at the babies they still held, but their gestures were awkward and the babies cried. The sailors wore uniforms looking to be from the mothballs of Russian Cossacks.

"Give 'em to me, boys," Castro said, regaining his boisterousness. The two sailors were glad to hand them over.

"Tell that old son-a-gun captain it is much appreciated he tell us that babies coming here. Okay, old friend?" said Castro.

B'chi nodded with a wink, then frowned. Castro asked what troubled him, was it the sick child. B'chi pointed through the wire fencing outside the compound. "Is that car there with you? The rich one?"

Castro shrugged. "No way."

"Well, my men they spotted it come in the fog. The man, he get out and he walk around with a flashlight, then he get back in, turn out the headlights. He is trouble, I think."

"Don't let it bugging you, dog," Castro said.

La Mariah's first mate hesitated. What now? Castro wondered. Something else seemed to bother him besides the sick child and the mysterious car, he could see it in B'chi's pitiful gaze.

B'chi said, "I don't know when I see you again, maybe never, my friend. Things are happening, the captain he say he not so sure we bring anymore business for you, for them. So, maybe goodbye … I make prayer this baby don't die."

Castro patted the smaller man on the shoulder. "You be good, then— you old dog meat. Pinch that wife's butt for me, too. Ha!"

Castro with the two Cossacks walking behind him loaded the babies into the cab of the truck, lining them in an even row sideways in the large bassinet so that he could see their little faces. Castro strapped the crib down with two leather belts he had put in for larger members of the tribe that he'd take into town often. He gave the belts a tug and, satisfied, stepped into the driver's side, which had no seat belt.

He pulled through the gate and waved at his cousin, the foot soldier.

He passed slowly by the car B'chi had pointed out, staring to get a look inside it. It was a late-model Lexus, black with gold trim, a vehicle too expensive to belong to someone in local law enforcement. Castro thought the bug-eyed man inside, definitely *norteamericano*, might be ill. Or just frightened. No sir, he was no cop. Castro didn't stop to speak; he would not have a hard time remembering the California license plates, some nonsensical letters—"SWABLAW."

Castro gunned the Chevy and took off across the railroad tracks with his eye on the rearview. He slowly approached the main highway just outside town. The speed breakers lining this main street into town meant business. He saw the Lexus move. The guy was following him. Castro was always ready for a race and so confident it didn't even occur to him that he was putting babies at risk; he had the streets of Ensenada down pat and considered it perfectly safe to hit eighty on those streets.

He led SWABLAW through the rich and hilly Chapultepec district, knowing it would stir his pursuer dizzy, taking the looping sharp curves at high speed.

But he couldn't shake the Lexus. He headed back to the bay and maneuvered through backstreet neighborhoods of the waking city with it perilously rough streets until, finally, he lost the fancy car. He had to give *Señor* SWABLAW credit for sticking it out that long.

As a reward for not crying during the race, Castro pulled over and fed the babies each a bottle of milk. This was no small feat with five of them since they couldn't hold the bottles themselves and one apparently too sick to eat; it took him nearly an hour to get them content. The babies settled, the Indian headed east into the hills.

CHAPTER THIRTY-NINE

The ten-minute traffic update was one minute slow advising south-bound drivers of a "slight tap of the brakes" before Del Mar Heights on the southbound 5. Another alert one minute later suggested all drivers should exit the 5 at Manchester Avenue, that a big rig had overturned just north of the Del Mar exit. That was nearly two miles down the road. Mendez had just passed Manchester and discovered on the same radio update that the only exit in between was temporarily closed. There was no way he could avoid the jam, nothing he could do but stick it out with all the other schmucks.

Mendez wasn't the only one to sit on the horn. A disharmonious symphony soon erupted. He stared with pure hate at drivers on both sides of his big sassy Continental. He mouthed profanities and they were mouthed back at him. One guy shot him the finger.

When traffic did start to crawl, he bullied his way to the right lane, a move that usually shuffled one along a little faster in slowdowns. But he fell four, five, now six car lengths behind his reference vehicle, a white panel truck inscribed with the logo "Diaper Dan's Baby Service." The irony was lost on Mendez in his road rage frame of mind.

Since entering I-5 South at Laguna Niguel, 80 miles back, he had been fighting traffic. He was returning from a half-day conference at Western Division headquarters. The meeting itself had left him out of sorts, as it had everyone attending. No one from the commissioner on down had a handle on how the agency would survive the move from Jus-tice to the recently created Border and Transportation Security division. The agency was in flux. It could get chewed up in that monster and turned into a toothless "enforcement" agency, little less than a bunch of schoolyard guards with whistles. Along with that unknown came the crucial element of job security from top on down.

The car up front suddenly slammed on its brakes and he had to do the same, as did cars behind him. He laid on the Lincoln's horn for a good ten seconds, then threw his hands in the air in an embarrassing orchestration of irrational disbelief.

Forty minutes later he reached the accident site. The Sysco eighteen-wheeler had been shifted to the shoulder and was surrounded by a light brigade of CHP cruisers and motorcycles, a fire truck, an ambulance and the wrecker that moved it over. Mendez gawked bitterly as he crept by the scene. The truck driver wasn't injured; he stood on the side smoking a cigarette and laughing with a patrolman and an EMT. Drivers in every lane gawked as well, perpetuating the delay for the long line behind. Diaper Dan had vanished on ahead.

Mendez sped up to eighty, as did every vehicle in front and behind him. The seesawing began, pushing and shoving just to flaunt aggression, and perhaps the freedom just to be moving that bird. Traffic quickly slowed then increased, slowed, increased. Every other vehicle wanted to get in a faster lane.

Mendez got off the 5 at La Jolla Village Road. It was nowhere near his destination downtown but he was compelled to take the exit and go into La Jolla proper by the quirk of nature that had made him the closet monster that he was. From La Jolla Village Road he could get to Fay Avenue much easier than if he took the Garnet exit in Pacific Beach. He had driven along Fay Avenue in La Jolla before about this time of day, mid afternoon. The thing that pull him there was Sister Madeleine's By-the-Sea Liberal Catholic Academy, a private school for elementary-grade girls, and it was located on Fay Avenue between Raymond Chandler Park and the La Jolla branch of the city library.

Off La Jolla Village he took Nautilus for a ways then turned onto Fay Avenue. His excitement began to rise. He passed Chandler Park and pressed on to Sister Madeleine's. At least the traffic hold-up had gotten him here when the second shift—the older girls in 4th, 5th and 6th grades—let out and Mendez wouldn't have to wait in the park. He preferred the second shift set, ages nine to twelve, when they were just budding. He breathed harder in anticipation, fighting to keep the car's acceleration down.

Approaching the reduced-speed zone, he was startled by his cellular. It went off on high-volume with a tune selection he had just recently added, an alluring Brahms lullaby.

"Richard Mendez speaking," he answered softly, without a hint of his previous annoyance. His eyes were on alert.

"Ricky? It's me. I, uh—I thought I'd better call."

Swabb's high-pitched voice drew a scowl from Mendez, and his voice changed. "You called. What is it?"

"Damn it, Ricky. You said eight."

"Don't go tongue-tied on me, Earl. What's the problem—because I *know* there's a problem."

He could hear Swabb breathing in quick pants, like a dog under a hot sun.

"I was there, just like you said. Even earlier. But, but—well, they got the babies. The Indian. You said—"

Mendez didn't hear the rest; he dropped the phone on the floorboard in the passenger's side and threw both hands on the steering wheel. He'd been seeing red and had not seen her.

One of Sister Madeleine's girls—the short plaid skirt, white blouse—the poor girl stepped off the curb in front of the big car. Obviously the girl hadn't looked where she was going. He slammed on the brakes harder than he had done earlier in traffic, which caused the big Lincoln to skid, bearing down on the frozen child—a lovely child, he noticed, shiny white shins. The damn lawyer caused it. He couldn't stop in time; he was going to hit her. He let off the brakes and yanked the wheel to the left across the on-coming lane between two parked BMWs. The Continental's tires bounced over the curb and the car came to a rest inches from a sturdy cypress tree, the park's prized old Torrey pine. He had somehow missed the girl, the parked cars, another pedestrian and the endangered tree. A miracle really.

He breathed hard and fast. His heart raced like a small animal's, pounded his ears. His immediate interest was on that sweet girl, and he searched for her through the passenger window. She wasn't in view; he hoped he had not scared her too much.

From the floorboard he could hear the slight sound of a toy voice shouting, "Ricky! Ricky, are you there?"

He craned his neck to look through the rear window for the schoolgirl, but she was gone. He got out of the car in a panic and looked under it and found no mangled body. He traced the car's path to where she had been standing paralyzed in the street, her precious but frightened eyes on him. He scanned all around, calling out, "Young lady? ... Young lady?"

She had disappeared. She must have been very frightened. He could soothe her fear; he could hold her ...

Once at his desk in the federal building, Mendez manipulated his cold, hard Chinese balls, cleansing his mind of the petty behavior back on the freeway. He tried to check persistent lingering thoughts of the girl—sixth grader, he guessed, skin pure as the untouched opening page of a hardback book.

The Chinese balls clicked and circled in his hand. He used his cell phone to call Swabb.

"I'm sorry," he said to the lawyer. It was the first time he had ever apologized to Swabb.

"Uh, that's all right, sure," Swabb said, sounding surprised, and doubtful. "What I wanted to tell you, Ricky, was I got there two hours early, just like you said, and I was *still* too late. The Indian, he—I tried to chase him, but—"

"Earl?" Mendez said softly. "Don't."

Even with the silver balls warm in the palm of his hand and the subject obviously important, Mendez had trouble focusing. It wasn't the girl now, and not the apprehension over his lapse of self-discipline on the freeway. He sensed it. He was losing control—of the business and of himself.

"Damn it, Ricky. Why was that damn Indian there, anyway? How did he know the shipment arrived early?"

"They have met the boat before; obviously the captain contacted them," Mendez said, still working the orbs, getting hold of himself. "Where are you?"

"At the border, it's a long wait today."

"It's a long wait any day, you idiot, when you don't have a SENTRI pass," Mendez said, then added, "All right, Earl. I'll put someone else on it. You need to destroy your files. I assume you can handle that much."

He snapped shut his phone and continued kneading the steel balls, now drifting back to the prized child. He had invited her into the car with a kindly "I'm going that way, dear," and in a flash she was down to the pink panties he imagined she wore. Two schoolbooks lay next to milky-white legs. She smiled; her lips were full, pink. The face just so smooth, so pure. *I'll see you get home. You can play the radio, only sit a little closer. Here, let me fold the console back so you can reach the radio ... Your last year before middle school, huh? That's so cool.*

Mendez had never felt sadness. He had never cried while eating. No tears had been in his eyes nor lumps in his throat throughout the entire simultaneous funerals of his mother and his father, him in his ninth year of Catholic prep school. He had never needed serotonin for depression, never taken tranquilizers of any sort nor supplemental hormones. But he was presently as close to sadness as he would ever get. The girl caused it. Causing the sense of helplessness, even when the ache to ravage such sweetness was his Achilles—and would be his downfall.

His cellular played the lullaby again. Rory Fitzsimmon, the Border Patrol dispatcher, bearing more negative news. Fitz had an eleven-year-old that Mendez once managed to embrace with no one the wiser, the girl fooled by her "uncle's" gentle roughhousing.

"Your man Cousins don't sound right," Fitzsimmon informed him. "I mean, he calls me wanting to know if the job on our girl is still on. Like that. Is there a reason he would think it's not?"

"No. What do you make of it?"

"I think he's trying to weasel out of the job. It just sounds like that to me."

"He hasn't called you yet to confirm?"

"Nope, only to inquire if it was still on. What do you want to do?"

Mendez took a cigar from his humidor and sniffed it. He didn't light it.

"Set him up," he said, making the decision that quickly. "For the *coyote* killing. Make it so the authorities down there can implicate him. He should be in possession of a good deal of money, use that angle—dope money."

Mendez kept the cell to his ear and stepped out of his office, passing Freida's desk with the I'm-leaving hand sign, and headed for the elevators.

Fitzsimmon said, "You sure? Cause he'll talk."

"Let him. He's in the dark."

"He knows *me*."

"He knows *of* you ... You don't get it, do you? He finds out he's wanted, he'll stay in Baja. There's nothing to worry about long as he's down there."

No one else was waiting for the elevator at 4:15 in the afternoon. "It becomes necessary, we can choose a more permanent solution later."

"Well, it seems necessary to me right now. Just the feeling I got."

"Your instincts are your best asset, Fitz ... Let's try it my way first. Get it arranged. The press should know soon as possible."

"I don't like leaving it at that."

Mendez sighed. "Then don't like it. That's your problem."

The elevator door opened and Mendez held it for a second longer. "Before I let you go, there's something else. I'm going to need your assistance tonight. Will there be a problem with that?"

"No ... What?"

"Wear dark clothes. I'll pick you up at the pier at eight-thirty."

"Dirty work?"

"Yeah ... " Mendez said, stepping inside the elevator and punching the button to the first level of parking, "but necessary."

CHAPTER FORTY

The tall columns of Benbough Sons Mortuary burned bright on West Main Street in the City of El Cajon. The white colonial stood next to Grijalva Chevrolet and across the street from Pussycat Theater. Next door to Pussycat was Denny's, then Pizza Hut, which used to be Bonanza Steak House. Looking farther down West Main, Myers saw the Night Owl Tavern, a Goodwill Industries thrift store, Discount Tires, Cousin Buck's Unfinished Furniture, and Whisky River Saloon. All that was on the one side.

Cajon in Spanish translates to "box." One of San Diego's satellite cities, it lay on a valley floor surrounded by mountains. The word probably gave Jack the idea to call his hamburger stand "Jack in the Box" when the first drive-in opened back in 1951 on El Cajon's Main Street.

Myers thought of another association: *el cajon de muerto*, box of the dead, or in this case, the coffin holding the body of John Frazier, which lay inside the sanctuary of Benbough Sons. This would be no open casket service.

Myers had parked on meter by the Pussycat Theater. He got there just in time to catch its marquee lights blink on. There wasn't a crowd lined up at the box office. Only one man was there, a bum about Myers' age lollygagging around the glassed-in previews. Inside the teller's cage a gum-chewing young woman watched the bum, her jaw slowing down when he moved. He wore imitation jungle fatigues, styled after Vietnam-era wear. Potbellied, a beard. Bearing of defeat. A man drifting through time, waiting to pass on. Myers decided the fatigues were not imitation.

He crossed the street in no big rush, eased up a couple steps and stood at the double doors of the blinding-white funeral home, taking more time before going in. Once he stepped inside, a wedge of sunlight entered the dark anteroom with him. A tomblike darkness replaced the shard of sunlight as the hydraulic closed the big door behind him.

The small congregation of people in the chapel sat with heads downcast, their mood probably deepened by the oppressive Dark Age music. Myers sidestepped the chapel and made his way down a hallway to the director's office, thankful he could use the excuse that he was here on business. When in fact he was not. He knocked and entered a dim, padded chamber. The director's room, well-observed as devoted to the home's theme, held a series of miniature caskets displayed in death colors under subdued lighting. Opaque, 30-pound drapes sealed off any remnants of the outside world and life itself.

Mr. Charles Van Peebles sat in a swivel armchair behind a polished mahogany desk that showed no evidence of ever having been used. Mr. Van Peebles had the appearance of a man mostly pleased with all things in life and beyond.

Myers introduced himself as the "reporter on the Frazier story," and the gangly undertaker rose a little stiffly to give Myers the fish handshake.

"How may I be of service?" was his line.

"Names," said Myers. "Parents, siblings, children, wife's folks. Correct spellings."

"Certainly." He handed the reporter a computer printout containing some of those names. "Anything else?"

Van Peebles wore flat-lens glasses that caught light and threw it at you like twin discuses.

Myers looked at the list. "Yeah," he said. "Who's paying for the service? Is the body being cremated?"

"Well, I'm afraid those arrangements are confidential."

"How come?"

"Anything *else?*" Van Peebles said.

"I'd appreciate it if you pointed out the parents."

"Of course."

"The daughter won't be here," Myers informed him.

"No?"

"She's had an accident ... But you might not want the clergy person—or whoever's doing the talking—to know that beforehand. You know, no need to upset these people anymore than they already are."

"Yes, I suppose," Van Peebles said. He didn't appear to be interested in the daughter's accident. He seemed more or less scandalized, bearing an expression that reflected not sympathy but condescension. That seemed odd for a man of his profession. That is to say, a man who appeared mostly pleased, comforting and assuring.

Myers had opened the door to leave but Van Peebles made a movement that meant to hold him a moment longer.

"I mean, she made a special request," Van Peebles said. "We are very obliging with requests, but this one, a song by a rock band? 'The End,' it's called. It's simply disrespectful—more than that, it's abominable. What could she have been thinking? Well, she's not here, so there."

"He served in Vietnam," Myers said with a marked edge.

"Oh? ... So?"

"How old are you, Mr. Van Peebles? Certainly old enough to remember The Doors. I think it's damned fitting—more than that, unselfish and appropriate—choosing that song as a tribute to a fallen soldier."

Myers slipped quietly into the small chapel, took a seat in the back row. He was uncomfortable. He was sweating, still hung over and still hurting. The room's dim lights soothed his aching eyeballs. That was all the comfort he would get here.

The service started and the medieval music mercifully stopped playing. Then, surprisingly, Myers heard the gauzy, sonorous vocal of Jim Morrison begin to fill the small chamber, "This is the end, my beautiful friend ... the end ..." Margaret Frazier had known the hell her father went through in Vietnam, and she knew the melodious, fatal words spoke only to him, of him.

A man of cloth delivered the eulogy. A surrounding jungle of flowers set the reverend's presence aglow.

Myers took a head count out of curiosity—23—while searching for anyone he might know. He'd seen no buzzhead corkscrew equipment out front where they liked to set up for promotional reasons. It appeared TV's interest in the story had waned already. He suppressed a grin spotting his colleague Tina Lubrano two rows in front of him. Hadn't Lubrano assured him she would not be covering the funeral? He recalled here words, "No way, buster." She scratched her head with the lead end of a pencil, squirming in her seat, anxious. Probably pissed. She turned and looked at him as though she knew he was behind her. He gave her a wink; she curled a lip.

Myers made a quick study of the aging minister. Watery eyes, either an asthmatic or a vodka drunk. He kept his hands clasped in front, as if to restrain them from a sudden burst of inspiration, or violence.

When he spoke it was only to the up-front mourners. He didn't dwell on pity or God's will, or God's kingdom, or all God's people. God didn't seem to have a lot to do with this particular service. A mark in his favor. There was anger in his voice as he spoke about the tragedy and the reprehensibility of death by provocation. Myers found himself listening to a eulogy that wasn't half bad.

He said, "I did not personally know John Frazier. I cannot attest to the disposition of his character, though I know what he showed of himself, and that portrait was of a responsible but troubled man. From all accounts John was a good, law-abiding, respectable person.

"I do not know why he was killed. I will not stand before you, his loved ones, and try to solace you by saying that sometimes these terrible things happen, that it is in God's overall design and we must accept such events as they are. It was *not* within God's design that this man's life be taken this way, so soon. God's design does not include senseless killings—by the police or anyone else, including by one's own hand."

The pointed rankle in his tone and words kept the tears down in the front pews. His voice was fluid, disarming.

"John had a blemish," he continued, moderating his voice as he took steps forward. His hands stayed together. "But who of us does not."

"He served his country at a time when it was unpopular to serve. He went, and he didn't complain about it. John fought and returned with physical and psychological wounds. He returned a decorated soldier, a Purple Heart soldier.

"Now I want you to try and imagine how difficult it must have been for him, for all of those young patriotic men—after fighting in war—to return only to be scorned. It was a time of dissent. Vietnam took that boy over the knee and whopped him a good one. War finally got him. It finally took him out behind the barn like an old dog gone rabid ...

"I grieve for him, my friends. I grieve for all of our unsung soldiers who to this very day are still ridiculed, yet take it in their hearts without reciprocity, without broadcasting their pain, just let it go. Men who live with their memories buried inside their hearts. But at this moment all my grief goes to the memory of just one of them, John William Frazier."

Myers listened stunned; his nose burned and his eyes welled. This was the reason he had come to the man's funeral. He needed to grieve, too. For that one common denominator he shared with Frazier, with all his comrades-in-arms. And for the pain he brought those gentle children he could not help and the ones he hurt.

The room grew smaller and darker. He felt the rising heat press down. His hands became a nuisance, cumbersome objects that blundered without cause. He stuck them underneath his legs.

Trying to balance himself, Myers thought cynically that such discourses would not get them flocking into the reverend's pews if he were on a membership drive. He decided the man of cloth had been a military chaplain, had himself served in the Republic.

The Reverend went on to give a short, reasonable sermon on the burden of carrying on after the death of a loved one, and then on to the bread-and-butter segment of his duties, turning to the familiar—intimacies meant to comfort the mother, the father, the sister, the one in-law, all of whom apparently were here, sitting in the front two rows. All but the deceased's daughter, who herself was now deceased.

In the anteroom afterwards Myers found Lubrano. "Tina, look at you." He couldn't help himself, the chiding was in his newspaperman's blood.

She didn't look friendly. She smirked. "You look like hell frozen over. What happened to your noggin? ... What're *you* doing here?"

Myers handed her the printout he'd gotten from Van Peebles. "For your obit. Since I won't be writing it."

She took it, said, "There'll be another before the week's out. Margaret, the daughter's dead."

"I heard."

"You heard? How?"

Myers sighed. "They call me 'Magic,' remember?"

"Well, I got one I bet you haven't heard. Wanna?"

Myers grinned. Nevertheless she bypassed the tease this time.

"The Border Patrolman you quoted from Ocotillo? Agent Cousins, remember him?"

Myers nodded again. "Curly redhead. Sure I remember him."

"There's a warrant out on him. Tell me what it's for, Magic."

He shrugged. True to himself, he wore the mask of disinterest. "I want to talk to Frazier's parents; maybe you could give me a minute before moving in on them."

"That's what I thought," Lubrano said, sounding superior, maybe irked. "You don't know. All right, that's all right."

Myers sighed again. "I'm sorry you got stuck with the funeral, Tina. I would've done it if I was still on the payroll, you know that."

"The hell you would."

"What'd the guy do?"

"Read about it in the paper … Get some sleep, Ray. Why are you here, anyway?"

"Hell if I know."

Myers re-entered the chapel. He didn't need Mr. Van Peebles to point out Frazier's parents. They were the couple still by the casket, both tearful, the woman crying openly. Myers approached. This time he didn't have to lie when he said he was the reporter who wrote their son's story. He offered condolences.

The mother responded. "Thank you. You have a job to do, I guess."

Polite but cautious. She clutched a handkerchief, used it on her swollen eyes. She seemed a little more bent than she ought for a woman who should be in her early 70s. She hadn't had sleep. She needed some.

"'Bill and Clea,'" the father said. "You can call us that in the obituary." They lived in Mt. Vernon, Indiana, in the same house Johnny had grown up in and was an all-star running back. He had a sister, Julie, who now lived in Buffalo, New York.

Bill Frazier said, "We're glad you're here, Mr. Myers. The funeral home faxed us your article yesterday. We were going to call you and thank you personally for the kindness you showed our son. But also, if I can be frank, we wanted to ask you what really happened in that lighthouse. I mean, why would Johnny go up there with a gun? I—we don't understand."

"I'm not sure that it can be explained," Myers said. "But you must know the whole thing was over the death of his son."

Both parents flinched, the mom gasped. They didn't know Minh had died, if they knew about the boy at all.

Bill said, "Truthfully, we'd kind of had a falling out after he told us about him. He was so—so obsessed over the boy."

"Minh," said Myers. "His name was Minh Nguyen."

"But your article didn't mention anything about the boy, about Minh," Clea said.

"I didn't know then. Your son gave me a snapshot and I followed up on it. He became despondent after Minh was killed."

"You have the picture with you?" the mother asked. "We've never seen the boy. May we look at it?"

Myers didn't ask why they had never seen a picture of their son's child, their grandson. He didn't have to, he knew why. The boy was half Vietnamese. These were conservative mid-western Christian folks with beliefs that didn't condone what their soldier son had done. But Myers guessed they had long since forgiven John the sin, only the son never knew it.

Myers took the picture from the inside pocket of his jacket and handed it to Clea Frazier; it was a copy Carol Finley had made from the original. Both of them held the picture together, touching it gingerly like a shared precious heirloom. Now they cared. Now that it was too late.

Clea said, "Julie, our daughter, has turned into one of those corporate women. She'll probably never have children. This boy was our only grandchild."

Myers frowned. "What about Margaret?"

"What I meant, a grandchild of blood," said Clea. "Maggie was adopted. Of course we love our granddaughter."

"Adopted, huh," Myers said feebly. He hadn't known that, either.

There was a dynamic involving Margaret that Myers thought best left alone. He could have told them she was dead, that maybe they'd want to go by her place since it was only a few blocks from Benbough's, take her belongings.

He couldn't get any further involved with their affairs, or hurt them more. Or hurt himself—even though he was the messenger.

Bill Frazier put an arm around his wife's shoulder, squeezed it. She still held the picture.

"Isn't he darling, so tall," she said.

She looked up at her husband. They posed a picture right out of the annals of Americana, Myers thought, and she said exactly what you'd expect a grandma to say. "He's so thin. They didn't feed him enough."

Myers studied the father a moment. Bill Frazier's measure of distinction was an inner strength that had so far kept Clea from falling apart during this time of sadness, perhaps a strength that for all their years together had been her shelter from hard times. But he too was affected by the picture of Minh, the only bit of tangible evidence of his only grandson, illegitimacy be damned, and the helplessness to console her now showed in the many lines in his face. Myers saw his pain as regret for rejecting the boy, for rejecting his own flesh and blood.

"We might have taken him," Clea said. Tears again welled in her eyes; her chin began to quiver. "We *wanted* to take him, didn't we, Bill."

"Clea," he said. "Honey, let's remember what we talked about."

He eased his wife into a pew and put a dry handkerchief in her hand, holding her other hand.

He turned again to Myers without speaking. He apologized with his eyes. What they had talked about was personal and did not include Myers.

"Keep the picture," Myers said and made his way out of the mortuary.

In the bright sunlight, he hung his coat over a shoulder and put on sunglasses. The air was fresh and he took in a big breath of it. The breeze caught a tuft of his thinning hair and blew it in his eyes. He brushed it back and the breeze immediately blew it back again. He needed a haircut. He'd needed a haircut for 30 years.

He glanced across the street at the Pussycat Theater. They still weren't lined up at the ticket booth. But the bum was still there, lolling in front of a tripod displaying the next XXX-rated feature. The tripod and poster were chained to the tiled floor. The bum wasn't chained to anything; he could move on if he wanted. Myers knew who he was now—one of Frazier's buddies from the VA who couldn't get up the nerve to cross the street, after all these years. Still too shaky to attend another service for another casualty of his war. Myers saluted him. He didn't have the heart to go to him, though, to recognize him, tell him, "Man, it don't mean nothin."

CHAPTER FORTY-ONE

The asphalt road east out of Ensenada ascended in no time, transforming the landscape from urban concrete and parched earth to spacious green as it opened into the foothills of the Sierra de Juarez mountain range.

Maggie drove. The Falcon's seat was stuck as far back as it would go and neither she nor Bubba nor both together had been able to move it forward. She rolled up the serape and wedged it behind her back to bring her close enough to steer. With her long legs she had little problem reaching to accelerate and brake. There was no clutch.

Bubba tried singing an Indian song he had learned from a crooning *cholo* he once busted, but it didn't help. Maggie was in deep purple and nothing seemed to help. She pushed his hand off her kneecap.

"You want some sweet cake?" he offered.

Maggie fidgeted. She lit a cigarette and glanced sad-eyed at him. She was beautiful when she looked at him like that, he thought, so vulnerable and fresh-faced. She rolled down the window and rolled it back up, rubbing her bare arm from the cool rush of mountain air.

"What's going to happen to me?"

Bubba said, "I used to feel like an orphan when I was a kid, the way my old man was."

"Hey. You *had* a father."

"Better if I hadn't, the way I figure it," he said. "When he was home, when he wasn't off mustanging some rig, he'd use his whip. A real one, with a Lash LaRue snap. Sis'd get it, too. *Por nada!* He'd send us to the train yards to sleep. You met some rotten people in the yards. A mean sumbitch, my old man."

Maggie tried to flick her ashes out the small vent window, which blew it right back inside.

She studied him a second. "You had a sister? He sent his own daughter out there?"

Bubba nodded, almost proudly. "Yep. He didn't give a shit about neither one of us. I had to look after her—and I did. She never got raped when she was with me."

Maggie sighed, wrenching her face. "That bastard!"

"You got it."

The road had narrowed and the slant-six engine pinged climbing into higher ground. The timber grew taller here. They saw splotches of snow in the shadows. The terrain turned rugged with washes and clumps of grass that scuffed the underside of the car.

"There was one family I liked, in Minneapolis," Maggie said at length. She'd gotten rid of the cigarette and her elbows were locked, hands gripping and whipping the wheel like a pro on the Baja 1000 circuit.

Bubba flinched and braced himself at the banging under the car but it didn't slow her down.

"I was five. I started calling them Mamma and Papa. They didn't want me calling them that, kept saying I would have to leave directly. Papa'd said that, 'd'rectly.' They were from the Deep South, Mississippi or some God-awful placed like that. They had three other children, all black, none of them their own. But me, they knew I'd have to go, and it wasn't that I was white. I was just older. But I got to teach school to the kids. I loved those people. For a little while I had a room to myself, right next to Mamma and Papa's room. Sometimes one or the other would come in for no reason other than to put my covers back on me. It was winter—in Minnesota."

"That the best you had, it must've been really rough," Bubba said. "I used to keep tabs on a few of the hobos. I knew they'd had it hard—bad teeth, bad livers, always one ailment or another. But I ain't never known a real bona fide orphan. Other than some poor *pollos*."

The strain on Maggie's face eased. She slipped a hand behind Bubba's head and played with his curls. She'd slowed to a livable gait, talking about that good time in her young life.

"I didn't have it so bad," she said, now in wilder terrain. "Compared to most, I had it easy. Never sexually mistreated ... I guess I was more the tomboy type."

"Could be you was just too mean to mess with."

He looked thoughtfully at her. "I'm sorry you're gonna miss your daddy's funeral, honey. I really am."

He regretted opening his mouth as soon as he uttered the words. He thought she would start crying again, but she didn't. She just squeezed her mouth into a hard grin and nodded.

Giant pines and thickets of juniper formed a canopy overhead and the path darkened.

Bubba said, "How much further we got to go?"

"We'll be there d'rectly," Maggie said, still mindful of that Minnesota family.

The occasional splotches of snow kept Maggie's reverie going. She thought of the snowball fights and laughing faces, the melting marshmallow in her hot chocolate, heavy blankets, a teddy she called Windows. Why that, *Windows*? She'd always wondered. Windows played in her dreams, things out there, things she saw and liked beyond her reach.

She looked at Bubba with a twisted grin. "I was good at my job," she said and patted her purse and bags where most of the money once again resided. "You should have seen me operate—Sylvia, I mean."

Bubba appraised her, grinned broadly. "Yeah, I woulda liked that, to see you operate."

Maggie stopped the car. She honked the horn three times.

"This is it?" Bubba asked. He didn't see the makings of a village, but there was no more road either, if the path they'd been on counted as a road.

"*Rancho Coyote*," she said.

"They couldn't think of anything better?" he said.

Maggie laughed. "Indians are literal people, Bubba. There's no irony with them, they are straight-arrow folk."

Bubba grinned. From what he could tell, they seemed to be on the edge of a timbered mesa.

She pointed to a half-constructed clay-brick house he hadn't spotted standing beyond the bisnaga cactus and scrub oak. Bubba figured the bisnaga grew in abundance alongside ten-foot clusters of prickly pear, there to keep out the wild cats and other unwanted varmint, like coyotes. It appeared to be a natural clearing until he pushed aside a hump of ivy and saw a low cut tree stump. Then he saw stumps all around.

A dark chesty woman appeared in the doorway of the structure. She wore a white cotton blouse and a burlap skirt. Steaming rags were draped over her arms. She was six feet, wide-hipped, square-faced.

Maggie beamed at the sound of crying babies. She hastily smoothed her jeans, as if whining babies alone made her take notice of herself. She walked quickly toward the woman. Bubba could see her excitement and wondered why.

The big woman returned Maggie's smile with one that transformed her dark face into genuine warmth. Bubba couldn't believe how a face could light up that much just by pulling up your lips.

Three tiny girls with dirty faces came running and attached themselves like crabs to the woman's skirt. The rags in her hands were diapers she'd been washing. Bubba saw the washbasin through the doorframe of the structure and the flame off a propane stove heating a large black pot.

Maggie said, "Margarita, are those babies I hear?"

The woman nodded. "Five little ones come. One is sick … Are you here for them?"

"I didn't know anything about them. They didn't tell me," she said. "But, no. I'm just here to—for a visit. Where's Castro?"

"Down the mountain, get medicine," Margarita said. She seemed perplexed. "The sick baby, it has the red eye and maybe she take the plague. I hope the evil is not with the others."

"I gotta go," Bubba said at Maggie's back. Both women looked at him. Maggie thought he meant to the bathroom, but he meant it literally, that he wanted to leave. He grinned at the Indian woman; she seemed to scowl at him.

There was no big reason Bubba had to rush off that very second, except that he felt out of place, a worm on a coffee table. He grinned, flustered, and walked back to the car and started unloading sacks with Maggie's new clothes and other items. He put the stuff on tree stumps, the tequila, pastries, limes, a lantern, Coleman fuel and some blankets she had bought for the villagers on the way out of town. Everything but the *piñata*, which he put behind a stump. Maggie ordered the kids clinging to Margarita's skirt to bring the things over. She took the purse full of money out of the car.

"We forgot your cigarettes," Bubba said, eyeballing the fat purse.

"That's all right, I'll make this pack last. I don't think I need 'em anymore."

After the items were put inside Margarita's house, Maggie went back to the old Falcon, where Bubba was squatting to look at the tires.

"They all right?" She knelt beside him.

Bubba nodded. "Don't worry about anything. Your boss will believe me when I tell him the money accidentally got burned up with you." He stood by the driver's door, and Maggie stood too. "We gotta take it a step at a time."

He slipped the room key to the Hotel Mexico into the front pocket of her jeans, as a way to sidle up to her. "Just in case it don't work out here, go on back to the hotel. I'll know where to find you."

Bubba held her in his arms. Mushy thoughts filled his head. "Well, I guess this is it then. It may be a few days, Maggie, but I swear to God I'll be back."

"I'll be safe here, don't worry," she said. "Castro can handle anybody that comes around."

He frowned. "This guy Castro, I don't like his name."

Maggie laughed. "Bubba, aren't you going to ask for any money?"

"Not unless you wanna give me some." He already had the little bit he'd stashed away.

She reached in the back of her jeans and withdrew some bills, then wrapped her arms around his neck and kissed his lips hard. He thought she believed him about coming back.

He got in another kiss before she pushed him off.

He lost sight of her waving at him in a gush of blue smoke.

~

Maggie sat on a tree stump and started crying.

Bending next to her, Margarita put a knotted arm around her shoulder.

"He's dead," Maggie said. "John was killed. The police shot him, murdered him."

Margarita gave Maggie's shoulder another squeeze and rubbed her arm without speaking.

"I didn't want to have to tell you."

Margarita took one of Maggie's hands. "I am sorry for you, *Poquita*. Is this the reason you are in trouble?"

Maggie looked at her, puzzled. "Why do you say that? What makes you think I'm in trouble?"

"All little birds come to their nest when there is trouble. I believe you think of our land as your home."

"Well, I hadn't really thought about it that way," she lied, feeling awkward that she could be made so easily.

"You are welcome here, always."

Maggie turned to face here. "We were so close to having the orphanage. I've worked and saved, and now—now, I no longer exist. I died last night."

She cried again saying this.

The broad-shouldered Indian twisted off the cap on a bottle of tequila and drew on it. Birds sang noisily. Children laughed. Babies wailed.

"Margarita, I don't know what to do."

The woman passed the bottle of tequila to Maggie, waited for her to drink, then took another slug for herself. Then passed it back to Maggie. "Your problem is about the babies that come here?"

"It is, and that man that just drove off. He was supposed to kill me for stealing some money. He didn't. But now I can't go home—at least not for a while."

The big Indian grinned. She looked girlish. "You are good with the men as you are good with the little ones."

Margarita looked up into the fading sky. A mockingbird chased a hawk for all it was worth but never touched the fleet fowl. A good sign, she believed. It meant no bloodshed today.

"Our land, our village, this is a good place for you, *Poquita* … You will stay with the babies."

CHAPTER FORTY-TWO

Myers' cat Angel lounged on the landing above the steps like the goddess of Giza. She appeared neither hungry nor lonely. When Myers passed her in a hurry, the half-Persian continued staring straight ahead. She didn't mew, she didn't flip her tail. No leg rub, no devoted flop on his shoe. Not after 24 hours of neglect.

"Aw, Angel," Myers said, picking up the wispy cat in one swift move that took her breath. "Come on, let's get you fed."

Myers put out enough dry food and water to hold her for days, then made himself a cold sandwich of provolone cheese on Russian rye and popped open a cold beer to wash it down. He sat at the kitchen table and listened to Angel breathe as she crunched her lamb-and-chicken nuggets.

If he left now it would be dark when he got to Ensenada, where he might or might not find an Indian who supposedly drew cartoons at an inglorious bar named Hussong's and who might or might not direct him to a place where some missing babies might or might not be found. He was tired. His scalp stung around the stitches along with an itch now, and he still had a nasty headache. His eyelids felt like lead shades.

If he left now he would end up like Margaret Frazier, taking the road to death on Gringo Pass. He wasn't going tonight.

He finished the sandwich and beer then went upstairs to clean up. He noticed the wall pictures were similarly askew, due to rumbling jetliners passing overhead. He straightened the frame nearest him, a portrait of his benefactor, Aunt Phyllis—"Auntie"—which he'd hung between bedroom doors. In it she stood suited and erect, a thin, stout-looking woman. Surrounding her in the picture were hundred-pound sacks of South American coffee beans inside the warehouse of the business she started in the 1940s. Import Coffees & Herbs was the source of her wealth. Phyllis was his father's only sister. Myers fancied the notion that he took after her because Phyllis was also a loner. Never married. She'd left Alabama to be a movie star about the time talkies started up, the native daughter wanting to play Southern belles in epic movies. But Hollywood already had its Southern belle in Tallulah Bankhead. That hadn't discouraged Aunt Phyllis. Travel then became her raison d'etre and she fared well; it was a time globetrotting Americans weren't yet ugly but by in large well regarded. Later she came to depend on her only blood kin in San Diego, Myers. She took a late-in-life last fling to Southern France and did not return alive. The riff in Myers' family over the house being willed solely to him alienated him even more than he had been from his Chicago brother and his sister who was married to a venture capitalist in Connecticut; she didn't need money and neither did his architect brother. Not like Myers, at least, who was a broken down reporter who at the time of Auntie's death had alimony and child support payments.

He went into the bathroom. In the mirror, his face looked gaunt, bags under the eyes. He removed the hospital bandage from his scalp. The break in the skin was uneven and purple, an ant line running an inch above the right ear. Pedroza could have used brass knuckles on him. Myers' jaw tightened as he made yet another mental note to someday take payback on a bully cop.

He undressed to the waist and opened the sink's hot water spigot for a lather shave. Waiting for the water to heat, he posed in front of the mirror, arms akimbo, muscles flexed, an angry fighter. Shadows outlined his ribs. He noted the pecs still held up nicely. Not bad for his age and occupation, he thought. He stripped off the rest of his clothes and let his eyes followed the shape of his torso below the navel until the mirror gave out. His fingers picked up and traced the line of scar tissue raised like blisters leading to the groin. This was the area where many men had hernia repairs. But his scar was jagged and it had been there since the age of reckless youth. He still felt a pull when he coughed or laughed hard—or posed like a he-man tormentor.

The material that had ripped into him—shards of tin and nails—was compliments of Charlie's sympathizers, the Viet Cong. Only a few people had seen Myers' scar, his ex-wives of course, some lovers in between, a few doctors. He did not advertise it and didn't like having to explain it. Sometimes he lied, telling of a stupid teenager water skiing around river stumps at night; he knew it was a dumb stunt, thank you, but he was drunk, just a boy. It was both scarlet letter and his badge of honor—or humility.

After shaving, he took a hot shower, and then re-bandaged his head wound.

~

When his phone rang, Myers realized he'd fallen asleep.

"Mr. Myers, that you?"

Myers moved from the chair to the desk. He squeezed his eyes trying to wake his brain. The voice was familiar but he couldn't place it. "Who's this?"

"It's me, Mr. Myers, Sid Rhoades … You know what we talked about the last time we spoke? You remember?"

"Uh—"

"Well, I got it wrong. There was no connection between John Frazier and any Indian tribe in Baja. That was something I *thought* John had told me, but when I re-examined my records, I saw that he got his pottery and stuff from a small family-run factory in a poor colonia in Rosarito. You know it, first town down the road from Tijuana. I wanted to clear that up before you tear off on some wild goose chase based on the wrong information and report something in the paper that isn't true."

He talked fast, sign of desperation—Myers didn't need to be awake to know that. But why? His voice was barbed and unemotional. Not the Sidney Rhoades he had spoken to that morning by phone when he told him of Margaret Frazier's death. That Sidney Rhoades had been genuinely upset, and that conversation had nothing to do with Frazier buying pottery; it was about Margaret Frazier and about an Indian reservation outside Ensenada that may have been used as the base to smuggle in foreign babies. Myers recalled Rhoades saying then that he would "run it by Captain Ahab," meaning his boss Richard Mendez. That was the thing that Myers considered now, as he fully woke

He grew cautious and alert, played along with Rhoades and let him go where he wanted with it. Myers said, "I see. The factory's in Rosarito, you say?"

"East of town, across the toll road," Rhoades answered quickly. "Listen, Mr. Myers, could you come over to my place? There's a lot more I need to tell you, concerning Frazier. Stuff I'd rather not talk about over the phone but that could really help your story. Can you come over now?"

Myers saw no reason to mention he'd been fired from the newspaper. He checked his watch: 9:35. It wasn't that late, he'd just slept hard.

"Sure, where do you live?"

"North Park. Twenty-three-twelve Olive Street."

Adding, "Could you hurry?" seemed to Myers a strange thing for any bureaucrat to say, in particularly one with the rarity of mellowness Rhoades seemed to have obtained in his long tenure as a servile government employee.

Myers wrote down the address then got out of his bathrobe and put on some clothes. He tied his sneakers without taking time to put socks on.

Angel had quietly sneaked to the overstuffed chair, now curled in a perfect orb, fast asleep or pretending to be fast asleep.

"Up you go, darling," Myers said and lifted the ball of graying fluff. He didn't like her there because of the hair she left on the cloth. He placed her on a leather couch in the foyer the legs of which she sometimes used as a claw sharpener, sometimes as revenge for neglect. Angel stretched to an impossible three feet from tiptoe to tiptoe, quivered radically, then curled back into the orb without ever opening her eyes.

He left the foyer light on and locked the door behind him.

North Park was an older residential community close to Balboa Park with less expensive real estate than uptown's Mission Hills and Bankers Hill, where Myers lived, but a decent area for families and older folks alike. Mature queen and king palms lined many of the streets here. Stately eucalypti abounded in back yards, as they did throughout the copious canyons ruling the city's vistas. Sodium lights cast a yellow glow down Olive Street, and the block was so quiet that Myers slowed to a creep to lower the whirring of the Land Cruiser's all-terrain tires. In the middle of the 2200 block he pulled over and cut the engine. He walked to 2312. The numbers were each in separate bright Mexican tiles on the outside wall under the portico. Rhoades had not turned on the porch light for him. The bulb was probably burned out, Myers guessed.

The house was set back thirty feet from the sidewalk. He tramped across the dewy lawn and on to the porch of the small bungalow. Low and broad in front, it had large eaves and abundant double-hung windows, cedar-shingle siding on the upper half, shiplap on the lower. The lights were on inside and music emanated from the living room, soft jazz that was inaudible unless you were at the door, where Myers now stood. He recognized the distinct jazz guitar of Barney Kessel, one of his long time favorites.

He also heard the faint sound of a ringing phone.

No one bothered to answer the phone or open the door when he tapped on it. Myers pushed the button. Between phone rings, he could hear the buzz of the doorbell deeper in the house, the kitchen maybe. He could not see inside for the closed vertical blinds covering the windows.

The door was locked, as he expected. He went around the side of the house and down the driveway. The property stood a narrow driveway apart from his neighbors. Myers didn't have to peek to see people through their dining room window seated at a large table, talking, eating. Late eaters. They didn't appear to notice the stranger pass in the driveway right under their noses.

Myers entered the backyard through a gate and found the back door ajar, a sliver of harsh kitchen fluorescence cast across the freshly mown yard that stretched 30 or more feet to a brick wall.

He slipped in and closed the door behind him.

The gallery kitchen was unkempt, cups and saucers stacked in the sink. Strange for a man who seemed to be neat, tidy.

The phone stopped in mid ring. No answering machine.

He heard a thump somewhere in the house, then a series of quieter thumps coming from a front room. He backed up against the wall next to the refrigerator, waited a couple seconds before stealing a glance through the dining room into the fraction of living room visible to him.

A shadow danced across the outer living room wall.

Myers called out, "Who's there? Sidney, is that you?"

No response. The shadow did not reappear.

His eyes at once searched the kitchen for a weapon, a block of knives, a glass or bottle. Nothing. He moved into the dining room empty handed. Another sound, one he now recognized.

Myers sighed and lowered to his haunches. He whistled quietly, "Here boy, here girl, c'mon now, come here."

An overweight collie mix waddled around the doorjamb wagging its tail, its uncut toenails tapping the wood floor in an uneven percussion to Kessel's two-five guitar. The dog stopped in front of Myers and whimpered, thumped its long tail against a built-in cupboard. Myers patted the collie's head then led it to the kitchen and told it to sit and stay, which it obediently did.

He got a bad, gut feeling of what he might find next. He took the living room first. The hi-fi set stood as a centerpiece on the wall opposite the street windows. He went to it and saw the tuner had been set to KJAZ, which played oldies in that genre. He turned it off.

On the wall above a desk where Rhoades kept his phone, and on two other walls in the living room, there were assortments of some twenty framed pictures. It seemed a curious collection, pictures of youngsters, a variety of ethnicities. All of them would be foreigners, Rhoades' past cases. In the photographs there were children with adults, children by themselves, posing, right hands raised to the flag, very happy to be citizens of the United States of America.

The dog's fleeting shadow had been thrown against the wall by an overturned lamp that lay on the floor near the front door, where the struggle probably started. Myers' synapses fired electric, his blood pumped faster. His instinct said leave, throw open that door and run.

But his senses commanded that he find Rhoades. He searched for a weapon, a fireplace poker, but found nothing suitable for defense. He moved through the dining room into the hallway and then the bathroom. There he saw a row of four bright lights above the mirror that lit up the victim like a stage production, crumbled and lifeless and wedged in between the tub and toilet.

Myers had guessed Rhoades weighed in around two-seventy. It would have taken a bigger and much stronger man to tame him into submission, throttle him, as the killer had done. There might have been more than one killer. Probably.

Standing over the body, Myers imagined the men who had done it, how Rhoades struggled, as he obviously did, from the living room through the hall and into the bathroom. They got him into the smaller room where he could be controlled more easily. He had finally been overpowered and brought down in a strangle hold with a length of stranded wire.

The bathroom mirror was smashed and pieces of silver-backed glass lay on the tiled floor and in the bathtub and in the bowl of the toilet. Blood smears swiped the tub and floor, apparently from the person cut by the shattered mirror. If that person was not Rhoades, the killer would soon be known. Myers squatted next to the body of Sidney Rhoades, listening keenly with the door and hallway in his peripheral vision. He took the dead man's limp and still warm hand in his. There was a deep cut on the fleshy part of the hand, no doubt accounting for the smear, or some of it. There was also a cut on his forehead, as from a fingernail. That would delight investigators. He checked the wrist for a pulse, knowing he would not find one. Rhoades' face was blue and bloated.

The wire used to garrote him was thicker than it needed to be, 18-gauge copper, the kind used in electrical circuitry. It had not cut into the skin. But it was drawn taut and invisible under the fold of flesh and exposed only at the back of the neck, twisted into a lock with two small lengths of wood fastened to the ends of the wire.

Myers continued to contaminate the crime scene. Grabbing a dry wash rag to hold the wooden handles, he untwisted the wire, pulled it aside. It didn't help Rhoades but Myers breathed a little easier.

He noticed a peculiar smell over the body, an aromatic fragrance something like glue from a model airplane kit. A little sweeter. A good chance it was chloroform that hadn't worked on the big man.

He knew now that Rhoades had been coerced into making the call, that he had tried to tip Myers off when he suggested their previous conversation was about Frazier's source of imported Indian wares. When it hadn't been. Myers should have called the police then. Again he found himself at the threshold, about to descend into that dark place. Again he had failed to save a life.

Who had done this thing, and why? And why had the killers wanted Myers here? Unless it was to set him up for the murder—or to kill him, too.

Myers stood and backed away from the body. He heard only the dog. He listened for the sound of breathing, footsteps, anything human. If the killers were still here, Myers would probably already be dead. He stepped back into the narrow hallway and looked in both directions. Bedroom doors at both ends, both closed, and no light behind either door.

He dashed into the kitchen and rummaged until he came up with a butcher knife from a drawer. It wasn't something he wanted to do, but he went back to the hallway. Seconds pass before he took hold of the doorknob to the bedroom in the back of the house. He threw it open in a rush. The thud that made him jump was the door striking the edge of a tall dresser, but no other sound. With the knife at the ready he turn on the overhead light. Nothing. He shuffled quietly along the hallway to the other door, did the same, got similar results.

He didn't check the closets in either bedroom. It seemed unnecessary.

Myers considered calling Detective Millard when something caught his eye, the edge of a notebook behind a wastebasket near a desk. He picked it up. It was Rhoades' address/phone book. He opened it to the "M" and found his name listed—via the business card he'd given Rhoades with his home number. It was taped to the page. Rhoades also had written in a phone number of Richard Mendez on the same page. Myers penciled the number on to a realtor's handout notepad and shoved it in his pocket. Rhoades had scribbled a message on the page opposite the first "M" page, probably when he had been forced to make the call to Myers. It read: *Ahab is smuggl—*.

Myers muttered softly, "It's him, Mendez."

Rhoades had only tried to seek justice for what to him had been an unacceptable decision by the agency. But the Frazier case was not the reason he had been murdered. He'd been killed for discovering that Richard Mendez was involved in the smuggling of babies.

Sidney Rhoades was too transparent; he would have given himself away when he approached his boss about the death of Margaret Frazier. That was earlier today, and the man he called Ahab had moved swift as a whale at sea.

Myers forwent calling the police. He did not want to deal with homicide detectives, in particularly Pedroza, though he knew the trouble coming his way for leaving the scene of a crime. What had Millard and company done for Myers lately? Besides put a hole in his head and send him to jail? They didn't have to know he was here at all, he thought. He had touched nothing but the dead man's wrist, the garrote used to strangle him, all the porcelain in the bathroom, the collie, the address book, buttons on the hi-fi, doorknobs, a butcher knife, the back door, left perfect prints with his sneakers from the dewy lawn out front and in back and inside the house, and probably dropped hair follicles all over the place, not to mention his sweat. To hell with them.

He would call Millard, turn himself in if necessary—but not before he made a trip south. He had a man to visit first, an Indian who drew caricatures in a Mexican dive, and there were some missing babies somewhere that could be in harm's way.

Myers saw this as a calling of sorts. Maybe, just maybe he could do something right. Help redeem himself. It was possible.

He left the way he had entered, from back to front. He again patted the well-behaved collie, now in its dog-bed in the laundry room. The dog was either tuckered or sad and he thought of taking it home with him. At that age it would not adopt out. He grimaced at the thought and could only hope it had someone to go to. He made a mental note to check later.

He closed the swinging kitchen-dining room door to hopefully keep the dog away from its dead master.

Myers went outside, leaving the outside door ajar for dog duties. The neighbors next door still sat at the dining room table, conversing. But this time all three, apparently bored among themselves, stared straight at Myers.

CHAPTER FORTY-THREE

Bubba got off the trolley at Broadway and E Street in Chula Vista. He went straight to the pay phone at a nearby 7/11 store. His employer wasn't picking up, so he left the number of the pay phone in a message then leaned against the wall and waited. Even with his Stetson held humbly at the knee, showing the world he had nothing to hide, people going in eyed him with absolute certainty he was waiting on his dope lord to call; dressed like that, in slick leather, boots, they knew his type.

Driving the old car north to TJ, he had given serious thought to his future, making decisions about Maggie, about Roxanne, his job with the BP and the other job, his evil work—which was over, never again, he'd decided that for sure as the pope prays. Away from Maggie, he saw things rationally. As much as he liked her, he could not just up and leave his wife and career. Rox wanted a family. There were plans and commitments he just couldn't bring himself to break by abandoning it all for what might or might not be true love on the lam.

He would visit Maggie, help her get her new life together. Hopefully they could still roll in the sack every now and again. He would help her get a new identity if that's what she wanted and then get her back in the country. It was possible she could return someday. Bubba figured at most there were only two or three people she would have to avoid. She could take on a different persona, which she was damned good at anyway, move to another city. Bubba Cousins' Protection and Relocation program.

By the time he'd ditched the Falcon in *Colonia Libertad* and crawled through a short tunnel he knew they'd never sealed, Bubba had made the no-brainer decision that he was done the moonlighting, *fini*. Killing people disturbed him. He'd only pulled two jobs, two men who were the lowest form on the human chain, thugs, slimeballs, the worst of the worst. Still, it haunted him. He was having nightmares too horrendous to think about. Who needed that?

His employer had gone too far wanting him to do Maggie. She had caused no real harm to anyone. His was no better than Taliban law. Bubba knew the moment he was given the job he was done killing, only he didn't have the guts to refuse the assignment—given the pressure the bastard put him under about his scamming days back in Sasabe.

The only upshot, he'd accumulated thirty thousand dollars for those bad dreams, which he had stashed in a secret account in a San Ysidro bank. Adding the twenty thousand he figured he had coming from Maggie was a pretty good start. He would have to talk her about that. After all, hadn't he saved her life instead of taking it? He deserved a cut.

When the call wasn't returned right away, Bubba went in to get a soda. Paying, he saw the newspaper in the newspaper stand that stood right there at the side of the cash register and doorway—and in one blink of the eye, everything he'd just decided changed. All those sober, righteous decisions erased. His future turned in an instant. The headline might as well have screamed his name:

BORDER PATROL AGENT SOUGHT IN TWO BAJA DEATHS

He calmly laid down an additional fifty cents for a paper and walked outside to read the story. He pulled the Stetson low over his eyes now. Not only was he getting the shaft for waxing the *coyote*, but that fucking Guerrero had accused him of murdering Maggie—Margaret. The story quoted that two-timing bastard, reading in part:

> ... *Chief Inspector Guerrero said, "There is evidence the death of the American woman [whose] car went off the highway Monday was not an accident. We believe a U.S. Border Patrol Agent named [Travis] Cousins murdered this woman and made it appear as an accident.*
>
> *"Our investigation also [proves] that the same U.S. agent murdered a Mexican citizen, one Miguel Sanchez, whose remains police found near Tecate only today. This man Cousins is dangerous. He must be apprehended before he kills again."*

They had run a Border Patrol file photo below the fold, taken when he had first been assigned to San Diego District, a little heavier in the face then and wearing a shitkicker's grin. But it was him. Anybody could tell.

The fucking rat, Bubba thought, his jaw clenched up tighter than a coke high. He looked around to see who was staring at him. The coast was clear at the moment but he stepped around the end of the building out of the direct light where his face couldn't readily be made.

First thing, Maggie was back on.

His second thought concerned the money in his secret bank account, which he couldn't get at until the bank opened tomorrow.

Unbridled anger seized him; Bubba felt the urge to smash and tear and scream out. It could only have been his employer who set him up for the *coyote*, since he was the one who contracted it. No one else knew, other than a couple of ladies of the night in a lowly Tecate bar. And it would never have gotten that far with the authorities down there. As for Guerrero, he sought revenge, Bubba figured, out of pure macho bitterness because Bubba had somehow insulted him or his fucking ancestors. Who knows—probably when he made him pull off that corpse's head at the morgue, how he tumbled from the gurney. Could be just the way Bubba had treated him, like the subservient scumbag he was. It infuriated Bubba all the more that he'd paid the bastard the rest of the money— $5,000 total. If anything the crook should have been grateful.

Right now Bubba needed to cool down so he could think straight.

He tossed the soda can in the weeds and paced near the phone as if the eleventh hour on death row quickly slipped away. Waiting on that last-hope phone call.

He had to pee something fierce. A sudden burst of headlights illuminated him, like an armadillo suckered by an all-encompassing force. He shielded his face with his forearm, pretending the glare bothered him.

When the phone rang, Bubba jumped as if struck by the car and pinned to the wall. He started to dance on his toes, holding it back. There was no public bathroom at the 7/11.

He jerked the receiver off the hook. "Talk to me!"

"Travis? ... You had me worried," Mendez said.

"How the fuck did this happen!" Bubba couldn't muster much self-control. "Christ, I did the woman, just like you wanted. And now *this*! What the fuck is going on?"

"I am sorry, Travis. It's shocking. I honestly can't say why the Mexican turned on you. You can probably answer that better than I."

Bubba took a breath, slightly more composed. He notice he wasn't dancing on his toes now, the urge deflated. He knew Guererro nailed him for the *coyote's* death but wouldn't bring it up since that was a dead-end street. He was more curious what plan his employer had worked out to get his money, the eighty thousand. Minus twenty for services.

"Has anyone talked to Guerrero? Fitzsimmon, maybe?" Bubba asked, softening his tone.

"He's not returning calls, we've tried," said Mendez. "The point is, Travis, it's done, and now we have to work on damage control. I will certainly try to get things straightened out for you. You must realize this hurts all of us ... Where are you?"

Bubba's lips grew tight as a wire; he didn't answer.

Mendez said, "You did get the money from her, didn't you?"

"That's the thing ... It's not like I get my cut, either."

"You want to explain?"

That was another item Bubba thought over on his way back to the States, knowing what he had said to Maggie about the money burning up in the car with her was unbelievable, unacceptable.

"It's in her bank account at First Interstate out in El Cajon, the one on Mollison," he said, sounding regretful. "There was no way I could get her to take the cash out, *then* take her to Mexico. She was too smart for that; you outta know that about her. But the upshot is I got her bankbook and the account number. All you gotta do is wait till morning, get a woman of your choice to go in a branch where they don't know her, make the withdrawal. But I wouldn't take the whole amount out—that raises suspicion ... If you could just leave my twenty in, I can figure out a way to get it later."

"Fair enough. The full amount's there?"

"According to the little black book I hold in my hand. I'll give you the account number after I get to my bank in the morning—if that's okay with you. I get the money I got stashed already, I'll call and tell you where to find the bankbook. Before noon."

"Noon, then ... I assume you'll be leaving the country?"

"You bet your ass."

"South?"

"Probably. For starters."

Mendez said at length, "I'm willing to offer you a proposal, Travis. Assuming I can use your services again, I will see that five grand is delivered to you in Ensenada. Call it a retainer. Would that work for you?"

Bubba grinned bitterly. "I like Ensenada."

"Good. Let the desk manager at the Hacienda Hotel know your whereabouts. Speak only to Jorge, the night manager. Your name is Gus Morgan. The money will be there in two days … We do business in that town, Travis. You won't go hungry."

Bubba, of course, was no bonehead. He knew a setup when he saw one, and he wasn't going to wait around till morning for the man to make his move. All he had to do was find him first, this fuck Mr. Earl Warren Swabb.

CHAPTER FORTY-FOUR

Bubba couldn't hold it any longer. He went around back of the 7/11 to relieve himself in the dark, by the trash. Then he hopped back on the trolley up to San Diego City College, located on the skirt of downtown, the trolley car empty but for a few people he figured rode around all night and who didn't read newspapers. He walked a little farther east on Market Street to a hole-in-the-wall at 13th Street, a cozy little Mexican joint with a blaring jukebox that played string-and-horn *mi corazón quebrado* tunes, which he wasn't presently in the mood for. But nobody there would speak passable English, much less read it. The place didn't have a television set either. But it did have a pool table.

Bubba walked in and went to the pool table first. He waited on the guy to shoot but still got a scowl when he placed a quarter inside the rail. He took a stool at the bar and was asked did he want a cold beer.

"Bud, *por favor*." He would be safe here and have a little time to put a plan together.

Fuzz Face, the hombre shooting pool, seemed to dominate the table. He was a hotshot with a personal stick that came in a silver case he'd parked on the windowsill under the light of a bright "Tecate Cerveza" neon.

When it was his turn, Bubba racked for eight ball. He gave the kid a couple of free shots then got bored and finished him off with four consecutive drops before slapping the eight ball off the rail into the side pocket. He didn't have to bank the black ball, as sometimes was a house rule; he just did it for the fun of it. He placed the stick on the rack and walked across the floor, letting the kid retain the table.

He took a sip of beer that foamed up into his nose nearly causing him to gag. He slapped the bar trying to swallow. "Damn!" he muttered when it was possible. Patrons eyed him silently.

"*Es calor*, sweetheart," he said to the woman behind the bar. "Dig me out a cold one if you can find one."

The female bartender glared at him. It was the reaction Bubba would've gotten no matter how nice and sweet he'd tried to tell her his beer was hot. She was pushing fifty, wearing a dress made for an eighteen-year-old, scalloped and sequined, tight as a prophylactic. Bubba felt pity just looking at her, the way she swung those big mamacita hips to tease these poor bastards.

The Dos Equis she handed him was barely cool but it didn't surprise him this time.

When the jukebox grew silent, Bubba walked over to a pay phone on the wall. Peanut shells crunched under his boots. He dialed.

"Hullo," answered a woman's sleepy voice.

"Rory in?"

"No, he's not. Who's calling?"

"He at work?"

"No, he's not. Who's calling?"

"It's work related. I'll try his cell."

He dished out some more change and hoped he remembered the number right. He did.

"Hullo," answered Fitzsimmon, same dull tone as his wife's.

"It's me, Travis."

Fitzsimmon was silent. But only for a second.

"You are in a world of shit," he told Bubba. Bubba could hear the drone of a car from the phone. "Don't you know that every agency in the land is out after you? The FBI, the CIA, us, locals from Oceanside to Imperial Beach, CHP, sheriff's department, plus the Mexicans."

"The CIA?"

"Like I said. They're working on a conspiracy angle ... Where are you?"

"Lots of people want to know that and I ain't tellin' nobody ... Rory, what's going on that made them throw me to the dogs? It don't make any sense. I did the job, like I was told."

Fitzsimmon went silent again, and that's what told Bubba he was in on it too.

"I wish I knew, Trav. But listen to me, you've got some other people nervous wondering where you are."

Bubba butted his head against the wall. Why hadn't he seen it? He had to think, he had to be careful what he said. Maybe they knew it wasn't Maggie whose body they pulled out of the Pacific; maybe they had beat it out of Guerrero. Maybe they didn't have to beat it out of the two-timing Mexican, he just told them on his own that it was a corpse from the morgue. That Bubba made him disrespect the dead, hurt his fucking feelings.

"There's nothing the law can squeeze out of me, Rory. Believe me, I don't know shit. Some guy I don't even know hired me. You know more than me. But remember this, Rory, I know you."

"Trav—"

Bubba hung up. What was he doing? He should not have said that. He took a long pull on the Dos Equis and walked a tight circle, thinking. He dug out some more change and dialed Rox.

"Honey?—"

He had to pull the phone away from his ear from Roxanne's sudden wail. He should have just sent her a postcard.

"Come on now, Rox, don't start that stuff. I know they're probably listening so I gotta be brief. I didn't do nothing, baby."

"They took stuff, Bubba, letters, bills, our wedding pictures!"

"They didn't? Those bastards! Some dirty people you don't know nothing about have done this to me, Rox. But I'm gonna clear it up. You just gotta hang in there. I'll understand if you want to go on back to Texas and I sure am gonna miss you, Roxy baby ... I gotta go, honey. Bye, bye."

"Bubba, I need the car!"

The twin schnauzers barking in the background made him homesick, even if he hated those two. He didn't tell her he loved her or where she could find the Chrysler. He couldn't. He just hung up.

He flipped through the frayed directory hanging under the phone. About half the pages were missing but there it was, the name "Swabb E.W. Esq.," only one in the book. Son of a gun! It even listed his address. That was ballsy of him, a lawyer. He dialed the number, got a human answer and hung up. The voice sounded nothing like that of his boss, but it was squeaky like Maggie described. He could've put on that other voice just for Bubba. But it was pure luck and he needed it just now.

He approached Fuzz Face at the bar sucking another can of warm Tecate.

"Rack 'em, amigo," said Bubba. "I'll play you for that little knife in your pocket against twenty bucks. Eight ball or rotation, your choice."

Fuzz chose eight ball with the grin of a fledgling hustler. Stupid boy, Bubba thought.

Bubba had him going with suggestions about Mamacita tending bar and he couldn't aim down the cue without smirking at Bubba, which caused him to miss cue more than once. Bubba let him have three shots this time, then he ran his balls and banked the eight again, three rails into the corner pocket, a shot that wasn't much if you were Minnesota Fats but one that impressed the hell out of the vanquished kid and even Bubba himself.

Taking the pocket knife, he said, "Say, amigo, you don't have a car, do you?"

CHAPTER FORTY-FIVE

Earl Swabb ate dinner alone at a sushi house in Little Italy then headed straight to his Mission Hills condominium. He drove slowly, a vigilant eye on the rearview as if someone were following behind him. He was spooked; he'd been petrified, in fact, since losing the shipment of babies to the Indian at the Port of Ensenada. He wouldn't put it past that snake Ricky to put a tail on him.

At home he threw his keys at the hallstand and moved into the sunken living room and circled the coffee table as if he were in the well of a courtroom. He had fashioned his living room retro '70s, with angles and parity. Everything was bleached virgin white, the furniture, torchiers, the faux-stone coffee table, the walls, bookcases, his two Gill Byrd abstracts. The marvelous original "Fourth Day Tumult" from Bill Bray's expressionistic-era collection was the only object with any color and any life, but the four-foot crayon-on-plank hung in the hall, not in the living room. Even the thick shag carpet was white as a German baby's butt. A cold but comfortable room admired by the sleek women he often had over. He knew for certain Hefner would dig his pad.

The ringing phone accelerated his anxiety, which eased when the call turned out to be a hang up. He thought about tracking the call to see if it was Ricky but he really didn't want to know.

Before getting into the shower, Swabb postured nude in the full-body mirror in front of his treadmill in the bedroom. He turned sideways for a view of the melon buttocks that women liked to pinch and sometimes slap. He removed a T-shirt and roughly patted his firm tummy. He had a thick mane of head hair styled for the moment after Gordon Gecko's, slicked back and held in place with gel but complemented with a four-inch ponytail, a symbol of defiance to rattle the adversarial courtroom clones he often faced. He'd been thinking, however, of going with the shaved head look. Really throw them.

Swabb strode naked into the living room and turned on the CD player. It was set at random play. "The World's Great Marching Songs" led off with a catchy, high-brass piece of German magniloquence—pompous, forceful, inspirational.

He got under the shower; the music was just as voluminous in there. He had paid dearly to have music piped into the bathroom through a waterproofed sound system.

He dried off in front of the body mirror, again admiring himself from side, back, front. He was every bit a man in the physical sense, from the tufts of hair on his shoulders and back to vaguely sculpted lats, pecs and the handful of genitals which he now grabbed and gave a little shake, like a ballplayer after stealing second. If only he was a little taller. His father, Earl Warren Sr., had been a short person, too.

He put on pajamas and then the Hef robe. The pajamas were made of silk, blue with yellow stripes, a designer name out of Neiman Marcus. The dark felt lapel on the robe coordinated vaguely with the pj's.

He heard a rustling on the balcony outside and opened the sliding glass door to satisfy himself that it was a gust of wind brushing the gangly eucalyptus branch against the railing. The wind could roar up the canyon and his unit took the brunt of it, being the closest in the complex to the ocean.

There didn't seem to be a wind of any consequence and he went back inside, about to make a Manhattan nightcap when his cell rang. Swabb stopped mid stride, nervously considering who might be calling after nine-thirty. The phone couldn't identify the caller.

He answered and a man's voice said, "Are you alone?"

"Who's this? Are you a client?"

"Ricky asked me to call. You alone?"

"Yeah—maybe. Why?"

"He has asked me to deliver a message. Don't leave."

"What do you mean, don't leave? Who is this?"

But the connection broke. He could not count the number of times recently that he'd been hung up on. He was even getting used to it, and that was just not right.

Swabb rushed into the bedroom to get some clothes on. He was terrified. He started to disrobe but didn't make it out of the pajama bottoms before the doorbell chimed. The chime was another charm with the ladies—a brilliant staccato bar from Chopin that got his dates immediately in the right mood. He dutifully answered the door, still in his blue-and-yellow pajamas.

"Good evening, Mr. Swabb."

"I'm gated. How'd you get to my door? … Who are you?" Swabb asked the question for the third time as the big man barged by him and stepped uninvited into the all-white living room.

Rory Fitzsimmon kept a hand inside the pocket of his jacket—fingering the strand of #18 copper wire attached to small wooden handles.

CHAPTER FORTY-SIX

Bubba paid the cabbie with a wrinkled twenty he'd gotten to break a hundred at the 7/11. He got out two blocks from his destination and walked to the address, a Mediterranean-style condo complex with a tall stucco wall surrounding it that supposedly reduced the noise off I-8 in the valley below and kept unwelcome visitors out. It did neither.

He easily shinnied a sapling eucalyptus with the help of the stucco wall and dropped on to the sparsely landscaped grounds inside. The Man, Swabb, had an end unit, good. Bubba thought of ringing the doorbell, just walk in on him, but if he had company or was on the phone the intrusion could be traced to a precise time. So he chose an alternate entrance. A mature, low-branched eucalyptus planted right up against the unit's balcony made his climb effortless.

He found the sliding door unlocked and entered quietly into a bright, perfumed bedroom that someone had recently been in. The perfume smell was more a woman's bite than a man's mulch scent. He thought at first it might be the wrong unit, despite the gym equipment in the room. In Bubba's limited experience with women, not many kept a Nordic slide and weight bench with 100-pound bell bars in their bedrooms; but then, there was that thing with the perfume.

He padded across the floor and quietly stepped through the opened door into the hallway and along the carpet to the staircase landing. He heard voices and stopped. He tried to match one of them to his employer's husky voice. One was familiar and he knew he'd gotten the right place, though it was not the voice of his employer. It was the voice he had spoken to earlier by phone, Fitzsimmon's.

He tiptoed down the stairs, hard-soled boots muffled by thick carpet. The boots were a little soiled, which would prove problematic if the condo became a crime scene. Even if he thoroughly scrubbed, Bubba knew there wasn't a chance in hell of escaping those crime lab pros, those guys who lived to nail dumbasses like Bubba Cousins.

The voice was definitely Rory Fitzsimmon's, the section dispatcher. Bubba listened closely and with a great deal of interest because the guy was talking about him.

" … Cousins may be on the loose now but he won't be any trouble to track down when it's time. We know where to find him."

It didn't feel right, Bubba hiding behind the wall listening to a man freely discuss when and where he was going to die. He felt his heart beating at every pulse point in his body.

Then the other guy, in a whiny and girl-like voice, responded, "Yeah, okay. But why didn't Ricky tell me himself? Why send someone over?"

Then Fitzsimmon again. "I'm getting to that. First, you were the one wanted Sylvia to disappear, weren't you? Asked him outright that Cousins pay her a visit?"

Bubba started to swell. *Sylvia.* That's what Maggie went by in the business.

"So what?" the munchkin voice retorted.

"He tells us only what we need to know," Fitzsimmon said. "He has a method … Say, you got a beer?"

Bubba felt suddenly embarrassed. The man who lived here, Swabb, the man with the voice, was not his employer. His man must be this cat "Ricky" the munchkin mentioned. Apparently, Swabb was just another messenger boy, another bubba.

He listened now as a fighter listens from his stool between bells, tense and eager, waiting for that moment he can pop into action.

Whiny voice said, "Uh, yeah, I guess … Why are you here?"

Bubba made his move before the second-round bell. Stepping into the light he grinned to hide the embarrassment, but he kept his hand close to the knife he had won off the fuzz face, now in his back pocket.

"Gents," he said. "What's up?"

~

It would have been a lot easier handling the two of them if he'd had his personal piece and cuffs. As it was he had to make do with his hands, hoping he wouldn't have to use his new blade.

Fitzsimmon, a big man as it turned out, was closer to him and Bubba surprised him with a high-impact straight-on punch to the throat that put the man on the floor gasping for air. Fitzsimmon didn't want to stay down and Bubba stepped closer, kicked him with a hard-leather-toed boot in the kidney under the ribs, then grabbed him by the shirt and shoved him against the wall in a sitting position. He delivered another blow with his fist into the cheek and nose. The head must have smacked dead center on a stud behind the drywall because he went limp and slid over to his right side, out cold.

He then turned to the other guy, girly-man in silk pajamas. Mr. E.W. Swabb. Maggie said the man was her handler in the smuggling business. He didn't look capable.

Swabb presented no trouble at all as Bubba went for him. He pretended to faint. Maybe he did faint.

"Stand up," Bubba ordered, as he would a collar, "get over here!"

Swabb moaned and made it to his knees. He crawled to Bubba.

Bubba pulled Fitzsimmon by the ankles away from the wall and rolled him on to his stomach by twisting the ankles. He searched his pockets, finding a garrote in the first pocket he looked in, and that was all. Nothing else of importance on him, a ring of keys, some cash, but no identification. He left him that way for the moment.

"You know what this is, Mr. Swabb?"

Swabb shook his head fiercely, scared to death, it appeared to Bubba.

"Garrote, used for strangling. Your bigger guys like to use it because they can. It's generally quiet and relatively clean." Bubba snapped the garrote and watched Swabb jump. "He planned to use it first on you, probably just about the time I barged in. Think on that a minute.

"And later, down in Baja, he would've tried to use it on me. Or he coulda planned on shooting me since I might put up a fight. Whatever, I just saved your scrawny ass and you are going to be nice in return— aren't you?"

Swabb went into shock, the pupils of his eyes disappeared behind the lids, his face lost its color. Taking it hard, Bubba thought. What a pussy.

Bubba tried to bring him around. He slapped his forehead, then propped his legs onto the coffee table to get the blood flowing to his brain. Swabb gasped and opened his eyes wide, trying to focus.

Bubba took a couple steps again to collect his thoughts. These men meant to see him and Maggie dead. He was disappointed too that this was not his employer. Swabb was a scumbag, higher class one but so what. Bubba had been trained in restraint and he had to apply that training now. He needed answers and later he could forget training, take care of this Mr. Swabb.

He got a glass of sink water and waited until Swabb drank it down.

"You know who I am?"

Swabb, wide-eyed, shook his head.

"You should know who I am, the guy Rory was just now talking about. Cousins, the Border Patrol agent … You read the paper today?" Bubba barked.

Swabb nodded.

"Then you know the trouble I'm in. Tell me who turned on me."

Swabb shook his head vigorously without speaking. Bubba thought he might not be fully cognizant yet and held off the physical stuff.

"All right, we'll start with you telling me a little about yourself," he said. "What does the 'E.W.' stand for? It's in the phone book. Like that: 'Swabb E.W.' I know you're a lawyer. Your girl Sylvia mentioned—just before I sent her off a cliff."

It got a response. Swabb said, "Uh, Earl Warren—she would talk."

"Like the Supreme Court justice?"

Swabb nodded.

"Your daddy's name is Earl Warren, too, I bet."

"He died last year. Heart attack."

"Then, you got a while to go," Bubba said, patting him on the shoulder. "Hard to take, huh, knowing you might've had a wire around your neck, gasping for air you weren't gonna get? But you're breathing, Earl … Tell me about this dude Ricky. He your boss in the smuggling operation? Anyone bigger than him? You with me, Counselor?"

Swabb began to heave and Bubba thought he might throw up. He quickly moved off the couch. But Swabb's heaves seemed to be of another kind, more of a drowning man's gasps or a child's breathless whimper.

Bubba sighed and stuck a finger under the crying man's chin, lifted it up. Not too hard he popped him one on the nose.

Swabb grew dead silent, caught off guard. Then the pain caught up and he began to wail in earnest. He pushed stiffly against the couch.

Blood from his nose found the white fabric. Red wine had been Swabb's stain worry until now.

Swabb stumbled to the kitchen sink. He grabbed a towel, wet it and covered his face, sucking air through his mouth.

"I think you broke it," he whimpered.

"You need to pay closer attention. Are you ready to do that?"

"Yes, yes."

"Okay. Why was I set up? Why did they want Maggie dead—that's Sylvia's real name you know? And, again, who's Ricky?"

Swabb took the towel away and spoke, his voice now a little more nasal. "I don't know."

Bubba used his index finger to thump the nose, like he was shooting a marble across the floor. Swabb screamed, his eyes tearing up.

"Are you some kind of masochist, Earl?"

Bubba sighed again. He found a dry towel and led Swabb back into the living room and sat him down again on the couch.

"Don't be a hero. Now, one last time, who set me up?"

"His name's Richard Mendez," Swabb said straightaway. "I—I just do the paperwork. That's the truth."

Bubba stared at him in dismay. "The Deputy Director of Western? *That* Richard Mendez?"

Swabb nodded vigorously, again.

"I'll be a wet cow chip," said Bubba. "And to think, I wanted to be just like him someday, big shot going around giving goose-bump speeches on patriotism and the need to clean up our borders for the sake of a better and safer America. Lord a-mighty."

"He's a dirty bastard, all right," Swabb said with conviction, which made Bubba smile.

"How come he wanted Maggie busted—and you too? No bullshit, Earl. Just spit it out."

"Busted? You mean—"

Bubba quickly grabbed Swabb's free hand, bent two fingers backwards; the lawyer squirmed off the couch.

"*All right!* She lied, she held back money. There were other things. She was a liability."

"What other things?" He kept the pressure on the fingers.

"You know, conflicts. That hurts! She had a crazy father helping her embezzle the company's money." Swabb tried squirming out of the grip.

Bubba eased off, then let go the fingers.

Swabb slithered onto the couch. He stuck his hand under his leg, as if that would keep Bubba from it. He suddenly gave Bubba a conspiratorial look. "You knew her, huh? … I mean you called her 'Maggie'."

Bubba pushed Swabb to the floor, about to kick him.

"She was the best operative we had." Swabb squealed out his words as if now realizing that Bubba must have liked the woman. "Honest to God. I tried to convince Ricky to just make her pay up, not to, you know, *bust* her."

Bubba stood clenched-jawed over the man, knowing he was lying. Again he restrained himself. It wasn't easy.

Swabb looked up at him and quickly averted his eyes. "It wasn't going to make any difference to Ricky one way or another," he said in a more level tone, "because he's dead set on busting everyone—obviously me included—who can implicate him in any way. He's crazy. He even wants to get rid of our latest shipment of babies! He wanted *me* to do it, to drown them at sea! Christ."

That didn't sound made up. Bubba figured the lawyer hadn't been so truthful in who knows when.

"The Indian camp!" Bubba thought out loud.

"Yeah, a damn Indian took them," Swabb shouted, then asked, "You know about them, too? Was I the only one who *didn't* know?"

Bubba held a finger to his lips, silencing Swabb. He looked at Fitz-simmon to see if he was coming around yet. Still out.

Bubba paced, banging things, the back of the recliner, the couch, his other hand. He knew Maggie would not let those babies go. Which meant she could get hurt.

He came back to Swabb. "Talk!" It was hard to believe anyone in their right mind would resort to killing babies.

Swabb lowered his eyes again. "Uh, I was supposed to pick them up and sell them, hopefully to one of my clients in Ensenada—immigration's my field. But I never got to them; the Indian beat me to it. Now I imagine Ricky'll send the Inspector to do the job."

Bubba stopped pacing. His grin was bitter. "Guerrero, that fucking police sergeant?"

"I don't know him personally, I sometimes make arrangements with—"

"Okay, Earl. Get me some rope. Or belts. The straps off your bathrobes."

Both Swabb's eyes had begun to swell and turn an unbecoming color against his pink-colored face.

After tying Rory Fitzsimmon's hands and feet with the belts and things, Bubba wanted a phone.

Swabb pointed to the kitchen. Bubba found the instrument and punched in Guerrero's number. Bubba wasn't normally a panicky man, but at this moment he desperately wanted the man to pick up. If the sonofabitch had made it to the reservation with Maggie sitting on all that money…

"*Hola!*"

Bubba identified himself and spoke in Spanish. "Hello, amigo, it's me again, *la migra*. Can you do me a favor—are the babies in your hands?" He frowned in anticipation of the response he didn't want.

"Maybe. Why do you call?" Guerrero said.

"Because I am your friend. I know you have done only what you were forced to do. No hard feelings. Now tell me if they are in your possession."

A momentary hesitation gave Bubba nothing to go on. "I did as I am told," Guerrero said. "I took the little babies, as I was instructed."

Bubba scowled, but he wasn't sure that he believed him. How could he have known so quickly where to find those babies? "Took them where?" Bubba asked.

At length Guerrero said, "They are safe. But what concern is this to you?"

"Don't do anything with them until I call you tomorrow. You will be well rewarded—more than what I paid you for the other job, for a lot less trouble … I am working on behalf of *Señor* Mendez."

Guerrero said, "This was not the plan."

"Fuck the plan," Bubba blurted in English. "If something happens to them, or to Maggie, I will—"

He stopped himself, went back to Spanish. "I have an offer for you. A large settlement. But I cannot get the money to you until tomorrow. Remember, no harm must come to those babies. Or the woman. I will call you tomorrow."

He put down the receiver and rummaged through drawers in the kitchen until he found a roll of duct tape.

"It's time to go," he said to Swabb, who sat on the couch with a twisted-up rag of ice cubes covering his nose.

"Wh—where? What about him? You can't just leave him here."

Bubba offered up a big grin. He said, "Don't worry, he's not interested in trashing your cute pad … Find your cell phone and car keys. You got any loose money, might want to take that."

Swabb complied with every command. Bubba pocketed the cellular with the car keys, then he gave the lawyer a private moment to powder himself in the bathroom. Bubba stood outside the half-open door.

He bound Swabb's wrists in back with the duct tape.

"Please, not my mouth!" The lawyer's eyes grew wide. "I have vertigo."

"You're a funny guy?" Bubba said. "'Not my mouth.' Lawyer would be pretty much lost without his mouth, I guess."

As the tape pressed against his lips, Swabb went into a panic, thrashing his head and shoulders.

Bubba could see the difficulty he had trying to breathe. "Nose won't work, huh? Okay, hold still. Curl in your lips."

Swabb's eyes bulged watching the knife in Bubba's hand come at him. Bubba held the lawyer's chin tightly and wedged a dime-size hole in the tape, apparently without nicking the mouth. He folded it in with a fingertip.

"I better not hear a peep out of you, Counselor, or I'll tape over this hole and tape your eyes to boot. Got it?"

Swabb nodded, thankfulness written in his swollen eyes.

Before leaving, Bubba found some stationary in a desk in the dining room and wrote Roxanne a note telling her where she could find the car and where the spare set of keys were in the trailer; he found a "forever" postage stamp and attached it. He would drop it in a box on the way.

"Your car, lead the way." He followed Swabb through the kitchen-connected steps downstairs to the garage where a handsome Lexus lounged like a sleeping black stallion.

He popped the trunk with the remote and helped Swabb in.

"I'll get you some covers, hang on. You want a pillow?"

Bubba was serious. He returned with an armful of soft material, ski clothing mostly, packed it around Swabb, lifted his head to place a pillow under it. He didn't fluff it first.

"You get some sleep now, Earl. We'll be off to the badlands in the morning ... "

Bubba felt a little worried seeing the fear in the lawyer's saucer eyes as he lowered the lid, wondering if he might suffocate or drown. Not much difference really.

He crawled in behind the wheel, took time to breathe in the new-leather smell, then raised the garage door and backed the stallion out into the cool November night.

CHAPTER FORTY-SEVEN

The woman poured Myers a drink from a bottle of scotch. Just one cube of ice, no water. She poured herself a drop as well. Flimsy plastic cups, compliments of the Lafayette.

He'd taken her for the night. For a man out of work, the room-and-girl package was expensive, but he could not go home and he wouldn't ask Tina Lubrano to put him up overnight. Same with Carol Finley, whom he had also considered calling but couldn't make himself. Things might advance with Finely in a direction that frightened him. Not ready for any kind of relationship. Max Cullen's wife might have turned him in. He wasn't ready to go back to jail.

The woman was somewhere under thirty, dark-skinned, kinky hair, smelling harshly of lavender. But her affectionate smile sold Myers. She had wide eyes, open and unabashed.

"Would you work my shoulders?" Myers implored, patting the bed for her to join him after getting the drinks.

"Cost you a bunch extra," she said. Teasing him, he knew, because of that smile.

The television was on but the local news had already had its run and all he could get now was CNN and there was nothing about the murder of Sidney Rhoades on it. He wasn't expecting any news outside local coverage, not until there was a bigger tie-in—which, ironically, he was going to provide. He didn't know what had been reported locally, if anything.

Right after he left Rhoades' bungalow he went to the Safari, had a drink and told Sam the barkeep what had happened. The bartender had not been exactly warm to Myers after the night before. But Myers wanted to know about Velma, how badly the impetuous detective had hurt her, and if Sam was okay, too.

"We can bring a suit against him," Myers suggested, seeing the extent of Sam's muted anger.

Sam said he had gotten Velma off the floor and back on to the barstool. She seemed okay, he said. "But, boy, was she pissed."

Myers didn't stay long; he thought Millard would be smart enough to send a uniform around, or maybe even Pedroza himself might show up again, this time looking for a suspect in a killing. Myers wouldn't put it past Pedroza to think he was stupid enough to show up here, after murdering a man. As it turned out, he would have been right.

"You smoke?" Myers asked the young woman. She nodded and he asked to bum one and a light. The first draw made him light-headed.

He asked, "You married?" Her name, she said, was Shawneen.

She got busy behind him, kneading the inside edges of both shoulder blades. She was good. He crushed out the cigarette and leaned his head back against her naked bosom, shut his eyes. He hadn't had sex with her. He was afraid of contracting something, HIV or gonorrhea or syphilis or bugs, any kind of germ. The real reason had nothing to do with diseases—he wouldn't let himself get intimate.

"Oh, you betcha. Got a kid, too. How about you?"

"Not for a while … That feels good, Shawneen. What can I do for you?"

It was past two a.m. Myers was exhausted. He needed sleep but he didn't want to sleep. He wanted to need someone. And this woman calling herself Shawneen would be the one upon whom he would try his newfound need for affection. If he could stay awake.

He could not.

In the early morning, before light, he felt the smooth warmth of Shawneen's naked skin pull him in. He was passionate, more than he could remember, using a condom as ordered, wanting to taste her lips, all of her, though she would not allow that.

He left the downtown hotel before Shawneen had finished her shower, just after the news at six a.m. in which he had been identified as a person of interest in the murder of a veteran Homeland Security deportation officer.

CHAPTER FORTY-EIGHT

Bubba slept in the Lexus. He'd parked in the driveway of a private residence southeast of the city. The lawyer lay hogtied in the trunk. A week earlier Bubba with a team of agents secured and sealed off the residence. The homeowner, a garment manufacturer, now sat in jail for using illegals to sew his imitation brand of Levi Strauss blue jeans in a San Ysidro sweat shop. The old man had lived alone in the big house.

The crow of a rooster woke Bubba, but he went right back to sleep. At eight o'clock he bolted upright, eyes burning in the bright glare of sunlight.

He looked around, sighed with relief seeing he wasn't surrounded by SWAT or shot full of lead by Blondies, the cartel now looking for the garment maker. He straightened his clothes as best he could, spit-brushed his curly locks in the rearview, chewed a stick of gum to cover his atrocious breath, then got out and spoke to his passenger in the trunk, "Good morning, Counselor." He spoke in a singsong but the birds weren't tweeting back.

By all accounting Swabb should have been cold stone dead, but he was alive and nodding as Bubba sprang open the trunk lid. His swollen eyes didn't look all that good, but Bubba could see a wedge of his pupils. His nostrils were swollen and crusty with blood. The hole in the duct tape covering his mouth had kept him breathing.

He helped Swabb out and cut the duct tape on his wrists so he could relieve himself, but left his mouth taped. He rightly assumed his hostage would poke the breathing hole wider. Bubba didn't care if he did. He tried to reassure Swabb things would improve if he didn't misbehave. The lawyer acted grateful, nodding rigorously as Bubba told him what he could not do. Such as try to run or scream. Nevertheless Swabb looked like the next victim of Leatherface's chainsaw as the trunk lid shut on him again.

Bubba drove to a Jack-in-the-Box near a branch of Wells Fargo Bank in San Ysidro. His stash was secreted away in a money market account, currently yielding a hardy four-point-one percent interest. The bank was less than one klick from the Mexican border. He felt the pull already.

He parked at the lonesome end of Jack's lot, got out and stretched. He spoke surreptitiously above the car trunk. "I've got some business. I'll bring you a Jumbo Jack if you're good."

He bought a newspaper from the vending box in front then entered and ordered coffee and orange juice and two breakfast burritos, a large Coke and the big Jack to go, then found a seat in the eating section where he could keep an eye on the Lexus. He looked at the paper.

There it was, another picture of him spread out for the entire local world to deride. This time it was a snapshot Rox had taken last year on their visit back home in Alice, Texas. The press had gotten it from one of those law enforcement agencies chasing him, he figured. The headline glorified his desperado status since last night's story:

Dragnet Extended for Border
Patrolman in Double Murders

He sipped coffee and read, occasionally glanced at the Lexus. He was affected by a bizarre sense of importance reading about himself as an outlaw on the run. He thought musingly of several historical figures. Clyde Barrow and Pancho Villa weren't bad guy before they headed into trouble. Most of the Dalton brothers were lawmen until they became killers. Just like Bubba. The problem had been how others saw these men, he reasoned, and that's what created the circumstances that caused them to go astray. Bubba didn't think of himself as a bad sort; he just got into a little trouble that escalated into bigger trouble. Most desperados were misrepresented in the press, their deeds exaggerated to sensationalize them and pump up their status as badasses, all to sell more newspapers. That was what they were doing with Bubba when all he had done was bust a couple of scumbags who proved they didn't deserve to live anymore in this world—you couldn't count Maggie as a victim because she was still alive. Okay, the law didn't know that.

Bubba thought of Jesus of Nazareth, another outlaw who had also been persecuted wrongly—but Bubba didn't think it fitting to relate himself to the Lord Jesus, regardless if he had grown up a God-fearing Southern Baptist who had been saved twice. He didn't know offhand but figured those other bad boys had religion too.

He guzzled his orange juice and read another article that interested him because he had met the guy. It said the reporter named Raymond August Myers was suspected of murdering a Homeland Security employee. Jesus, he thought, "murder" had gone rampant in the news. Bubba remembered the guy because he had gotten right everything Bubba told him at the site of that massacre in Ocotillo Wells. In his experience, that wasn't the case with most reporters. Frequently, they bent things, sometimes exaggerated what he told them. The *real* number of deaths, that sort of thing. Inferring a human foul might have contributed to the deaths of border crossing immigrants when the only thing foul had been the weather.

But something wasn't right about this guy out murdering someone. Why would a reporter want to kill this agent? Why was the man killed, anyway? It felt awfully close to the trouble Bubba was in. Then he read that the victim, Rhoades, had died by strangulation, garroted. Fitzsimmon had brought a garrote to Swabb's place, intending to use it on the lawyer—and then on Bubba sometime later. Fitzsimmon was the one who killed the ICE agent, not the reporter. The reporter knew something about all this, had to, and he had been set up. Just like Bubba.

He scratched his head, on top in the middle. That was the place that always itched when he was figuring something out, and when he ate jalapeños. A lot of the time he had to remove a hat to scratch. Who was setting everybody up? Easy, he thought. Director Richard Mendez—a onetime idol of most of the sector's field agents. He was the man who had instigated all these murders. Bubba had it figured out. He stopped scratching.

He ate the burritos hungrily and finished off the coffee.

The bank opened at 9:30. He was there at 9:20, knowing that bank robbers don't show up early. He was aware that bank employees get a fast-track training course from any number of law enforcement agencies on how to spot would-be robbers and other potential perpetrators. So he was being Your Average Customer, polite but anxious as they were over money matters.

The door opened and he stepped up to a teller's window unrecognized, so far as he could tell. He showed the clerk a pleasant expression and the false driver's license with the name under which the account had been set up. He said he wanted to close out.

"Fifty- and hundred-dollar bills only, please. Mostly hundreds."

The teller, a young woman who seemed nervous about the request, had to call on the manager, who had no problem with Bubba being Thomas Conroy Collins. The problem was that he had not opened the account at this branch and could not close it out here.

"Okay," Bubba said, holding the smile. "Why don't we just leave five bucks in. That work?"

"I'm sorry," the slender manager said, pithily. "The minimum balance for our Saver-Thrift account is fifty dollars."

"Okay, then let's make it fifty."

The other problem, he wanted cash.

"Perhaps a money order would be safer," the manager suggested. He was giving Bubba a suspicious glare now, which Bubba didn't like.

"That costs, don't it?" Bubba said, shooting the suspicious look back at him.

"Well, yes. Ten dollars," the manager said. Condescension this time. "We could give you a bank note. There is no charge for that."

Bubba stood his ground, gently shaking his head, still with the smile.

"Currently the account has thirty-two thousand, one hundred fifty-one dollars and fifty-one cents in it," the manager told him.

Bubba grinned. "Okay, give me all of it but the fifty-one bucks and change," he said, leaning forward, drawing the manager close. "See, I've got a deal on a sailboat, a steal, and the guy ain't American; he wants cash."

That was all it took. The man was just nosy. His mouth formed the big O and broke into a grin, showing he wasn't being snide with the customer.

Bubba asked for a double plastic bag to carry the bulk of cash.

Stepping out into the sunlight, he once again did not encounter SWAT. He hadn't been recognized; he now didn't have to make a run for the border. But that was still where he was going.

He diverted from the Tijuana crossing to Otay Mesa, still nervous as hell over this last obstacle. U.S. officials might have a controlled checkpoint before crossing, a possibility less likely at the less popular Otay. The didn't and he breathed easier. Mexican officials didn't give a hoot who crossed. Of the two countries, Mexico had the truer open-arms policy. Come on over, *bienvenidos*.

He drove to the *colonia* where he had left the '62 Falcon, figuring the car would still be out back in the dusty pottery yard. He figured right.

He caught up to the smuggler's kid brother in the painting shed, a boy about twelve at work detailing dry clay pots in colorful peacock-tail strokes. The kid was apprenticing in the *Talavera* style, a young artist in the making.

"Hey, little man, come over here a second," he said, trying not to breathe in the high odor of shellac.

Bubba pointed out the vehicle. "See that car?"

The boy had a paintbrush in his teeth; he looked, he nodded.

"You think you're big enough to reach the gas pedal?"

The boy nodded hard.

Bubba opened the door and took the car key off the floorboard and pitched it to the kid.

"Tell your sorryass brother it's yours. He gives you any grief, tell him I'll see he gets a stay at La Mesa."

Bubba just liked the kid's looks. Kinda reminded him of himself when he was a hustling youth.

CHAPTER FORTY-NINE

Margarita Herlinda stood with a fist on her hip in the doorway of the room where Maggie lightly snored. The Indian came to wake the lazy white woman, but didn't. A small cloud of dust rose on the dirt floor when she tossed a pair of heavy boots that might fit Maggie's long Anglo feet.

She sat in her rocking chair in the common area, tucked snuff inside her lip, then spoke to the girl on the floor who tended two babies. "Go to the store for some milk. I'll look after the little ones. Get yourself some peanuts and a Pepsi if you want. Here—" She handed the girl five pesos and an empty Pepsi bottle.

The ten-year-old used her toe to brush dirt over a line of approaching ants and got up, leaving the babies on their mats. She rubbed her eyes and grinned sleepily. Robalba had been up most of the night with the babies. The sick one hadn't slept well.

Margarita picked it up. It had conjunctivitis. Margarita cooed and bounced it as the other child lay sleeping at her feet. The sick baby's fists reached out of the swaddle and shook. Its red-streaked eyes were open wide, fixed and teary. The child was also malnourished, light as a clump of kale.

She spat dark juice into an earthen pot. Her thoughts about the child's mother weren't good. Any woman who would give up her baby so young, and when the child was sickly, was no mother. She was a whore. No matter how much she'd been paid, no matter what her reason, she had no right to send her baby away unhealthy.

The Indian woman spat again.

The three children Margarita birthed and raised had been nourished like babies were supposed to be nourished and they'd gotten heavy as sacks of beans right away. Maybe they didn't get enough education growing up, but they were healthy children. They didn't run off until there was nothing left to hunt—after the *norteamericanos* with their roaring machines and the filthy drug dealers with their crops cleared out the wild mainstay of deer and wild pigs and goats.

She stood over Maggie. "Do you want to help with them, *Poquita*?" It was time the city woman got up. "They need changing, feeding."

"You bet I do," replied Maggie, suddenly appearing in the doorway rubbing her eyes.

Margarita looked warmly at her. There weren't many gringos she liked, but she liked this one; *Poquita* had brought life to her village. Margarita had liked her father, who put half the no-accounts on the reservation back to work making the stuff that John paid them a handsome price for. "You rested well, then? Mountain air good for the mind and the body."

"I feel wonderful. Where are they?"

"Follow your ear, your nose," said Margarita with as much of a grin as she would ever show.

Maggie got busy with the most basic of domestic human work, the routine chores of mothers and caregivers far and wide. Her thoughts didn't dwell on being officially dead, or that she had missed her dad's funeral, or that her future looked dim. Working with babies was a consuming labor of love; the mess she had made of her own life didn't much matter. Attending to babies put her in a wondrous frame of mind, giving her a sense of purpose and joy. She made time to tease a cute little Asian baby with a rattler, poke the skinny doughboy belly. The baby beamed.

She heard a commotion, the squealing voices of the bigger children outside. Then the door suddenly swung open and Castro entered in a flurry, stooping to get under the door. He stood for a moment, as if to adjust to the darker interior.

"Hey there, boobaroo," he said in a singsong addressing Maggie. He wore a Viking-like sheepskin coat with a fox-and-squirrel collar that blocking light from the doorway made him appear bigger than the door itself.

Maggie said, "Castro! Boobaroo yourself. Hey, where have you been all night, amigo, huh?"

The big Indian was a good sport, easy to tease.

His perpetual good-natured grin grew wide. "You catch me, oh boy. Maybe my wife she don't want to feed me now, huh?"

"I'll feed you. Here, take this bottle."

"Boobaroo, you know I only drink the Hawaiian Punch, Diet ... But I am tired from working all night."

He pulled out a fistful of wadded greenback bills. "Many pictures. Big group and everybody want a picture from Castro Herlinda, big native injun chief."

"I was there the other night; how come I didn't see you?"

"Ha! You too busy with the *muchachas bonitas.*"

"All right, not funny."

"Ha!" Castro said and turned to his wife.

He handed her two bottles of medicine he had gotten at the *farmacia,* a children's liquid analgesic and a solution for the eye infection. His face grew serious and his wife asked, "What is it, husband?"

Castro said it would wait until the children displayed. Six children stood outside Margarita's door, waiting patiently.

Margarita gave the sick baby a spoonful from each bottle then handed the child to Maggie. She went out. Castro followed, stooping again through the doorway. Maggie knew something wasn't right; Castro hadn't even asked about her father. John Frazier, she knew, was his favorite *gringo macho.*

Castro had the children fall into a line military style. As part of their regimen, each child stepped forward to show Margarita his or her take, a burlap bag, today containing either pine cones and needles or a dead small animal. One smiling boy's bag contained a red hawk, which Castro allowed—the hawk would be the last of four birds of prey allowed under tribal rule to be downed every year. His was the last haul shown because it contained the hardest to get.

The children were excited with their draw. The pinecones would be made into Christmas ornaments and hopefully sold to a *norteamericano* merchant; some of the ornaments they would keep for their holy season. The hawk would provide ceremonial feathers.

Castro released the children with a clap of his hands and watched them scurry off.

"Now, what is the matter, husband?" Margarita asked. She placed two squirrels and three quail into a single bag which she would skin and pluck then refrigerate. Cleaning the carcasses was up to her because everyone knew how Castro turned ill at the sight of blood. No one kidded him about that.

He said, "Why is Miss Maggie here without John?" He pronounced it *Joan*.

Margarita frowned. "Something is wrong. It is the babies?"

Castro nodded. "Some guy wants to play chase with me for them, you know. Then I saw a man I don't want to see. He want to take them, I think. He is coming here today, I think."

A moment passed before Margarita said, "The Inspector?"

Castro nodded again. "You know what it will mean if we defy him."

She said, "We have money. We can pay."

Castro shook his head frowning. "He will only return for more. He would not stop."

"Then we must find a way to hide these babies from him."

"They are not ours to hide, wife. What choice do we have?"

"A baby is sick! We must take it to the hospital—" Margarita stopped speaking when she heard a noise in the nearby woods, a flush of quail.

Castro said, "Maybe he is here, I think."

He went inside for his rifle.

Margarita's flat eyes moved rapidly around the outlying scrub.

Castro held the rifle facing the ground as he emerged. He saw the alarm in his wife's face and nudged her. He grinned, as if unconcerned, and said, "Maybe he will find one big surprise waiting for him. Huh?"

CHAPTER FIFTY

Myers eased the Land Cruiser along the drowsy street of Avenida Ruiz, cruising past Hussong's Cantina. The saloon appeared listless, which it ought to since it was mid-morning. He turned at the next corner and parked and got out.

He was still in last night's clothes—jeans and a collared shirt under a sweatshirt that read "Life is a Beach" on the front. He was not overly concerned that he might be made as a wanted man. He knew Baja law enforcement didn't much care about a gringo fugitive who wasn't part of a drug cartel or who had not assaulted a Mexican citizen. It was pretty much live and let live unless you did something to cross a Mexican cop— or woman.

Myers felt fresh from his relatively sober night at the Lafayette Hotel with Shawneen enlivening him with some good loving—never mind the three-hundred bucks it cost in ATM cash or the needling thought of exposure to some bad bug.

Rhoades' murder mostly occupied his mind. He tried to divert a nagging sense of guilt that he could have somehow prevented his death. Rhoades was not a typical bureaucrat. He was a man of conscience, genuine and overly generous. He had a moral sense of indignation for what Myers remembered him calling the "system's unwitting victims." One of those victims was Madelene Schaefer's housekeeper, whom he could easily have gotten into trouble but didn't. He had even risked his career and pension when he defied his sworn duty, and in the presence of a news reporter.

Myers hoped what he learned down here would turn out to dignify and validate Sidney Rhoades. It had better come to something as he was violating a court order to stay put in the good old U.S. of A. Rhoades had told Myers if he found the Indian sketch artist, "you'll find the village" and finding the Indian village might help him learn the fate of some missing babies, maybe lead to a smuggling ring.

Myers walked through the cantina's swinging doors. It was dead quiet but not empty. A few locals leaned against the bar as if attached to it. There were no mariachis plucking strings and tooting horns for these gentlemen. Myers didn't hear snarling dogs or gamecocks clucking out back. The air was stale but clear. The sawdust floor had been swept down to the planks. This was no way to see Hussong's. It shattered the myth.

Myers overlooked the hard stares. He browsed the multitude of pictures nailed and stapled to the walls—good-humored satirical charcoal depicting rogue American cowboys and yahoos, somewhat individualized. Probably took six, seven minutes per drawing, he figured, though not being a fast-sketch artist himself he really didn't know and shouldn't guess. He did recall a drawing of his son Richie long ago; that didn't take long.

He stepped up to the bar, keeping a distance from the locals who had now bunched up like hens in the presence of a fox. Myers took note and got friendly. *"Tequila por mi amigos, señor!"* he exclaimed to the barman, a slight man so old he might have been the original Hussong's bartender that invented the world renown *margarita*.

He waited until the men downed the shooters then spoke in Spanish, "Friends, can you tell me who the artist is? ... When will he be here? Tonight, maybe? ... What tribe does he belong to?" Myers was not sure how to say "tribe" so he said *familia* instead. "Does he live in the mountains? The *ejido*? ... "

Blank stares notified him to mind his own gringo business. But the shot glasses were empty and he called for another round. He was not deterred.

In English, he asked, "Does the man come at night, when the gringos are here?"

Nada. The hens weren't talking. Myers got the bright idea to take a closer look at the drawings. He found a name taking up lots of room across the bottom of a sketch, "Castro Herlinda." Clearly written. There were a few other names but mostly the sweeping signature was "Castro Herlinda" or "Chief C. Herlinda." A sense of humor to go with the frivolity in the caricatures. He already liked this guy.

Myers called for a third round of tequila shots all around, plus nine long neck chasers this time, including one for the bartender and one for himself.

Then he waited, unhurried, fixing himself to the bar like the locals.

"Old Castro, he is Pai," a man soon blurted out in English. Myers wouldn't have bet on this particular man speaking, based on the intensity of a scowl that hadn't changed. He wasn't so old as he was gnarly.

"Yeah? Would the Pai be anywhere I can drive to?"

The man nodded his head once, not a big talker. Myers bought that individual another shooter. With that, the man broke through the scowl and grinned at his buddies and, head tossed back, downed the tequila. He kept the stolid demeanor telling Myers he might look for the tribe's village twenty-five kilometers east off *"Ojos Negro,"* or *"Black Eyes,"* apparently the name of a road.

"Only one there is," he said. He said you would see a sign saying *Rancho Coyote*, or maybe it was *Catarina*, he wasn't sure, he never went up there, too dangerous with the drug bandits.

Myers filed some of that to memory. He bought the big talker another shooter and cerveza before saying *adios*, dropping Great-Grandpa tending a $20 tip. It was quite reasonable to drink here. But he couldn't keep this up, a man without a job.

Local farmers had no use for dune buggies and Hummers in Baja, nor any other type of off-road gringo vehicle, which might as well include a 30-year-old Land Cruiser, even though it was a utility vehicle, not a toy. So Myers was careful not to run over any living vegetation that wasn't weeds. He headed east keeping to the road and then to the trail and then the cow path that the trail became after fifteen or so klicks into big tree country. There was some wild growth he could not avoid running over and persuaded himself it was only weeds.

The sun flickered high through tall timber as the road steadily ascended. The drive turned slow going, then bogged down as he maneuvered in four-wheel drive over boulders and across narrow, eroded ditches. He kept track of the kilometers. He'd driven several miles farther than where Ole Gnarly had told him the sign would be, and he had seen no signs at all.

There was nothing that could be called a road and the terrain here appeared too rugged to travel any further. Myers got out of the car. He walked a couple hundred feet to the mesa drop-off. Surrounding him were inclines with large boulders, small and large trees. Maybe he'd taken the wrong cow path. Maybe "Black Eyes" was a cute little send-up for a gringo with too many questions.

It wasn't cold but he could tell it would be by dusk. He walked in the direction of a clearing, then into the tree line across the clearing. Nothing to indicate humans lived here. The gentlemen of Hussong's were having a good laugh on him about now.

The thought had him distracted and he had not seen it coming, though he should have. Something consistent with the weight and shape of a shovel slammed into his back, driving the wind out of his lungs. Stars shot from his eyes like nighttime sparklers. He bucked forward, losing his balance.

He knew what struck him. He knew just before when his shin brushed against a twig that didn't properly give. He'd tripped a booby line. Shiny metal blades underneath him flashed in the afternoon sunlight; he twisted in an effort to defy gravity. But the years had slowed his reflexes and when he hit ground he felt blades clip his ribs. Instant pain.

The trap was not designed for just any animal. It had been built to do exactly what it had done, knock a man into a bed of steel stakes, knife blades. Its intent was to kill that man. It was a coarse setup, much like the VC's booby traps Myers had encountered more than once, functioning on a three-way leverage system rigged to the stiff twig he'd tripped which released the length of four-inch cast-iron plumbing pipe from a tree branch above, its force creating enough power to knock a large man into the leafy shallow pit. Hate and probably vengeance and protection were behind its construction.

His vision darkened, as though the forest had suddenly grown another canopy. Some time seemed to pass before he rolled over and raked a hand along his side. The hand came up bright red, shiny. He rested his head back against the leafy ground; his head felt light as a wave of heat and his vision lost color before he closed his eyes and drifted ...

He glimpsed a burr-headed VC dashing from tree to tree. Then gone, like a phantom, déjà vu. Delirious, he searched the ground for his weapon, which must have flown out of his hand when Betty exploded. He didn't move or look down at himself, not beyond his bloody hand, for fear he would find no legs to get him out of there. He spotted his buddy Danny now, out there. No, not him. Visions. Children running, screaming. Flailing arms, the cries. And he lay helpless …

Slowly the shadow of a figure moved above him. Who … ?

The man now straddled him, tall as a tree, brandishing a rifle.

"Who you are, friend?" Castro said.

Myers glimpsed the blue-steel barrel of the AK and rolled onto his wounded side, drawing in his legs. Time to die. In that moment before death when you can clarify the important things past, he thought of all the people he had loved and how he had failed them. In the negative. *He had failed them.*

Another moment passed and he sensed himself still breathing. He rose onto an elbow, then to his knees, and then tried to run.

Castro grabbed a handful of shirt at his back.

"Whoa, take her easy, friend," he said. "Who you?"

Castro then saw the blood on Myers' shirt and let go like he was holding a snake. Myers dropped to the ground. And that, the pain of it, brought him to his senses.

He got to his feet again. "Who are *you*?" he asked the big, dark Viking while lifting his shirt and evaluating the damage. Several inches of flesh lay open in two parallel gashes, exposing the angelic ivory of bone. The blades had skimmed along the ribs and not punctured a lung even though it felt like it had.

He glanced at the Indian wearing a smile on his chiseled face and grinned out of embarrassment for losing himself to another time and place.

"Yours?" Myers said, nodding toward the steel stakes and the dangling section of iron piping.

"Hey, sorry, Chief. That trap was for the mothers I think coming for no good. Sorry. Can't say no more than that." Castro kept his eyes above Myers' head, squeamish of blood.

Myers grimaced. He sighed and then perked up. "Are you Pai?"

Castro nodded eagerly. "Full blood Pai Pai. All injun."

"Your name Castro, 'Chief Herlinda?'"

"I draw you before?"

Myers felt the wound on his head from last night leaking under its bandage; his spine was bruised, it felt like. He needed to get these new gashes cleaned and sewn. He wasn't ready to evaluate, but he was beat up pretty good.

He asked, "Do you care for babies here?"

Castro frowned. "Who you, man?" His tone turned harder.

"Nobody that's going to bring you harm. I've come looking for some missing babies."

Myers stumbled and Castro took his weight. Myers thought he could walk on his own but he let Castro hold him. Shortly they came to a clearing with a low-slung adobe structure. Children were running around playing some kind of battle game with sticks as swords and guns. Myers had been steered right by Ole Gnarly and his drinking buddies at Hussong's; when he could travel no farther, he had arrived at *Rancho Coyote*.

Two Indian women stood bent at the waist over a mixed-vegetable garden of string beans and cabbage and carrots. They stopped what they were doing to stare at Myers.

Then a white woman appeared holding a baby on her hip. A colorful bandanna covered her hair. She wore a long burlap skirt. In her free hand the young woman carried a bunch of carrots by their stalks. His mind raced but came up empty for an explanation why Margaret Frazier wasn't on a slab in a morgue, what was left of her. Her eyes shone bright with contentment, not the look of sadness and disillusionment he'd seen at the lighthouse. But there was no mistaking who she was.

"God, you're hurt!" Maggie said, recognizing the reporter as well. "How did you get here? Why?"

Myers held up a hand. "Asking the questions is supposed to be my job."

"Come on inside," said Maggie.

Margarita entered and called on two girls to look after the infants. She made Myers lie on a yellow formica-top table. She helped him out of the sweatshirt and shirt underneath and then handed him a bottle of tequila to suck while she prepared. He asked and she told him the blades in the pit were not contaminated with bacteria, and he breathed a little easier. He lay shivering on the cold table as she cleaned the wounds with biting antiseptic and gauze. Maggie used towels and applied pressure above and below the gaping wounds, suppressing the bleeding. Myers raised his head to swill down tequila. Castro didn't come inside.

"Be still," Margarita said. "Take this."

It was a smelly mud-colored goo in an old amber pint-size bottle; it tasted worse than it looked and Myers had to sit up and gulp more tequila to keep the goo from coming back up.

"This will sting, *señor*, but it hold you together."

Myers tried to concentrate on Maggie's explanation for Castro's booby trap. It wasn't easy with the big Indian woman poking his skin with a fat needle and jerking the string as if tightening down buttons, but he heard something along these lines: Castro and some of his tribesmen had modified a non-lethal trap to discourage the invading drug lord's mules. They had modified the trap again, just this morning, to stop a man they thought was headed here to take babies from them. The babies arrived yesterday from Indonesia, Maggie told him in confidence, and Castro had grabbed them off the ship before some other people, the same people who wanted Maggie dead. She explained all this in such abbreviation Myers needed to figure it out.

"They aren't the babies from the Ocotillo tragedy?" He spoke between gasps and moans.

Maggie waved a hand in the air. "Oh. No, that group has already been placed. Those babies are safe, thank God."

Myers lay back hearing that. He yelped. "How many of those are you going to do?" he asked the big Indian woman.

"You have bad time before this, huh?" she said with a frown, touching the top edge of his shrapnel wound in the groin. He had no response.

He didn't ask Maggie to explain her resurrection, the reasons why she wasn't actually dead. He didn't ask why they wanted her dead in the first place. Those questions could wait.

It took Margarita ten minutes to insert thirteen nylon stitches along the rise of two ribs. The job looked to Myers like a T-Day turkey he might have sewn. But the bleeding had stopped. She re-bandaged his head wound too.

"Okay, amigo, you done," she told him. "Maybe you want to go into town for shots."

Myers had had his last tetanus shot four, maybe five years ago. Yeah, he'd better get shots. He didn't feel much pain, only when he breathed and moved. He felt a sharp pull now, lowering his legs off the table. He sucked more tequila. He probably had had enough to be drunk but couldn't tell it.

"Thanks," he said. No slurring the word; Myers could hold his liquor. He did wobble a little taking a step, but he could do it by himself, thank you.

Maggie gave him a shirt she had bought for Bubba and forgotten to give him, things being so daunted and rushed. It was a cowboy shirt, red, white and blue, with buttons of pearls and wing-flap pockets flaps.

Myers got to say thanks again and gingerly slipped on the shirt. He crept outside. He saw Castro wheel in the Land Cruiser and park it under a sprawling black oak next to a shiny 1953 Chevy pickup. Classic truck and well loved. Castro had a gun in his hand.

Myers moved across the yard. The pain wasn't so bad if he kept his feet moving, if he didn't kick a stump or stumble over the pecking hens.

Castro handed Myers the keys along with the handgun. "You need this. The Inspector he is a dangerous man. You be careful."

Myers took the meaty gun, a snub nose .38 revolver, saw that the cylinders held shells, and slipped it under the driver's seat of his car. "This the guy's got everybody spooked?"

"Bad hombre," Castro said, losing his ever-present smile. "Ole Castro has ears. I hear he come to take them. No time to talk."

CHAPTER FIFTY-ONE

A sense of urgency took hold throughout the Herlinda compound. People moved with purpose.

Castro sent the children down to the village central. "Go on," he said, prodding the reluctant ones. "Robalba, you are in charge of them. Go now!"

He walked after the children along the road to see that they hurried.

Outside the house, the sick baby bounced in its pouch against Margarita's chest. The child wasn't crying. It slept soundly even as Margarita rushed across the yard. She slipped off the pouch and lay the sleeping infant on the seat in Castro's pickup.

The other babies were in the large pink bassinet that sat on the outdoor table, waiting to be loaded into the truck.

"Will you come with us?" she said, turning to Maggie.

Maggie looked at Myers and back to Margarita. "He may need me to drive."

Margarita nodded. She saw Castro on the other side of the truck and she climbed in behind the wheel. She cranked the muscle Chevy, ready to head down the mountain and to safety when a gunshot rang out. It was close and clapped hard in Margarita's ears. She looked but didn't see Castro now. Instead, through the passenger window, she saw the Inspector and a younger man not in a police uniform.

~

Guerrero stood silently, as he stared at the ground by the truck. The young man with him was armed with a shotgun, the gun he'd just fired close to the truck.

"José, you stupid son of a whore!" Guerrero bawled at the young man.

José batted his eyes fiercely. He tucked his head. "He was going to shoot us, one of us," he cried. "He aimed at us. What was I to do, Uncle?"

Guerrero pulled a gun out of his shoulder holster, as if he might shoot his nephew, his own flesh and blood.

On the side of the Chevy Castro lay mortally wounded in a heap on the ground. José had shot him in the back with a load of buckshot from a twelve gauge.

Guerrero kicked his nephew in the shin with his steel-toed boot, sending him into a dance. He looked at Castro then at Margarita, said he was sorry, then moved hastily around the Chevy to the others. Castro didn't hear the apology. He was dead.

Margarita did not speak. While Guerrero cursed his nephew, she had slipped the baby out of the car and hid it along with the carrying pouch underneath the truck. Oddly, the gunshot had not awakened the sick baby. If he did not know how many babies there were, maybe she could save at least this one—if the child would only remain quiet.

Guerrero waved his handgun lazily at Margarita then at Myers and Maggie in a motion for all of them to move close to each other, as if to gather them for a photo or a mass killing.

He ordered them to their knees and called to his nephew.

~

Myers glanced more than once at the Land Cruiser, estimating it would take three very long steps to put a hand on the .38. He didn't know if the safety was on, which would take a precious moment he didn't have. It was the trigger-happy kid and his big gun that stopped him from trying it. The kid idly guarded them with his shotgun hanging ready in the crook of his arm, the end of the barrel still smoking.

Guerrero said to José, "Can you get these babies into the car without choking them to death? If you hurt them, in the name of the Virgin, I will shoot you, just as you shot this great artist."

They all watched as José took the bassinet and walked carefully off the compound and into the woods.

"Where is the other one?" Guerrero said to the woman.

Margarita said nothing.

Guerrero grunted and looked in the truck, holding the group at bay with his handgun. He glanced back at Margarita, shook his head and bent on his haunches and looked under the truck. He pulled out the bundle. "Is a crime to lie to the Inspector, woman."

Margarita stood off her knees and spat. "This baby is very sick. It will die if—"

Guerrero gun-butted her on the front of her head, dropping her to the ground.

Myers moved in time to throw a leg under Margarita, partially cushioning her fall. It didn't help his just-sewn ribs, but her head didn't crack open on the hard ground.

Guerrero's knees popped as he lowered himself now in front of Maggie. He said, "Where is *la migra?*"

Maggie didn't reply, nor did Myers. She scooted next to Myers; Margarita's head now lay on his lap and he had brushed back her hair, revealing a large bump above the ear with a small gash that appeared only superficial. Her eyelids fluttered.

Guerrero sighed and stood. He tucked the bundled baby under his arm and walked off to the wood's edge. He might have shot holes in some of the car tires but he didn't. He might have taken the souped-up '53 Chevy truck for himself since the car's owner was dead. He didn't do that either. To the citizens of his jurisdiction, he was a considerate inspector of police.

"Don't try to follow, amigo," he said, turning to Myers. "I am *policia* on official business. You will be arrested. Or shot."

CHAPTER FIFTY-TWO

M aggie had dreamt in the night something so remarkable she woke without realizing she was awake. It was a simple dream. Through a kitchen window, she watched her son climbing in the low-slung branches of the tree out back. The dream had blessed her with a biological son. Her own flesh and blood—that's what it felt like, anyhow. In the blue sky there were white clouds. A golden retriever wagged its tail and barked playfully at the boy in the tree. Her hands were wet and warm, her eyes were dry and clear. A snapshot really. It was the feeling of comfort and security she had at that moment that was remarkable. The feeling of being home.

She held on to the dream until it faded in the morning noises and then she took a deep breath, threw off the blanket and got up to face the uncertainty of her shady new life.

She slipped on her jeans and shirt and opened one of the French doors to let in the bright morning light. Myers was standing on the balcony next door, five feet from her, and for an instant she fancied him her loving husband, father of the boy in her Rockwell dream, having his coffee and morning cigarette outside so as not to disturb her while she slept. They were on holiday in Rio after all.

"Good morning," she said, stepping out onto her own balcony. "How did you sleep? Do you hurt much?"

Myers had a cup of coffee in his hand but no cigarette. The balconies of the two rooms practically touched; one could easily step across to the other's.

"Sore," he said and smiled, "but only when I whistle."

"You whistle for that coffee?"

"Room service, believe it or not."

Maggie grinned. "Bubba said the place had class."

"Come on over, they sent a carafe."

Maggie tidied herself then locked up Room 203.

Coming off the mountain last night, she showed Myers her cross-country skills behind the wheel. She pushed the Land Cruiser as hard as Myers' injuries would tolerate, but they never saw the cop's vehicle. Even if they had caught up to the kidnappers, she could have done nothing more than follow. It was best, they'd decided, to start the search fresh in the morning.

"Why'd you come here, I mean how did you know to come to the village?" Maggie had asked him. He looked sleepy but he hurt too much to sleep on the rough road. "I hope you're not just after a story."

He grinned best he could. "What a story. Certainly put my name on the front page."

"Again. You're kidding, right?"

"Well, to answer, I'm not here for a story per se. I wanted to find these missing babies, so that there's no big story. Now there are *still* babies to find, so there's still a story."

Okay," she said and drew quiet.

She found a hospital, *Centro Medico Moctezuma*, and Myers was re-sewn, inoculated and bumped a notch with codeine. He paid with his Visa. He wanted a drink, and over gimlets in the Papa Doble Lounge at the Hacienda Hotel, Maggie had said, "I guess you want to know what's going on with me."

"I was wondering."

"They wanted me dead and sent Bubba to do the job," she'd told him without getting emotional. "It was his idea, faking the car accident. I died to save my life. Funny, huh?"

"Bubba? You mentioned that name before."

A little sparkle came to Maggie's eyes. "Yeah, that's what he goes by. Real name's 'Travis Cousins, Border Patrol,'" she said in a low, mimicking voice. "Like that, he talks that way. Joe Friday. 'Just the facts, ma'am.'"

"I know that name. He was the agent who didn't mind talking at the Ocotillo tragedy. Nice guy, talker. I like talkers. Who was it wanted you dead?"

Gimlets had been Maggie's suggestion in keeping with the old, shadowy feeling she got from the bar, the hotel room, old Ensenada all the way. She nursed hers and told Myers some startling things about herself—she had sold smuggled babies and explained that a corpse went off a cliff instead of her. Telling that one made her a little squeamish, recalling that bowling ball bag. Without pointing fingers, she said Myers' newspaper article was the main reason her boss, Mr. Swabb—Earl Warren Swabb—had sent Bubba to kill her, that after Myers quoted her father talking about missing babies and smuggling, she stood accused of violating their "stupid code." Maggie barked saying it, "I broke the stupid code." She didn't tell him she'd embezzled eighty-five thousand dollars from the same baby-peddling gangsters. He hadn't asked, she didn't see any reason to mention it.

Myers listened with interest, even as he dozed. She could see it had been a long day with a lot of wear and tear on him.

She said, "Let's go. I have a place," and drove to the Hotel Mexico where Myers took Room 205, next to Maggie's, and they said goodnight.

~

Myers picked up with last night's unfinished conversation. Maggie had finished a cup of black and very strong coffee and taken another. They talked inside Myers' room.

"Swabb was probably working for Richard Mendez. You know him?"

Maggie sat on the bed with her coffee; it squeaked more than hers in Room 203. She said she hadn't heard the name, Richard Mendez.

"Where is Cousins now?" he asked.

She frowned. "He went back up."

"Then he's probably seen the papers."

"What's the paper say?"

Myers studied her, trying to get a read on her feelings for the man. Myers needed her to help him find those babies without getting all lovesick over a fugitive killer and clamming up on him.

He kept it short. "We were both in the news. The police want both of us. Me for questioning, him as a suspect." He added, "He'll be hiding out somewhere."

Maggie brightened. "If he runs, he'll run back here, to Ensenada, to the hotel. What do they want him for?"

Myers poured the rest of the *Combate* from the decanter and left her question unanswered. "Have you given any thought to going home?"

She nodded. "I don't know if I want to go back. There's my job. If you can call leaning over tables in a V-cut a job. There's my dog and stuff, but other than that, I just don't have much reason. Nobody left to call family."

"There're your dad's parents, your grandparents. They seem decent enough—I went to your father's funeral … Sorry, I didn't want to have to mention it. They gave a very nice service, most of his people were there, and quite a few people came."

She smiled generously at Myers. "I like them, but I don't think I could live with them. I'm grown, they're old. Excuse me," she said and went into the bathroom.

The Hotel Mexico installed its phones long before the invention of touch-tone and hadn't changed them. Myers had no choice but to try a thing called patience as he dialed and waited. It wasn't easy. He got through to the *Journal* and spoke with Tina Lubrano instead of Cullen. The city editor wouldn't appreciate that he was out of the country, violating his bail.

He growled at Lubrano, "What idiot editor didn't tie Rhoades' murder to the Frazier story? Don't tell me, lame-brain L.C. Right?"

"Good to hear from the Magic we all love so much," Lubrano said. "Especially important to have a good sense of humor when one's up the proverbial creek … Wanna know what's going on? You up to it?"

Myers didn't hesitate too long, on account of talking long-distance. "Break it to me gently, Tina."

"They traced your prints, of course, and your shoe prints. Found a piece of mirror from Rhoades' bathroom in one of your footprints out front and, I guess, in your shoe at home, too," she said. "You *do* wear rubber-sole shoes, don't you, Ray, size 12? Rockports, aren't they?"

"It's a common brand. I was in his house, no denying that … Tina, I want you to call Detective Millard for me—I can't let him trace my number. Tell him the man he wants is Richard Mendez, works at ICE, division deputy director. He killed Sidney Rhoades, or had it done. The guy's my size, little larger, probably the same shoe size. Good looking as me, too. Think Ricardo Montalban. Probably had an accomplice—one man couldn't take Rhoades down. I'll explain it all when I get back. Tell Millard that."

"Back? When you get back from *where?* Where are you, Ray?"

"Are you listening? Tell him that Mendez operates a baby smuggling ring. Lawyer named Earl Warren Swabb is part of it. A little investigating on these individuals, things'll fall into place. Those people who died at Ocotillo Wells were caretakers for the babies Mendez was smuggling. Incidentally, the babies were recovered alive."

"That's good. But I really think Millard wants to talk to *you*, Ray. In person. That's the impression I get."

"Tina, I've got a story that's going to make us famous." Myers spoke in a monotone. "You've heard of the Pulitzer."

Tina said, in a monotone of her own, "I think they're putting out a cash reward for information leading to your arrest. I can contact the guild for you. But, frankly, I don't see it doing any good."

"You want I should give the story to the *Times?*"

"I know you didn't do it, Ray."

"You gonna give me an answer, Tina?"

"Sure, Ray, sure. I'll call him."

"I mean about the idiot that didn't tie in the stories. I know you'll call."

"Aw, that. Yeah, you were right. It *was* L-the-fat fuck-C."

~

Maggie brought her belongings to Room 205, heeding Myers' advice that if Bubba showed up it might be better if he didn't know she was there. He could lead them to the babies and if he knew a reporter was around he might not. Reasonably, she agreed, and let Myers talk it up with the dufus desk clerk.

When Myers went to the bathroom, she hid the money she'd brought. She only carried a few thousand in cash down from the mountain, the rest she'd left with Margarita. She stuffed it behind the dresser and put some in her purse. For shopping and things.

She did herself up, dressed Mexican in a multi-colored, shin-length dark skirt and white cotton blouse embroidered with blue sailfishes on the upper front and back. Big, looping earrings. Some blush on her cheeks and ironed waves in her ash blonde hair—Okay, the getup was gringa Mexican, but she didn't care.

Myers said, "You look nice. Like the sailfish."

"I'm partial to fishes … Ray, can I ask you something?"

"Why not?"

"Why are you interested in these babies? I'm curious to know since the ones kidnapped in the desert are safe now, so I know it's not just the story."

Myers looked at her. "You might be wrong about that."

"C'mon, there's more to it. You're genuinely concerned about them when you never saw them. You must like children … You're a father, right? I can tell."

Myers didn't like the subject and gave her a dismissive answer. "Twice over. Didn't take."

"Why not? You're a nice guy. A great guy," she persisted, applying a bit of Sylvia Fischer.

He gave her a sharp look. "Okay. The first one might've been my fault. The second was sure as hell my fault. I let her go, my son went with her."

"Where do we start?" she said, seeing she might've stepped out in a wrong place.

"The way I figure it, if Guerrero has any sense, he'd get the sick baby taken care of," Myers said. "That baby's worth its weight in gold. But he wouldn't take the child to a hospital; it would be some medical practitioner he controls. Doesn't leave us much to go on."

"We've got to try anyway. We can check some medical clinics and call doctors' offices. Pharmacies maybe?"

Myers picked up the phone book. "We can start with this."

"No, wait," said Maggie, "there's this dentist I'm sure is on his payroll. Got false teeth, a dentist with false teeth. You want to try him?"

"Choppers, huh. Good idea."

No one answered the listing under Dr. Lopez's office number and his residence wasn't listed. Myers started a list of possibilities, the dentist included. There were four hospitals and 12 medical clinics in the phone book. They had visited *Centro Medico Moctezuma* last night to get Myers' treated and he had asked, but no luck. He wrote down names of the other clinics, then he began the tedious work of phoning them. He did it himself since Maggie's Spanish wasn't up to it. They all wanted to help, but none of the places could confirm admitting an Asian baby with an eye infection or fever in the past twenty-four hours.

Maggie's anxiety level seemed to grow each time Myers cradled the phone shaking his head. She worried the baby might have died and Guerrero dumped it.

"Let's try the local paper," he said after the fifth call. "Hit some of the clinics in person."

"Sounds good."

El Mundo Hoy wasn't far from the hotel. Myers stepped into the newsroom and stepped into the past, drifting in time to the small weekly in southeast Georgia where he got his start in the writing end of the newspaper business under the tutelage of a wise old editor named Dick Moore. Tricky Dick Nixon was in the white house back then. *El Mundo Hoy* took up more space, but he heard the click-clack and dings of early century Underwoods. The paper went to bed on a hot press in back of the office, just like that little weekly of Myers' past. Smelling of paper and lead, men with ink-soaked, calloused hands performed the tedious and delicate work of inserting each six-inch lead feeder for each letter of each word of each paragraph for each story into column racks. Everything that picked up ink was upside down and backwards. Took half a day for half a dozen people to set type for a 12-page paper. *El Mundo Hoy* was much larger than that.

Myers noticed a nameplate on a desk in the rear that read, "Wilford Reynolds/*San Diego Journal*."

"That's the stringer who wrote the article AP picked up on your car accident," Myers explained to Maggie, who didn't seem to get the stringer part.

"The guy's supposed to be long retired and sipping margaritas on the *bahia de todos santos*. But here he is still hacking out articles. Gets in your blood."

It was their bad luck Reynolds wasn't here. He might have been able to help them. He could have at least been trusted not to turn a comrade in to the local police.

A man who had the editor-in-chief look danced out of an office that identified him as such. The man was short and pudgy, had sixty-plus years on him, a smoking cigar in the side of his mouth. He had no hair on top of his shiny head. The paunch, the slouchy attire and worn wingtips, the intelligent if not cynical eyes probing—there was no mistaking him as the M.E.

Myers said in English, "We have a medical emergency and need your help. A policeman by the name of Guerrero shot and killed a man yesterday at *Rancho Coyote*—it may be called *Catarina*—a village in the mountains east of here, Pai Indian reservation. An Indian took buckshot in the back. The policeman kidnapped five babies. One of them is very sick. The people were bringing it into town at the time for emergency care. Can you help?"

The editor went through a couple of facial changes as he listened, as though he might have picked up some of it, but played the typical skeptic. He said nothing to Myers. He glanced several times at Maggie.

Then he said, "Who are you?" in English.

"We are adopting one of the babies. We're very concerned."

"The woman?" the editor said.

"My wife, of course," he said quickly. "We're here to find out what happened to our baby. There are others worried sick over the other four. You understand? Murder and kidnapping are serious crimes."

"Why didn't you go to the police?"

Myers dropped his shoulders. He ground his words so that they crawled out. "Look, we could not very well go to the police, a couple of gringos, and accuse one of their own of murder, see?"

The eagle-eyed editor did what any self-respecting, cynical newspaperman would do in that situation. He called the police. He used a phone on the desk closest to him. Myers put his hand on Maggie's elbow. The editor turned his back and muffled his voice so Myers wouldn't hear, but Myers heard him say, *"Por favor, puedo hablar a Inspector Guerrero, eh?"* He drummed his fingers and turned and stared at Maggie as though trying to place her but seemed to have no luck doing it.

Myers said, "Let's get out of here."

They heard in their wake the editor shouting, "Hey, stop."

Myers couldn't run too fast but he hobbled behind Maggie across the street to the car. Maggie drove fast.

Maggie said, "Are they all crooked down here?"

"Tight's more like it, particularly when it comes to gringos throwing around such accusation. Wasn't too bright me taking you there."

"You think it's any use, Ray?" Maggie seemed despondent—except when she stepped on the gas.

Myers nodded encouragingly. "I never really thanked you for your help yesterday," he said. "Thanks."

CHAPTER FIFTY-THREE

Swabb survived the night only by averting panic when it surged. It surged a lot—every time he tried to breathe, the way he'd been crammed fetus-like in that dark tomb of his own car trunk. The duct tape over his mouth felt like a living thing, a pulsating hand tightening against his face in an ever-constricting grip. He'd made it through the long night only by thinking of the women he had nailed, in his suave apartment of course, pretending his face was buried in the bosom of first Jan Obermeyer and taking it from there to bury himself in other warm places. It had worked. He may even have slept a little. He was still breathing when the trunk lid flew open and the pupils of his eyes disappeared in the blistering, wonderful sunlight. He thought for sure he now knew better what women wanted.

After a long rough ride south, he found himself in a dismal hotel room where his abductor had re-tied him to a high back chair. He didn't know what was going to happen. He didn't know what the hell to expect.

His distinguished Nixonesque nose had lost what little arch it had. Its swollen bridge was now thick and purple. His eyes were swollen but no longer closed shut. The rest of his face was puffy from duct tape and from bawling. His lower lip quivered at will. He couldn't make it stop. At least the tape was off.

He felt suddenly nauseated and began to rock the chair in the direction of the bathroom. One of the legs collapsed under him and tossed him forward, smacking his cheek on a filthy carpet. He was close to swooning.

Standing in the French doorway, Bubba saw him flip over. He sighed and grabbed hold of Swabb's miniature ponytail and lifted his head off the floor. "You okay, Counselor? ... Need to potty?" He untied him from the broken chair and let him go unaided into the windowless bathroom.

Bubba tried Guerrero's mobile number again. Still no answer. He called the city's main station house and was promptly put on hold.

In a moment Guerrero answered and Bubba told him to call back using his cell, which the Mexican did without question.

The room phone rang right away, a loud, bona fide ding-a-ling, a ring of antiquity. Bubba let it go through a third ring just to hear its shrill clarity then picked up, said, "First thing. Are the babies okay?"

Bubba took it for granted the cop had lied in their last phone conversation, when the Mexican said he had the babies. Now, he wanted clarity.

"Don't worry," Guerrero replied. "They are in reliable hands."

"Cause they fucking better be … What about my woman Maggie? Where is she?"

"I do nothing to her or the other gringo—"

"What other gringo?"

"The one with her."

He didn't know who that would be, but it didn't sound like anything made up. "Never mind about that. Is she at the Indian camp?"

"I am your little soldier? … You don't care she have another boyfriend?"

Bubba took a breath, telling himself the sorryass Mexican just wanted to harass him. "I know you have your instructions, but you are not going to get paid anything because the man you take your orders from, *Señor* Mendez, will be dead before you see a dime from him. But deal with me and I'll see that you get real money and lots of it. I am prepared to buy the babies from you for five thousand dollars each—in greenback. I have the cash with me. How about it, pardoner? Show me the babies, I'll show you the money."

Guerrero didn't answer. He was thinking it over, a good sign, Bubba thought.

"Why you say *Señor* Mendez dead?"

"I didn't say he was fucking dead, I said he will be dead … Where do you want to meet?"

Guerrero didn't hesitate. "The place for the last job. It is quiet there."

Bubba supposed he meant the paupers' morgue, making another pathetic joke. "Not there," he said firmly, figuring it for a sure setup. "Hussong's. I'll meet you there at nine o'clock tonight."

A brief hesitation, then Guerrero said, *"Sí. No problemo,* Okay."

"Have all the babies nearby. I will give you the money, all of it, then and there. Think about it. Twenty-five thousand greenback dollars. That's a lot of money for a police inspector. Eh?"

Bubba slapped Swabb on the shoulder as the lawyer stepped out of the bathroom. "We got him," he said. Fire burned in his eyes.

He made another call, dialing "0."

"*Hola, amigo ...*" He moved outside the French-doors so Swabb would not hear the conversation. Whispering into the phone, he said he wanted a sack of smoking weed. Yes, he had bought it many times in the past, didn't the hop remember? Yeah, numskull, two ounces, a full bag. Of course he knew it was hard to come by, that it would be expensive—so charge the going price plus twenty percent if it could be done quickly, and tack on ten percent more for yourself. Just deliver.

Bubba never smoked the shit himself. It was for protection, when and if the time came.

Swabb emerged from the bathroom. Bubba grinned at him, saying, "You look thirsty," and pitched Swabb a plastic bottle of water.

The lawyer drained the bottle in one tilt.

"Okay, Earl. It's time to pay the piper. You're going to call your boss. I want you to speak clearly, with authority. Tell him you've been kid-napped and it will take fifty thousand to keep you from going to the DA. The press too. Say you're going to spill the beans on the smuggling ring. You'll swear on the grave of the great Chief Justice that he is the ring-leader, and that he ordered people murdered—men, women and babies alike."

"Whoa, wait—"

"Yeah, I know. You're thinking there's no way in hell he's going to pay, that he'll go along with whatever you say, and then lay a trap to si-lence you ... So, you're going to have to convince him you mean busi-ness. If you don't convince him, then *I* will kill you. That's what I do."

Swabb had looked a little better when he left the bathroom, but a sickly pall now snatched away that burst of rose color on his cheeks.

"But—but, I don't think—think I—"

"Don't get your bowels in an uproar, Counselor. Don't think, just get it done. Here."

He gave Swabb a piece of Juicy Fruit gum, noticing his lips were sticking to his teeth and causing a disgusting smacking noise, like some method actor. Bubba encouraged him further. "Look, you've got the goodies on him, right? Last night he sent Fitzsimmon to take you out. That should motivate you right there; frankly, it ought to really piss you off. He even ordered you to murder innocent babies. Good God, man, doesn't that do something to your gut? And you know he ordered me to kill Maggie and that murdering *coyote* that murdered those immigrants. He's got to figure she's still alive since he ain't seen any of the money she siphoned off, right? So tell him you've talked to her and she's agreed to point the finger, too. Tell him to bring the money to Hussong's tonight at ten o'clock. Make sure you tell him ten ... He'll come through if he wants to save his ass."

Swabb listened attentively, nodding like a bobble head. He said, "Yes, that sounds good, smart ... But, ah, one question. Why don't you talk to him? I mean—"

"Fair question," Bubba said. "*You* are the lawyer, the mouth of drama and sincerity, so to speak. A plea bargainer, right? ... I'm liable to get mad and lose sight of what's at stake, and that wouldn't be good for you."

He extended the corded phone.

Swabb took it and dialed. He got through to Mendez' mobile.

Bubba listened approvingly as Swabb put his professional experience to work: "Ricky? It's Earl—surprise! I'm still alive! ... No, *you* listen, Ricky. Mr. Cousins has kidnapped me and is requesting you bring him fifty thousand dollars—don't tell me you don't have it ... Yes, *requesting*. But that's just polite talk. He means it."

Swabb's voice was all nasal with his swollen nose, and his lips were sticking together and smacking again but he sounded true. Bubba watched him with arms crossed, chin up. He moved nearer Swabb. Maybe he could hear something, get a read on the man's attitude.

"Ricky, Mr. Cousins is going to take a deposition in front of a witness that will state my knowledge and participation in the smuggling ring that you run. You'll sink on that alone. But I'm also going to say that I can prove you commissioned the assassinations of both Sylvia and me as well as Agent Cousins himself. You made your mistake when you sent Mr. Fitzsimmon to my house, Ricky. You will find him tied up in my apartment, still alive … You should *never* have tried to have me murdered! Bring the money to Hussong's Cantina tonight at ten o'clock sharp. If you don't come through, you are going to burn—you know, by lethal injection? They're working on getting the appeals process shortened in California. I'm fucking serious, Ricky. *He's* serious …"

Bubba beamed as Swabb assured Mendez that Sylvia had not been killed, that she was mad as hell and would also swear, in a notarized recorded complaint, that Mendez tried to have Mr. Cousins drug her and make her murder look like she got burned up in a car crash. Swabb said that unless he pays, Mr. Cousins would plea-bargain and testify that Mendez paid him cash and a promise of cash to kill a Mexican citizen named Miguel Sanchez as well. Did he want to save his ass or not? Tonight. Hussong's. Fifty thousand dollars.

After he hung up, Bubba said, "Counselor, you can represent me any day of the week … What was your read?"

"Locked it," Swabb said. It was as succinct a comment as the lawyer had ever made, in court or out.

There was a soft knock on the door, like the flap of moth wings. Bubba slipped a hand under his jacket and onto the handle of the serrated hunting knife he'd won off the drunk Mexican kid at pool. He flung open the door, irritated by the boneless knocking, and stepped quickly into the hallway.

"Let's see it," he snapped. "How much?"

The hop looked boneless all over. He stuck an appendage out, presumably for the money, and said, "Four hundred. *Dólares*."

Bubba saw the paltry contents in the baggie, amounting to less than one ounce, he guessed. "For this much you get three hundred, and that's counting the fucking tip."

He grabbed the pleated sandwich bag of seed-heavy marijuana and stuffed it into the front pocket of his pants, shut the door on the guy counting his money.

Swabb asked, "Who was it?"

"That? Just the bellhop, thought we might want some pussy. I told him no, we're sweet on each other."

"But, didn't you just a while ago call him?"

Bubba shook his head in amazement. "Earl, I swear. Sometimes you don't know when to keep your mouth shut."

CHAPTER FIFTY-FOUR

The sun danced across the blue bay without a care. Gulls dangled from invisible strings above the sterns of arriving fishing boats. The marketplace air was redolent with fresh catches. The smell carried into the parking lot where Myers and Maggie sat inside the Land Cruiser having bonito ceviche in plastic cups and sweet lemonade from paper cups. They watched the boats lurch into slips without banging the floating docks.

Until recently Ensenada was but a quaint fishing village, sportfishing the big draw. Now the city was a major Pacific Rim player, a key cargo port on the west coast and a senior partner in the global marine economy, producing high yields of yellowtail and albacore, spiny lobster, yahoo and bonito. Ensenada tuna was king.

Maggie drove them back into the city and to the dental office of Dr. Julio Lopez. She parked in the alley where Bubba had earlier parked, then directed Myers around the corner to the door under the big-tooth shingle. The door was locked, a sign pronouncing the office presently closed. The blinds had been drawn tight.

"Isn't this Tuesday, a normal workday?" Myers said.

"Is it a holiday?" asked Maggie.

"Siesta time?"

"You kidding?"

The street was busy with cars parked at expired meters, *"Abierto"* signs stood in doorways up and down the sidewalk, people striding in and out of those shops. A bustling metropolis, busy at mid-afternoon.

Maggie stood back from the storefront and looked at a row of windows on the second story. "Listen. You hear that, Ray?"

Myers shook his head. His enthusiasm didn't overwhelm her.

She said it again, a little more resolute. "There's babies up there, let's get them."

Myers frowned and pointed out a big, flourishing sign next door, not five feet to the right of them. The sign read, *"Manuela's Niños Del Cuidado*

Del Dia." The day nursery's window was painted in candy cane letters in broad-stroke pastels.

"Babies are here, not in the dentist's office."

Maggie grinned sheepishly.

"We'll find them," Myers said.

"Yeah. Okay, let's blow."

It was mid-afternoon when they arrived back at the Hotel Mexico, out of ideas, needing to regroup.

Myers reached under the seat and brought out the snub-nosed revolver that Castro had given him. Maggie curled a corner of her lip but she said nothing. Stepping out of the car, he slipped the gun into the waistband of his pants. He tried to keep his wounded side from knowing it was hurt but that failed on a flash of pain.

Maggie followed Myers up the hotel stairway, holding his arm. He felt her grip tighten as they ascended the dark stairs, then loosen when they reached the landing.

The skinny clerk snoozed behind the desk, his head thrown back so far his Adam's apple poked out like the toe of a four iron.

Maggie stopped at Room 203. She put her ear against the door, then waved her hand to silence Myers, who was opening the door next to it. She caught up and followed him inside the room.

"He's in there," she murmured, "Bubba. Someone's with him."

She shoved her ear against the wall and listened.

Myers laid the gun on the bedside table and stepped on to the balcony. Room 203's French doors stood open and Myers could hear talking despite the street noise. He determined the voice was a man's, if somewhat nasal and high-pitched, trying to weasel his way out of a jam. "I—I can't tell you *what* he'll do." Sounding just like Peter Lorre, same liquid singsong. Miffed, as well.

"It's Mr. Swabb," Maggie whispered behind him. "What're they talking about?"

Myers shook his head. "Listen."

They heard Bubba's Texas-twang, "You can bet someone's coming with him," and then Swabb, again sniveling, "Oh, God, he's bringing *that* bastard. Why didn't you disable him when you had the chance?" and

Bubba mumbling, then finally saying, "He'll eat it soon as I see those little babies."

Shuffling, some indistinguishable sounds, then quiet. Then Bubba's voice again mentioning Hussong's Cantina, then saying, finally, "You can do it, Counselor, I know you can. C'mon now, look sharp."

Myers moved back inside the room, Maggie right with him. He said, "They're taking off. Sounds like they know where to find our bad guys, or our babies."

Maggie said in a rush, "Or both. He mentioned Hussong's. They're probably meeting whoever it is there. Let's go."

"Does Cousins—Bubba—have a car?"

"I didn't see it on the street. It would be an old jalopy, supposed to be red but it's mostly rust."

"I'll go—it's better just one person follow. I'll call soon as I know something. Hang by the phone" He didn't know how she would react if he had to square off with Bubba Cousins. And if Cousins were to see her, it might get in the way of finding the babies.

"But you might need help—your side." Maggie sighed and nodded. "I guess you're right."

He entered the hotel's phone number into his cellular, reading the number off the rules-and-regulations notice on the backside of the room door. The notice had been inked in over the typewritten notice. His mobile service didn't cover frontier Mexico but having the number on hand would save time on another phone.

"Stay put, I'll call this room when I know something. If anything goes wrong, Maggie, find your way back to the village. Do you have money?"

"Some, enough," Maggie said with a straight face. "Ray, don't let anything go wrong, please."

Myers glanced at her, his eyes briskly taking her in. He wanted to pull her close. The yearning startled him.

He shut the door behind him.

~

Maggie dashed onto the balcony in time to get her first glimpse of the man who had ordered her killed, Mr. Swabb. Was that *pajamas* her boss wore? The sight might have been amusing at another time. The two men were crossing the street just below her. Like little boys, both men duti-fully looked before stepping into the street, Bubba with his arm around the smaller man's shoulder, being the good Boy Scout. Swabb didn't seem such a big shot lawyer now. He looked frail, pitiful. But that was the man who wanted her dead. Her jaw clamped hard.

Bubba swaggered, a man in full command, she noticed. He still had a bedroom effect on her. But she saw him not like that now. She was look-ing upon her would-be executioner, someone who had killed for money, a crooked cop. A married man playing around. The titillation of the wild carousel ride had slowed. She was getting a truer fix on things.

The muscular gun wavered in her hand. It was crazy; she had shot a gun only once in her life, blasting a can in some airy Minnesota woods, a long-barreled gun that bruised her shoulder and deafened one ear.

She thought about shooting Swabb. She wanted nothing more than to put a bullet into him. She played it out in her mind as if she were a char-acter in a script requiring her to shoot—hold the gun in both hands, ex-tended, lean forward so your forearms are supported on the ledge to steady the hands. Aim carefully, until you're sure. With the short muzzle you could easily miss the target from sixty feet, so aim for the torso, not the head. Don't breathe, don't panic, squeeze the trigger gently. If she hit him and killed him, what then? Since she was officially dead anyway, she saw no reason she couldn't get away with it. Simply walk away.

Myers appeared under her, crossing the street a short stroll behind the two men. It stilled her. His presence dampened the flame for blood. She lowered the gun, put the script in an easy-to-reach quarter of her mind, a place to pull out at will.

Tears gathered and clouded her eyes.

CHAPTER FIFTY-FIVE

Mendez sat behind his office desk. He was on the phone with his secretary who sat just on the other side of a thin wall. In his free hand the metallic Chinese balls clinked. He worked them hard, as if their kinetics could produce a solution to his problems.

" … Tell her I can't make the dinner, she'll have to go it alone. They've called me to Washington … that I'm terribly sorry, can't be helped."

"It's the budget thing, isn't it, sir?" said Freida. "They're cutting jobs. *I'm* getting cut, aren't I?"

"You know better than to ask, Freida. Tell her I'll be home tomorrow."

"Yes, sir."

"Better make the call now. I'm on my way to the airport."

"Aren't I supposed to make your reservations?"

"Saved you the trouble. But you're a sweetheart, Freida. What would I do without you."

"I knew it!" she exclaimed.

He packed a change of clothes from the closet—brown field attire of the Border Patrol grunt—into a small suitcase along with a pair of high-laced boots and a dark brown cloth jacket on his arm, the same jacket he wore to steal across Sidney Rhoades' unlit lawn.

He put the Chinese balls into a case and into his suit coat pocket and left the office, granting Freida a quick nod. She looked at him pleadingly. He took the janitorial elevator to the underground parking lot.

An anxious and angry attitude shadowed Mendez, carrying with it the kind of impatience that invariably affected him under real pressure. He reminded himself to stay focused. He could get through this, he told himself, if only he thought out his moves and kept a step ahead of his adversaries, that weasel Swabb, the traitor Cousins. That woman and that goddamn rat reporter.

Hopefully, things wouldn't be as difficult with Fitzsimmon along. Fitz was smart for a tough guy, and well disciplined from years as a cool-minded dispatcher and martial arts practitioner—although the incident at Swabb's condo when Cousins put Fitzsimmon on the mat, that troubled Mendez to no small degree. Apparently Cousins had done it quite easily. It just made him more wary of Cousins—the way he would be wary of any man who would return with his victim's ear as evidence of his kill. The same man who then double-crossed you by faking his next assignment and lied about it to keep the eighty thousand for himself. That man was slicker than Mendez had thought.

But Guerrero could be useful dealing with Cousins. There were some things he had to work out, and quickly.

Once off the elevator Mendez tried phoning the Mexican cop. If he could still trust Guerrero, and there was no reason to think otherwise, then he'd have Guerrero locate Cousins, see that he kept him and Swabb under surveillance until he arrived, which would be well before their 10 o'clock meeting.

Guerrero wasn't answering his phone.

He called Fitzsimmon to let him know he was on the way. Fitzsimmon was at home on a bogus sick leave excuse that the palomino spooked and bucked him. The "accidental fall" had left him with a swollen, bruised face and a prescription for bed rest. Mendez had to be careful when the play came that Fitz not lose that disciplined detachment with Agent Travis Cousins, the man who caused his "accidental fall."

"Hullo?" Fitzsimmon said in his normal voice.

"On my way."

"All right."

"We'll want to get out some munitions."

"All right. I'll clear the horses from the stable."

As he talked, Mendez threw the suitcase into his car trunk. He tried Guerrero again without reaching him. Then he drove his big vehicle out into the sunlight and headed south on the 5.

CHAPTER FIFTY-SIX

At 5:32 on this November afternoon a sudden burst of light exploded along Ensenada's streets reminiscent of the festival fireworks you'd see on the Day of the Dead. Bubba and Swabb both looked heavenward, as if some miracle was taking place up there. At first bewildered, they glanced blankly at each other, then realized that, Oh, it had only been the streetlights turning on. Both men shrugged with slight embarrassment and continued on their way. Bubba didn't think he would ever get used to the fluorescence they used to light everything with down here.

He steered the lawyer into a department store that displayed window mannequins outfitted in the latest mainland Mexican fashions, both sexes. Dorian's didn't rank up there with Neiman Marcus, but it was one of the classier emporiums in Ensenada, comparable to Macy's. They stepped through the automatic doors and a hundred thousand watts of cold fluorescent light hit Bubba like ice water. The light struck Swabb as sunlight strikes a vampire. He dipped his head and covered his damaged face with his arm in a single move. Shoppers nonetheless glared at the man in his bloody pajamas and kept their distance, moving out of the way as the two passed by.

Fluorescence was omnipresent in Baja, in restaurants, hotel rooms, sport booking arenas, cathedrals, upscale bars and jails. Everywhere but in the confessional where there was no light at all. Bubba had determined some time ago that Mexico's craze for fluorescence had only one purpose—to prevent teenagers from falling in love by exposing every pimple, blemish, nick, bruise and psoriatic peel known to the human skin. It baffled him why merchants would purposely want to expose their older, already hitched patrons in the worse light, parade their sagging skin, their fat shadows.

Bubba hadn't really wanted to drag Swabb into this but neither could he leave him in bloody pajamas or unattended while Bubba shopped for him. He hustled Swabb down aisles and between counters to the men's section and shoved him into a changing room, hoping no one had called security. He hurriedly grabbed clothes off the sales racks.

"What's *that?*" Swabb said distastefully of the red-and-yellow polyester plaid pants Bubba handed him.

"Said you played golf, didn't you? It's Rodney Dangerfield's label. Here, this shirt ought to go okay with the pants."

Bubba handed him a ruffled pink guayabera long-sleeve, the kind Mexican waiters and casino card dealers wore, sometimes with black bolo ties.

"Mush, mush, Earl."

Swabb stood in the bright dressing room, naked but for his BVD's, the fluorescence turning his skin blue in the mirror and his bruised face black.

"Put this jacket on when you're done. You're freezing, man," Bubba said. "You got chill bumps all over."

He held out a shiny crocodile-green vinyl jacket for Swabb to slip on. It was the jacket of a '70s Bronx pimp.

Once dressed and out of the booth, Swabb appeared more presentable. "The new Earl Swabb," Bubba said approvingly, "guy'll paint your car for—what is it now, 99.99?"

Bubba handed the pleasant and nicely dressed woman at checkout two one-hundred dollar bills from his own stash and was returned twenty-seven dollars in change.

The new clothes perked Bubba up more than Swabb. Swabb still wore a look of doom. He seemed to float rather than walk, moving only because Bubba was guiding him along. "Wh-Where are we going? Where are you taking me? It's not time to meet him yet."

"You really need to learn how to relax, man." Bubba eyed him. Just last night, he had wanted to bash the man's head in, and he almost did, but Bubba had gotten over that initial fury. He only felt disgust now, maybe a pinch of pity for the poor scoundrel. He tugged on Swabb's arm then gave him a little goose to keep him moving.

"But—but, I mean, where're we going *now?*"

Bubba grinned. "Dude, we gotta eat."

They were a block from the Hacienda Hotel, where a message from Mendez might be awaiting Bubba under another name. Didn't the man say something about five grand waiting for him? He considered: Would he only be playing into a trap if he went after it? But what did he have to lose?

"We're gonna make a quick stop first," Bubba said.

A moment later he opened one of the hotel's two front doors, towing the burdensome lawyer. Bubba sat him in an easy chair in the small lobby with a big staircase. The deskman wore the same color guayabera as Swabb.

Bubba was friendly. "Don't tell me. You're Jorge, right?"

Jorge twitched a corner of his mouth for a nod, then grew alert when Bubba asked if there'd been a message for Gus Morgan, a package maybe. He stood up tall behind the check-in counter.

"*Sí señor*. A man he call for you. Maybe twenty minutes. He say for you—"

"Shh, keep it down," Bubba interrupted him, nodding toward his companion slouched as if passed out drunk, the one dressed like Rodney Dangerfield in punk. "What did the man say?"

Jorge furrowed his brow, as if a little confused. He was pudgy and had a chubby face with a thick mustache that reminded Bubba uncomfortably of the two-timer Guerrero.

Jorge rubbed the mustache and now leaned closer to Bubba. "He say plenty money for you to help him. He say he need you to take a *Señor* Slob fishing. He say you know what he mean."

"He say when he would be here?" Bubba asked.

"He say you call him after you fish. Tonight."

"Okay. *Gracias*, Jorge."

Mendez *was* playing the angles.

"He say you pay me," Jorge added with a forced grin.

"He say how much," Bubba said sarcastically, grudgingly slipping him a twenty.

CHAPTER FIFTY-SEVEN

Mendez gassed up the Lincoln at the ARCO on Bonita Road, the last gas station when taking Otay Lakes Road out to horse country in Bonita where Fitzsimmon's ranch was nestled in the valley. He placed a long-distance call to the Hacienda Hotel in Ensenada in Baja Norte and gave the evening clerk a message. Who knows, he thought, maybe Cousins would take the bait and get rid of Swabb for him. One less problem for him to clean up.

He first filled a five-gallon container from the trunk, then fixed the gas pump handle into the car's tank and let nineteen more gallons of high octane flow in.

Mendez walked halfway around his car, admiring its enormity and shine, the old Continental's exquisite lines. It was black—black on an automobile announced wealth, power. He noticed that the left front tire appeared low but then the gas handle snapped off and he moved back along the side of the car, removed the handle from the tank's throat and hung it up. Disgusted at the dollar amount charged to his American Express card, he forgot about the low tire.

He estimated a time table for the evening: counting the gas stop, give thirty minutes out to Fitzsimmon's, half an hour there loading up, quick half hour to the border, count on no delay crossing, at tops an hour and a half down to Ensenada via the free road—Mendez preferred the more challenging but slower old road and always took it when there was a choice. Arrive at the docks roughly at seven-thirty. Plenty of time left to set things up. Time to kill.

He hadn't brought cash money for either the ransom or the job on Swabb. He never considered it. He carried only incidental cash, about three hundred dollars. No one was fooling anybody. Cousins knew he wasn't going to pay out any ransom for the lawyer, particularly not if he got curious and went to the Hacienda Hotel. Cousins was in so much hurt already that he was in no position to "request" anything. He did have brass, though. Mendez gave him that. Those days in Sasabe with Agent Cousins, starting up his fledgling smuggling operation—only pot then—showed Mendez that Cousins was not the country bumpkin he seemed to be. Rather he was sharp and cunning and mean. Those were the reasons he too had to perish.

Before Mendez made his turnoff, his cell phone played a dreamy rendition of "Daddy's Here," the Brahms' lullaby signifying an unknown caller.

"Mendez," he said.

"Eh, *Señor* Mendez, it is I, Javier Maria."

"Hello, Inspector. Been trying to get hold of you."

"I have news."

"I'm all ears."

"Eh? … A certain bird, he tell me where some *bambinos* are. *¿Sabe?*"

"I'm still listening."

"I cut the long story and tell you I have five *bebes*, take them from the farmer Herlinda. *¿Usted comprendes?*"

"Like you say, that's good news. I've been looking for that particular merchandise."

"Is not all, *senor*. The dirty *migra*, he want to pay me for them. He say he give me thirty-five thousand in U.S. money. I meet him tonight. But I think maybe I call you, see how much *you* give for these *bebes* now. Eh?"

Mendez thought, *The man is chum.*

"I'm certainly glad you did, Inspector. I'm sure we can work out a better deal. I'll be there later tonight. Where are you keeping this merchandise?"

He heard a chuckle over his phone. He wasn't getting an answer.

"Eh, one thing more, *Señor* Mendez, sir. *La migra*, he say you are a man who is dead. If this is so, how then can you give me the money?"

Mendez had his steel balls out in a flash. "Nonsense. Don't you know when you are being duped? … Don't be the fool. And don't forget who keeps your wife in gambling expenses, Inspector."

It was all he could do to keep his voice even. He added, "The other thing you can do for me? Agent Cousins will be with another man. His name is Earl Swabb. Arrest both men and call me when you have them secured. It's worth another ten thousand. Both men. Do you understand?"

"Sí, this will be easy. But the *bebes* go where the money is, *señor*."

"Don't worry, I will be there. Rest assured I'll be alive. Call me when both men are in your custody. We'll set up the meeting."

"*Bueno.*"

Mendez drove the asphalt strip working the Chinese balls. His thought had shifted now to the merchandise. If he did not get rid of it all, in time there would come the repercussions. Not the lost shipment before this one, those were "legally" adopted into the country. But these, no. It would do no good to simply place them in homes outside the country. It would be years before one or more of them applied for U.S. citizenship, and when they did their papers would reveal their illegality. The unsolved disappearance of Swabb, whose name would be on those records, could be linked to him. He knew how immigration worked. He had to act.

He winced and his hand flew open, the silver orbs falling at his heels on to the floorboard. A bruise formed in the palm of his hand from gripping the balls too tightly.

Must collect myself, he thought pulling into Fitz's property.

Fitzsimmon and his wife operated a pinery at the convergence of Bonita Road and Otay Mesa Road. The acre patch of evergreen seedlings took up part of the pasture in front of their ranch. Christmas trees were ready to harvest but Fitz said his wife, Gabby, who actually took care of the grove, would not open for self-cutting until the traditional Christmas shopping season began after Thanksgiving. Mendez noticed they hadn't put out the signs and colored lights yet. The business made no money but Gabby loved her "little forest," so she had kept the cyclical business going.

The ranch house sat further back, bordered by a row of eucalyptus on one side and a venerable oak grove on the other. Mendez pulled onto the gravel-and-dirt driveway past the tree farm and turned off his headlights as he pulled toward the stables. He spotted Fitzsimmon heading back to the house from the horse corral. Fitzsimmon was dressed in camouflage. He honked and Fitz turned to meet him.

Noticing the Explorer parked by the house, Mendez said, "Gabby's here, I see. Bernie, too?"

"Cooking dinner, I guess. Told her we'll be bird shooting, gone couple nights."

Gabby was a nosey one and Mendez had concocted his reason for driving to the stables instead of the house. He wanted to hide a gift for the couple's young daughter, Bernadette—"Bernie." The gift was a horse bridle for her filly. He knew her birthday was coming up in December.

Mendez backed the car up to the stable's wide doors. He heard a horse whinny nearby and the flutter of sparrows settling for the night on the overhead power line running through the airy oaks. He quickly changed into his browns behind the car, threw his suit clothes in the back seat, laced up the boots.

There was evidence of the eleven-year-old all around, the tire swing, a motorized miniature pink Jeep, the bright-colored playhouse, a Schwinn bike on its side. Where was she? He wanted to see her, but secretly, without her seeing him. Secretly spying on them made for future fantasies. He'd gotten his first touch helping her climb on to a Shetland when she was nine, and as often after that as he could. She liked his hands on her, tickling, caressing. She even wanted it, he'd made himself believe. In his perverted sense of things, she hadn't been just another skinny tomboy girl, but rather a prick-teasing pubescent yearning for something she didn't yet understand. He had seen other girls like that.

The stables smelled of stirred-up hay and Mendez tried to keep from sneezing but couldn't.

"Here we go," Fitzsimmon said, raising a door in the floor concealed under loose hay. It was inside the palomino's stall.

The hidden chamber apparently had been the creation of the previous property owner, a Mexican with dual citizenship affiliated with the Arellano Félix drug cartel. A BP Special Agents squad in connection with an elite Tijuana police unit caught the bastard in a sting and the property was seized and put up for auction after he had been sent to federal prison for 40 years. Having an inside line on these events, Fitzsimmon took out a home equity line of credit against his Chula Vista home and won the bid on the estate. The weapons pit was an unexpected bonus, and it remained a secret to all but the two men now standing over it and the Mexican dope smuggler in federal lockup, who would not live long if he talked.

Fitzsimmon let the door drop back, creating a small dust storm in the stall and a staccato sneezing fit from Mendez.

"Sorry about that … Here we are."

Mendez got on his knees over the open dugout and surveyed the small, potent arsenal the Arellano guy had amassed. The stockpile included handguns, Kalashnikov assault rifles, loaded banana clips, dynamite in cases, plastic explosives. Mendez figured that one or more of the four Kalashnikovs had been used in any number of unsolved gangland killings in Tijuana.

"I'll pick us out some playthings." He grinned as if he'd made a funny. He stepped onto a stationary ladder inside the dugout and disappeared into the earth.

He handed items to Fitzsimmon in twos—Kalashnikovs with clips inserted, .45 automatics with boxes of ammo, a wooden box holding a dozen sticks of dynamite, timers, detonators. Fitzsimmon stuffed the material into a duffel bag, all but the handguns.

Just before Mendez shut the Lincoln's trunk, Gabby Fitzsimmon, silent as the moon, appeared behind them.

"You boys want some dinner before you go out huntin' your birds?"

Mendez was disappointed it wasn't the eleven-year-old.

CHAPTER FIFTY-EIGHT

Myers wasn't thrilled watching his two charges go into a department store. Agent Cousins of the U.S. Border Patrol was wanted in connection with two murders, but did that keep him from traipsing into the town's busiest-looking store with a guy in bloody Liberace pajamas? Myers asked himself that and shook his head in amazement, though it was reasonable that the little guy had to get out of those clothes. Myers stepped inside, into a blast of fluorescence.

He found them in the men's clothing area, of course. He watched Cousins pay and the two scramble for the doors like Laurel and Hardy escaping from another perpetrated disaster. Myers was amused, then curious, then confused why Swabb would dress himself as if he were on Saturday morning TV.

A few blocks later, outside the Hacienda Hotel, he tried to make out the conversation between the desk clerk and Cousins but couldn't. He did catch Cousins slipping cash to the desk clerk.

Myers crossed the street before the two men left the hotel, turning his back as they exited. He tailed at a safe distance. They entered a restaurant on the same block as the Hacienda and a maitre d' greeted them. Myers shifted his weight three times to try and ease his troubling wounded side. He watched through the painted glass window. He gave them time to be seated then he stepped back to the hotel and spoke to the pudgy clerk.

"You know that guy just gave you money?" he said, using a cop's don't-fucking-lie-to-me tone.

The man wasn't intimidated. He snickered.

"Who are you, sir?" he asked in good English.

"He's wanted for double murders in San Diego. You know that and you took money from him. That makes you an accessory. Accessory means hard time, amigo … Tell me what you talked about and I'll forget I saw it and leave you alone."

Myers put his weight on one hand, leaning in on the man. The clerk gave, backed off.

"I don't know this, *señor*. Is true?" he yelped, his English not so good anymore.

"You lie. I think I will take you in. One last chance—now *talk*!" Myers raised his voice so only he would hear.

"Sí, *señor*. He supposed to go fishing with *Señor* Slob. Is all I know, sir."

"How do you know he is supposed to go fishing? And who is this person you call Slob?"

A film of sweat made the clerk's face as shiny as the counter reflecting his image. "A man call, he tell me."

"Who's this Slob guy?"

Myers wasn't too slow; he only had to say Slob twice before figuring out he meant Swabb. "Okay, my friend, tell me the man's name who called with this information and you are home free."

"I do not know, *señor*. He is gringo. He say he call *desde* San Diego."

"What's your name?"

"Jorge Campo Ramirez, sir. I do not lie."

The man probably earned no salary to speak of from his clerking job, mostly what he scrounged from tips and bribes. He probably had a family to feed and clothe and shelter. He probably made confession every other week.

Myers patted the man's shoulder and nodded, then slipped him a twenty and a ten.

"Okay, Jorge. *Gracias*."

Swabb did not appear to have an appetite. Myers saw him drink water in dainty sips, like a refined Peter Lorre drinking English tea. Cousins, on the other hand, put it away, going at his carne asada and *papas* and washing them down with a bottle of Dos XX. Myers did his spying from the shadows outside. Only the soft-colored neon above La Quinta Restaurante & Lounge cast light on him, and it was too dim to show much of Myers' face or his soaring anxiety to act on the fate of five missing infants—and hoping Maggie Frazier was okay by herself.

CHAPTER FIFTY-NINE

Maggie stood before the dresser mirror turning her lips dark with a shade of smear called Night Redemption. Her hand trembled applying it. Over her shoulder a reddish hue off the city ignited the edges of black sky, burning hellishly through the French doors. The night was balmy and warm-blooded and she felt it calling her, like Dracula.

She smoothed rouge into the hollow below her eyes. She paused and took a moment to imagine the desperate people who had occupied this room before her, women gazing at the same glow through these flung-open French doors. She imagined some gangster's moll making herself up before stepping outside into a hail of bullets. It was a room with a barrelful of dark stories, hard-luck people running for their lives from a world that didn't understand them and didn't care.

Not me, she thought. She had to act; she couldn't sit by any longer and do nothing. But she felt sinful making herself over for the malice that lured her out into the vibrant night.

A teary blur caused her to miss her eyelid and rake mascara instead up onto her eyebrow. She flustered. She dabbed her eyes with a fold of toilet paper, blinked several times to clear her vision, then quickly went on to finish the face.

She dressed in a sweet-girl-white Mexican blouse that fell just over the beltline of her tight rhinestone jeans. She put on heels to make herself taller than the men she knew would come on to her soon as she stepped into Hussong's Cantina. She wanted them to make a play; her power worked off the desires of men.

She screwed the lipstick shut and slipped the cylinder into her pants pocket, then strapped the fanny pack she'd bought around her waist. The .38 snub nose fit snug inside it. She slid the pouch around to her backside. Its weight tugged at the thin strap against her stomach but she'd get used to it soon enough. She then slipped on a colorful red-and-white serape that hung low in the back.

Standing tall now before the mirror, Maggie took a stance, her feet apart, planted. She showed the mirror a hard face.

"Don't beg, you sorry piece of ... " she said through contorting lips. She practiced with the gun, drawing and aiming it at an imaginary figure in front of her then returning the weapon to the rawhide fanny pack.

She practiced until she could get it out without the barrel tip snagging on the satchel's zippered corner. Confidence to pull the trigger was a different matter, but all she had to do was remind herself that he was the coward who ordered her murdered, that he cared no more about those babies than he would dolls on a store shelf, just how much he could get for them.

"Say your prayers, you are fucking dead, *Mr.* Swabb."

She meant it.

She stuffed a few twenties into her pocket along with a length of folded toilet tissue. She positioned her purse behind the mirror and knee-shoved the dresser against the wall to trap it there. She wasn't worried if she couldn't get back to the room; the bulk of the money, more than seventy thousand of it, safe in a Pai Pai bank called Margarita's Hospicio Trust. She shut the French doors, turned off the overhead fan and lights and locked the door behind her.

The desk clerk snapped to when he saw her. Lust rose in his eyes as if he was seeing a tender concubine of the Great One, all primed and ready for the taking. But she wasn't giving; she stared him down with the silent message that she was off limits, and so was her room.

On the street she breathed in the city, ready for it. She felt strong, even anxious.

She walked in the direction of Hussong's on now familiar backstreets, north on Gastelum, passing El Dorado, turning east on Ruiz. Journeying through these dark passages, provocatively dressed, only enhanced her sense of self. She now felt close to the city, as though she belonged to it. She didn't need Bubba at her side.

Across the next street was Hussong's with it's faded neon.

She held the serape together stepping between federale guards, two stone-faced gargoyles brandishing retrograded U.S. Army M-16s, their weapons at the ready. She noted their eyes feeding on her as she entered the hall.

The place was smoky and clammy and loud. A sullen Mariachi group corkscrewed around tables, swaying their bulky instruments dangerously close to the heads of patron, playing to a crowd that couldn't hear them over itself. Most of the customers were locals and most of those were the Don Juans. Maggie could easily tell the pretty boys by their embroidered, dark polyester attire and imitation crocodile boots with elevated soles. They wore shirts opened to the navel, just above big medallion belt buckles that matched the medallions hanging around their necks. Dozens of ten-gallon Stetsons bobbed around the room like thimbles on an agitated sea. Maggie thought of bantam roosters, the way they strutted.

There was no delay in her getting noticed, a drag on her cigarette, the look in her eye. She tossed her hair and struck a curvy pose, then stepped down into the din. Her audience had formed as fast as that drag on the cigarette and a way was cut for her, like waters parting. She walked the short gauntlet to the L bar expecting some groping or maybe even being tossed in the air and moved along like a rock idol. For a moment the place stood eerily quiet, even the music died, but only until she threw back the first proffered tequila shooter, followed daringly by another.

The four instruments broke into a blustery vaquero rendition of Herb Alpert horns. A sound impossible to produce on a *guitarrón*, sour notes gone unnoticed in here.

She would have seen Ray because of his height, and maybe Bubba, but not Swabb, who was about the size of most of these bantams. It was him, Swabb, she wanted and nobody else.

Maggie didn't see any other Americans.

"Another," she called.

The husky one who bought her the shooters nestled up to her and drew a trick smile out of his Stetson meant to tell her he knew exactly how to handle a woman like her. His parting lips revealed a tiny diamond in the middle of a front tooth. *Charming*, Maggie thought, and then wondered if she had said it.

When he spoke all potential evaporated, like the bitter tequila shooters she threw back.

"My beautiful lady." He had the Omar Sharif accent. "I see you once again. You have no man? It is all right because now Juan Castillo is here, eh?"

His roaming eyes were opaque. He seemed to float before her.

"*Don* Juan?" she heard herself say in a giggly voice. "Thanks for the drink, José, now beat it."

Undaunted, the Mexican moved closer as though she'd said, *Come get me.* He showed her the big Chiclets leer, eyes rendering the deepest yearning for her. He said in a devilish singsong, "You dance for me, my lady, huh? My wild American woman."

A sea of men now surrounded her. A fast and odd sensation had drifted over Maggie, like fog off water. Racking sounds from a trumpet bellowed out some melody that imbued her with musical wine. She *was*, she now thought, she was the wild American woman.

Diamond Tooth raked Corona bottles off a table with one sweep of his hand, then in dramatic fashion offered the platform to Maggie.

"Dance, Wild One! Show me how you do it—for me, my lovely. For all!"

She stepped out of her heels and out of herself. Her clouded eyes followed his lead to the tabletop and there she saw *him*, Count Dracula, extending a hand to take her.

CHAPTER SIXTY

Myers needed to rest. The pain in his side resounded like a cymbal clash every time his foot met concrete.

He watched Cousins and the lawyer leave the restaurant and saunter along one of an Ensenada's avenues popular with tourists. They browsed a leather-goods store, moved through novelty shops without touching a thing; they passed a pharmacy and a liquor store uninterested, sidling along in no particular hurry. A couple of bored tourists.

Myers thought about stepping inside the pharmacy to use his prescription for Tylenol with codeine but figured it would be his rotten luck that just then the men he'd shadowed all night would move things along. Maybe they weren't going to Hussong's. Maybe they were going to the babies instead.

He tagged along behind the two lackadaisical tourists who shortly thereafter entered the cantina. Myers sighed. He stopped and tried to gather himself.

He wasn't going to get any rest in there either. He was tired and losing steam, losing hope as well of ever finding those baby children. He thought of Maggie waiting anxiously back at the hotel. Any fool could see she was despondent and he should not have left her alone. He should not have left the gun. A gun in the hands of an emotionally mixed-up woman had a way of changing the balance of anyone's world. He thought that now, but not when it counted. She was fine, she'd said so herself— and he was supposed to be a bright boy, too.

He waited another minute then crossed the street and went inside the joint. He didn't find what he expected. He didn't expect what he found.

~

Nothing spun before her eyes, not the men around her, not the columns holding up the ceiling. Maggie didn't feel nauseous or slow-witted from the effects of the drug Diamond Tooth had to have slipped into her shooters. That's what she thought happened. She leaned against one of the columns long enough to determine these things.

Then she saw him, by the bar. Bubba was with him, protecting him, it seemed to her. He played with his little ponytail, curling it around an index finger and thumping it off then curling it again. Nerves, she figured as a woman. She stood off the column and squared herself and marched his way full of purpose.

Nobody moved to make way for her now. They had gotten their amusement out of her and now she was just another spent gringa. She slipped the snub nose out of the fanny pack and raised it. The shot she fired staggered the crowd and a sudden berth opened for her. With the gun held in both hands, she walked untouched up to the man who would tell her what she wanted to know or who would die.

She leveled the gun at the area of Swabb's chest, the place a heart would be if he had one.

"He's not the one you want," said Bubba, not moving his arm off the bar. Staying calm at a frantic, dangerous moment. "I'm getting the babies tonight, Maggie. I was gonna come get you right after I got them. All right?"

His words stilled her. But they didn't soften her. "Where are they?" she said directly to Swabb, as if not hearing Bubba.

Swabb dodged a phantom bullet. He drew himself in, becoming tiny. "I didn't do it. It wasn't me!"

"Where are they!" Maggie said louder.

Her face reddened, her chin quivered. The crowd seemed to comprehend her instability and sense that anyone could take a bullet, just like that.

~

Myers stepped in front of her, in front of the gun that trembled visibly in her small hands, delicate, feminine hands that looked obscene holding blue steel. "Maggie. Put it down."

She looked fleetingly at him.

Myers shifted when she tried to peer around him. He shifted the other way, cat and mouse, his larger frame concealing the lawyer from her. The snub nose wavered but its barrel didn't drop.

Myers took another step. "He's going to jail," he said. "Give it to me."

He was calm, cool even. If he had tried he couldn't have swallowed. "We won't find your babies this way. This man doesn't know where they are. Maggie, listen to Cousins. Listen to Bubba."

Maggie's eyes appeared to soften but she didn't alter her stance or the aim of the gun.

Myers reached, quickly, his hand ducking under the gun, taking her wrist and rotating her hand skyward. Colt revolvers weren't factory set with hair triggers and that meant if she pulled the trigger it would be intentional, not by accident. He could not fit his finger between the trigger and guard; he chanced she wouldn't pull the trigger again. She did.

The sound peeled through the barroom and Myers' ears. The crowd backed off, stretching out the circle like a stone hits water. No one fell to the floor or yelped or gushed blood.

Myers twisted her wrist again and pulled the gun away, putting Maggie on her knees. Both her hands raced to her face and covered it. She slumped in a heap.

CHAPTER SIXTY-ONE

Mendez drove with both hands on the wheel in the Driver's Ed position, which may have accounted for him continuously jerking the wheel. His driving had Fitzsimmon uneasy. Fitzsimmon glanced at him again, then dropped his irritated gaze to Mendez' lap where he viewed under the glow of dashboard lights two lumps that were the Chinese marbles in his pants pocket positioned atop his thigh like a set of oddly dislocated testicles.

"Next time we take my car," Fitzsimmon said. He was eating a machaca burrito and bits of it spewed out as he talked.

The big car shivered to the left as Mendez took a hand off the wheel to wipe his cheek. He looked at the spot of egg on the back of the hand and scowled.

"You're a pig. Hurry up and finish that thing, it's stinking up the car."

They were on a narrow, winding hillside road south of Tijuana in the dark of night. Fitzsimmon was less interested in eating than watching the curves Mendez took too fast and too casually. He was one lousy driver, Rory Fitzsimmon thought. He wadded up the rest of the burrito in its wrapper and folded it inside the paper bag it came in. Maybe he would finish it when he could get a soda to wash it down.

Mendez wasn't interested in Fitzsimmon's concerns; he was thinking about Guerrero. He tapped his fingernails on the steering wheel, considering how dumb or smart the Inspector might decide to play things at tonight's meet. First and foremost Guerrero was a dirty cop on the take, very capable of double-crossing him. The increasing bloodshed caused by the Arellano Félix gang and other drug lords finally had united law enforcement to clean up some of the corruption down here, which meant Guerrero would be worried about his job and maybe even his life. All of which gave Mendez cause to think the Mexican cop might have his goon squad along. Scoring a drug bust, even if it was by an American, would put him in with his new chief of police, a guy too new to be on the take yet.

Guerrero was still alive and on the police force, and that meant he was no moron. The man wasn't going to simply hand over the cargo and expect to collect thirty or forty thousand dollars for it.

Mendez said, "Guerrero'll get there early, get his men spread out. We've got to hit fast."

"What if he don't have the babies with him? Should we hit him anyway?"

Mendez took his eyes off the road for just a second. "We do everybody but Guerrero. But I expect him to bring the merchandise—to show good faith. It's in his culture, get us hopeful before he cuts us down."

"Lovely … What makes you think he'll agree to meet at the pier? You don't think he'll be suspicious?"

Mendez' face loosened and fell slightly, adding years to his vain appearance. "He knows what I intend to do with the cargo. It's the natural place I'd choose for the transaction."

"He thinks that of you, he can't think much of your chances in the afterlife."

"I don't suppose he much cares which direction I take … But it's a curious observation."

"Yeah, I'm kinda artistic with my thoughts at times."

A simple subtle smile restored Mendez' aging Hollywood looks, a slight lift of the face was all it took and he was Ricardo Montalban again. He gave thought to the artistic nature of his accomplice, how skillfully his garrote had put down big Sidney Rhoades. Too bad he hadn't managed to apply some of the same art on Earl Swabb as he'd been ordered to do. Mendez could almost feel sorry that after this business was settled he had to take Fitzsimmon fishing with all the others.

CHAPTER SIXTY-TWO

Automatic gunfire erupted. Loud, *da-da-da-da, da-da-da*.

The diverse assembly of revelers—the cretins and sex-craved, the alcoholics, bartenders and mariachis, good-timers and a few northern vacationers involved in crimes both south and north of the border—everyone doubled over as though caught in the streets of Baghdad. Dust and plaster rained down.

The two federales rushing in behind blazing guns were nothing but scared boys in the menacing black clothes of soldiers, wielding assault weapons that could wipe out the entire barroom in seconds. The first shout came from the federale with the most pimples. "Who has the weapon? Speak up!" His dialect was backcountry, Myers decided.

Some eyes settled on Maggie but the armed guards did not pick up on it. She was still on her knees. She stayed there.

Myers moved to the hollow in the crowd, as if taking the stage, and raised the handgun by its barrel. "An accident." He spoke slowly. "It was on the floor. Here, take it."

Someone showing off, he explained in Spanish, some guy drinking a little too much, but nobody's hurt. He shrugged, as if baffled.

The young federales lowered their weapons and moved their fingers to the front of the trigger guards. One of them took the proffered revolver.

The crowd remained silent. No one stepped up to argue against Myers' explanation. He thought that odd but didn't push it. He stepped through the idle crowd and helped Maggie to her feet, then moved her over to the bar and joined Cousins and Swabb as if nothing unusual had happened, no gunfire, no destruction of property other than holes in the plaster-and-wood-plank ceiling, just a bunch of diverse, deviant people having a good time getting drunk together, everything just hunky-dory. It's Hussong's, people, forget it.

The soldiers didn't forget it. They asked questions, speaking to local good-timers and the cretins. There was little chance any of the four Americans could up and walk out just then. They all had reason why they wanted to do just that.

Bubba's reason would be the most compelling and he felt the walls closing in. He thought now might be a good time to start praying for a miracle, hoping that Maggie or Swabb or the reporter or any one of these miserable gigolos who could read or had watched television and knew he was wanted by the law would do him the favor of saying nothing to the pimple-faced conscripts, that they would see no one had been hurt and let it go as typical Hussong's rowdiness.

The culprit turned out to be Swabb, who played his card with a lawyer's flair for urgency. "He's wanted for murder!" he shouted in Spanish, vehemently jabbing a finger at Bubba. "He's the Border Patrol agent they're looking for in San Diego. He killed two people and is planning to kill me. Arrest him!"

Both soldiers at once whipped their weapons toward Bubba, sharing similar expressions of confusion and hostility.

Bubba considered smiling pretty; he considered running like hell. Bad thoughts, both. He couldn't outrun bullets and he knew these minimally trained teenagers would not hesitate to cut him down.

Still, he reacted quickly. He waved an objecting hand in the space between him and the barrel tips of the M-16s as if to outright dismiss the accusation.

"This man," he said contemptuously, "he was a Baldie with the Sinaloa cartel until they discarded him for stealing from them. He talked his way out of floating on the river; he's a good talker. Now he is on his own, selling meth and weed and crack—you name it—to children in the neighborhood, at the schools, cathedrals."

He drew close to the pimple-faced troop who seemed more appalled by his words than the other kid. As if selecting the guard as his confidant, he whispered, "Yes, I am *la migra*, but I am not a killer; I am down here to take him back to the states on smuggling and murder charges ... Search him, you will find illegal substance even now. *You* can make the arrest, get yourself promoted. We just want scum like him off the streets. Your sergeant does too."

The young man threw persuaded hard eyes on Swabb. Bubba knew that federal *policia* were particularly keen on curtailing drug trafficking. Everyone did. The soldier ordered Swabb to get his hands up high and step forward, his comrade responded in turn with a gun barrel poke in Swabb's back.

Swabb was flustered by Bubba's outrageous invention. His face a tantrum of incredulity, his mouth opened to speak and the guard lifted his rifle as if to butt him. *Silencio!*

Swabb raised his hands as commanded.

Pimples dug into a pocket in the lawyer's shiny vinyl jacket, drawing nothing. He searched the other pocket and pulled out the sandwich bag of marijuana Bubba had moments ago planted there, opened it, sniffed, then grimaced. A collective grunt resounded around the room, bolstering contempt for the drug dealer. Someone spit by Swabb, the crowd drew closer, swelling like a gathering storm.

Swabb turned sick-looking, ready to faint. His eyes dimmed. Both guards roughly seized his arms and forced him to the dusty floor.

After a meticulous search that turned up only a few crumpled pesos that Bubba had given him from dinner change, Pimples clasped Swabb's thumbs together by plastic tie behind his back and yanked him to his feet. Swabb had turned almost ashen now, like the vacant color of a dying leaf before it falls. His still-swollen nose began to bleed again. His tears were ignored.

In the midst of the activity, a group of burnt-faced Orange County vacationers wafted in on the oddly quiet scene. Taken back, the foursome started to turn and leave when one of them, the late-twentysomething brunette wearing Lolita sunglasses, shaped her mouth into a big O of recognition.

"Holy shit, Dwayne, it's the guy," she said and invited Dwayne closer to see for himself.

A patron in a Stetson seemed fascinated and sidled up to the brunette. "Who, my lovely?" he asked.

"The guy on the front page of the paper, *that* guy," she said. She pointed out Bubba as she would a suspect in a line up. Apparently she hadn't seen the following day's paper that featured Myers' picture.

Word translated quickly and the guards again eyed Bubba, then quickly handcuffed him with no further words. The young soldiers appeared pleased with themselves. They had made two big-time arrests, a drug dealer and a murderer. Their sergeant, as Bubba had suggested, would be proud.

Bubba now spoke quietly and rapidly to his captor. "Do me one favor, amigo. Let me speak with my wife first. It's not much to ask."

The young soldier appeared baffled. He grinned. "Why should I?"

"I will speak to your commander and commend you for your alertness making the arrests. Please, just give me this moment."

Pimples grinned like the coach had just called him in to play. "Okay, but be quick."

Bubba drew Maggie aside and got close enough to notice the sleep rheum still in the corner of her eye from the drug she'd been fed.

"Reach inside my shirt," he said softly. "Don't look suspicious, just do it slow."

Maggie gazed forlornly at him and unsnapped one button midway down his shirt, reached in and put her hand on the thick belt. He'd purchased the military-fashioned pocketed belt in men's accessories at Dorian's while Swabb tried on shirts. Combat-style gear and clothes was the in thing in Mexican culture, as were paramilitary gangs.

"Good," said Bubba. "Put it under your serape. Slow now. It's thirty-two grand, Maggie. Use it to buy the babies off Guerrero. And, ah, maybe you could see fit to help Roxanne out some." His voice was as humble as a mouse's in a mouse house trap.

"You're a good man, Bubba ... Where is he?"

"Guerrero'll be here, outside maybe. Dark little tick with a pot belly and a stupid walrus mustache."

"I know him, he killed my Indian friend Castro."

The belt hung loose on Maggie's hip but it stayed up. "Oh, Bubba. I'm so sorry."

"Yeah, me too, honey. Ah, could you maybe get in touch with this dude Ruben Juarez? A lawyer I know in San Diego? ... God*damn*, I had hoped I would never need one of them."

Maggie got teary-eyed. This was it for her cowboy. What a trip it had been, she thought. She hugged Bubba. She kissed the side of his face where a tear, apparently, had dampened his whiskered cheek. Her words were thick with lament. "I wasn't going to shoot *you*, you know."

"I know that, Maggie. Boy, I'm gonna miss you. Be careful, trust Guerrero like a snake. Don't even blink at him."

Bubba turned on the soldier's insistent tug and disappeared through the saloon's doors, not too far behind Swabb.

The eclectic throng of Hussongites hooted like a gaggle of high-pitched baby owls. "Who—yoo, who—yoo, who—yoo." Crazy as loons.

Sam, the bartender at the Safari Lounge, had nailed Hussong's infamous character. It was the Sodom and Gomorrah of the modern west, and more.

CHAPTER SIXTY-THREE

The streetlight shifted on a gust of wind, making stationary objects appear to move. Myers imagined nighttime flares throwing shadows on the riverbanks of Can Tho.

They held Swabb at gunpoint. The guard had let him sit against the wall. A white-striped military van pulled up and double-parked in the street next to a civilian car and two federales jump out. Hurriedly, they lifted Swabb to his feet and pushed him inside the van through the back doors.

Maggie applauded with quick, hard handclaps. "Put him in a cell with no window," she hollered to deaf ears.

Myers glanced sharply at her, still troubled by the extent of her vehemence for the man. He said, "I don't see Cousins?"

"They took Bubba into that taco shop. Down there, see?"

Myers didn't see him. "What was it you took from him?" he asked.

She told him. Money, thirty-two grand he told her, she said. She didn't ask where he got it but he was going to use it to buy the babies back from Guerrero. "Bubba was supposed to meet him here to make the exchange," she said. "*We* will do it, the two of us. Bubba said he would be here, any time now."

"Give me the money," Myers said firmly. "You're going back to the hotel and wait there. And this time, I want you to wait."

"It's going to take both of us to handle that many babies."

"When I find them, I will call you. Promise."

"There's Bubba," Maggie said.

Cousins stepped out of the taco shop, shoulders droopy. He stood by the pimpled-faced federale, who was biting on a rolled taquito. The soldier ate as if starved.

Myers spoke with urgency. "Maggie, you've had a rough night. You need to go, let me handle this."

"Well, yours was worse." Maggie was frustrated and peeved. She nodded, frowning, "All right, you're right. I know I haven't acted sensibly."

"Nothing is sensible. I have to follow this through, alone, no matter how it turns out. That's not sensible, either."

"Make it turn out right, Ray."

He waited until the shadow took her at the corner then he walked over to the van, keeping an eye on Cousins still standing by the taco shop. A window in the back of the van was halfway open. Myers said through it to Swabb, "I'll call the Consulate, see what they can do for you. It wasn't that much dope, can't be that bad."

Swabb was a small and beaten animal, sitting on the floorboard. "The Consulate won't do anything," he said morbidly and grew smaller, a shrinking man destined to demise in this country's convoluted legal system.

A soldier about five feet tall stepped out of the van's driver's side. He gave Myers a shove to move him along. Myers' eyes were leaden but he stepped onto the sidewalk.

A police jeep sped by and squealed to a stop in front of Cousins and Pimples. Myers recognized the passenger. Guerrero, the killer, the kidnapper. He jumped out and the jeep sped away, burning rubber as if the driver was the only cop on duty in the city and had to get somewhere else fast. Myers stepped back into the shadows. He considered his options—jump in now or wait till he saw the infants. He wasn't armed, Guerrero was. He waited.

Guerrero placed the full of his arm on Pimples' shoulder, cajoling the young guard, it appeared. The street light pitched shadows and Myers wasn't sure that he saw the corrupt cop hand Pimples something that looked a lot like a sliver of folded paper, the kind of origami-fold holding a quarter gram of something. He couldn't be sure that he saw Cousins shake his head or not shake his head. He did see Pimples and Guerrero each pull a weapon on Cousins and he saw Cousins turn his head away and down as if expecting to be shot right there. Myers saw Guerrero shove his handgun into Cousins' kidney area. He watched Cousins walk off, Guerrero guiding him with a gun to his back.

They walked south from Hussong's like that, the cop in step with him. For three blocks Myers kept pace along Ruiz through light pedestrian traffic, hanging a half block back. Guerrero led his prisoner north onto a darker street that had no street sign. A few short blocks farther along the dirt-and-gravel course, they came to a road paralleling the four-lane avenue where traffic flowed into the city from the north side highway.

Just then there came a great explosion from some distance away, possibly at sea. Then the immediate western horizon turned bulbous in bright reddish yellow. A secondary, larger explosion flew by him on a violent airwave. The mushrooming brilliance momentarily blinded him. Then it diminished to high yellow flames.

His eyes saw spots where his subjects had been and he sped up to cover the gap. What had been a dull ache in his side turned into sharp pulls. His shirt turned damp at the wound. *Crap.* A mutter under his breath.

He turned on a street that seemed the logical direction they had gone. A little farther behind a Cyclone fence there stood a three-story brick factory and on stilts atop it stood a worn, unlit sign that read, *Fábrica Atún de Ensenada*. It would have been the old processing factory, Myers figured. A sharp scent of fish wafted on the air. Lights streamed through rows of multi-paneled windows at the entire front of the building. The tuna factory was up and running on the swing shift, it appeared.

He listened to the noises associated with processing, the dull hum, clanging, the whir of motors.

The back end of the building was dark.

Then he saw a light flicker back there and he moved toward it. He came to a dock with an industrial-size aluminum door. Stamped in yellow print above the battered door was *Recepción de Cadaveres*, the reception terminal for cadavers. A morgue.

He tried the door. It gave. He slid it back slowly, trying to keep the rumble down and vaguely wondered if Old Leatherface waited on the other side with his sledgehammer. It was a thought. He slipped through and left it open behind him. The light came from the long narrow corridor where he stood. He peered in both directions at a series of closed doors and two elevator shafts. The elevators were the kind with accordion gates that closed against each other one at a time, Otis elevators dating to the earlier part of last century. He could hear one of them in operation, going down.

He started to descend the staircase when he saw a man standing on the next landing down. The man was lanky, bony arms and legs. He apparently had stopped to get his breath as Myers heard him wheezing and holding onto the rail. Around his slender waist was a Roy Rogers gun belt tied to his leg just above the knee. A big gun with a bone-and-silver handle. The old security guard may have been 85 years old, asthmatic, rheumatic. Myers stepped out of his sight and waited. The old man didn't seem to be going after anyone. It may have been him who turned on the light. But it wasn't him on the elevator.

The seconds stampeded by. Myers thought he'd have to be a Boy Scout and help the old guy up the stairs. But then the guard continued his climb. He didn't stop again on Myers' floor to catch a breath but continued up the next flight holding onto the rails on both sides of the narrow staircase.

Myers took three steps at a time down the stairs until they ran out. He opened the door in front of him and found the basement.

It was all concrete and had no windows. It was wet and dank and smelled of Pine-Sol. The elevator's interior light reflected on another, smaller aluminum door, the reception for cadavers. Myers noticed himself in the mirror-like aluminum; he couldn't see how tight his teeth were clenched but didn't let the sunken eyes discourage him.

There was another light, too, coming from under the door. A shadow inside moved across it. Myers put an ear on the cold metal. He took a breath and grabbed the doorknob. He thought it would have been nice if he'd borrowed Roy's big gun.

CHAPTER SIXTY-FOUR

Bubba wished like hell he had held on to part of his cash money. Cash worked miracles, even on a man who had a personal vendetta against you. Five thousand. If he'd thought to hold on to just five grand—well, he might not be looking at corpses again.

Guerrero hadn't brought him here for a night on the town, two crooked cops out celebrating and gloating over their richly rewarded endeavors. He'd had it in for Bubba since that night in this very cellar where he had forced the superstitious Mixtec to help him cut the head off that corpse named Julieta. He told the bastard no names. Don't tell me the goddamn name. It had jinxed him, he knew it then.

And now, with no bargaining chips, he didn't hold out much hope of seeing the morning fog.

Guerrero wasn't talking, and that's what worried Bubba the most; he didn't want to deal, he had a plan. He used the gun barrel to nudge Bubba along. He was guiding him along the wall to the rear of the room, toward the closed door to *"Preparación."* Bubba felt a rumble in his gut, a serious tightening in his throat. They passed the gurney where the corpse named Julieta had once lain. The mounds of covered dead staring at Bubba, inviting him to chill, stick around. It spooked the hell out of him.

Bubba considered where he had gone wrong and knew it started long before meeting up with Guerrero. His first days on the take in Sasabe had followed him to this very moment. He hadn't done anything dishonest until he joined the BP, just got by through his youth and up till then. So it wasn't that long ago, relatively speaking. After that first time, you start thinking you might as well take as much as you can cause there ain't no going back. Turning a blind eye to the cargo entering the gate became easier the more you allowed it, the more money you picked up. And then you took that leap. Bubba lamented his past; he had become no better than that *cholo* junkie he wasted in the Tecate desert.

Bubba missed his chance when the end of the gun slipped from the nape of his neck. He'd been thinking and did not seize his moment. The next time that happened he would make his move, let the bullet get him through the neck or shoulder muscle, the collar bone maybe, but give him a split-second to turn, chop, grab the gun. Give him a fighting chance.

If the bullet didn't hit the spine, didn't take an upward trajectory, if the potbellied slob was slow as he looked. It didn't leave Bubba much to work with, but he wasn't giving up. He wasn't finished yet.

Guerrero finally spoke as they drew closer to the far side of the room. "I will tell you I did not want the man Castro to be killed," Guerrero said. "It was that stupid nephew of mine, he is hot-headed. He has no sense. I am going to see that he makes payments to the family for his evil sin."

"That's the right thing to do," Bubba agreed. "They're good people. They take in abandoned street kids." He couldn't figure Guerrero. Why cry to Bubba about the Indian? Maybe it was as simple as he just needed to confess. Repent.

Keep him distracted.

Bubba said, "Much braver than you and me, amigo."

He tried to turn around to look at the man but Guerrero clamped surprisingly powerful fingers around Bubba's neck to keep him facing ahead.

Bubba said, "The babies are here, aren't they? I have got your money, the money we talked about. You remember? … Well, if they are not here, then what purpose did you have for bringing me here, just because of the other night?"

"There are plenty rich Americans who can pay very good for these babies you all worry so much about," Guerrero answered. "I know. You know. Our good friend *Señor* Mendez, he knows."

Suddenly, Bubba had his chance handed to him. The lights flickered out.

He found out then how slow the fat cop was.

Roxanne appeared like a bright light on a road he couldn't turn away from. But there was nothing to regret there. No children, no home mortgage to sweat. She'd make out all right; she still had her schnauzers. His big loss was Maggie. He had meant it, he did love that woman. If only they had come together in another way. But Maggie would find her peace. He mostly reflected on his Texas youth under the thumb of a vicious father who really had sent him and Bonnie to the train yards. But he wasn't copping out by blaming his old man for his own criminal undertakings. He'd done that to himself. The old man was probably dead now, the way he was going the last time Bubba had tried to help him out of the gutter. Pathetic. That man was his biggest regret, his biggest shame.

The jar of it was what Bubba noticed most, most surprised him. A failing vision of Maggie, and then a mutt he'd had at age ten that bit his old man's hand, of his little sister's sweet face. The force of the bump, a great ringing, dimness cloaking his vision. The black hand of death closed in on him so swiftly he did not even know he had fallen, the floor, the earth opening up below him.

CHAPTER SIXTY-FIVE

Myers cracked the hinged door part way open and quickly slipped in. He dipped and glided against the cellar wall careful as a cat. The morgue burned under cold fluorescence. Corpses lay beneath sheets on makeshift platforms in no apparent arrangement, some elevated higher than others. He surveyed the entire room in a millisecond, spotting the two men on the far side of the room, 40 feet from him. He threw a nearby light switch as Guerrero turned his way.

A halted muzzle flash and a muted clap of gunfire rang out where the two men still stood in his after-vision. He knew what had happened and regretted having fallen behind and lost track of them. He might have saved Cousins.

He heard another shot, the coup de grace. An instant later, a mallet pounded the wall much too close to Myers' ear. Hard particles of concrete cuffed the backside of his head. He dropped to the floor and rolled under a corpse on a wooden slab. He moved on hands and knees among the corpses, toward the gunfire, its white bursts now an imprint lingering in his vision. He followed the vision until it mutated into a useless road map of white lines. He fell on top of a stiff corpse, a mannequin covered by a sheet.

Guerrero called out in Spanish, "Police, do not move. You will turn on the light or I shall be required to shoot to kill."

The voice came closer, moving toward the door. Myers could not let him get to the light switch. Another flame lit up a space in the dark and airmailed pulverized concrete near him again. The flash gave him an exact fix. He crawled to a place that should intersect with the cop before he reached the door or light.

Myers bumped something with wheels, saw that it would roll, waited one-one thousand, two-one thousand. Now! He shoved gurney with everything he had.

Simultaneously, the door opened. Framed there, big as *High Noon's* hero, stood the old guard, innocent and curious. Roy Rogers turned on the lights.

The lights flickered to life across the ceiling like flares and Myers' inner voice said, *Fuck me.* He felt pinned, a butterfly under glass. Guerrero had only to put a bullet into him.

Myers' nemesis had bad timing. But that was its M.O., to strike when defenseless. Myers' eyes dilated, grew deluded. He saw hands in flames. His maybe. That old foe stepped in, took over ...

Plodding through weed, enemy swarming. In your haste the snap of a wire against your shin. A sickening sound that leaves but a moment, then ... You are in great need of intercession. That was the terror of it, your life depending on your buddy. And likewise. The burst of fire and wind ripping at everything, tossing you like a leaf.

Danny dies, you live.

The seared-in-memory of him was ghost-colored but it wasn't a ghost.

Myers stepped aside and ducked, then jumped back hoping a miracle would keep away the bullets. It came, it did. The gurney hit its mark and dislodged the revolver from Guerrero's hand.

The old guard tried to shout, "*Que esta pasando aqui, eh?*" and then coughed and coughed more.

Myers went for the gun. Guerrero went for the gun. Roy Rogers went for his big sidearm in the tan holster.

He acted like a security guard and ordered both men to hold still, to stand up, still trying to get the big gun out of the holster, coughing. He said, "You are under arrest, raise your hands." His voice was feeble, croaky.

Fumbling with his revolver, the guard inadvertently tripped Myers, allowing Guerrero time to retrieve the gun. He got to his feet holding the weapon gently, as if it were the woman he loved.

Myers let go some air. He felt suddenly very tired. "I am only interested in finding the infants," he said in a strained voice. "I have money."

Guerrero grunted, his face sweaty. "How much?"

"Ten thousand U.S. dollars," said Myers, "just outside in my car."

The Mexican raced his eyes up and down Myers, as if evaluating a formidable opponent he was about to meet in the ring. "You insult me, *señor*."

Myers wasn't as versed in this game. "I can get more."

The old guard voiced a command to give over the gun and show some identification. The crooked cop glanced at the guard, who still could not pry the gun from his hard-leather holster and had given up. Guerrero gave him a look that resembled a satiric grin, snorted, then turned and left the morgue, giving Myers not a hint or hope to work with in search of the babies—but handing him a second miracle. His life.

He wondered why the crooked cop didn't take his offer or ask for more, which Myers would have given him; the bartering had to start somewhere. He wondered why he didn't ignore the hapless guard and shoot Myers. And why not kill the guard, too. Maybe whatever contention had been between him and Cousins could explain it but Myers couldn't figure it. There was some reason he had executed the man. And let him go.

Myers forced himself to confirm that Cousins was not still alive. He confirmed it without the need to take a pulse.

The wooden guard began wrestling with the gun again. It would not come out. He said, now solicitously, in Spanish, "What's going on in here? Who are you, *señor*?"

CHAPTER SIXTY-SIX

The drive over the mountain at night in the dark took longer than Mendez had planned on. He had chosen to take the less traveled but longer route south out of Tijuana through Garcia and over to San Miguel on the coast. This curvier route was more exciting than puttering around the slow, boring little burg of Rosarito and along the nondescript nighttime toll road. The road smoothed out before reaching San Miguel and then became a smooth ride on in to Ensenada. Ensenada was now close by, its horizon aglow. He estimated another fifteen minutes.

Fitzsimmon sat quietly. He hadn't spoken a word since the near miss with an oncoming truck whose headlights weren't on. That had been this side of Garcia, about an hour ago. Mendez overreacted and swerved too far to the right trying to avoid a collision. It was their good luck that the guardrail at that point was built strong enough to prevent the Continental from tumbling over the hillside. But the impact jolted both occupants. The incident had not left Fitzsimmon at his best. His response, though low-keyed, would have gotten him suspended had he been on duty. He said, "My daughter who doesn't even drive could handle this vehicle better than you. Pull over, let me drive."

Mendez conjured a lustful vision of the eleven-year-old but let it fade. He otherwise ignored the comment. But he would not forget. The insult would make it easier to retire Fitzsimmon when the time came.

He watched the moon race alongside the car across the galloping pearl carpet of the endless ocean's surface. Ensenada lay just ahead.

"We've lost time. We'll have to move faster setting up," Mendez said. "Check the gas level in the boat first. Get the five gallons out of the trunk and take it with you to the boat."

"Okay. You want all the fireworks on the water?"

"Not the sticks. Take the plastic and automatics. We'll set the plastics up where it will jar them loose, and we knock them down."

"Simple as that, huh. Ducks on a pond." Fitzsimmon wasn't one to think things worked that easily.

Mendez gave him a dull look, "Just do what you're told."

They came into the city on its main artery, Lázardo Cárdenas Boulevard. The boat yards were up ahead on the right just north of the marina where Santiago docked his speedboat. The plan was to get to the rendezvous spot covertly by water and set out the plastics—for their entertainment and pleasure, as designed by Mendez.

Fitzsimmon eyed the driver curiously. "What the hell is that noise?"

Mendez took a hand off the wheel and used it to try and open his cell phone, which was performing the Brahms sleepy-time tune, the tune that denoted unknown callers. But he knew who it was. He made his voice sound cheerful but business-like. "Hello, Inspector, what can you tell me?"

Guerrero spoke in a low voice that sounded like he was whispering. "I am taking your law man somewhere right now to discuss this business with the money offer."

Mendez turned up the volume on his phone. "Make it a final offer. Understand?"

"No problem."

"Where is the lawyer?"

"With the federales. They belong to me here. I will get him later."

"Sooner than later. We cannot do business until it's done."

Guerrero quipped, "*Sí sí.*"

"How long will it take for you to finish?"

"Soon. One hour."

"Let's say we get together in an hour and a half from now. I should just be arriving in Ensenada then."

"You have the money?"

"Down to the peso, amigo. You have the merchandise?"

"I do, *señor.*"

"Good. Bring them to the park on the bay, *la Bandera*. At the flagpole. I'll be wearing a white hat. Can't miss me."

"There are people in the park."

"Who cares? Only the perverts at that hour … It is the place we will meet." Mendez's tone was resolute. He listened to the double-dealing cop complain a moment before relenting to a murmur, as if deciding to do Mendez a great favor.

Mendez snapped the instrument shut. He scowled at Fitzsimmon. "It's not noise. It's Brahms … He's taking care of Cousins and Swabb. That'll give us enough time to get there before his goons."

"What if he's playing it straight?"

"Fine. He'll die by himself."

Fitzsimmon shook his head. "Oh, man. You're a hard one, Mister Grinch."

Along Avenida Lázardo Cárdenas, the "40 kilometer/hr" signs meant business. The thoroughfare had serious speed bumps that would give those who didn't slow a good headache, even a knot.

Streetlights illuminated the boulevard and roadside businesses. The glare might have been the reason Mendez didn't notice the speed bump warning sign. He was also talking on the cellular, not regarding his driving.

He even accelerated a little, tense over his conversation with Guerrero.

Two young girls inside a bright laundromat window played a hand game, a universal pastime that Mendez remembered from his own youth in the cattle fields of east Orange County. He played the game with a runt cousin in the slaughter yards where they would sneak in to watch the cattle get shot in their brains.

The Mexican girls were in their sweet years, seven or eight, dressed in the skimpy plain cotton dress ubiquitous to poor village girls, exposing creamy brown skinny thighs and shoulders.

He hit the first speed bump at sixty-five miles an hour—or over 100 kilometers per hour—and the impact caused the tire with the low pressure to fail in angry protest.

It wasn't that that caused Mendez to lose control.

Fitzsimmon shoved his foot into the floorboard. His hands shot forward and pushed the dash. He screamed, "Look out!"

Mendez saw it then. So fast. A child in the street in his lane, two of them, and for a moment he froze and the two children in the windshield before him also froze.

The girl had thought the highway was clear when she told her companion, the boy, "Let's go, hurry up." The children had scrounged some remnants of croissants and half eaten barbecued chicken breasts out of the trash bin at the rich marina and were in a hurry to get to their shelter behind the laundromat to eat it. The boy had lost a leg to polio. He was six now. He had a mother somewhere in the slums of the city but hadn't seen her for three weeks. The girl had run the streets for thirteen months, since separating from her caretakers. She was eight and somewhat of a guardian to the boy.

The boy threw his crutch at the oncoming shiny-black monster. The girl put her skinny arms around the boy and stood there and waited, her innocent mind not comprehending the fierceness of her imminent destruction.

The boy had never made the pilgrimage so the Virgin of Guadalupe came to him. His eyes grew bright. He first smiled, then he laughed as the black dragon swerved and left him fighting to balance himself against the monster's rush of wind.

Mendez had had some recent self-training at dodging children in the street—that Catholic girl in La Jolla whose life he had saved because of his quick reflexes. He did it again now, defying the laws of gravity, it seemed. He saved the two children but flipped the off-balanced Continental when the front wheel with the destroyed tire hit a foot-high curb. A colorful comet of sparks followed the upside down vehicle still speeding across the highway onto the concrete space of a Pemex gas station.

Had the Pemex driver not stopped for watermelon in San Miguel, the tanker would now be through filling the subterranean tanks and on its way. The driver was paid by the hour and used to taking his time on these cross-state trips. He had parked the tanker vertical to the boulevard and in line with the charging two-ton Continental. The first explosion blew the gas tank quickly followed by the five-gallon can in the car trunk, which then ignited the sticks of dynamite. Mendez and the BP dispatcher were blown all the way to kingdom come, bit by bit.

As Ray Myers shadowed someone on Avenida Ruiz a few blocks east, his first thought as an American with memories very fresh of the crumbling twin towers, was that terrorists had hit the cargo docks.

CHAPTER SIXTY-SEVEN

Back in the paupers morgue, Roy Rogers' gnarly hand went into a muscle spasm trying to undo the tight cowhide eyehook that held the gun in the holster.

"Let me help you," Myers said to the security guard.

Myers slipped the leather hook aside and removed the big .44 revolver with the pearl handle. He balanced its hefty weight and wondered if the old man could actually lift and fire it. He popped open the cylinder and looked at six gold-ringed metallic shells.

"I need to borrow this. I will return it."

Roy looked forlorn, like he had lost his wonder dog Bullet.

Myers didn't see Guerrero but he heard the sound of boot heels striking the steel steps of the staircase. Halfway up the stairs he heard the distinct rumbling noise of the outside door sliding on its overhead rollers. The Mexican had fled the building and Myers was fast losing hope of finding the babies.

He jumped five feet off the loading dock onto concrete, clenching teeth in anticipation of the pain sure to follow. On impact his yelp was involuntary. He saw the faint shadow of a door closing at the west end of the same brick building and he picked up his pace. Running wouldn't make his wounded side any worse for wear since the last stitch had already pulled loose and he was bleeding again.

At the busy end of the building, he opened the door cautiously and looked inside. He saw a brightly lit factory at work. As best Myers could make out, management hired only women. The women wore broad slick-rubber aprons and heavy yellow gloves and used filleting knives to cut large fish on bloody aluminum tabletops. Stationed along an assembly line, some gutted the fish, others filleted or chopped out steaks. They had sure, swift hands. A slow-moving conveyor took the finished cuts through a wall. What was left over, Myers guessed, went into tuna tins for humans or pet cats.

The conveyor ground to a lull as Myers moved closer; the workers saw a bleeding man brandishing a gun with a barrel too long to stick into his pants. None of the dozen women shrieked or ran. The gun didn't seem to bother them. They seemed more interested in Myers' midsection.

He spoke to a woman whose broad face was hard-edged as her knife.

"Where is he, the man who entered?"

She raised an eyebrow and nodded and pointed her long blade to metal stairs leading to an upper station that looked out over the ground floor, the foreman's office. His eyes traveled the stairs upward and saw the distinct figure of Guerrero there, as he entered that office then closed the door. Venetian blinds snapped closed inside the window. A slat in the door blind lifted and in a moment dropped back into place.

"Do you know him?"

She shrugged and he took that to mean he was no stranger. But it could have meant the opposite.

"*Gracias,*" Myers said. He reluctantly headed for the stairs, the vertigo setting in simply at the thought of the climb.

"You need help," said the woman.

"Not yet."

The women were all back to work before Myers began his accent. Maybe men with guns ran into the factory all the time. Maybe drug lords showed up with their Uzi-toting goons. The factory most likely had been condemned years ago. Maybe it was a sideline for a small-change operation that packaged mackerel instead of the tuna to sell as "solid light," shipping it to Oaxaca and Chiapas and other states too poor to enforce government oversight.

The stairs were wobbly. He tried to ignore that. He stopped on the thirteenth step and looked up. Dust sprinkled down from the loose screws holding the stairs to the concrete wall thirty feet up.

Guerrero had to go through him to get down but he hadn't come out of the office. Myers saw fish come down a chute from behind a wall onto the conveyor below. It half circled around the workstations where people did their jobs, tossing entrails into a huge central pool of dark liquid, acid by the boiling reaction.

He stopped again on the twenty-fifth step and squeezed his eyes shut; there were 39 rungs in all. He had counted them after the thirteenth. The stairs seemed to sway now and the paralysis grew but he pushed on and made it to the catwalk near the office. Never look down.

Myers called out, "*Señor* Guerrero, come on out of there. We're not finished."

No response. Then, suddenly, Guerrero opened up and stepped out. He was ten feet away pointing the revolver at the thickest part of Myers.

Myers held Roy's .44 against the backside of his buttocks, knowing he could not get it around in time to fire.

"I give you life and you don't take it. You don't want to live?" the cop said, voice soft as slush.

The catwalk swayed under their combined weight. Myers sweated now.

"There's the matter of those babies you took from the Herlindas—and the murder of two innocent men. But all I want is the babies, and I will still pay you; I will pay you thirty thousand dollars."

But he didn't think money was the issue since Guerrero shot him.

CHAPTER SIXTY-EIGHT

A half-dozen pairs of startled eyes looked up after the clap of gunfire. The women saw the Inspector—as they knew Guerrero—thrust his gun forward like he might shoot the man again. But there was no crack.

The women watched the motionless American on the metal grate as Guerrero moved slowly away. Then they saw him move, try to lean against the catwalk rail. Some of them thought the American would topple and that caused a collective gasp. The group as a whole seemed to waver, as if duplicating Myers' slow motion stagger up there. The wounded man collapsed onto the metal landing again and slowly push himself up until he stood all the way to his feet.

~

Myers saw light but all the crawling things in his vision broke it up. The wind exploded out of him with the impact of the bullet but he dare not faint. It was 40 feet to concrete below. The bulk of pain centered somewhere in the middle of him, like tightening barbed wire. He teetered on unconsciousness and had to stretch flat on the metal grating. He fought for air.

Momentarily he rolled and looked up to see Guerrero still there. He looked into the gray-metal eye at the end of the Mexican's revolver and gritted his teeth. There seemed nothing else to do.

Click, then, click click.

Myers grinned even with a thousand daggers in his torso. He gripped Roy's .44, now under him, and tried to lift it out of quicksand.

Guerrero took a vertical ladder up to the ceiling. His revolver lay on the catwalk where he dropped it.

Myers low-crawled two feet without collapsing, then tried standing. Wobbly, but up. He thought it was a good idea to look at the damage before climbing higher. Under his shirt warm blood seeped at the top of the money belt. He lifted the shirt with a grimace and gave it a sheepish look. He wasn't losing blood in gushes and his insides weren't outside. He reasoned the money belt took the impact, diverting the slug. There was a puckered, gray-bluish path along the skin. The bullet had lodged somewhere under the ribcage, opposite side of the knife wound. He would have a triangle of scars to think about when—and if—he made it out of this mess he'd brought on himself.

Guerrero could have fled back down the ladder. He had the advantage. It puzzled Myers why he didn't. But Myers now had to go up there and bring him down.

The wall ladder led to a wide metal I-beam that might've been to change light bulbs and clear roosting birds. But that would be about it. Maybe for circus practices. It traveled below the girder and joists straight across to the far wall. You couldn't get much higher up and still be inside the building. Myers grabbed hold and took a step up and the ladder immediately pulled away from the wall, one of its concrete bolts flying by his head.

Myers tried to spare himself the misery of going any higher. He said, throatily, "You've got no where to go but down, amigo … The cannon I have can knock you off that beam. I won't shoot you if you come down—I will if you don't."

Guerrero stood on the I-beam joist like an over-the-hill acrobat. There might have been a grin under his walrus mustache. He said softly, as though he might lose his balance if he shouted, "Let me warn you, my men will be here very soon. You do not have much time. They will show you no mercy. You better run."

Myers didn't look down. He didn't look anywhere but into the wall and the paint peeling off it. He scaled gingerly upward until he was there, then forced himself to crawl out onto the I-beam. He moved on his knees, holding on dearly and tried to mask his growing panic. He bled from both sides of his ribs. He took his mind off the wounds but still wondered if he might lose his balance before he passed out or after, but then thought how ridiculous since it wouldn't matter too terribly much which happened first. There was more than fifty feet of air and space between him and there. He looked down. And that froze him. Never look down.

Guerrero stood tall and confident, facing Myers. He took a step, then another, one foot in front of the other, fearlessly. He laughed and it was not a gentle laugh. It was loud, it ricocheted off the rafters. It was a mistake.

Myers grew blinders around his eyes and crawled into empty space, charged now by anger and defiance of his own irrational phobia and the fool coming at him. Ten feet out on the beam the men met. Myers was still on his hands and knees. The killer carelessly stood there, looking down on Myers. He had no leverage, nothing to hold onto. It was another mistake. This one just plain stupid.

Or so Myers thought.

A quick, hard fist smashed against the left side of his head above the ear, the part of the skull that could take a punch. A white flare seared his vision. The next blow only grazed the top of his head. He had had enough. He pulled the gun from his pants, aimed in the right direction and fired blindly. It had a bigger kick than he counted on and the gun jumped from his hand, landing somewhere spongy. A burst of screams down below.

The killer groaned and Myers got no more rock fists thrown at him. The flare in Myers' eyes died down and he re-focused on the space where his enemy had stood or crouched to pummel him. Except he wasn't there.

"*Por favor, señor.*" It was a whisper coming from beneath him.

Myers reached under the joist and touched Guerrero's forearm before he actually saw him. He was hanging by the fingers of his small hands onto the bottom lip of the I-beam. He wasn't looking down either; his now-contrite eyes looked up at Myers with a new, beseeching stare. No smirk, no walrus-lip grin. Myers traced down the path he would fall, which took a route into the big round vat of acid. He glimpsed the audience of animated faces that huddled too close around that spot. The women were caught up in the theater above them, so much that they had yet to back off.

Myers manipulated himself to get a better hold on the man's wrists, his balance guided by the hot spear driven sideways through his ribs.

Then, moving by gravity over his armpits, globules of blood began their run downward along with drips sluggishly falling from his sodden shirt.

The killer's fading eyes suggested to Myers it was time for confession. The irises showed too much white. Myers didn't know where the bullet had hit Guerrero but he didn't seem to be losing blood and he should have been, a slug that large.

"Where are those goddamn babies!" It was no longer a question. "I will let go of you!"

The threat didn't mean much. He didn't answer. Guerrero's small hands could not hold his own weight. His left hand went first, slipping from the beam and forcing Myers to let go that wrist and use his forearm against the beam to support the grip on his other wrist. But it was a tenuous hold at best, as blood from the gunshot Guerrero had put into Myers now began its run in earnest to Myers' own wrist and onto his and the killer's joined hands. His grip, like holding a peeled mango, turned slippery very fast.

Myers said in a calm and condescending voice, "Shouldn't have shot me, dude."

Dangling, Guerrero then grinned, a glimmer of himself. "*Mano a mano, eh, señor?*" Macho to the end.

"Talk to me. It might get you into heaven."

That seemed to touch the crooked cop because he moaned and expelled all but enough wind to utter, " … Lopez. Dentist. Like babies—got no teeth … I—"

And that was all. On the descent, he may have been repentant. Only his maker would know for sure. Myers wasn't interested.

The women below him smartly had already scattered when Guerrero hit the acid as a huge melon might. The splash of thick, black liquid rose from the pit in the shape of a king's crown. It turned the area into a smoldering gas chamber.

Guerrero had apparently lied about his thugs being on the way. Or, Myers mused, someone might have decided to let Sergeant Guerrero's situation play out with no intervention, a subordinate uniform looking for a promotion perhaps.

Myers now faced the toughest challenge of his life. Getting down. Again he froze and now as if he and the thin steel beam had fused as one.

Two younger, thinner women climbed the rickety stairs without collapsing it and with alacrity and soothing persuasion guided Myers down before he blacked out. The others swarmed to attend him. They cleaned his face, gave him water, helped him out of his blood-sodden clothes. A woman wrapped gauze around his ribcage. They put him into a rubber raincoat. He asked an older woman if she would make sure the security guard got his gun back, and she said, "*Sí sí,* yes." He held firmly to the money belt. They got him into a car belonging to one of the women, and three women rode along. They took him to the same hospital where Myers had been treated for knife punctures, *Centro Medico*; the nurses weren't pleased with the negligence he'd shown their work. He called the Hotel Mexico and told Maggie she was right when she heard those baby cries at the dentist's office, that Dr. Lopez may be holding them and to get on over there. She said, "You did it, Ray, you did it!" It took the ER staff less than an hour after his arrival to put him under general anesthesia.

CHAPTER SIXTY-NINE

The five very vocal babies in Dr. Lopez' upstairs residence were a pampered bunch, but the dentist was grateful to turn them over. Dr. Lopez told Maggie whenever she needed her teeth cleaned, come see him, he would not charge her a penny. "So relieved" was how he put it when told of Guerrero's fate. He said it was like having a festering tooth yanked. He laughed toothlessly at his own joke.

It took a month to bring the sick child back to traveling health; the best treatment for meningitis was not available at Margarita's hospicio. But the child recovered there and all the babies, over the weeks and months to follow, with Robalba and Maggie's vigilant attention, were brought to full health, the Australian three gaining more weight than the smaller-boned Thai girls. Maggie drove Myers' Land Cruiser around while he waited extradition in federal jail in Ensenada. She brought him agave pecan pies to share and that helped his time go by easier.

~

A year after Castro Herlinda's murder, Maggie opened *Casa Libre* in San Diego. She did not post a city license on the premises. Her first orphans were five multinational toddlers without papers. Maggie would eventually adopt them out but there was no hurry.

She found the perfect house for her orphanage, a grand Victorian with a yard behind a fence two blocks from Balboa Park with all the open wonderment it had to offer kids young and old. The house had 27 rooms, which she separated by function—romp, day naps, bedrooms, arts and crafts, nursing, rooms for breakfast and for lunch and dinner, music appreciation and practice, movie watching. There was a giant banyan tree outside the kitchen window where she could watch the children climb in the low branches or swing on the big tire Ray had been so sweet to put up; it was a scene taken out of her dreams and made real.

Myers wrote out a two-year lease for *Casa Libre* and gave her full run of the Juniper House for the cost of taxes, upkeep and a token charge for rent. Myers moved into the old servants quarters on the other side of the banyan tree, the one-bedroom cottage he had in the past rented to San Diego State college girls.

Angel did not forgive Myers for letting dogs and children into the house; the half-Siamese could no longer lounge on the cloth furniture or hang at the front steps without getting chased by tail-squeezing toddlers. She was kicked out and left to scuffle with the old collie that Myers picked up from the Sidney Rhoades estate, plus Maggie's goldie and the neighborhood tom, the feral creature that jumped Angel at unexpected times, like Cato Fong jumped his boss Inspector Clouseau.

Initially, Richard Mendez rose from the ashes a public hero, honored in both Baja Norte and San Diego up to L.A. for sacrificing himself to save the lives of two handicapped homeless children. The *Journal's* own retired Wilford Reynolds broke the story—

Ensenada Crowns ICE Official as Child Savior

The worship for Mendez, however, was short lived once Earl W. Swabb was allowed to talk to U.S. authorities. All his U.S. and Mexican accolades were quickly rescinded, buried.

Swabb's talking also loosened the noose on Myers. Local police had first retained him after the hospital reported the gunshot wound. No evidence came to light of Myers breaking any Mexican laws; the bullet removed from Myers could not be matched to a know weapon and any crimes. There were no reports of illicit activity at the old tuna factory. Sergeant Guerrero simply disappeared.

A person by the name of Sylvia Fischer paid a funeral home to prepare Bubba Cousins' body for shipment to Alice, Texas, embalmed and with some miracle work performed on the head and face in case Roxanne wanted an open casket service. Ms. Fisher inspected the final work much as Maggie Frazier had done with her father's cold body.

Now cleared in Mexico, Myers still had to answer to authorities in the states. The feds had no case against him. The San Diego district attorney's office wanted it explained why Myers should not be charged with obstruction of justice in the Rhoades murder case, one that never had the chance to develop as a result of that obstruction, and separately for withholding information in the internal police investigation of the

Frazier shooting incident at Cabrillo Lighthouse, as well as violating a court order when he traveled out of the country. At the grand jury hearing into Rhoades' murder, Myers' lawyer cleared things up for $3,287.60 in 9.40 billable hours. Cheap really for not having to do all that explaining. Myers was glad he hadn't seen Pedroza in the hallway, waiting to give his lying testimony, or Myers may have gone to jail again, this time for a long stretch. He ended the whole legal mess with a guilty plea to a reduced charge of misdemeanor B&E. He paid no fine and no court costs. He was put on one-year's probation with a strict warning not to leave the country during that period.

The judge did not take his passport.

Myers flew to the capital city of Guatemala. It took a week working through various government offices and humanitarian organizations to discover there had been hundreds if not thousands of missing persons from just the countryside. One village in the backcountry named Quezaltepeque stood out because it had no record of missing residents except for a handful in the fall of last year. He traveled into the high mountain range in a rented old Nissan sedan. He encountered no roadblocks on the winding hundred-kilometer trip, which he had expected and brought extra Q notes for necessary bribes he'd figured on. He found the village in mid-afternoon, a poverty-stricken community of sheds and lean-tos. It surprised him that the village had electrical power. There were not enough teens living here to have a street-gang problem. He'd bought a cooler and filled it with diet Coke and Hawaiian Punch back in Guatemala, drinks he thought they might have liked. He brought along words of condolences that the American authorities had not offered because the Americans had not identified any of the victims.

He located four of the victims' families. The families of the others, he was told, must have lived in another village. No one could tell him of any other people, young or old, who had left the village at the same time the victims had. The children were not going to *el norte* these days, he was told in confidence because the *coyotes* wanted more money that anyone here could ever come up with. Those missing, the rumor held, had been paid to care for babies. The rumor was right, Myers said and told them what happened.

He bought six *chuchitos* in the main square at the stand where the slain Jovita Mendelez made her *perros poco*, best ones on the mountain. "*Delicioso*," he told Jovita's daughter. The children liked Coke better than Hawaiian Punch, but both were gone in his first couple of hours there. He spent the night on the ground under a blanket next to the lean-to shack of a victim's family of seven. The victim was the patriarch. He wanted better for them, they said. Before Myers left in the morning, a boy told him in private that a young girl about his age had disappeared at the same time as the others, a girl named Carmela who shamed the community by having a baby, did Myers know anything about her. The boy was very interested to know. Myers told him no young girl was among the victims which encouraged him.

Myers had nothing more to offer the families but the bribe money he'd brought along and to express his sorrow for their losses as well as a promise to make people aware of these kinds of atrocities, the heartaches they bring to families and entire villages. Even to him the promise sounded hollow.

He wrote a human-interest story on the families, describing the degraded living conditions and dead-end lives of the *campesinos*. In it he tried to explain why they kept coming to America, braving the horrors on determination and hope they could make it to the bountiful work fields. They had no choice if their families were to survive. The people could either wilt in the poverty of the land or succumb to narco pillaging; that, or the challenge of a deadly trek through a hostile and murderous desert—a ray of hope, even when they knew nothing of desert travel.

Only after Myers had been cleared of the criminal complaints and Esquire published his story did the *Journal* take him back. The publisher bristled at the thought but leaders in the powerful Chicano community convinced her majesty upstairs it was in the city's best interest to have the reporter back on board. L.C. accepted him with a thankful snarl. Max Cullen, Lubrano and Carol Finley and most of the staff welcomed him back with open arms. Sports and Soc didn't much care one way or the other.

That the massacre at Ocotillo never came to an official resolution neither surprised nor deterred Myers from the reporter's foolish drive to get back into the next provocative story, in Myers' case going back to something that had haunted him since the beginning of this episode—the police shooting of the unarmed homeless guy that got Myers out into the desert in the first place for the puff story on flowers. It would probably kill his career in this town to go after the city's finest for their cowboy style use-of-deadly-force policy. But it needed questioning, developing. Changing.

Then again, reflecting on the physical and emotional inconveniences placed upon him doing these hard fought stories, he softened and considered instead taking Angel and roaming the lovely, lonely roads of Baja and beyond in search of something elusive.

ABOUT THE AUTHOR

In the late 1980s, Ronald Argo published one of the more important novels on Vietnam, *Year of the Monkey*, a story that paints a comprehensive and human canvas of that war. Before and after he served as a military correspondent in LBJ's lost war, he had worked as a psych-ward aide, a prize-winning photographer, a Florida Keys boat captain, a special-needs bus driver, a stock trader, an award-winning newspaper reporter, and a newspaper editor. He has restored several historical houses. Those among other constructive and nefarious occupations. He was never a bartender, boxer nor preacher.

Argo is the author of *The Courage to Kill* and *The Sum of His Worth*, both historical and thriller novels, and both recipients of awards for literary fiction. He spent some time working for three university degrees including a bachelors in Journalism, the Masters in English Lit and the MFA.

Argo was born in Alabama and now lives with his wife Mary and their cow dog in San Diego where he tends his garden and continues to write.

Please visit Ron Argo's website at www.ronargo.com.